Published by Semiotext(e)
2007 Wilshire Blvd., Suite 427, Los Angeles, CA 90057
www.semiotexte.com

Special thanks to John Ebert, Noura Wedell.

Cover Photography: Francesca Woodman, *Untitled*. Rome, Italy 1977–1978. Courtesy George and Betty Woodman.

Back Cover Photography by Penelope Pardo
Design by Hedi El Kholti

ISBN: 978-1-58435-120-7
Distributed by The MIT Press, Cambridge, Mass. and London, England
Printed in the United States of America
10 9 8 7 6 5 4 3 2

THE SAD PASSIONS

Veronica Gonzalez Peña

this book is for my mother, Luz Peña Courcelle

A person, scattered in space and time, is no longer a woman but a series of events on which we can throw no light, a series of insoluble problems.

— Marcel Proust, *La Prisonnière*

The sad passions always amount to impotence....

— Deleuze on Spinoza

(2005)

Sandra

I WAS BORN THE YEAR Julia was given away. And though nobody knew it at the time, I was there when it happened; because, as I figure it, our mother, Claudia, was three months pregnant with me when that severance occurred. It didn't help that of all my sisters I was the only one who looked like Julia, the other two having the black hair and green eyes, the sensitive light skin, too, handed down from our father's Irish grandparents. My eyes, like Julia's, are large and dark and our skin is golden brown; we have deep auburn hair which with some sun can go to golden too, so alike that it is as if my sister herself had magically passed these things down to me before she left, or was forced to leave, as if through me she intended to be felt there, to be continually thought of, even in her absence. So that well before I was born, afloat in our mother's turbulent belly, I was already a remorse-ridden image of Julia. I know this. I was a shadowy mirror, a sorrowful replacement, a sick doubling. I was the image of the girl who was not there, my missing sister, though to my mother and grandmother and aunt I must have seemed a hope for absolution too, even as I was a constant sad reminder.

Julia was not yet seven when she was sent away from our family home in Mexico City, to live with our uncle David, in the United States. A big black car came for her, on that fateful morning, my paternal grandmother its single sinister passenger. It would be only hours later, after the solemn midday meal, that my grandmother Marina would take Julia from us, on that day staining us all forever. Rocio, the oldest of the four of us, tells of how they all stood in an uneasy grouping, feet shuffling, watching bewildered as my terrified sister was led away, her hesitant steps painful to behold. My grandmother Marina and she would ride to the airport together, Julia not daring to cry; and then the two of them would board the plane, my grandmother's stern hand pressing down hard, clear and authoritative, on my silent sister's shoulders as they inched their way to their two seats.

My sisters and my mother with me in her belly had only been back from the desert for a few months, had seemed to be just settling in, when Julia was taken away. My mother and three sisters had arrived at my grandmother Cecilia's home in a cloud of confusion, scared and defeated. My uncle Felix had been sent to fetch them. He'd spent a whole dutiful night driving the vastness of that northern Mexican landscape and had reached them at dawn, mere minutes after passing the lagoons, the sun just rising on the distant horizon. The desert floor was covered in long-legged spiders when he arrived that early morning. They'd hatched the previous night after the first long rain of spring and now they were charging for safety in ranks, blanketing the ground, that vast rush of an arachnid army. They marched across his fine leather city shoes as he stepped out of the car, with divine indifference to his presence there; and for a while he watched that sacred march, as they moved from east to west as if on special order. And then he walked, with halting steps at first, crunching whole troops of them as he made his way to the house, which stood small and desolate in that big desert landscape.

Inside it was a hostile mess; and she in the midst of it, filthy, sitting in a corner staring at the wall, her long hair tangled, her head turning sharply, eyes going from blank to fierce as he walked through that weighty threshold. *What are you doing here?* she angrily breathed.

Come on, he said. *I'm taking you and your girls back to the city.*

It had happened in steps. But Rocio, who was nine, had finally found it inside herself to call my grandmother Cecilia. And immediately my grandmother had sent Felix to fetch them. My uncle Felix, who had no job to speak of, did it for a small fee. The money folded neatly in his pocket, like a filial bounty hunter he had gone to collect his sister, to bring her and her three daughters home to his mother.

He gathered those girls, though he fastidiously held them at arm's length as they rushed to hug him, a single unruly mass, insisted they bathe before he'd allow them into his car. Clean, they were permitted to jump in, without any of their belongings, however. *I'm not taking that junk*, he said dryly, wiping at the desert dust left on his shoes, *leave it here*. He made them leave the cat too, though Rocio and Julia cried out at the injustice.

Then, the whole ride home, my mother wept in the front seat.

I don't want to, she repeated again and again. *I don't want to…* and no one dared ask what it was she didn't want to do.

To Rocio it had become clear slowly, but then one night Claudia forced them to sit in a bath for hours on end. She never made them bathe at all so this was strange. Their bodies grew cold and shriveled in that late night water, and so they began calling to where she sat in the other room, begging our mother to let them get out.

I don't care, Marta said when Claudia didn't answer. *I want to get out.*

Not until she tells us it's okay, Rocio warned.

I want to get out, five year old Marta insisted, *What are you so scared of? You chicken baby.*

Stop it, Rocio said, and then she turned to Julia for help and saw that Julia was absently playing her fingers upon the surface of the cold water, then moving them slowly to an inch over her own arm to drip, drip, drip there on her skin, before running them back to the pliant surface of the cool bath once more. Rocio pulled her eyes away from Julia's hypnotic slow and measured gestures and looked back at Marta, *She told us not to*, Rocio said.

But why? Marta answered. *I don't have to listen to you, you big chicken baby. Or to any of you*, she added, defiantly beginning to rise.

Please be quiet, Marta. Sit down, Rocio begged.

Instead, Marta shoved Rocio away and got out, her round bottom dripping all over the floor; Rocio panicked, but when nothing terrible happened, she got out too, her long thin limbs.

Should we go to bed now? Rocio, her hair still wet, asked our mother who sat staring into blankness in the bedroom.

I don't care, Claudia answered, hollow.

And then the next day she was gone, locking the door behind herself.

Claudia locked the door behind herself, bolted them in from the outside, and then did not come back for nearly a week. Rocio had had to find scraps with which to make simple soups to feed my sisters; she had fried eggs. And then the three of them would climb out the window and run around all day as if there were nothing strange in this, as if it were normal to be locked in your house by your mother; they'd simply climb out the window and spend the day, as always, running and playing in the garden, eating prickly pears and desert plums from the neighbors' trees. Making up games with the neighbor boys, whispering in a huddle first, before splintering into groups which chased and tagged and accused each other. At night they'd crawl back in the window, never mentioning our mother at all.

When she finally returned, Claudia moved from ordering them around with erratic, screeched commands, to completely ignoring them. She would cry and cry all day. She made no sense at all. Her dark eyes were fierce and her long black hair, uncombed, looked fuller than ever. Our mother was terrifying, but beautiful, Rocio knew. After a few days of Claudia's yelling, of her crying, Rocio went to the neighbor's house and called my grandmother Cecilia. The thin, sad-faced elderly neighbor handed Rocio a bag full of plums before she walked out of his front door. *Thank you*, Rocio whispered politely to him, reaching out for them without lifting her gaze.

Silently, the sad man stared at her.

Two mornings later, the sun just coloring the sky red, my uncle Felix was at their bedroom door.

Wake up, he repeated again and again, *wake up*, as he shook their shoulders, first one then the other two, then back again.

They had only been back in Mexico City a few months when my mother gave Julia away.

She disappeared my sister, sent her off from our family home, never to return again for more than an occasional weighty and always too short visit.

She got rid of one of us, Claudia did, just like that.

And then I was born. Mere months after Julia was given away, born into that gaping hole that was my missing sister. I was born into all the empty spaces, all the regret-filled secret places of the women—my mother and aunt and grandmother— who surrounded my childhood. In which childhood I lived an image of the absence, her absence personified, Julia, my sister who had seemed to pass herself down to me. Except that I was not her.

Yet, in that mirroring world I was born into, there was never a possibility of my being anything but a sorrowful echo, anything but that other girl who was not me.

And though this was how it had always been, how I was written into things from the first, it all took on an increasing weight for me last year. This is when I went to join my mother at a friend's home at which she was a guest. It was there, on that visit, that it became clear to me that everything, all of it, was conspiring against me, that nature, even, was working to turn me into Julia.

My mother had asked me to come and stay a while, and though at first I refused her, for I worked hard to keep my distance, she convinced me by saying I should at least see the place where she and my sisters had once lived. The woman she was staying with, Carla, had just been left by her husband and though she wasn't crushed by this fact—he had been a tough and angry man—nonetheless, she had called my mother and my mother had agreed to go and stay with her for a few months. To console her, my mother said, though I suspect Carla just wanted someone new to care for now that her husband was gone. She was big boned and strong with thick black hair and clear direct eyes and my mother, of course, always needed tending.

It was the town my family had lived in nearly twenty years before, I knew, at the foot of the lagoons in the Coahuila desert, when my sisters were just girls, in the months before Julia was sent away. My father, M, had come into some money, gambling probably, and had rented this pretty little house, fully furnished. He smugly put the money down for a full year and then picked them all up from my grandmother Cecilia's home, where they were living. He moved them from the relative safety of my grandmother's house in Mexico City to that little house in the desert, proud, as if they were a real family, and he the accountable head of it; he'd even stuck around with them for a while before, as usual, he could not sustain it and so took off, disappearing from their lives once more.

And, as Rocio tells it, one day they were out in the yard, playing, running with and chasing the neighbor boys and their big dog. It was a male dog and she remembers being a little afraid of it. It was really very large and a few days prior she had seen it having sex with another dog, had seen it climb on top of her, the bitch from three doors down, and then what he did to her, and how, growling and biting at her neck repeatedly as he did it. And when, the day after she saw this, that dog chased after Rocio in the garden she imagined it wanted to do the same thing to her. This terrified her and she jumped up on a picnic table for safety, but he circled and circled with his dripping red tongue hanging out; and he would not leave. She cannot now recall how she finally got off that table, how that stand-off ended. But on this day she was in a group of children, out in the yard playing, my messy long-haired sisters in their tattered, hand-me-down, satin dresses, well worn shoes, and the wiry neighbor boys, all of them chasing and being chased with their big brown dog running right behind them, when suddenly what seemed to them a large black curtain became visible up in the sky, at a distance; and it appeared to be coming their way, traveling fast. Very quickly the day began going dark around them and as they continued staring up, they saw the entire sky being closed in by this heavy black curtain which grew and grew so that they now saw that it was rushing toward them, moving miles forward by the instant and that it would indeed soon be upon them. *A tornado!* the boys yelled, though it did not look like any tornado my sisters had ever imagined, nothing like the V-shaped whirlpooling tornadoes they had imprinted in their minds as the image of that thing they were all now supposedly gazing at; this was a fast moving and quickly growing black expanse, overtaking the sky, smothering the sun and coming to swallow them whole. But those boys had always lived there, in that lagoon bordered desert, and they had seen this before and so they called it what in fact it was and then they ran for home. And as those boys ran, Rocio and Marta and Julia just stood there frozen, staring up as if enchanted, hypnotized by that going dark sky, as if it had already blackened and stolen their souls; and it wasn't until my mother, Claudia, ran out, yelling at them to move—What were they crazy? *Run in, run in!*—that any of the three of them was able to stir herself.

What was that? Rocio wondered, that thing that had enchanted her and her sisters, which had held the three little girls in place? The source of that paralysis which could very well have killed them all?

But instantly then, with Claudia's yells, the spell was broken and they did begin moving, running fast, shouting and gasping for air, and then in a mad rush of terror-filled cries, they were in. Though they soon realized they had forgotten their cat and so Rocio, who was not usually brave, ran out and found him, shaking under a bush, and she yanked him by his hind legs and though he scratched at her she grabbed him up and held him tight to her and then she whipped her head about and saw the laundry room which was detached from the rest of the house but was the closest place to where she now stood in a panic, grasping that cat tight to her chest. She ran into that room and kicked the door shut behind herself and then she waited that thing out, alone, the whole sky going black and things which she could imagine but not see flying into the walls with loud bangs in that blackness, smashing and crashing into the house.

And then it was over and the fat gray cat turned his face toward Rocio and started licking her nose and Rocio began to weep with fear and relief and a deep love for that big dumb cat.

Rocio says she remembers their faces, dirt and tears having mixed and smeared across their cheeks, their trembling eyes looking up at her from the floor where they lay under the table when she finally walked into the house, her wild youngest sister, Marta, and Julia, and our mother, staring up with scared wide eyes; and it was Julia's terror filled eyes that drew her, Julia's brown eyes that showed a real and deep love-driven concern for her and to which she was thus drawn. And then, overwhelmed by the intensity of that gaze, Rocio pulled her own eyes away and looked down at herself and she saw that the front of her satin dress had ripped, probably as she'd pulled that cat out from under the bush. And, as if in gratitude, the cat regarded her with his bright yellow eyes, reached out his tongue again, and licked her tear-streaked face.

She remembers that day in strong, sharp pictures, she says: the felled trees, the boys running home, their fast moving legs, broken glass, Claudia's screaming face going to red, the distress in her eyes that Rocio does not remember ever having seen before in regard to them. Our mother, Claudia, who was so often absent, who was a blank, mostly, when she was there, this same Claudia, our mother, had worried about them, their well-being. She had saved her daughters with her yells, had pulled them out of their spell with her screaming; she *was* a mother, in fact!

And then Rocio looked around herself again, still holding that cat, and she saw that the dust and dirt had come in under the door and through cracks in the windows and all the other small openings in that house too. Mirrors had fallen and shattered. Dishes had come crashing down. Julia, her eyes still full of fear and concern, came running up to her then; and when her little frightened sister threw her arms tight around her body Rocio knew that of the three of them—Claudia and Marta and Julia— it was Julia who really loved her. Without saying a word Julia softly touched the scratches the cat had scored upon Rocio's arm, as if to confirm them as a mark of their mutual affliction. And then it was Rocio and Julia who cleaned up that mess, Claudia having become lost in herself once again.

———

I had only been in Coahuila for a week, the days long and lazy, dust streaked; desert mice and slithery lizards scampering in that heat, under bushes and in between cacti or digging down with frantically moving limbs into the cool foundations of that house, me watching their crazy jagged motions while lazing on the porch, lost and bored and sluggish there in that land where my mother had lived with my sisters; and now it was me with my mother and Carla in that dusty place, wondering how it was that anyone ended up here, in this barren land; and, as I said, it had been only one week, one eternally endless, stagnant week, when there was a tornado. I looked up, heard Carla's deep voice as if from a great distance, yelling at my mother to run in as she herself noisily herded in her many dogs and cats, the sky going to black by degrees, exactly as Rocio had described it.

Carla yelled at me when she saw me standing there in front of that porch, motionless, her tone going to anger when I continued, immobile, staring up at the sky, mesmerized.

How could I tell her that I was my sister? How could I tell her that Julia, her paralysis twenty years ago, had somehow entered my body, that I *was* Julia and that right then a part of me wanted to die?

I realized then, in that moment of dread, that I must have been conceived there; that this was where I was formed. Had my mother given Julia away because I was coming? I was weeping when Carla was finally successful in dragging me in, though I fought her for a while, struggled against her in a deep dark fury as she violently pulled at my body, wanting nothing more than to stay where I was and be swallowed up in that storm. And when she yanked me in and slammed the door behind us I collapsed into her strong arms, knowing that she could not ever have guessed at what it was she was fighting, never have guessed at the depth of my anguish, of my guilt and burden, at why it was that I so deeply wept.

And yet she hugged me tight.

It was then, after that storm passed, that I decided to go. It was on that same dust-written day, a mere palimpsest drawn over Julia's story, that I decided I had to leave Mexico. I would have to lose everything that was Julia, I knew, to find a place from which to start again as myself, as Sandra.

It was on that day that I decided to sell my grandmother Cecilia's ancient rings, the three she had given me, and to use that money to go to Spain. It was then that I decided to pull it all off, like a heavy coat, the weight of my family and what it had done to me, their sadness; then too that I decided I must get away from Claudia, and her unsteady mind, the way it had written itself into all of our lives, me and my three sisters. I tried hard to steer clear of her, but somehow, always, she drew me back in. I had to go, as I could think of no other way to stop her from further inscribing herself into me. I had to go, for it was Claudia—her erratic nature and what drove it—was it not, who had disappeared my sister.

Julia

IT'S NOT TO SAY that things were always terrible. They weren't. Most of the time they weren't and I was happy, lots of people around me, aunts and cousins and friends, my grandmother. We would eat together often, all of us, big meals prepared by the housekeeper. My grandmother, the sole adult in that house, really—her children all still in their twenties and continually rushing back to her home after the always futile attempt of a few months out on their own—worked her job at the National Palace, so was gone most of the day every day, and on weekends loved to play cards, poker for small change—her glasses on, deep concentration, a cigarette in her mouth, three fingers tapping, everything flowing in and out of her and she herself focused on her hand—so that every week there was a parade of folks streaming through the house, old people mostly, but often with children or grandchildren in tow so that they weren't always uninteresting to us, those card games, my grandmother laughing and joking and sipping wine or coffee and picking at olives or nuts or dried fruit which somebody had brought; we would play too sometimes, piles of change in front of us, scheming, trying our hardest to cheat, never really knowing if they were letting us win or not.

These nights were for staying up late, for running in groups through the house and all of its secret insides—the rooms of our uncles and aunt, full of candles and little bottles holding tonics and perfumes and dark colored paintings and drawers stuffed with treasures which we dared to open only once or twice. And then we'd go outside, to the little enclosed garden which transformed into dim unpredictable wilderness in the dark of night, the bunch of us planning and hiding and spying, peaking through windows, trying to get at hints of what it was that drove the adults' unpredictable lives.

Sometimes a group of my estranged father's friends would show up for those card games too, though he was rarely with them, and they were thrilling to us, young and handsome like he was, in skinny black suits and thin ties and even back then we could tell they were serious in their gambling though in my grandmother's presence, out of respect for her, they held back. There was one, he was tall and had light colored hair, was often in the center, the others orbiting around him, and this one would occasionally send gifts meant only for me, not for my sisters, but *for me*, and we never thought to question the apparent injustice of this, we were used to inequality, though for a long time it remained fuzzily unclear; it wouldn't be until I was older, thirteen or so, that I would come to understand what was driving those visits, driving those just for me gifts.

No, things were not always terrible. I remember laughing, like other little children laugh, until I couldn't breathe sometimes, chasing my sisters or cousins around the couches in the living room, shrieking with *You're it!* delight. Later, after I'd gone to live with my uncle David, he would—for his own difficult reasons—sometimes send me back to my family during school vacations, and during those warm summer months so many people flowed in and out of my grandmother's house that there were free-flowing gatherings and simple get-togethers almost every night. Throughout these teenage summer visits there were also parties where we moved those couches into corners and I danced with boys I had a crush on and were now miraculously in our house—who had invited them, their green eyes, who knew these boys I liked?—or with boys I hadn't had a crush on at all until I danced with them, the thrill of closeness taking over, of a body focused on mine.

But I'm getting ahead of myself. In those early days, still a small child, I remember running wild in the streets with friends, getting glimpses of boys or girls who were god-like to me, older and beautiful, the gorgeous Sebastian whom none of us yet knew was gay, and whom I can't think of now without seeing Mantegna and his saint, arrows piercing holy flesh, and then the slow walking girls, their perfect clothes and hair. Or a sighting of that other boy, whom I'd only seen once or twice at the corner store or walking toward it because he didn't inhabit the streets like us, his family strict, my same age or just a little bit older, beautiful with dark eyes and milky skin. His lips were red and my eyes had locked with his once, him up at his window, like a princess caught in a tower, and me down below, the dashing and wild one—the prince with the promise of freedom in the very air which floated around me and I delighted in my male vigor then, my chivalrous offer of pure love, my saving from towers in exchange for a kiss from those beautiful lips. I parted my own lips then and his mother, as if alerted, called from within that big house and he dropped my eyes and I rode off on my dragon, and then I was merely a girl again, inexplicably controlled by the shadowy intrigues of the adults around me, my mother, unaware of her secrets, the dark sad places—sometimes terrible—from which she roamed.

But on these warm summer nights it was as if there were no adults for miles, and I could be anything—a dashing young prince—on these long warm summer nights. Running wild in the streets. Those Mexico City summer streets.

I was blindly happy, too, when he would show up out of the blue, our handsome father, with a pile of cash in his hand, a game played in his favor, a night of gambling turned right, and off we would go into the country, the rest of Mexico, my younger sister and me innocent and trusting, after months of not seeing him, and now we were disappearing like our mother, like she did so often into dark unsettling nights, her unexplained absences extending into weeks sometimes; but now it was us, leaving with almost no notice, shoving things into a bag while yelling out at our aunt Sofia that we were going with our father, *Yes, of course it was alright, he was our father!* and then riding off in his VW out of the sprawl of the city and into a forest where at a restaurant in which we stopped once for a late dinner they kept a pet deer, a fawn, huge black frightened eyes staring out at us, her neck tied by a long length of rope to a tree just outside; I reached out to touch, but she was so shy, backed away in such terror, that I drew my hand back. Or to the beach, one time, a tour of those beautiful Mexican beaches, endless swimming, floating atop rising rolling falling waves, letting ourselves go for a while, Marta and me out further and further until the people left behind on the beach seemed so small, tiny there before us, and a fear would strike inside us that we may become irretrievably lost so that we would lap our way back toward the shore, yelling out, alarmed though joyous screams that were lost on the crests of waves while our father disappeared with newly made friends. But we didn't need him, for it was us in water forever, nearly naked at ten and eleven, at the edge of knowing what being naked meant, what it might imply to some of them, the old and judging catholic ones.

He always traveled with boys, teenagers mostly, and on this particular trip my father had Pablo with him, a boy four years older than me, fifteen at the time. He would become a poet and a mathematician, was already brilliant and thoughtful, and decent, and what was he doing with our dad? I remember Marta and me sitting over him on his bed in the room we'd gotten for the night—where was our father? We sat near him as he lay propped up by a pillow and we teased him about loving our older sister, Rocio, who was the one everybody always loved because she was the sweet and strikingly beautiful one. He didn't answer our teasing but talked on and on to keep us there and in a stolen moment, Marta having gotten up for some water, he stared into my eyes and without knowing why I touched his nipple for one second while I continued to tease about Rocio though he said he didn't like her. She was not the one he liked.

His tone had dropped, was low and serious, and I saw that there was hair beginning to grow around where I had touched. And though I was just a child, deep inside me I felt what it is I felt.

Six years later, during my longest return visit, Pablo and I would sleep together—it meant something (was even grave and weighty, perhaps) though I pretended it did not—at my mother's apartment after an afternoon sitting in a park and he would tell me that he'd had to work hard to keep from touching me indecently back then. But on this trip he lost the keys to the VW in the ocean, they fell out of the pocket in his trunks, and my father had to hot-wire the car. Marta and I were impressed that he knew how to do this, our dad, and while he worked before our marveling eyes my father laughed and said he'd done it many times before and of course we believed him, we knew there was that side to him, knew that side was maybe all there was, and then we teased Pablo forever, how clumsy, look at what he'd caused! Afterward we sat on the beach eating fried fish which the old women cooked on the open flame, served with salt and lime, picking at that fish with our pruned fingers which we licked after each bite while our father played his guitar and sang.

He was terrifying in his own way, in a way different than our mother, our father, and on this particular trip I was introduced to that.

But I feel I've been working hard to convince of something here, to depict and prove it: my childhood joy; or perhaps I'm trying to absolve myself of something, something that I shouldn't need to be forgiven for. Why do I feel the need to explain that we were happy, mostly, the need to justify it? And why should my happiness be something for which I feel guilt, for which I feel I need forgiveness, for which I feel the need to apologize?

It is because of Claudia, of course, our mother. She who ruined everything and who makes it hard for me to be guiltless even in the mildest case of childhood contentment. I am bound by remorse though it is she who would disappear for weeks, sometimes months at a time, who was erratic when she was there, and cruel, somehow foggy and cloud-like; and still we were happy. Of course we didn't know what she was in those days. Little kids then, we didn't understand, and even into our older, teenage years we didn't have a clue. In fact, I don't think anyone around me knew what she was, who she was, what it was she was capable of, and if they had a fleeting idea, a sense of something they thought that they might grasp, they would never have put a word to it. And this I understand. For language seals things, makes them seem much clearer than they really are, makes things seem, in their very denotation, makes things seem less aqueous, more stable, constant, continuous even in their motion…. But we weren't sure, are still not sure, perhaps, so changeable and motile, so slippery and ultimately hard to define: she was this, yes, but she was also that and that and that. And her blood, that murky and confounding blood in her veins, whatever we decided to name it, was also mine.

What was this thing inside her, the inside? Maybe my grand-mother Cecilia, maybe she had seen something, or enough things to satisfy a definition, and so maybe she had tried to put words to it. She did cry to me once: I was angry. I was eighteen and it was dark and I was leaving. My mother and I had, two days earlier, had a terrible fight. And beaten down and fully injured, I ran to my grandmother for solace, for her support and under-standing. She was lying in bed, and though I don't otherwise ever recall her lying down, there she was, overcome, while I stood at the threshold, the door to her room, that room like a cave on that dark night, she already on the other side of something, inside it, me at the mouth of it, struggling my way out; and my grand-mother's voice traveled to me through that great distance, from out of that darkness, some sick sort of truth there with her, invisible to my eyes; and instead of walking into those terrible oracular depths, offering myself up in sacrifice to help her bear it—to understand and know it and then to want to surrender myself to live there with her in it—I pulled back from the chasm. As if to save my soul, I pulled back. Though I felt adrift and fully lost then. I had just turned eighteen and I'd had a dreadful fight with my mother. She had been biting and cold, and I had yelled back at her; with tears in my eyes I had begged her to tell me how it was that a mother could give a daughter away, how it was that *she'd* given *me* away. My voice breaking, my hands a shaky mess. My wet beseeching gaze. She turned toward me. My mother gave me a long and hardened look, said things that were searing and cruel, and then she walked away. And rather than forgive her, rather than chase after her and force her to help me understand, rather than stay and struggle with her, I decided to go. Once, long ago, she had given me up; and now, at eighteen, I was leaving. And I would not return.

My grandmother cried when I told her, said I should stay, and so asked that I please forgive her.

"Forgive your mother," she cried.

"She was horrible," I answered. "She was biting. She has not changed a bit. She is cruel."

"She doesn't know what she is doing. She is your mother and she does not know what she does. Please. Forgive her."

What I knew of my mother was that from the time that I was very small she would disappear into night shadows, in her tight knit skirts and kitten heels; my mother almost always wore black, dark glasses at her eyes, a flowing scarf tied around her neck, waving in the air behind her as she darted off again…. I recall her mostly in her comings and goings, a twilight silhouette, a beautiful black clad, unpredictable being. Shadowy, she was now made darker still by the fact that when I had tried to speak to her, had tried to get her to explain my childhood to me, to make some sense of it with me, she'd said hard and spiteful things, and then she'd walked away. And instead of helping me, instead of offering me the solace I had come for, my grandmother was defending my mother, asking me to forgive her. But I couldn't. In her presence—I already knew it—I would be always drowning in her. She would drown me. And so I had to leave.

And the next day I was on a plane.

Yet, I can hardly recall her. Was she so important? Did I really leave because of Claudia? I can hardly recall what she was then. A shadow. A dark and violent cloud. Between us a thick black Barnett Newman line, dividing the canvas but also connecting the two sides, defining them as different, of course, but then inevitably illustrating that they are alike—each a part of the whole, me and her the two sides.

I think I do remember how I felt about her though. From the time that I was very little I hated her and that insane laugh, her get-away shoves as she struggled to get out the door, pushing one of my sisters back while she herself groped for her freedom, eyes darting, arms reaching toward the outside; I never asked her to stay, never grabbed at already walking away legs, tears in my eyes, begging her to come back, sit with me, come back. It was Marta, mostly, who did all that.

My sister peed once in protest; she was so angry at that leaving. All her attempts had been so futile, my mother's eyes a blank even in the face of my tiny sister's tear-filled four year old cries, and so Marta stood in the middle of the floor and peed, her hands little fists at her sides, her short black hair and big green eyes, her face squeezed tight; and still my mother was soon gone, barely a glance back as she rushed to get outside.

Was it me who helped to clean up that night? Who pulled Marta away from her banging at the door in her ferocious urge to follow her mother? Did I rush to get rid of the evidence of that humiliation, that pressing need, the bodily failing my sister in that moment, or, more confusingly, perhaps coming together in a concentrated way, in a primal expression of love thwarted, her pee the image of love thwarted, of mine too, and so I rushed to clean it all up.

I never begged, for she was cruel, the way she spoke to my grandmother; how could anyone speak to her like that? cold and biting, those dark tones, that thick murky underside, to my grandmother Cecilia who was always laughing, who told jokes and gathered people around her and sang and played cards, my grandmother who worked all day and was not like other people's grandmothers most of whom solely cooked and took care of houses and snapped angrily about all the things you should be doing and were not. My grandmother was not like other grandmothers. She had, courageous and daring for her day, left her husband for cheating on her, and she smoked cigarettes, and read books late into the night. She'd had the honor of shaking the president's hand once, and even if he was a crook, Lopez Portillo, she'd had the honor of shaking his hand. And to her, my mother spoke like that.

Like something unseen and yet there, the pressure of the outside affecting all that is within, like gravity, a concealed force. Though when I left I tried to float unburdened, alone, swim, a drop of water set free of that dark sea, away from her, her large motions, her engulfing devastating force, swim to different waters, struggle free, unrestrained, wash her out, move into other currents; like a single cell in that pool of undulating blood, struggling to escape her presence or absence and my staged indifference at both: all of it to end in a thick dark line of nothing between us, a thick dark line I could not help but draw.

Picture the trunk of a tree giving out a branch, on that branch a pod and in that pod a seed set in a cottony fiber, breaking free; I am floating out over a landscape measureless, larger than anything in either one of us, drifting out alone into that vastness, my wings spread in an Icarus prayer, that thick line I have drawn stretching larger and wider until it is a dark wash, the line becoming the full canvas, an Ad Reinhardt black which references nothing but itself, a vast abstract, a black that is black because it is black, all of that, now, the border between us; and as I flow and glide, my Icarus wings, I tell myself that Medusa is not there, that she does not exist, because looking at her directly, we all know, could turn me into stone.

And there is nothing in my memory that balances it, this need to blank out, black out. What I mean is that I don't remember moments of love to set off the anger, the confusion, the resentment, or anything surrounding those feelings, any other feeling I might have had for her that might have cushioned those darker emotions. Though if I'm truthful I have to admit that there was a longing, sometimes, because I would cry with missing.

I remember having stayed behind once, I was small, five or six at the time, and my sisters and my mother and my father who had appeared unexpected, a fistful of cash, went to live in the desert in another one of his out of the blue, grab your things now adventures. They were going only for a month, they said, but then they stayed much longer. And I'd been left behind with my grandmother and my aunt, and I remember missing them in the day, but crying for her at night, my grandmother hugging me, saying it was alright. Shhhh, she would say, shhhh. It's alright. And through my sobs I told her I was only crying for them, for my sisters, though at the center of the crying—I didn't have to tell her for she surely already knew it—was her daughter. My mother.

I did eventually join them there. Though by the time I showed up it had all fairly disintegrated, my father's money having almost run out.

Still, there must have been more than just this once of longing, though I'm loath to admit it, there is never just one time. Yet even then I knew I was crying for something she could not give me, something I had never had. Six years old and I knew it. The longing was false, a fantasy longing, for there was nothing on the other side of it; my mother had offered me nothing. And then five months after returning from the desert, she gave me away. She sent me to live with my uncle David.

And now as I was leaving of my own volition, as I boarded that plane for New York, I knew that the confusion and resentment and anger were the only real things. The only things I could hold onto. The only things which I still, clearly, have.

Claudia

IT WAS 1964 and we hitchhiked through the middle of the United States. We slept wherever we could, on floors mostly, in the backs of bars or stores, barns or garages, wherever people would put us up. Just like that, like people without a home, with nothing to show of where we came from. Like hobos or ramblers or de-centered beings, beings without pasts and no notion of futures because it's not like we thought about those things and no one asked us questions, no one cared about our pasts or about our coming plans. He'd just pull out his guitar and start to sing his Mexican songs of love and yearning and eyes would turn dewy and soft and we would all sing along and sway and sip at beers and then after awhile they would show us our room or barn or storeroom, a blanket to lay out on the floor.

We got picked up in Dodge City, late at night. He came upon us in his car, the sheriff, though he didn't turn on the flashing red lights and then he stepped out his door, his gun at his side, and he cocked his head while he asked us questions in the beam of his headlight. Like someone very curious, like not a sheriff at all, a cat eyeing a bird, his head cocking from side to side. Side to side to side. And that look of his made me think that he liked us, and I guess I was right, I guess he really did because he let us sleep in the jail, though not together of course. He could get himself in trouble for that he said. So he put M in the men's jail and me in the women's jail, though we were the only ones there. The sheriff said it wasn't good us wandering the streets in the middle of the night, and so we slept there, the doors locked though we weren't locked up.

And I remember as I lay on my cot, a musty blanket the sheriff had brought for me from who knows where, I remember thinking then that the sheriff hadn't been making eyes at me. It wasn't me that he had liked, cocked his head at. My blanket smelled of dampness, of long wet nights, though it was dry and I turned my face from that smell and up high toward the tiny window in that cell and it was as if I could see M in his cell, see them, see them talking, whispering secrets, late into the night. I closed my eyes and tried to sleep though my mind ran circles and my heart raced, the door locked, damp smelling blanket, the sounds of the night, life rising and falling all around me, crickets and cicadas and all those other deep dark insects and hot breezes running through the weeping willows, or dusty ash trees, or sycamores, or whichever those trees of Dodge City are, the wind whispering mournfully through them, their leaves, outside the jailhouse, whispering leafy secrets, nature's susurrations, deep into the night.

In the morning the sheriff woke me with a shake and then he took me to where M was but M didn't even reach out toward me when he saw me walk in, barely lifted his eyes, so I turned away from him for a long hurt moment, and then I sat, trying to swallow my anger, though all I ever really swallowed with him, though it seems stupid to say it, was my pride, my legs crossed under me yogi style, close to M but not touching, and for a while we all three sipped our coffee together, like friends or neighbors, without asking too many questions, without talking too much about the previous night. Then the sheriff cleared his throat and in a low slow voice he did begin to inquire, about us, what we were doing, what we had planned. We didn't tell him too much though. We'd just gotten married.

Weren't we awful young? he asked.

Yes, we were awful young, should have waited, M said, should have thought better before acting.

What were we doing in Dodge City? he asked.

Well, we had gone to Kansas City where M had a friend and we'd stayed there on this friend's couch until our money had run out, and then for a little while longer while I worked a job cleaning a bar that this friend's landlady ran. I didn't like the cleaning part, but that bar was a place to go, a place to be and I liked that, the clear direction it gave.

And then we stopped talking.

What I didn't tell him, what I didn't tell that sheriff was that one night a woman came up to M while we sat sipping at drinks in that bar and she bent down into him, her breasts near his face, and thanked him for the beautiful necklace, completely ignoring my presence, her hand playing at her own neck which was bare at the time; and later when we were alone and I showed my anger and then cried at M he said, What, do you think you're the only one I ever had? And then cruel and with a smirk he began to name each one. I threw myself at him then, my nails bared, and when he laughed I broke a bottle and threatened him with it and when he laughed louder I lunged at him but he just grabbed my wrists and held me hard and then he was not laughing anymore;

the next day I quit my job at the bar, though the landlady had been kind, had stroked my hair as she talked softly to me. And though at that time I mostly didn't understand her, her English, she had said things to me in that soft warm voice whenever I cried. But I was glad to be leaving; that friend of M's had beaten his wife. Not every night, you understand, but enough to terrify. And the wife, that girl was so quiet and mouse-like there was nothing I could ever say to her; I was afraid of being her, becoming her, though with pity I would smile at her from time to time. Once or twice, while she cried, I stroked her hair, like the landlady at the bar had stroked mine.

So with no jobs and no money we left Kansas City and began to hitchhike our way back to Mexico City. And it had been good again; I even told myself it'd been the place, that city, that Kansas City had been the badness I told myself; and I was hopeful once more, because it had been good again, so far, our voyage home, no one bothering us and people taking us in like they had.

I have to tell you now, make it clear right now, that it wasn't me, not my idea. I just followed him; I'd never done anything like that. I followed him because he knew what he was doing, M said. He said he knew what he was doing; barely twenty and he'd been hitchhiking for years, had moved all over two countries for years like that, since he was ten, he said, or maybe it was even nine. The Sheriff told us to be careful on our voyage, not everyone was like him; it was clear he wasn't talking to me. And anyway, we already knew that. He hadn't had to say it. He hadn't had to say anything; I knew it all, the way he looked at M.

You have to understand. It wasn't my doing, wasn't my fault. I'd never done anything like that, wandered around like a stray dog, like a person with no home, with no past. M was so gorgeous.

He played the guitar and sang his songs so sad or loud and joyous and everyone came close when he sang though his voice was not a beautiful one; he was alive and had eyes like an angel, blue and clear as water, the Irish eyes of his mother, her wry smile on his lips at all times. It was like he had borrowed his mother's mouth, her eyes, and though I hated her, and always would, I followed him with no reason, like a girl who had lost her mind. I'd started following him in Mexico City almost two years before; he lived three blocks away and had befriended my brother, Felix, and when I first saw M standing there in that group of boys my middle melted; he turned his gaze on me for just one weighty second—his liquid blue eyes pulling at my center—before quickly turning away in feigned indifference, and I didn't know how I would ever stop thinking of him again. In the midst of that group he stood laughing and teasing; my brother was there too, surly at the edges as always, but they all disappeared, even the black hole that was Felix, all seemed to fall away, so that it was as if it were only M standing there in front of me, floating before me, the others having vanished from right in front of my eyes. My middle melted and then forever my head remained not right.

But it was all his fault. It wasn't me, I tell you. I wasn't like that. I'd grown up in a very strict household, though no one could say I was innocent because I was always the wild one, the one who took risks, the one who ran and climbed trees and fell and injured myself. I was always the one with the outrageous friends and the loud laugh and the anger at my sister for being so quiet and perfect and well loved by my father. My father who was now gone.

My father was serious, was a businessman, and was directed and clear, not like M's father who was himself a sort of vagabond, who skulked and hid and lived in secrets and half lies. It was his father who first took M to Kansas City, when he was eight or nine. But when I met M I didn't really know anything about his father, his family, the stories, of which I became a scandalous part at a later time. My own father managed a bank and was so straight and right and proper in his dealings that when a German lumber giant needed someone to go into business with him in Oaxaca, he went to my father. My father, who had always been so frank and serious in all aspects of that German's interests at that bank; my father, who seemed to know the ins and outs of Mexican money, my father who could also drink, and joke and laugh. I will put up the capital, the German said to my father, and you will manage the enterprise. We will be partners, he said. It was more of a statement than a request and my father said yes. A German had helped him before at least once.

I was about to tell you about my mother, she is (she's now very old, but still alive) the granddaughter of French immigrants, but now I feel I should first explain to you about the German who so long ago helped my father. Before he was even born. This is how it was, in Zacatecas, near the silver mines: My paternal grandmother was a tiny woman, and my father was big in the womb. Everyone said she would lose him, at five months it was already clear. This was a long time ago, 1909, you understand. She stayed in bed, but somehow it was believed she might lose him even then.

There were two daughters at home, my aunts, and so they, without complaint, stepped into most of the management of the house, though they were still young girls, twelve and thirteen at the time; they knew their mother would lose the baby if they didn't learn how to stay on top of things. Even worse, their mother herself might be lost. So they told the cook what to prepare at every meal, and made sure the housekeeper kept things orderly and they tended their mother themselves, dressing her in the morning even though she never left the bed, feeding her, knitting and reading with her, bathing her at night. The German doctor made a sling for the baby. It sounds very simple, *is* simple nowadays, I suppose, but they all acted like he was a god, this doctor. He made an elastic sling, and maybe it was the elastic that made it fantastic in those days, elastic in 1909 only recently invented for clothing, fantastic, the fact that it gave. He adjusted it to her groin and every week or so he would come see her and he'd adjust it again, and so she was able to keep the baby inside. And then when it did come out it was a boy. A beautiful boy with those two older sisters who'd had to grow up when he was still in the womb so that by the time he came out they were miniature adults, had been caring for him already for nine months; and then there was also his mother and a grandma and that cook and the maid, all right there in that one house, all those women. Babying him. Well, he'd never had to do anything, you see, my father. The gorgeous boy. The golden one.

So, many years later, when this lumber man, the German lumber man, offered to move my father from Mexico City to Oaxaca, to make him the partner in this great enterprise, my father said yes right away and left his job at the bank. This was a sign, he believed. Because a German had given him life.

My mother was a granddaughter of a French engineer who had come to Mexico to help set up the Mexican railroad. My mother's young life had been incredibly cloistered. She'd still get excited by candies and balloons at fifteen. 1931 and a balloon was all it took. And she was moral, had principles. When she found out my father was cheating on her with the maid in Oaxaca she threw him out. He had grown distant and cold, was coming to visit us in Mexico City less and less, and when she found out why this was she threw him out. You must understand, nobody ever threw them out for cheating with the maid. Every man cheated with the maid; this was Mexico, 1950, so it was a pre-ordained fact. Plus, it was in another state. Nevertheless, she threw him out and then she raised all of us on her own. Her own parents had long since died, tragically both of them. Carlos Courcelle had been bitten by some kind of infectious horsefly and died a month later, his daughter only five. Her mother died nine years after that and then my mother was raised by her aunt.

And this part gets very confusing, because her mother had already asked her sister, *If I ever die*, she had said, *you must take my daughter*. And her sister pushed right by her and into the kitchen while in a rushed voice she said, *Yes, of course I would take her, but please do not talk like that*. And then just a week or so later my grandmother contracted a fever and she did die. How had she known? And her sister, my mother's aunt, did take my mother in. But we all know that a mother and an aunt are not the same thing. Especially when a girl is fourteen. They just are not the same thing, a mother and aunt.

My sister and I—I don't at all like her, you might as well know it now, so you probably will not be hearing much about Sofia from me—my sister, Sofia, and I went to visit my father in Oaxaca, two or three times, my brothers refusing to come along because they hated my father's new woman. When we did go to visit, this is how it was: He was a silent man, spoke very little unless it was to command, even at dinner during which he merely gestured and grunted as that new woman held forth on some inane topic—she was very dull—while absently passing him the various dishes and sauces he pointed at. He merely gestured at what he wanted and she stupidly placed things in his hand.

I watched him as he ate, chewing hard like him.

After a short nap my father would set off to work again and in the afternoon we were allowed to follow. When we set into the woods there was dark and there was moist. My father trudged, trudged, ahead of us and we always kept him in sight—he might disappear we both feared—even when we seemed fully involved in something else. So that we were this: a serious man who walked with the heavy monster steps of slightly arthritic knees— moving forward through his toil, in what he professed to be the straightest of possible lines—and two small girls, circling about him, stopping to chase and catch and dig, to look and observe and wonder and fall back, and then run forward again to catch up and even get a little ahead of the insistent plodding steps of that man, our father.

I guess what I'm saying, what I'm trying to explain, is that this wasn't what I'd been brought up for. Sleeping in jails in Kansas. It was thrilling, yes, the wandering. M was beautiful, drew people to him. People wanted to be around us, to help us. They looked at him like that. But it was his fault. Everything to come was his fault. Julia. All of it. Everything that came later. Everything that would eventually happen, Julia. Don't ever forget that. Though things had started out well, the trip to Kansas City exciting, almost immediately it had all begun to get confusing, what he would get involved in on those dark nights, skulking like his father, his friends and the gambling, the long list of women. Those drawn, dark nights. But on our trip back it seemed good again; I thought we had left the confusion behind and again it seemed like he was mine. But only for a short while. A tiny little while. Because again things started feeling not right. We would get into a new town and M would disappear for long stretches of time. And then my mind started slipping in ways I didn't remember it doing before, in ways I didn't understand, and in these different towns I panicked; my mind would slip and my heart would race and I would panic. In these many different towns the dust tasted the same, the thick hot air, the sun beating, that sun beating down hard; and I cried and I cried. My thoughts started running in circles; these towns were all the same place. We would stay in a town for a day or two and then we would move on, but were we really moving? Were we really going anywhere at all? Getting any closer? All the towns were exactly the same. Was it in fact the same place? My judgment grew confused, my mind slipping, my heart racing for no reason at all, palms sweating, breath coming in heaves. He had a bit of a streak, then, and so we stopped in Amarillo for a while and on the third day there he gave me money to buy some groceries, things for the little hotel room we were staying in. He was lying in bed, propped up like a sultan, completely worn out from another late night, and when I approached him on that third Amarillo day he didn't want me to touch him. I looked at him with broken eyes and then I walked to the store instead, the dusty hot streets, and I came back thirsty from eating that dust and empty-handed except for a pretty little dog collar I'd found. I'd seen it in a shop window on the way to the groceries, so pretty and bright. But when I brought it home for him, it was a gift, he was mad. It was red leather, studded with diamonds, fake of course but so pretty. Luminous like his eyes, I told him. Bright and clear like the water which was his eyes, I told him; I was so thirsty and still he yelled at me while he held it in his hand. What the hell was I doing spending his money on a leash and a collar for a dog we didn't have? I blinked three times to make sense and then I tried to look into his eyes, those liquid blue eyes, I am so thirsty, I said to him, I need a drink, I said to him, but he just came up to my face and he grabbed the bag from my hands and stormed out with it so he could get his money back. And, confused, I stood there and I cried, staring at his receding back.

It was soon after that I started not sleeping; I paced and paced all night. I tried crying, but my eyes would not cooperate, so that there was no relief, now, a blank, nothing to let out. I tried screaming, my voice stifled. He would be gone sometimes for days at a time and so I had no one to run to. No one to find and to whisper to, no one to warn that there was somebody coming, someone was after us; I didn't know who, don't ask me who I would have said if he had asked; I had no idea, had not seen their faces, could not see their faces, but I heard them sometimes, whispering, and I knew that they were there, knew they were going to descend when I was not looking; and so I looked and I looked. I had to keep looking. I searched and I searched. I tried screaming. I would stand in the middle of the room, sometimes, and it would finally come to me, my voice, and so I would scream at them to come out, to just come now. I could not take it any longer. I would no longer wait! And sometimes, with my voice, this same voice, I yelled for them to go away. Get the fuck out of here!

In Galveston he took me to a hospital. It was not really a hospital, I don't think; no one there was there to help out, there had been no oath taken in that place. He slapped my face when I scratched at him and he pulled me into the car though I was kicking and when he got me there he spilled me out and they scooped me up off the pavement and they took me in and they tied me down. They tied me up liquid and held me down solid and shoved something cold and hard into my mouth and then they gave me those shocks in my head. They held me down tight and tied me up hard and gave me electricity shooting into my head and he watched them while they did it. I was seven months pregnant with our first baby, you understand; I don't think I've mentioned that. Did I already tell you that? I was pregnant. And I held on to Rocio with my steel legs gripping tight. I'd been sporty, the wild one, remember? and I was strong and I gripped my legs tight like clamping hard steel. And he, he let them do that to me. He watched while they did it.

It is his fault, I tell you. It was all his fault. Everything. All of it. I was not cut out for that life, that skulky wandering life.

Then, still drooling, he drove me back in another one of his borrowed cars, where did all of those cars come from? from whom did he borrow those cars?, to my mother in Mexico City. He dropped me on her doorstep, savagely spilled me out there too, and she picked me up soft and then she fed me gentle with a rounded spoon and she loving wiped away the drool while I stared straight with my eyes all full of blankness for many many months; to me she sang each night and then it was months before he came back. Rocio already squirming about in my mother's overly engulfing swallow me up arms when he finally came back.

Rocio

MY CHILDHOOD MEMORIES ARE mostly fuzzy, milky, like a watery dream. Yet some things do come back to me clearly, rise up inside me—painful, relentless—almost as whole scenes. One of our returns to my grandmother's house, for instance. I see myself at seven or eight, bouncing from foot to foot, anxious, waiting outside the front door of my grandmother Cecilia's house. The day was grey, with menacing clouds above, and my mother down below them, a dim dark presence there, her pencil skirt hugging her hips tightly, cinching her waist as she leaned forward, knocking furiously, ringing the bell again and again, then fisting her hand to pound once more.

Very soon, her voice, hysterical, began accusing through the mail slot: "Open up! I know you're in there!!"

She screamed it loudly and then paused for a few heaving moments before repeating the whole mad process again.

"I know you're in there!"

My mother marched over to the sealed tight window now and leaned her head against the pane: "Open up!" she yelled once more, her eyes wildly searching the silent insides.

Julia and Marta, already in the midst of some game, seemed oblivious to all this; but how could they ignore this behavior, my mother's angry arms hammering on the door, her fury filled voice screeching in windows? They seemed to take no notice of any of it, as they played, carefree, in the middle of the street. I turned and saw their four skinny legs chasing swiftly, unkempt hair bouncing in the breeze. They stopped suddenly then, and screeched in delight as they spotted an old washed-out hopscotch on the ground before them, "Me first! Me first!" they yelled almost in unison before throwing themselves down on all fours to search for pebbles. Within seconds they were jumping after those newly found pebbles tossed from number to number, in succession, joyful hopping from one to ten on their flamingoed legs.

I saw them, always, was constantly watching my sisters, though, perhaps because they were younger, they rarely saw me, never noticed my unease; how could they possibly see it now, my fingers nervously scratching at my own neck, or feel the tightness in my throat as I attempted to speak, to calm our mother, or sense the mortification I felt at noticing my Aunt Sofia's angry eyes looking down upon us from her bedroom window? I caught her there, scrutinizing, judging, wishing us away with her hard, determined eyes.

"Mami..." I implored, grabbing at her skirt, but when my mother turned to gaze at me with all the rancor she carried inside, I grew silent. My hand went back to my neck.

Did my aunt really think we would just leave? Where would we go? Didn't she know her sister, our mother, would never give up, never just go? A sudden fear rose inside me that I might soon draw blood and so I forced my clawing hand off myself, then checked under my nails for bits of disengaged skin.

Eventually, my aunt did come to the door. "Be quiet, Claudia," Sofia hissed. "Everyone already thinks you're insane. Do you have to constantly confirm it?" She collected herself then, and in full composure opened the door very slowly, clear and directed in her motions, purposely—or so it seemed to me—drawing a sharp contrast between herself and my mother. But as my mother fitfully pushed her way in, my aunt couldn't help but roll her eyes. "Back so soon?" she asked, ironic as she made way, my mother jerking her body inside that threshold, "Will you be staying long this time?"

My aunt turned from my mother and seemed to forget her for an instant as she ran her fingers gently through Julia's hair, gently, a further contrast to her sister's volatile motions, and my own little sister, hungry for it, paused before entering, melting for a moment in our aunt's soft caress.

What was my aunt Sofia doing there alone that day? Any of the others would have opened faster than Sofia, sparing me some of my mortification, she and my mother really hating each other the most and so finding any way to torture each other.

Yet, I liked my aunt, and didn't blame her even then. My suffering, I knew, was not her fault.

Was everything a mess from the beginning? It is all so murky, but it seems to me it was. A shameful mess. The past does rise up in me, sometimes, though there is nothing good calling me there, nothing warm, nothing to nostalgically long for. My mother and father had never been happy. I knew it even then. It had never been so. No one had ever been happy. Ever.

———

My father was rarely around and because of this my memories of him are extremely vague. It was because of this absence, of course, that we had to follow our mother like a bunch of sick puppies. We lived at my grandmother Cecilia's mostly, in the house my mother and uncles and aunt had grown up in. But then he would show up out of the blue, disturbingly boisterous. He almost always wore skinny suits, but the legs and the sleeves were often too short, so that he looked more like an overgrown boy in those suits than a father. He wore his hair slicked back, like Elvis or James Dean and he was always joking, his broad mouth smiling, his blue eyes dancing with a deep love of himself. I would see him offer that smile up, barter with it; what could he get in exchange? I rarely saw him angry, probably because he could get most of what he wanted with that wide open mouth. My father was fast talking and I knew that other people loved him, though I mostly feared him and worked to keep my distance. I didn't like the way he showed up, boastful and conceited, full of himself, descending on us, hugging us too tightly, throwing us up in the air, laughing loudly, then shouting at us to feel the muscles in his arms. Maybe we hadn't seen him in six or seven months, maybe we needed a moment to warm into it, needed to take it a bit slow, needed to center ourselves a little first, but there he'd suddenly be, instantly crowding us, overtaking us, sticking his face into ours and brazenly joking, and then abruptly, swiftly, as if to prove his manliness, he'd pick us up and carry us around on his shoulders, two at a time like some show-off tarzan.

He'd appear out of thin air, my dad. He'd even pretend at being a father, sometimes, ask us what we were up to, maybe even try to lower his voice a bit, give us advice, try to claim authority over us, as if we were a real and legitimate family, *his family.* But it never felt real, more like he was trying to prove something to someone, who knows who.

He would disrupt things. Disrupt us. He'd show up with a bunch of his friends, bring his guitar and play and sing during my grandmother's card games. He'd get everyone else to sing too and then he'd tell some jokes and make my grandmother laugh; he'd put his arm around my mother, lean back on the couch with his arm on her like that, his woman. He was so handsome in his suits, his slicked back hair, his big arms. He'd lean further back, his feet crossed at the ankles, chest puffing out. Claudia would smile a lot, laugh at his boisterous jokes, then run and throw on a tight wool skirt. A little sweater-set, pink or gold or red, and kitten heels. And off they'd go off. And over the course of that date, they'd decide to live together again. *Come on,* he'd say, *we have to try.* He would convince her to try again. Again, though they'd never for more than a couple of months lived together before. If he needed to he would insist; she was his wife. He'd get an apartment, or borrow one from someone he knew. He had lots of friends, my father. And then they'd gather us up and off we'd go into false dreams, my sisters squirming with the joy of it, my father belting out some raucous song as he drove us away from our grandmother.

I recall him putting his lying arm around our mother as he led her through the door each time. I can picture it as a series of photographic stills, almost. The guest house in Colonia Roma, behind the lonely old woman who lived in the front; she was the mother of one of my father's best friends and loved my father and would often hand us stale candy from her shaky hand, the bony fingers of which we were scared to graze as we took it; the apartment in Tlatelolco a year later, a place I especially liked, because it was modern and clean; the little house in the desert in Coahuila. And each time Claudia was pleased, for a while, before she began criticizing things, the size of the bathroom or of the kitchen. A smell no one else could smell, or how some dark shadow fell.

"I don't like the light," she would suddenly say. And within days she'd be crying about it. Weeping about the bad light. "That smell. Can't you smell it?" and we would shake our heads no, three baffled girls. "It's bitter. A bitter bitter smell!" She would insist. Start screaming it. Demand that we help her find it. And so we would follow behind her, Julia and I, scared, sniffing into corners, under tables and beds, in closets, truly frightened, really trying to help her, aching to find the source of that thing which we could not smell but that so clearly tortured our mother, while she wept and Marta ignored it all and ran around and around the house, climbing on and jumping from the furniture, barking at us from under the table, growling even, like an angry dog, striking out at us with bared teeth.

Very soon Claudia's complaints were filling whole days. Whole days were turned into her wet and weepy truths, her truth, repeated and repeated until we felt we were drowning in it; until we felt ourselves near death: three confused girls, variously drowning in the mess that was our mother's soggy repetition.

We only ever kept those places for a short while. But in the mixed-up, confused days of hopeful beginnings, my sisters and I would quickly find other kids in the building, or on the same block. Marta was especially quick to make friends. She would start games that all the other children wanted to play and almost always she would win though she was often the youngest. She could climb better than any of the boys, like a little monkey, so often her games had quite a bit of climbing in them. If the object of her invented game was to have someone throw a doll far into a tree, a lost baby in peril, she would always be the first to reach and save it, scrambling up that tree like a wild beetle, all her limbs moving quickly, one leg stretching, an arm reaching, a pull and a push. Though once saved, Marta just brutally threw that baby down, a heavy blow, its movable eyes shutting sharply upon landing. She never carried that baby carefully, or whispered to it, or cuddled and comforted in the descent, as I would have done. Of course, I never got a chance to show her how to do it, how it should be done right, the saving of a baby, because I was afraid of heights. And so I never did it at all, save a baby.

Unlike Marta, I almost always just stood back and looked on. I was so often scared as a child, even when there was no real threat in sight. And because of this fear, I was always watching, my green eyes wide and expectant of danger.

One of these times of pretending at family, of his pretending to be a real father, he moved us to a house in the Coahuilla desert. On that occasion we moved out of the city and to that lagoon bordered desert, into a small two story house our young strapping father had rented for us. Immediately Marta and I made a game of sliding down the stairs on a flattened out cardboard box, and even after she fell and hit her head hard on the wall and then cried and cried from the blow, they did not tell us to stop. This time we lived together a bit longer; seven or eight months perhaps, though initially we did not bring Julia. She at first stayed behind with my grandma and my aunt Sofia. I remember leaving her, packing into the car without her and wondering about this; it made no sense and actually made my heart hurt, but when I asked they ignored me, and when I asked again my father shushed me. Julia waved sadly as we drove away, trying to keep from crying, and then there was no one who looked at me the way she did; there was no one who followed and grabbed at my hand unexpectedly, or raised her eyebrows with me when my mother and father acted crazy. There was no one who imitated the way I skipped rope or brushed my teeth, or whom I could rush into our room when Claudia started screaming or crying, no one whom I could whisper to to calm each night. The days soon turned into one big gray cloud and I cried and cried myself to sleep at night, completely alone, though she was the one who had been left behind.

But it is true too that Claudia was less fierce without her there. There was no focus to her volatile energy when Julia was not around.

And then, suddenly, she was with us, and I recall being over-whelmingly happy when I saw her, so so happy when my grandma and my uncle Felix pulled up in his car, and her little face looked out at me from inside it, those sweet brown eyes, seeking me out. She ran to me, it seemed, before the car had fully stopped. To me. And I put my arms around her tightly and then pulled her by the hand, showing her the garden, where I made mud pies, then inside where we slid down the stairs, and the small room Marta and I slept in, the mattress on the floor in the corner. My grandma Cecilia and my uncle Felix left the next morning, but Julia stayed and I understood that they had come just to deliver her to me. And then I slept with her each night, whispering her into dreams. I had my Julia back.

On her third night there I couldn't help but ask it, though I knew I shouldn't. Though I knew it might hurt her, I asked anyway, "Did you miss us?" And I looked into her eyes for proof.

She pulled her gaze away from me and looked up at the ceiling instead, "Grandma Ceci took me on a horse ride through the city with Nico," she answered. "She told me they were taking me out and so I put on my beautiful polka-dot dress, the one with the big skirt, and Nico told me I looked very pretty. I couldn't look at him then, but soon we were in line for the carriage and the horses that pulled ours were white, the only white pair, and Nico lifted me up into my seat and then we rode that carriage behind the palace, and as the driver told stories about the Aztecs and the conquistadores who'd killed them, I leaned into Grandma Ceci's arm and whispered for her to point out what part of the palace she worked in while Nico held her other hand. The buildings behind the palace are all very old and the streets are made of stone and are narrow and crooked and Nico told me that those streets were made to be traveled like this, by horse. We ended up at a beautiful restaurant and I counted ten big chandeliers in the three rooms and when I turned from my counting I saw Nico kissing Grandma's cheek. They let me order chocolate cake for dessert and then we took another carriage back to Nico's car. And in that carriage back, Nico pointed out one of the buildings and told me that the walls there were covered in gold. A Spanish prince lived there once, he said, and then it became a school, and now it is a museum with murals on nearly every wall, and I will take you there some time, he said, when your grandma says its okay for all three of us to go out together again."

———

And then it was me who was jealous, though I tried not to be, me who felt the gray metallic tinge of having been left behind, who wanted to be out with grandma Ceci and her friend Nicolas, instead of having been sent off to live with the strange erratic ones.

And maybe it was then that I learned to stay away from him, to stay away from her, to never go anywhere with my parents again.

The garden which had seemed almost boring without her, became magical when she arrived. Julia saw something everywhere and could catch the lizards who scampered and hid in the cactus, "You have to be patient and get them by their middle" she said, "so their tails can't break off. Most people don't know how; they just grab at the tail." She knew how to get tadpoles too, from where they hid at the edges of the lagoon, tadpoles that she would then put into a small jar to turn into frogs in our bedroom. "Isn't it funny that things can change, Rocio?" she asked me. "Isn't it curious that a thing can become another? Isn't that strange, Rocio? that a silent swimming thing can turn into a big jumping one. That the big noisy jumping one can have a deep voice that sings so loud across the dark sky."

Once, we heard Bicho, the cat's low growl rising up from some deep part of him, and we rushed over, Julia leading the way. When we got there we saw that Bicho had cornered a tiny gray desert mouse. Upon seeing us he immediately pounced and instantly it was in his mouth, and Julia was suddenly on him, prying his jaw open, though Bicho tried to squirm back and away from her grasp. She did get that little creature out, "It's okay," she whispered tenderly to that half dead thing, ignoring where the cat had scratched her. "You're alright," she said as if to convince it, and then she set it down and we watched over that tiny mouse, squatting there for what seemed hours, Julia whispering warm encouragements from time to time, before it gathered itself up and darted off. "He could have died," she said when he was gone. And suddenly I was overcome with the thought that there was something in her, that it was her will that had saved that small creature, Julia's quiet force and attention and the way she had concentrated it all upon that little dying mouse. In some deep and magical way, Julia had poured herself into that struggling life.

I saw it then, the way Julia talked, the way she looked at things, the way she held them inside herself and did something with them, extraordinary and beautiful, before she put them back out into the world; even with her words she could do this so that a simple lizard was for her an adventure, a full emotional life, a slithery reptile that you could capture and feed and make into a pet for five minutes; she would touch at its skin, turn it over, inspect its little feet with their perfect nails, and seek out its pumping heart, the only thing moving in that lizard who lay fully still in her grasp; while touching at his belly she told me about his wife waiting for him at home, their three children, one of whom was an opera singer, and how they fed on fireflies so that their bellies shone in the night; and then she turned him over and let him go. Julia took things inside herself and she added something there, some sort of beauty, before she spilled them back out.

Where I saw danger and felt a need to hide, she reached quietly into things and made something new and hers which she then shared.

"Naughty cat," Julia gently scolded Bicho when we saw him sunning himself near the house hours later, his stomach exposed, his legs sticking up. She bent down to scratch at his ears, "He's just a simple kitty," she said to me, "That's just how simple kitties are. They can't seem to help themselves."

I loved Julia, but could share her too and there were other kids on the block and though it was a desert we all swam in those lagoons full of water that came down in springs from the big mountains in the distance and gathered as pools there near us, only four or five blocks down from our house so that there was this magic water very close, this place for us to float and paddle in; and it was beautiful; we played and played all day staying in that water for hours as if we were made of it.

And like this we forgot that not long ago they had separated us, we forgot, too, the last time we'd all lived together, our mother and our father and us. We forgot all the last times of newness and excitement at being a family, and how it all always ended in misery and blight.

Each time, my father's money would run out. They would start fighting more intensely. My mother would lose her secretarial job, if she had one. She would snap at the boss, or make one of the older women angry with the way she so openly flirted. Or else our father would just start not showing up at night. And then not showing up at all.

I remember in Coahuila sitting at the table ready to have dinner and he would simply not come. It was never a real meal like we ate at my grandmother's where meals were two or three courses always. With my mother it was inevitably something thrown together, quesadillas with no cheese or thin soups, sliced cucumbers on an otherwise empty plate, or a tortilla and a fried egg. Yet, we were acting at being a family, our little legs hanging inches above the floor as we sat there, Julia's and my hands properly sitting in our lap, though Marta would often just run around and around the room, making strange noises. We were acting like we thought other families acted, acting at having real meals together. And we would wait and wait for him to complete the picture, give shape to the illusion. But he would not come. And we would sit there. And then the next morning he would still be gone. And Claudia grew angrier and angrier with each passing day so that we knew not to approach her. I knew to take Julia's hand and lead her and Marta outside, away from the dark cloud that was our mother; and once out Marta would initiate some loud game, a screaming shrieking hide and seek. The boys from down the block would come over and pretty soon there'd be a big and furious game of tag too, my sisters in their short outgrown dresses, mad chasing legs, the boys and their dogs running circles around them, screaming and shrieking. I would nervously try to settle us into something quieter, like jacks or mud pies, I was so afraid of further aggravating Claudia with our noise. And then at night I would try to silently lead them both in, but often Claudia would fling herself at us in anger, throwing her hand about, connecting with Julia's head more often than not. "Don't look at me like that!" her mouth would yell at my sister. And though she had not even looked in her direction, Julia would never protest, never even try to defend herself.

There is nothing you can do. How can you do anything? But in your terrified silence you are incriminated. I was the oldest, yes, but I was only nine. And if you were like five year old Marta you were openly fanning the discord, fighting to get all of the little there was for yourself. So that though we were just children, we were put into the camp of either cowards, or traitor sycophants. Little tiny girls, and in the war that was our family already our sins were being written out for us.

I don't really know what order any of this happened in, truthfully; the timing of it all is so confusing, but I learned to cook some basic things when I was still quite young, too young, perhaps, fideo soup, and eggs. I would take Julia to the little store two blocks down and get tortillas and mangoes and cucumbers and limes. I'd set the money or the vitamins down on the counter, things I had found or else taken; sometimes the grocer would give me my groceries and hand my money back. I would catch his eyes looking at my clothes, the stains and tears in my hand-me-down dresses, or else at Julia, her long unruly hair, and I would clench my hand tightly around that money.

At some point Claudia had stopped even trying, and so I would feed my sisters. And while Julia followed me around, holding my hand, telling me stories about some bird she'd found, or a giant beetle that had swam next to her in the lagoon, Marta would go off to play, fiercely, with some group of street kids. She was always being adopted into some family or other; those other mothers falling in love with her fiery green eyes, what they thought of as her cute grown-up manner, scolding rules into the other children, No! she would say, and wag her finger at the other little girls who looked up at her with big obedient eyes. The way she would strut. She would make them laugh, those other mothers, so that she was always chubby with a belly full of another family's food, even as Julia and I grew thinner and thinner.

Eventually we would get kicked out of our place and of course we would end up dragging our feet back to my grand-mother Cecilia, me holding Julia's limp little hand, my mother pulling fidgety Marta along. And then, after some furious banging on the door to let us in, we would be right back where we started from, living at my grandmother's house once again.

I was the oldest so I noticed things my sisters probably didn't. I knew my grandmother's other children, my uncles Felix and Adrian and my aunt Sofia, hated having us back. It was our mother they despised, not us. I saw this even then. Though their unmasked irritation at our arrival still hurt. *Here they come again, Claudia and her unruly daughters*; I could almost hear it. Though only one of us, Marta, was truly unruly. But we were all three in need of washing, with uncombed hair, skin and bones except for Marta. Those hungry eyes. None of her siblings liked Claudia at all, and, of course, we were an extension of her, whether we liked it or not. Yet, their irritation with her was well founded, I knew. She'd always needed so much, taken so much. She always pushed herself into the center, no matter what. And my grandma Ceci defended her always, even I could see that.

Soon my mother would start flirting with Sofia's boyfriend's brother. The two guys would just be in the living room, nicely dressed, greeting my grandma, nodding their heads in respect, making a joke or two, waiting on my aunt Sofia, and my mom would descend from her room and start up, speaking slowly, in a low voice, or else laughing a lot, loudly, staring straight at the men while draping herself over the couch or a chair. Sofia would be furious. The last thing she wanted was my mother enmeshed in Antonio's family. "Stay away from him," Sofia would warn later that night and my mother, in her flimsy black slip, would instantly be at Sofia's throat, yelling, "Who do you think *you* are?" her eyes blazing, the veins in her neck flaring out like two angry snakes. "You can't tell me what to do!"

In a calm voice, slow and calm but deadly serious, Sofia would repeat again, "Stay away," and my mother would start shouting, calling her names as Sofia, in a forced stony composure, walked away.

One time my mother found out my uncle Felix had locked Marta in his bedroom. It was only for a minute, to teach her a lesson. He'd found her in there rifling through his drawers, his things strewn all over, "You want to be in there so badly? Now you're going to stay in there," he shouted as he shut the door. The lightbulb in his room was red, and he had a skull and other tomb-like things on little shelves all over, so that it was terrifying in there. Marta screamed and banged on the door and wept and screamed some more. And my mother flew at him when she found out. Instead of telling Marta to stay out of their stuff, she flew at Felix like a wild animal, leaping on him as if Marta were her own life force, and had been truly threatened. He almost hit her back, I could see it, but he controlled himself, even though his arm was bleeding from where she'd scratched.

"Lunatic!" Felix yelled as he retreated. "Keep your brats out of my room," he added, and though they were my mother and my sister it hurt me to be included with them.

And then we were all meant to console her, as she cried and cried, spent, in a heap on the couch, even though she was the one who had enacted that violence, the one with blood on her hands, her fingers, under her nails.

My grandmother would come home and find my mother weeping after each of these incidents, and she would go and yell at my uncles and aunt.

It injured them deeply, to be yelled at by their mother. They worshipped my grandmother Cecilia so that, though they were not in the wrong, they never said anything back.

I always wondered why my grandmother defended her. What was there between them? Once, my mother and her youngest brother Adrian were in the kitchen. I nervously ran over to peek in from the edge of the dining room when I heard him yell at her to tame her beast, meaning Marta, who had left his honey spilled all over the table. It was a special black honey from the Yucatan his girlfriend had brought him; she was serious and shy and she'd brought it back for him from a family trip, and we all knew we were not to touch it. He had made it very clear. We called it the love honey behind his back. "Oooooh, the love honey! *Do not touch the looooove honey!*" but Marta had not only used it, she had left it smeared all over the table as proof of her disregard, the container open, sticky remnants all over its side. "Tame your beast!" he yelled at my mother as he picked up the jar, and when she went at him he grabbed her hands and held her there, squeezing tight, laughing in her face as she feebly tried to pull free. My grandmother was home that time. And she flew past me into the kitchen at the sound of Claudia's yells, and I was immensely relieved that she would soon be stopping all this. "Let her be," my grandmother said to Adrian. "Let go of her."

"Get the hell out of here! Leave us the fuck alone!" my mother shrieked at her. "Leave me the fuck alone!" Claudia turned and stared at my grandmother with such hatred in her eyes that I ran.

My grandmother was only trying to defend her. And I could not fall asleep that night.

Her brothers and sisters had always hated her and now they were all in their twenties and as soon as they'd settle into the relative quiet of the house without her, their handsome boyfriends and slow walking girlfriends and the easy rhythm of the days and of those long warm nights, the simple flowing in and out of that house, there she would come again. Tromping in. Their mess of a noisy sister, being trailed by the three of us.

There we always were, in that house, bouncing off the furniture, screaming and chasing and crying and screeching. Our eager eyes, inexhuastibly needy, because our mother was gone half the time, disappearing into dark nights just like that.

Yet, they did always soften. Sofia would begin to put her arms around Julia, to tenderly comb her hair. She would whisper at her to come along when she was going shopping, in her ear only, or to a movie. She would take her out to eat often. She and her boyfriend, Antonio, loved pretending she was their child. And though I often felt left out, I knew this was good, was important even, because except for when she was being cruel to her for no reason, or what I at the time thought was no reason my mother ignored Julia completely.

But then again, what did I know then about her reasons, my mother's sick reasons; what do I know about them now?

Sofia would buy Julia clothes to replace the old worn dresses, the tattered shirts and pants. Julia was so neat, so quiet, so serious. She folded and cared for things, even her very old and threadbare things, in a way that only served to further break your heart. Sofia bought Julia lots and lots of colorful clothes and got Julia a new haircut, too. This was after, completely unannounced, my mother had taken the huge craft scissors from out of the drawer and pulled little Julia's thick long hair up high above her head and then cut it all off. It was the night before the last in the house in Coahuila, a few weeks after the tornado, right before my uncle Felix showed up to take us back to my grandmother's house. Claudia grabbed Julia's hair balled up in her fist like a piece of crumpled paper. And then she held it up high and cut it off in two big swipes so that it was all uneven. I would have cried, having my beautiful hair cut like that. But six year old Julia just stared straight when our mother was done. She didn't even look in the mirror, just silently walked out of the room like that. It was the next day that I called my grandmother. And then Felix came for us and when she saw it my aunt Sofia fixed Julia's hair. She got her new shoes too, a pair of red patent leather clogs that I remember still. And she would let Julia sleep in her bed most nights. Though on other nights we all slept together in the one bed, me and Julia side by side, Marta down at our feet. From down there Marta was always trying to warm her toes by putting them up our pajama shirt or pants, even up into our panties sometimes, her wormlike toes squirming about in there.

Though I can't remember the order in which things happened, though it is all unclear and fuzzy, we did grow up like that, pulled along and mostly unwanted. Yet it does seem we were wanted enough for them to pick sides, my parents' families, for them to have further cause to dislike each other. Of course we didn't know why they treated each of us so differently, the two families.

I was chosen by my father's side, my grandma Marina and my aunt Mina. Because I looked like him, I believed—my father—like them, tall and light skinned with green eyes, and though we all want, wish and hope that things are not so basic, in fact most of the time they are. The color of skin, of hair, of eyes, the most rudimentary biology determining whole lives. I was with them often as a result of how I looked. But they all made it clear where we belonged; Julia was most often with Grandma Ceci and my aunt Sofia. Marta, it seemed, was mostly with my mom. Marta was Claudia's favorite, and though my mother had little to nothing to offer, we still silently hated Marta for it, and of course she hated us back. Though, I believe, being our mother's favorite ended up being as much of a detriment to Marta as anything else, because it simply did not work in your favor with anyone else. And, like I said, my mom didn't have much to offer. A dark and sneaking sickness, she could certainly offer that.

Julia was six years old when my mother gave her away. Just like that. This I do remember clearly. We had just gotten back from Coahuila. It had only been a few months. There was the tornado in the desert and then Felix came and got us and then a few months later my sister was gone. I recall the day, I'm ashamed to say it. Julia was wearing a beautiful blue dress; I remember it, though I can't say who got it for her. And a big bow in her hair. She may even have held a little bag, white to match her bow and her crisp bobby socks. She was so skinny. Her eyes long and drawn.

They had told us she was going for a visit, my father's brother, our uncle. He was a nice man, this uncle David. Though because he lived in the States we didn't know him that well, we knew that. David was nice. He and his wife lived in California and we thought they had a lot of money (of course, we believed everyone in the US had tons of money back then) and Julia was getting to go and I wasn't; and I was jealous. I remember the black car that my grandmother Marina came to get her in. Though she wasn't close to Julia, because David was her son, Grandma Marina, would deliver Julia to him. It was an event. My grandma Ceci almost cried when she said good-bye; you could see her holding it in. And I remember wondering why she was letting Julia go, if it was going to make her feel like that, her body stiff from holding those tears in. And then I remember Julia's small, frightened face turning back, looking out the rear window of that big black car; at me. She was looking at me as they pulled away. She must have had to get up on her knees at that point, to continue looking back. And then, as they kept driving, her little hand went up and she waved, back and forth, like a wipe, her searching brown eyes a straight line, firmly set on mine. I waved back, tried to smile, though, shamefully, I was very jealous. Because Julia was at the center of all this fuss. She was the one in the middle of all of this commotion. And she was getting to go, and I wasn't. They had been preparing us for a few weeks. My uncle was rich, we believed. She would get wonderful toys, they told us. Beautiful clothes. Long green lawns. She was getting to go and I wasn't and I was jealous. Though as soon as she was out of sight my grandmother Cecilia cried.

I was supposed to be the good one. The one who never made problems and was kind and generally gentle and caring. I was pretty, even, as if that were the outward sign of my inner goodness, they said. And quiet. I was helpful. I was the one everyone got along with. I never fought. Innocent, and though I was cautious, I was eagerly gullible too, even I knew that. It was a joke I was in on. I fell for anything anyone told me. If you cut your dolly's stomach she will talk my cousin told me, and though I knew it couldn't be so, I wanted to believe in things so badly, that I cut my own doll up the next day. If you swallow three cherry pits your wish will come true, my uncle Felix said once, and though Marta rolled her eyes, I swallowed, nearly choking on each one. I will not tell you what I wished for on that day, for a part of me believes it may still come true.

Gullible, yes, but my goodness was never an issue: I was shy; I was kind; I was caring. Yet, now, instead of feeling bad that my little sister was being taken away, instead of being wary when they said that she'd be coming back, instead of trusting my own initial disbelieving, that sick black hole in the middle of my stomach, my queasy morbid intuition, I ignored all that and was terribly jealous instead.

I knew she loved me more than she loved anyone else, trusted me more deeply, more fully, and, even then, knowing there was something strange in this awkward and sick parting—my grandmother crying, my aunt Sofia refusing to be there at all—I was full of resentful jealous feelings. Her little hand waving, a wipe, her sweet dark eyes.

I lifted my own envy-filled hand, then, and with it I waved back, a green-eyed coward.

Good-bye.

And then I didn't see her for four years. And when I did see her again, everything had changed.

Julia

I ENDED UP IN NEW YORK, far away from the Los Angeles I had grown up in with my uncle David, but far from Mexico City and my mother and sisters too. And with this distance, in this place where I had no roots, I tried to invent myself. This is where, at eighteen, I began my adult life. This place is where, in desperation, I attempted to erase my history and studied instead the history of art. It is where, now nearly two decades later, having recently ended it with Joaquin, I am choosing to start from again.

Only now, instead of living in the city, I live on Long Island. It is solitary here most of the time, and that seemed okay until recently. Until recently I liked the aloneness, deeply believed the solitude would help me finish my book, all of the summer people gone, the leaves turning and beginning to fall off the trees. I have my dog, a cream colored mutt I found at the shelter here, and we go for long walks every day. He leaps about my legs at the sight of his leash and then we go to the Long Island Sound and I throw sticks into that gently lapping water; he dutifully wades in after them, joyfully trotting those sticks back to me, over and over again, like a job. I wander into town once a day. I go to NY nearly every week, visit galleries, have drinks with friends. I do my internet from the local library, and have become friendly with the librarians. I read a lot too. And in the mornings and early evenings I force myself to sit and write.

Daily I feel I should just quit, but after six years working on this book it is almost as if I have quit already, and so the point becomes moot, until I force myself to start again each night. Every night, almost, I have a moment of dread, and again I must tell myself it doesn't matter, that it is like I've already quit, and somehow through this nightly ritual of deprecation the pressure eases a bit and I can begin. But last night none of this worked and I sat at my desk in a panic, unable to start. I never quite know where I'm going, never quite know what attracts me to an artist, why it is that I am drawn, but I have to trust something, start somewhere, or else there is nothing, and so I let myself go where I need to. I can usually begin by writing about this or that work and after a while, usually, I become further drawn in; through one piece I move to another and sometimes, when things are going well, I understand the line between what came before and where I am headed. But last night was terrible, I was suddenly and inexplicably very anxious and soon felt overwhelmed, so I allowed myself, finally, to get up from the table, my heart racing. And this morning, after a bad night's sleep, I find myself wanting to write about Robert Barry, wanting to write about gas, about the way in "The Inert Gas Series" we are being asked to look at this invisible substance. But how do you photograph that which is to the naked eye not there? We look and we look but all we see is the paraphernalia surrounding that gas. In one of the photos Barry bends over a flask. In the photo that follows he stands back, away from the flask, hands on hips, looking on as that gas, which we are being asked to believe is there, disperses. The next picture is of the flask alone in the desert landscape; this is evidence too, no? We trust that he has released it; we believe the gas is there, even if we cannot see it.

And as that indiscernible amorphous presence shifts and flows it becomes constantly some new mutation of itself, something altered. Just because you can't observe it, just because it is going on in an invisible realm, this does not mean it isn't happening, the photos seem to say. The gas, Barry tells us, "continues to expand forever, constantly changing and doing so without anybody being able to see it." This idea of change is as important as the fact that it is unobservable; change, or process, or transformation as central to an artistic practice, even when imperceptible, mirrors the workings of the psyche, the way we are constantly in process too, being shaped through time, or formed by it, and the events therein. Barry's work, in its simplicity, speaks to all of this.

Robert Barry's respect of the tiny motion and his understanding of the way that a minute action can continue to affect everything forever, however invisible, however small, is pointed, and poignant as well, his notion of process, of change.

Recently, this philosophy of process has come to mean something in the world at large too, outside the sphere of art. Developments in neuroscience are leading to an idea of neuro-plasticity, the notion that the brain keeps developing and thus forming throughout an entire lifespan. That change opens the door to new possibilities, that there is always an option for something different... I have to believe this. I have to believe that things can shift and flow, that there can be motion, a rewriting of possibility. That I am not written by my past, that I am not bound to be some sad image mourning a mother... I have to believe that I will finish this book, not for anything other than the knowledge that I have done so, that I can do so... through the tiny motions I make on the page each night, however small, unobservable, or seemingly inconsequential. That struggle means something to me.

For some artists this motion is marked by a repetitive line, Hanne Darboven and her minute shifts in repetition; for others a body struggling with matter, Ana Mendieta covered in mud and the expansion of the elements around her, so that she is that mud and different from it at once. How do we name all the things that make us who we are, all of this work seems to ask; all that which affects us, which moves us to struggle with the outside, with the ineffable, the inexpressible? To become it, even. And what saves us from slipping off the edge, the terrifying end where things do seem unspeakable, the place where time does seem to stop, where development ceases, where language doesn't reach or suffice, the place that is the same as death? The place that mimics it so completely that we are the walking dead, the living dead, the stiff, the zombified.

The tiny motion, the rubbing in earth, the repetitive mark, a symbolizing of something that otherwise seems impossible to define, impossible to take grasp of, a making of meaning through some small action, an insistence on the voicing of something which can provide at the very least a decentered understanding, a knowledge which is constantly moving and thus maybe never really a knowledge at all but an idea which, just as it is almost graspable, is always shifting and changing and melding into something else, that speaks to this need to transform, this conviction that transformation is always taking place. The same painting painted over and over except for some tiny gradation, Agnes Martin, like Gertrude Stein's repetition, always this, but also always already on the way to becoming that. The inside and the outside and how they develop into each other, how they are always already one, being and becoming.

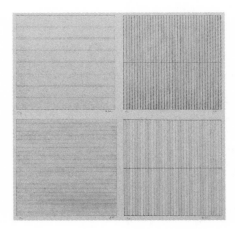

But what does this all mean for someone like my mother, for whom process never builds, for whom process and time only equal a chaos that never adds up to anything at all. Even as I deeply want to believe in transformation, I also wish for definition, for the stories—of which there are many—to add up to something, to someone, to a thing or person intelligible, sayable. Something, or someone, to hold on to. A centered presence. A definable being. A meaning. Someone knowable. Graspable. A mother. Or the story of a mother, at least.

And yet they do not. The various segments do not add up. And I can't really speak to her, nor to my long ago need to flee from her, nor to my continued want of her. Not to any of that. My lack is the only thing I can speak to, that absence as set against my deep and gnawing need.

So, instead of her, because she is too painful, I will tell you about myself through him, as he is less complicated, simpler for me to grasp, if less compelling, somehow:

Though he hadn't lived with my mother for years, the summer I was thirteen my father was around more than usual. I think I've mentioned that he always moved around with teenage boys; sometimes there would be only one, though often he traveled with many. He was older than them, of course, so he teased them viciously, openly, in front of us, some dumb and callous joke tossed out at their expense, "Oyé F-f-f-f-flaco," he'd call out to the very fat boy with the stutter and that boy himself would laugh even though the mocking was cruel and gruelingly stupid. He would tease those boys about us too. One day he arrived with six or seven of them, and before disappearing into my grandmother's house he noticed one of his younger boys staring at me. Lalo was my age, with big lips and big ears too, his hair pulled back in a loose ponytail, "You like Julia?" my father asked that boy, nudging him with his elbow. "Act fast; she's only visiting; she's the one we released." Then, facing my sister he added, "Don't even bother looking at La Virgen, Rocio. You might as well just go pray at her altar, she's so uptight." Red faced, I looked toward my sister, who, without saying a word, had turned and was walking away, toward her friend Amanda's house, while I stupidly stood there and watched my father in his skinny pants and white t-shirt, the sleeves rolled up to show off his muscles, cigarette dancing in his fingers, walk into my grandmother's house to ask for something.

And then that group of boys acted like they weren't standing around waiting for him; they bunched and shifted near us, as if they'd just dropped by to hang out for a while. A couple of the older ones lit cigarettes, and nervously glanced back and forth between the house and their feet, while the three youngest punched at each other and laughed a lot; ugly Lalo, the big eared boy, stood apart and stared over at me. Pretty soon though, the other five had pulled him into their group and they all hunched further in around each other, whispering, smoking cigarettes, an occasional and to our ears lewd group laughter rising up and then falling uncomfortably back down around them as it transitioned back to murmured whisperings.

Marta, our friend Bubbles, her sister Laura and I pretended they weren't there, forming our own little group, whispering about the boys we actually liked, boys from our neighborhood who were handsome and funny or smart and were not friends with our father. And then I felt something at my back. It was Lalo, suddenly behind me, his hand in my hair. "Oooooooh!" Marta screeched and Laura laughed loudly, both of her hands flying up to her mouth in shock.

"What are you doing?!" Bubbles yelled. I stood there, struck dumb, my face a bright red. Lalo looked startled, completely confused, as if he didn't at all know what it was he was doing, his big lips working to form a word which never came.

My father walked out, having finished his business, ignored our shrieks, threw the boys a nod, and off they all went following behind him without another word, ugly Lalo too.

"Gross!" Marta and Bubbles yelled together as those boys walked off with our father, throwing an accusing look my way, as if I'd asked for that strange attention.

Marta and I didn't question the lack of a good-bye from our father, and we didn't look up from our teasing to bid him a farewell either.

The next time he showed up he brought a boy we'd never seen. He was younger than the rest, only about twelve or so, and handsome too, with wide shoulders and a straight nose, high cheekbones and honey colored eyes, so light they were yellow, and a deep direct gaze which made him seem much older. Marta walked over to him on some dare and unflinchingly lifted her shirt for him to see, and though she had nothing there yet, he stared at her intently, like a man. When she had long pulled her shirt down and the rest of us had settled into a game of *Name That Tune*, taking turns humming a few bars of some popular song while the others screamed out titles to guess, he kept silently staring at Marta so that it made me nervous, though she clearly liked the attention and noticeably flirted back, humming extra loud while looking right at him. And later, when my father walked out she ran up to him, begging, hanging off his arms, trying to get him to take her along with them. Rocio and I were relieved when he said no, for we had seen something sinister in that boy's yellow cat eyes.

We thought of them as degenerates, not the kind of boys we'd really look at ... or what we thought of as that. Though sometimes we did sing whole songs together, belting them out in broken English as they rose loudly from the radio ... *the cat's in the cradle and the silver spoon...* or, *baby you can drive my car...* and skinny Sergio, the funniest one of the boys, would, on cue, leap into my father's car with his rubbery body and begin steering the wheel madly as if he were really driving, his hands flying all over that wheel as the car sat fixed in its parking spot, my father finally reaching in to slap at his silly head a bit, sending all of his long unruly hair flying about, while Sergio acted as if he had genuinely been hurt by that clownish smack, rubbing at the spot with an injured Stan Laurel expression, the rest of us laughing loudly at his mugging.

Once, when they arrived we were in the middle of a show. This was something we did mostly for each other, though sometimes we were able to cobble together an audience of our grandmother and uncles and aunt. We were intently working on *Jesus Christ Superstar*, though some of the lyrics, Judas's especially, scared me a little. We were yelling at each other about when the key twirl should take place, already in our costumes, which we'd fashioned out of flowing pieces of material we'd found in the closets, capes and long skirts, and head-dresses with flowers and lots of streaming parts and though they were mostly just taped and stapled together, those costumes were very glamorous. Suddenly an older group of these boys was in our midst. Why they had entered the courtyard I don't know, for out of respect for my grandmother they usually stayed outside the gate while my father slipped inside to give a greeting, ask for money, beg my uncle Adrian to get him re-hired at Pfizer, or to at least give him a box full of samples, whatever it was he was involved in on any given visit. But on this *Jesus Christ Superstar* day they were daringly inside that gate and they even helped us make a little stage out of some bricks and large planks and then they sat back on the grass and watched as Marta and Rocio and Bubbles and I performed. Rocio almost instantly ran out of the gate and to Amanda's, clearly mortified. But Marta and Bubbles and I twirled and held our short sticks up to our mouths as we sang about how we didn't know how to love him, and those boys, along with Laura who we never let perform with us, cheered and laughed all through our act.

They were probably high, slapping their knees and hooting like that, Mario even smacked Laura on the back once and, startled, she laughed even harder to keep up with him. Marta and Bubbles bowed and bowed while I blushed from the attention.

And then my father was out of the house, nodding tersely to those boys, and just as stealthily as they had entered, they were off, while we looked after them, a sudden and atypical hush falling over us girls for two or three minutes before Bubbles and Marta began to fill it with their bickering, arguing about who had danced more beautifully while I fingered at my beautiful skirt. Their senseless squabble died away as I thought of Pablo, that memorable trip through those Mexican beaches, me and him and Marta all together for nearly two weeks, wandering over Mexico, floating over that land in our father's VW, inhabiting those beaches where we would swim together all three; and how even though we had been a tightly wound group for a while, though we had lived together in and out of that car for twelve or thirteen days, even so, at the end of that time we were the ones who were dropped off first, my sister and I, and then my father and Pablo went off together, not much more than a wave good-bye.

We stood just outside the gate and watched that car drive away, all our belongings in palm-frond bags we had bought from an Indian woman on the beach and which we now gripped in our hands, our only souvenirs, their radio blaring till the sound became distant... *baby you can drive my*.... Marta simply shrugged and went in, but I stood and looked after them for a long time, in disbelief at that brief good-bye, and then Pablo stuck his head out to look back one last time, his hair tossing in the breeze as he stuck his head way out. He put his hand to his mouth then, paused it there, and blew that kiss out to me...

I remember I had tears streaming down my face.

In the end we never questioned the presence of those boys, their friendship with our father, or anything around it, though our grandmother and aunt would whisper sometimes. Those boys were older, nearly twenty, or younger, pre-pubescent; they had caramel colored eyes and curly hair, or straight long hair and deep black eyes. There were the green-eyed twins he'd brought to my grandmother's house for a party after a wedding; one of them I'd lain with, behind the couch, whispering into the night. I would never admit it to my sisters, but I liked him. His hair was straight and black and long, down to his shoulders, and his dark-lashed green eyes leapt out against the golden brown of his skin. He was rumored to be magical with animals, dogs and horses and he had once brought a hummingbird back to life, tenderly holding it in his cupped hands until it recovered from a blow inflicted when it flew into a window. He rescued bats trapped inside of houses too. The first time he'd caught a very small bat that was hanging from a ledge inside his house by putting a bowl over it and then quickly sliding a piece of cardboard under the whole thing to keep it from flying away as he calmly walked it outside and set it free in the garden. After that he would get called whenever someone found one in their house. He became famous for it and once, he told me, the bat he released flew around and around him in the yard, sending off high screechy sounds that were like little thank yous each one.

He seemed tender and proud both as he told this part of the story.

I looked at him and told him my own animal story, "Our cat Paco was terrified when he first got here," I said. "I think he was feral. Maria brought him home to hunt mice—she is a real hater of mice—but when she got him here he immediately ran under the refrigerator and wouldn't come out. It made her very angry, his laziness. But I worked and worked to get him out from under there, tempting him with cheese and fish and milk and calling to him very softly, *Come Paco. Come on Paquito*, over and over. Eventually he did come and soon I was hand feeding him. He let me pet him a little, coming out a bit further each day; and after a while I was able to grab and pull him fully out and I forced him to sit in my lap. He's used to me now, and comes out whenever I call. He even lets me brush him. But only me." I looked into that twin's eyes, "He's very shy," I added. "But I think he loves me now," I said.

The twin nodded, "He understood your patience," he said. "He appreciated it, you know; it said something to him about you. Cats and dogs have a language too, you know, all animals have a language; you just have to watch and learn it." He got very serious then, and so I stared into his eyes as he talked, "We all expect animals to understand *our* language," he said, "we shout orders at animals and expect them to react, but very few of us try to learn their language, which would make more sense if we're supposed to be the smarter ones. Instead we expect them to be smarter than us, to understand us, when we can't understand them." I nodded as he spoke. "To a dog you're just a dog too," he said. "And you have to teach them you're the leader of their pack. Never ever let a dog pass through a door before you," he said gravely. "This is part of their speak. And when you take him for a walk, always make him stay respectfully behind you. Don't ever let him lead, because this means something. Talk to him in a voice that sounds like a bark. Short sharp commands," he said.

I knew this boy understood language and power and how you have to adjust to others, to each situation. And his eyes were like my sister Rocio's. She was the most beautiful person I'd ever seen and I wanted to make this boy's eyes mine. I wanted them to stare at me just like they were now for the whole night.

But then I had a moment of curiosity driven weakness, "What do you do with my father?" I asked. "Why do you all like to be with him so much?"

He looked away for a moment, but then turned his tender eyes back on me, "I don't have a dad," he said. "We live in a pretty small place. My mom works all the time. Your dad's always around. He takes us out, me and my brother," he said, "and some-times he buys us things. Clothes sometimes. Food. Cigarettes."

My breath caught in my chest, and I noticed my hands fisting. My father had never bought me a gift.

"Last week he took us to Avandaro," he said, "and we went swimming in the lake and afterward we went to this place he knew about where the women make these amazing carnitas. They cook the pork in a big hole in the ground, and they sit making tortillas while you eat. We were all wet, still in our bathing suits, but it didn't matter, the old women were so nice, and your dad told jokes and we were all just kind of happy."

My body was fully tense now, how could he not have noticed, but he kept going.

"He bought me this shirt," he told me.

It was a beautiful shirt he was wearing, green like his eyes, and when he tried to place my hand on it I leapt up, furious, from where we lay behind that couch. My sisters saw me then and teased me about liking him and though I did I never again got close to him, for aside from my jealousy at his time spent with my father, at some level I had understood something I did not know how to think then; something about him and my dad, all those boys and my dad. Still, his body had been warm and his heart had been open and sympathetic and kind. And before he'd told me it had been a gift from my father I *had* wanted to touch that shirt, had admired it, had noted how it played with his eyes.

For my father there wasn't a type and for me only with Pablo was there anything like a real and sustained crush, or an interest which would, from time to time, rise into a crush. I, in fact, still wonder about him sometimes.

My father took me to Pablo's home that 13th summer, the only one of these boys' homes I ever entered. I met his mother, and one of his sisters too. His mother cooked for us and my father spoke to her respectfully. Pablo and I went for a walk while she prepared our meal and he made me stop and look at things in a way I rarely had before. He named trees, told me about the poplars which were planted by the hundreds on the order of a Spanish Viceroy. They were meant to remind him of Madrid, but when they weren't growing fast enough for his liking he'd had them all removed and then had replaced them with ash and willow trees instead, Pablo said. "This is why there are so many willow trees in Mexico City now," he said. I looked at him as he stared at the trees in the Alameda, his long curls, his deep black eyes and beautiful brown skin. "I like them," he said, "its a cliché but they do make the whole city seem wise and melancholic."

And, cliché or not, I saw them that way too then, for the first time.

We were near Paseo de la Reforma. "Did you know that Maximilian had Reforma built as a gift for Carlota?" he asked as he turned to look at me, "For her golden carriage?"

"No," I said.

"Can you imagine me having a street, the biggest street in the whole city, built just for you?"

"No," I breathed, fully flushed. He was four years older than I was and seemed already a man to me then.

"Ridiculous," he said. "Deserved the firing squad for that alone," he said.

My heart dropped; I had thought he was being romantic. But he took my hand as we crossed the wide street and I felt it there, though he let it go as soon as we got to the other side. My middle had gone hot as he'd reached for me, but we kept walking as if nothing had happened, as if that had not just occurred and then in front of Bellas Artes he started talking again, told me about how they had drained the lake that Mexico City sits on, Lake Texcoco. "In the 17th century," he said, "because the city kept flooding; it was all growing too fast, kept hitting up against the banks, so they built waterways to drain it all. And now all the canals the Aztecs used to move on are gone, except for in the South, where you can still rent little boats to paddle through them."

"Xochimilco?" I asked. "I've been there with my Grandma Marina."

He nodded. "That's why Bellas Artes is sinking," he said. "The clay from the lake table is saturated and so soft that these huge buildings can't be sustained."

Pablo led me down to the center to look at the Cathedral and he used words I'd never heard and when I asked him to explain things he was patient and clear and kind. When we got back to the little central park in his neighborhood he told me that each neighborhood—each colonia—was modeled on the Spanish and French city, with a central park out of which all the streets radiated. He explained that all of Mexico City was built like that, each little park representing the sun with the streets as rays spanning out of it. He said the Zocalo was the main square, the central sun out of which the rest of the city shone, and that this mythic center had something of everything in it, of the Spanish and French, yes, but that the heart of it, the stones which those other peoples had used for their imposing religious and civic buildings were all Aztec, their great temple stones. "This is what makes Mexico fantastic," he said, "the way that things get incorporated and pile up on each other so that the past is always present, never fully quashed, often not even hidden."

My uncle Felix, who was often high or in a bad mood, was the only other person who spoke to me like that, who made me think about how things worked, what they might mean, and why. And though he was not kind like Pablo in his lessons, often using them to humiliate me for my ignorance, still I appreciated them. For, everyone else I knew just took things at face value, never questioned anything, never wondered how or why.

Later Pablo became a poet, I heard, and this made sense to me. My uncle Felix had been an artist, and though he never found his way, it was a form of thinking, a form of questioning the world, which I liked.

At lunch that day, the lunch his mother cooked for us, I understood that Pablo was too serious for a simple crush. I looked at his mother as she spoke to my father and I knew things had not been easy for her. She had raised them alone, his brothers and sisters, in that tiny apartment, a kitchen and front room and then two small bedrooms, one for the brothers, the other she shared with her daughters. She was a housekeeper, yet even my father spoke of her in reverential tones. And it was for her, I understood, that Pablo and his brothers struggled to put themselves through school, serious and studious, brilliant and beautiful all of them. His sister too, was unapproachable some-how, and I could barely glance her way, not daring to say a single word to her though I was friends with her brother. I did watch her though, as she ate, her careful manner, the way she would slowly and patiently work her utensils, how gently she pushed her long black hair out of her face when it fell forward. The way she got up to put water on for coffee, so her mother would not have to get up again.

My father knew two or three phrases in five different languages, an insult in shorthand usually, so when we were included, when he did decide to take us on one of his weekend trips, we were delighted by the fact that he could walk up to strangers and make the foreign ones laugh. Or else they'd walk up to him while he played the guitar and he'd stop strumming and yell out a joke about la belle petite avec le bete, or Fraulein Frida und grosse fetter wolf, a playful flirt with a young wife. And then the Frenchman or the German would laugh and sit at my handsome young father's side, a slap to the back, and my father would reach for a beer and grab his guitar and la petite et la bête or fairy tale Fraulein would sit and laugh and sing along until the whole lot of them were close to drunk while we watched from the sidelines, late into the night.

In bed at a beachside cabana one night, Marta whispered in my ear. We were supposed to be asleep, "Go to bed," he had slurred out from the side of the pool. "Get out of there and go to bed," and though we did it slowly, we did finally pull ourselves out of the water. And then as I tossed and turned in bed an hour or so later Marta worked to convince me to get back up.

"No way," I said.

"Come on, you coward. No one is going to see us. We'll sneak real quiet. Don't you want to see what they're up to?"

"No," I answered. And though I was scared, she stared me down, her eyes glaring even though it was dark.

"Well I'm going alone then, you chicken shit," she said.

And of course I followed her.

The group was by the fire, drinking still, even though it was deep into the night. But it was only a little while before they rose up and stumbled toward a room that wasn't our room, wasn't our father's room, sliding drunkenly in and out of each other's arms the whole way, the wolf and his wife with our father, or was it the beauty and the beast laughing wildly with our dad, the glow from their cigarettes guiding our terrified if curious gazes deep into their cabana. My father had beautiful dancing blue eyes; he had a big willing smile and wide shoulders; his tone was always jokey.

He was not a man to say no, my father. He was not a man to ever say, That is enough; I have reached my limit; it is time to stop; my daughters are waiting; my daughters might be looking in through the window right now, might be seeing that which they will later find unspeakable, might be perplexed beyond language, and so it is time for me to stop.

My father was not a man to say, Stop. It is time for me to go to bed. It is time to say good-night.

My father was not that man.

Playing in the street with our friends, we would run in groups, the sun shining down upon us, the ball of us yelling at each other, calling out, trying to set the rules for a new game. Bossing and screaming and crying. And up he would creep in his red Volkswagen bug. Appear out of nowhere, no forewarning. We'd see him from a distance, moving toward us, me and Marta, and Marta would begin jumping up and down at the sight of his car, wildly joyous. We'd stop our group running, abandoning friends mid-tag and we'd yell out and dash up to him proud and excited. Marta would be shrieking. He'd honk his horn once though he had already seen us, had already seen that we had seen him, so it was a show-off motion, and then he'd step out of the car and have us, me and Marta, hang off of his biceps in front of our friends.

By the time she was twelve or so Rocio always hung back with some boyfriend or other, tall and graceful, her bell bottoms flaring, leaning back against a wall, never making an erratic motion, never rushing or screaming or showing any excitement at all. He'd make his muscles dance for us, me and Marta, his sleeves rolled up to show their bulge. Our friends would stare too and we would beam at his clowning. We adored him, his wildness, how child-like he was, like an overgrown boy, our father, his shining eyes and laughing mouth. He would make a big show of giving us money which we would stick deep into our pockets and then he'd take us out for ice creams; he'd pick two or three of our friends to come along; he did the choosing, and the others would be hurt and disappointed at not being selected and this was the whole point, to mark some as special and make the others envious, prostrating them in their desire. He knew how to make us popular, knew the rules of the game. And then off the little group of us would go, envious eyes boring holes deep into our backs. He let us and our friends ride around on the footstep of his VW bug, holding on at the open window, grabbing the frame as tight as we possibly could. He'd drive crazy, zigzag up and down the street, us hanging on for dear life, screaming out at him to stop, stop, it was time to stop! It was inevitably me who wanted off first, Marta always the last one to get off and if she fell she never cried.

One day I was alone as his car turned onto our cloud darkened street, coming back from the corner store, a paper bag in my hand. The bag held some tea my grandmother had sent me out for. I was quietly singing to myself as I walked, humming and singing, and walking, but I stopped short at the sight of him, and fought an urge to hide behind the willow tree. I felt something like dread begin to spread inside me in that pause, my feet unable to move. At thirteen I was still small, skinny legs and arms, deep and serious eyes, my hand holding that bag tight. It turned into terror, that thing spreading so inexplicably through me, and it wasn't until Marta ran out at the sound of his horn that I felt the excitement rise and wash over that terror, an excitement that was like an extension of hers, was like a learned or forced reaction, an imposed jubilation, something I was obliged to feel.

That night in bed I lay awake, unnerved because I had not felt it, the thrill: alone on the street, his red bug inching toward me, the terror like a wash extending itself through me as he approached slow and threatening, a sickness like nausea coursing through my insides. Until my sister appeared, her black hair bouncing as she ran, her eager eyes gushing, her shrieks drowning out my more complicated emotions.

Which of those two things was real, I wondered, unable to sleep. But I turned my head and shut my eyes and forced myself to think of other things.

Still, those more complex feelings do easily rise up inside me now, those dark emotions. The big black hole which can now only be filled with disappointment, with disgust, and anguish, and anger.

My father's mother, Marina—Grandma Marina—did not love me. She had four sons and one daughter and, though my father was a drifter, he was her favorite. He was shiftless, a gambler, and she knew he would never work for anything, so she bought him a diploma. It sat prominently displayed on her wall. Her son was a doctor. My father was a *doctor!*

My uncle Adrian, my mother's brother, had landed him a job at Pfizer, and he was maybe even good at it for a while, salesman; it made sense given who he was. It was after he got fired from that job, for who knows what, that my grandmother got the idea. He'd been hawking drugs; that must have seemed close enough for her. He'd carry boxes and boxes of the free samples he still begged from my uncle Adrian when we traveled through Mexico; he'd open the trunk at the front of the VW and hand them out in the little villages. We'd be greeted with open arms by the women of the town and he'd give them the vitamins or antibiotics he'd gotten for their children. They would surround the car while he handed them out, and they'd give us places to sleep and cook for us, a chicken or lamb killed in his honor. I think he may have set a bone once. The doctor, they enthusiastically called him. The doctor has arrived! And this I genuinely liked about my father, his cowboy spirit, the way he handed out those drugs in the little villages. A Robin Hood of sorts, with dozens of Indian children jumping up and down at the sight of him, then hanging off his legs and arms, their mothers bashful, the men respectfully removing hats and glancing up from lowered heads.

Rocio had turned sixteen a few months before I arrived that summer. My father gave her a huge chunk of cash, hundreds and hundreds of pesos, for he had missed her quinceañera. We knew he'd had a big win, and though it was a birthday gift, we were jealous of Rocio.

"That idiot always gets everything," Marta said.

And though I was envious as well it was hard for me to feel too badly toward Rocio, she was so kind, though I didn't say anything to defend her. Still, I knew I would always side with her over Marta. I *was* jealous though, as my aunt Mina, my father's only sister and Rocio's godmother, had brought her many beautiful birthday gifts from her trip to Holland, gorgeous dresses, and jewelry and boots. I coveted a Lucite bracelet, striated brown, and though she let me borrow it whenever I wanted to, I was jealous over that pile of gifts.

Marta and I were playing in the garden; we had a pair of chameleons we'd gotten at the outdoor market.

Our uncle Felix had taken us; he'd offered to take me, really, but Marta had begged along, and though he disliked her he'd given in to her promises to behave. It was the day once a month when the Mazahua Indians came from Avandaro to sell their crafts in the market, and also the man who had birds and rabbits and chickens in cages, and he was the one I was really going to see.

"Please, please, please," we begged when we saw the chameleons.

And my uncle Felix, in an uncharacteristic act of generosity, though not until giving us a long and boring lesson on reptiles, finally said yes. "The birds, all birds, are descended from reptiles," he emphasized, as he paid for one for each of us. "Did you know that? In fact, there were dinosaur birds, dinosaurs that could fly," he added. "And chameleons are the most special of the reptiles, since they can change color, did you know that? And it's not just to blend in like some people think, it also has something to do with how they're feeling, with their mood. Did you know that?" He stared into our eyes, "I'll get them for you but I'm going to test you on your facts in a week," he said as he handed them to us, our hands greedily reaching. "And don't forget, you have to feed them only living flies. You don't want them to die, do you?"

"Of course not, uncle Felix," I said and reached my mouth up for a kiss. He reluctantly bowed his cheek down to receive it.

"Don't slobber," he said as I kissed him.

We loved those horny toad chameleons dearly—they were so ugly—and were in the garden playing with them, letting them wander a bit amongst the plants, giving them a false sense of reptilian freedom, our delimiting hands appearing god-like to grab them up and place them back within the bounds we had decided on, when our father appeared. We were excited to see him, stuck our pets in the aquarium with a brutal drop and ran up to him, screeching. But he dismissively told us he was there for Rocio. He was terse and I was once again forced to be jealous of my beloved sister and Marta was openly angry and yelled at him that Rocio never even wanted to do anything with him, that she had hidden under the bed last month when he showed up to take us to Taxco for a long weekend away so she wouldn't have to come, so she wouldn't have to leave her stupid boyfriend.

"So she won't have to spend any time with you, her own father! She can't even leave her stupid boyfriend for more than a day!" she yelled. "She can't even choose her father over her idiotic boyfriend!"

My father ignored Marta.

"And now you only want to see her?!" she went on.

He ignored Marta and then barely looked my way as he passed so that I felt truly invisible and then he came out of the house with Rocio looking beautiful in a yellow dress. He was taking her out to lunch. And only her.

"Idiot," Marta spewed as Rocio glided past, tall and gorgeous.

Later we found out that during that lunch he had asked her for that money back. She had said no at first, a show of uncharacteristic strength, but then he begged. She turned away from him as he did so.

"Please. Pleease," he said, his eyes firmly on her. "I need it. Don't make me get down on my knees," he said.

He said other things too, apparently.

"I will get it all back to you soon," he desperately promised; but though she was gullible, she was not stupid enough to believe him.

She made him drive her back to the house. As soon as I saw them enter the gate I quietly rushed to the bedroom window from where I often watched my sister. I saw Rocio pull up the panel she herself had put in her drawer. With a screwdriver she pulled it up while he stood, eagerly watching. I saw her hand the money to our father, without turning to face him. He leaned in to kiss her, but she turned away.

And my stomach balled inside me, sick at the jealousy I had felt in the garden. I was wretched and selfish and my sister, who never asked for anything, who was gentle and decent and kind had had to give the little bit that she had ever gotten from my father right back. And I was a small and wretched creature.

My mother… she is something else entirely, unspeakable, perhaps. When you draw her make her liquid fragile tissue, a gaseous substance, diffuse and undefined. Make her a watercolor in deep dark shades, with tones spilling into others, and marked by lack of line.

Just because you can't see something, Barry tells us, that doesn't mean it is not there. Just because you won't speak the thing, can't speak it, cannot find the words to speak it, just because you don't know at the time what things are or what they will become, just because you have no language for it, the undefined and fluid changeability, this does not mean it has no impact, that it will not affect you, shifting and transforming, infecting and affecting, turning things in on each other and then in on themselves too, on you too. Like the gas, Barry's gas.

I spent two summers with my family after I was sent to live with my uncle David and his wife when I was six. I was allowed to return for those two visits, when I was eleven and then again when I was thirteen, two full summers with them. And then I came for a whole year when I was seventeen. And at some point between these two final visits I found out that M, my mother's husband, was not my real father. But, by then, perhaps, it was a relief. Or else it no longer mattered very much. For nothing much did then.

Marta

THEY WERE THREE SISTERS TOO. Gigi, and Bubbles and Laura. Bubbles and Laura were the two I hung out with most on account of they were my age. Besides, Gigi was older and was mostly not around. Their dad was divorced but had remarried and Tere, their step-mom, was very cool and mostly just left us alone. Laura was kind of stupid and very skinny and pretty ugly, but it was fun to have her around as a kind of clown. A willing slave. She would do anything we told her to. We'd be lying around gossiping or listening to music and would get hungry and so we'd send her down to the kitchen for snacks. She never said no. And then, if there wasn't enough sugar in the lemonade she'd made us Bubbles would make a face and loudly complain and Laura would go and stir in some more. I'm cold, Bubbles would say, hand me that sweater, and though Bubbles was closer to it herself, Laura would always get up and get it for her. Bubbles and I spent a lot of time making fun of her, her knobby knees and bony arms, her ugly face and wig-like hair, and Laura just awkwardly laughed along, trying to make herself a part of the fun instead of just the object of it.

Bubbles was a year older than me, the same age as Julia but not cowardly like my sister was, and she's the one I got into boys with. Maybe it's true that the boys liked Julia, but she was so stupid and slow and fake-innocent that it never really amounted to much. But Bubbles was right there. She would kiss the boys back. Chase after them, even. And she knew how far to go to get them to come after her. When to pull back, when to stop. They'd come running. You know, she really knew things.

Gigi, who was three years older, had taught her a game that Bubbles and I would play together sometimes. Bubbles called it practice. Let's play practice she'd say and then she would pretend to be the boy and lie on top of me. Then she would rub her body up and down and back and forth and we would pretend to kiss. Her tongue dipping deep into my mouth sometimes. Just pretend, she would say, and sometimes she would be giggling but other times she would be super focused and dead serious, her tongue in my mouth. This is how you do it, she would say in a low whisper, how people do it, and then she'd rub back and forth on me. Her body on me, hard and rubbing. It was a sort of practice. I taught Julia too, but it embarrassed her and she'd whip her head from side to side when I pretended to kiss her, as if I were really a boy trying to stick my tongue in her mouth. Though she did let me rub my body on hers a few times. It's just a game, I would say, frustrated at her stupid prissiness, wanting to hold her down and just force my tongue deep into her mouth.

Bubbles and I would take baths together and then play the rubbing game, but Julia never let me play it with her naked. Sometimes we'd cut the hair off of Bubbles' dolls and would glue it onto their pubic areas, their armpits too. Bubbles would laugh and laugh at how funny it looked, and I would pile it on thick to entertain her, glue on big chunks of it till it really was ridiculous looking and I'd laugh loudly too. Laura would eagerly dart her eyes back and forth from the dolls to Bubbles and me, adding to our fun with her nasal guffaws, those bony elbows jutting out at her sides as she doubled over. Julia never understood why it was all so funny, but she was so stupid we didn't ever really expect her to understand anything. And we never bothered to explain either.

I spent most of my time at Bubbles' house. Because they hated me. My uncles and aunt. Even my grandmother kind of hated me I think. They were always telling me to do something ridiculous like clean the balcony, just to keep me busy, or they'd yell out in anger just because they thought the TV was too loud or something. Who do you think you are? they would yell at me. But I would yell back. Who did you think you are?, you're not my mom, screaming at me like that. You can ask me nice if you want me to turn it down, I would shout. Instead they would stomp toward me all puffed out, with raised hand as if they were going to hit me over something as stupid as the volume on the TV, but I would stand up to them, actually stand up, and they would always back down. Brat, or sometimes, Fucking brat, they would curse as they made their way back to their rooms. That's right, I'd say, and don't you forget it.

I would stand my ground.

Julia and Rocio were always quietly tiptoeing around that house, pathetically crawling into laps, cautiously taking hands, sniffing about like some kind of pet, a begging dog or cat, starved for attention, starved for love. I didn't need it. I certainly wasn't going to beg for it, that's for sure. Who cared if in the end my grandmother and aunt took Julia's side all the time? Or if Grandma Marina adored Rocio so much? Or if Aunt Mina gave her gifts she brought all the way from Holland? In the end what did it get either one of them? Rocio married to that pathetic husband of hers at twenty and Julia given away at six.

And who cares what either one of them have to say about me or any of what I did or still do, really? My sisters are both always so full of shit anyway, pretending to be so pure, working so hard for approval, with their fake innocence. Who cares? I, for one, have never cared what people think. I early on decided not to have anything to do with any of that. And it's not like it was even a decision, really. It's just the way it was. They did what they did and I did what I did and mostly what we each did didn't mix or mingle. I was busy with my friends anyway and the one who was closest to me in age was Julia and though she partially wanted to be involved in things, partially wanted to be out having fun with me, when I did let her come along she was mostly just complaining, slowing things down, telling me and Bubbles to be careful as we were spying in some boy's living room window, so that we would have to turn and angrily shush her, our fingers up to our mouths, our eyes cinching furiously. Idiot, I'd hiss at her as I shushed. Or else she'd start calling out to us to watch out when we were jumping the fence to pick some plums in Bubbles' grumpy old neighbor's yard; or she'd be yelling out are you sures as she chased behind us, trying to keep up as we ran to the bakery with money we'd stolen from Bubbles' dad's pants. Yeah I'm sure, you dimwit, Bubbles would say, He has no idea what's in his pockets. He doesn't keep track of shit. But of course Julia'd instantly take her piece of cake or candy or ice cream or whatever we'd bought with that money, no complaining then, her mouth full of our hard earned sugar.

She was super frightened and nervous all the time so that, although I was younger, I was always having to stop and convince her or to tell her it would all be okay, or something else to calm her down and in the end who really gave a shit if she came along anyway. In fact it was much more fun when she wasn't around, slowing things down, making everyone worry. Sometimes I would just turn around and stare her down and tell her to just go home if she was going to whine so much.

Like Bubbles she was a year older than me, but she acted like such a lame ass it infuriated me. We'd all be getting ready to climb the fence into the public pool, and out of the blue she'd suddenly change her mind. And you always knew it was coming; she'd be fidgeting so much, shifting from foot to foot, so that you just knew it. And then there it would finally come, she'd nervously tell us, her eyes turned down, and everyone would groan, and we'd have to figure out who was going to stand guard now, even though she had agreed to do it. I don't want to anymore, she'd suddenly say, and she'd start walking home. It embarrassed me in front of my friends, the idiot. It just really made me want to hit her.

So, though I could sometimes talk her into doing things, usually she was just plain scared and I would get sick of the convincing and end up taking off without her. Though she always had a good time when she came along. So what was she whining about? The wimp. And Rocio was even more of a wimp. She is a full four years older than me and still she was afraid of me. You barely even knew she was alive because she was always hiding out with some boyfriend or other, always looking for someone to huddle with, someone to whisper to, someone to take care of her. And Julia worshipped her: Rocio this, Rocio that. It infuriated me when she wanted to stay home with Rocio instead of coming out with me. But then again, who needed her? And who on earth would want to be like either one of them? The idiots.

And that scar on Rocio's hand, if you ask her about it she will immediately tell you it was me who gave it to her, who cut her up, but that is a lie. The door broke when I slammed it into her. The glass shattered, and that's how she cut her hand. To hear her tell it I took that glass and carved that crazy scar into her with my own hands.

They were hypocrites too, are hypocrites still. They acted so pure and innocent all the time, getting all the love and caring from my grandmother and my aunt with their sweet girl acts, yet Julia would light up with me when I pulled out the cigarettes. We'd be up on the roof terrace, and my aunt or Maria would start loudly coming up the stairs and Julia would hear them coming and right away she'd stomp her cigarette out. But I would stand my ground; I wasn't about to hide and lie and pretend I was something I wasn't. And so I would of course get caught. She'd just look down with her stupid sorry assed eyes, and no one would say a thing to her. That idiot. I just told them, Yeah, I was smoking, so what? What were they going to do about it? There was nothing they could do, nothing that would make me act any differently than I did, than who I was. I wasn't going to lie about who I was. I was just telling the truth. But that made them hate me more. And then my uncles and aunt acted like they were trying to break a horse. Like I was a beast and they could break me.

But there she was, right behind me, Julia, if she thought she might actually have some fun. What else was there for her to do? I remember once flirting with some older boys who weren't from the neighborhood and there Julia was, all innocent-eyed, and of course guys always fall for that soft, pure girl crap so the most handsome one liked her, though he wasn't her type. What's your name? he asked her. He was tall and had dark skin and full lips and black hair, really nice big arms, strong, and she acted all coy; Julia, she said softly, and then—though the sun would soon be going down—we hopped on their bikes with them, on these stands one of their brothers had welded onto the back wheel, so that we were upright behind them, and we rode through the city like that, hanging on to them tight. And there was such a freedom in that. I loved it, not feeling tied down to anything, acting like we didn't belong anywhere, that kind of freedom, seeing my sister there in front of me, looking wild and without ties and knowing I looked like that too, Mexico City flowing past us as we held on to those boys tight. Julia's lame hands barely touching that boy's shoulders when we first got on, but by the second or third block holding on nice and tight. My arms immediately rounding the boy whose bike I was on, though he was not the more handsome one. But the feel of his body in my arms was nice, and I felt free and open like nothing mattered but me here on this bike with my arms around this boy who was riding me far. After a while, though, we weren't too sure where they were taking us and the guys just kept going and going while they talked and laughed and talked. We were ten and eleven and they were older, fourteen or so and so finally we jumped off near Tlatelolco. Even I felt we had gone too far, and who knew when or where they would ever stop. Where they were taking us to, what they had in mind. We had a cousin who lived in Tlatelolco and I remembered which of those many apartment buildings was his and so at a stop light we jumped off the bikes and ran though the boys called after us, Come back! Where are you going? Julia! Aren't you having a good time? but we just kept running. When we showed up at the front door of my cousin's house well past 10 o'clock at night, his mother, my aunt said he was asleep and then looked at us, horrified. Our faces were red and hot and flushed. What are you doing here? she asked. We told her what had happened, that we'd spent more than three hours riding around the city on the backs of those bikes but then we didn't know where we were headed and when we saw Tlatelolco we jumped off; she stared at us with disbelieving eyes and she called our grandmother and then fed us while we all waited for her to come to pick us up. We'd never met those boys before, so when my aunt asked us about them we didn't have a thing to say. We didn't know them, but the one Julia had ridden with was really handsome, strong, with a wide back. She had pulled her inno- cent doe-eyed look on him, and I think he wanted to fuck her, though she was just a kid. And of course if she was going to fuck at eleven then I was going to have to fuck at ten, but in the end it didn't happen.

I started smoking cigarettes that same year. I don't think I was really smoking then, though all the adults around me did it, including my grandmother, and there was nothing I wanted more than to be grown up like them so I could get the hell out of that house, and so I started smoking cigarettes. Just blowing in and out, really. And Julia did it with me, though of course I was the one who got caught. My uncle Felix came home one day, and because the cigarettes we were sneaking were his, and since he assumed it was just me doing it he yelled at me and then as a punishment, and to make me sick from it too, he made me smoke a whole cigarette in front of him while he watched, as if somehow that would deter me. He sat and watched me, with his legs crossed like a woman, sat there in that chair facing me, Go ahead, light up, he said. And then he shook his head in shame while I lit the match. Who taught you that? he asked. It's just a match, I answered back, No big deal. And he just kept shaking his head while I lit up and when I didn't puke and in fact looked quite happy and satisfied while smoking that cigarette, he just walked away in disgust.

Where do grown ups get their dumb ideas? They try the same stupid tricks over and over again, even when they don't work. I'm sure some adult had pulled that shit on him when he was a kid and there he was, smoking pot like it was going out of style and now he thought that same lame punishment would work on me? Progress.

When I was twelve one of the boys in the neighborhood came out of his house with this electricity machine. He wasn't the smartest kid we knew, had a jaw like a chimp and little rat eyes, and I'm not really sure what that thing he brought out was for, cars maybe, maybe his dad or uncle was a mechanic of some kind, but it had a surge of power that ran through a couple of long cords, probably meant for charging something. And another one of the older guys in my neighborhood got the bright idea to turn it into a game of chicken, knew from school that the more of us there were standing in a circle holding hands, letting the electricity run through us, the lower the charge each of us got. Of course kids would start dropping out pretty fast, and the ones who were left really felt it and were somehow the winners, you know. There would be something like twenty or more kids, all ages, at the beginning, and Julia always dropped out right away, if she played at all; I was always one of the last. It was intense at the end, the surge.

That says a lot about her though. She was never willing to risk anything. She was a coward. That said, everyone still loved her, plus all those idiotic boys liked her too.

This one night that same summer we were all playing, who knows what, what were we playing that night? ... and this boy, Oscar, kissed her right on the mouth; it was like a dare, and I couldn't believe they both took it. It wasn't spin the bottle, which we of course also played, and god was she lame when we played that, acting so shy and sickeningly awkward about every little peck on the cheek. But on this day we were all standing around in a bunch of little groups, boys in one area, girls in another, the really little kids kicking a ball around were a sort of third group, then somehow we were all suddenly together, and Oscar kind of ambled up to her and she acted like she didn't know what was coming, though we all knew it was coming on account of his friend had just asked her if she liked him. We were all standing around, kicking it, just hanging out and then suddenly there was a buzz and we all knew Oscar was going to kiss her, because his friend had asked her, and because she hadn't said no, though she hadn't exactly said yes either. She acted shocked when Oscar came right up to her and kissed her there in front of all of us, on the mouth, for kind of a long time. And though at first she acted shocked she didn't pull away. We couldn't believe it.

I was relieved when it ended up not meaning anything. When Oscar didn't become her boyfriend or something. He was my type, not hers, strong, with a wide back, and quiet, though not too serious. I'd liked him for a long time.

One night, we were older, 16 and 17 I think, we went out to a bar and these guys were there; it was clear that they were rich. It was one of those bars. And there were six or seven of them and three of them were pretty good-looking, though two were very overweight; it was me and Julia and my friend Anna, and they talked us into going back to their place. Parents gone, you know, like that. It was a little bit of a drive and most of the guys were pretty drunk and were a bit lewd, but we were tipsy too and just kind of laughed it all off, their hands grabbing at us, their stupid dirty jokes, though the cars did kind of swerve a lot as they traveled down those empty city streets. And then as soon as we got there Julia was strange; she'd gone in the other car with the guy that owned that place and now she was refusing to go inside the huge walled-in house. She stayed in the big garden looking up into all those trees with that guy that lived there while he tried to find a pet owl he said he owned. He was her type, kind of thin and sensitive looking, kind of girlie, if you know what I mean. He had longish hair that he parted on one side and a mole on his cheek and he was wearing a nice sweater. She was really into seeing that owl that he supposedly kept as a pet and was peering up into all the trees, her long hair swinging all about as she looked up. Anna and me thought it was stupid and went in with the other guys, and we kept on drinking and pretty soon their clothes had come off, except that one of the fat guys kept his on and he was scary that guy, looked creepy just kind of standing back and watching with his hands moving around in his pockets, though it was easy to see that he was really drunk too. One of the other guys came up to me and said, That one's worth his weight in gold, and I thought it was supposed to be a joke on account of he was so fat but when I looked over at the kid who had said it I saw he was serious. And then, from one moment to the next, they were all tearing Anna's clothes off of her and she was laughing as they smacked her ass around and I knew that anything could happen here. These guys were rich; I mean really rich, the huge walled in house, that ridiculous garden, big as a park. They could do what they wanted with us and no one would ever say a thing.

A shot of fear ran through me for the first time in my life. This was Mexico, after all; we could disappear and these boys they had fathers who could make anything they did alright. And then I remembered Julia, I was worried about her, a spike of electricity running through my insides, and when I called out to her the guy who lived there, the guy with the longish hair and the pet owl said she had gone home.

She split. Just like that she left me behind. Anna was fucked by two or three of the guys, right there in front of me, while the other ones watched, and though at first she was laughing soon she was gasping and begging them to stop. And somehow, I'm not sure how, my head spinning, I got out of that.

That was Julia too, you know. Don't let anyone tell you she was the high and pure one. She left me there. And Anna, though at first she looked like she was having a good time, was basically raped that night.

Sandra

I ARRIVED IN MADRID, dizzy and tired and when I got off the plane I found my way to the center of town where I went and slept in a park. A car bomb went off in the late afternoon, a few blocks away and though it was small and had hurt no one the park filled with people anxiously discussing it. I had never experienced anything like that and, though I was groggy still and had been planning on spending some time in Madrid, I got on a train and took it to Barcelona that very evening. From there I would continue with my journey to Mataro where I had heard my father's friend Pablo was living. Though I barely knew him and wondered myself if this casual acquaintance with my father's younger friend was enough of a draw, in my lost, untethered state—I was floating confused, and needed a place to land— this distant friendship seemed as good a way as any to pick a destination. Besides, it was the only thing I had.

I sat in that cramped train compartment and in the middle of the night—the air full of the smells of all those people around me combined with something being burned in the surrounding fields, something sweet and heavy and sickly decaying, a scent that went on and on for miles, something like the smell of flesh burning—I became so dizzy and ill that I wobbled my way to the small bathroom where I threw up again and again, the walls and floor and ceiling shaking all around me. From Barcelona I took another train to Mataro, that tiny Spanish town on the coast, near the border with France, and as I arrived the air seemed to finally clear, and that seemed a good omen, for it was in this town that I would try to clear myself too.

It's true that I'd stupidly hoped that simply by leaving Mexico, that just by leaving my home, my family, my life—everything that was familiar—I would no longer have to be my sister. It is true too that I needed to get away from my mother, from Claudia's sad and desperate need. And like a foolish child I'd hoped that by surrounding myself with foreignness I would instantly be able to leave the unspoken but deeply felt expectations, the formed ideas, my pre-figured being behind, in Mexico, with Claudia. It is also true that I dimly felt I would then be open and empty enough to be free to invent myself. I had imagined that by vacating myself, unbinding all ties, I would then be able to build upon that emptiness—and shape a newfound selfness. Only then, I believed, might I be truly open to finding my sister, Julia, to coming to understand her as a separate person. The actual other, not just the one I carried inside myself.

I found a low level posada in a family home where the father was stern and the proper young daughter spent hours practicing the piano; and though I didn't like the sound of the father's low and muffled voice ordering her about, I did love hearing the same songs repeated over and over, with different slips each time, seeping up through the floorboards and emanating from the walls. I stayed in bed listening to the sounds of that house for three days running, only leaving my room to wander out for something to eat. But on the fourth morning I felt the terror of being completely rudderless start to rise inside me. It was then that I decided to finally go see my father's friend, Pablo, who had moved to Mataro to write poetry. I'd heard he was trailing another poet and for some inexplicable reason when I arrived at his place I told him I wanted to be a writer too, though I had never even thought this before and felt myself a liar. But in the face of his cold reception, this had seemed the only excuse I could provide for coming to see him. How could I tell him the truth, that I was there because I was completely adrift, and terrified, and alone? Still, I was surprised when he seemed to take my statement seriously, a writer. He regarded me differently then, looked me up and down for a few moments before turning from me there in his living room; I watched him as he walked to and then leaned over his table. I liked the determined way in which his body moved, the strong veins in his arms, his long fingered hands, the way his thick hair fell forward as he leaned into that table. He searched out a paper there that he then handed to me. It was a map on which in red he'd circled the pension where he suggested I stay, much cheaper than the small hotel I'd been staying at he said; and then he moved to his shelves from which he pulled a book that he then handed to me too. It was a copy of Nabokov's *Lectures on Literature*. He did all this for me and still he remained distant, and when I looked at him with what must have been eagerness in my eyes, he walked me to his door and told me he would talk to me when we had something to discuss, when I had finished reading the book. For now he had to work.

For the next week or so I read that book slowly, and hoped that somehow the author's words would enter my body, that they might give me a new shape, a narration, a line. I had read most of the books Nabokov spoke about, had read some of Nabokov himself, nonetheless, I preferred reading novels and it all seemed a bit abstract. But Pablo was almost always too busy to spend time with me, and besides he had said he would not talk to me until I'd finished the book, so that when I wasn't staring at the yellowed walls in my room at the pension, I wandered the town, Mataro, alone.

The tiny old woman who owned the decrepit house which she ran as a pension seemed to be always buried in the depths of its rooms so that I rarely saw her. When we did happen to pass each other in the halls, we rarely exchanged a word and the old woman seemed to make a point of not looking my way. It was always a surprise, once out, that the sun shone so brightly on the other side of that heavy front door, the house itself seeming to be made up of a series of ancient shadows, the old woman herself always dressed in black. Why would Pablo have sent me there, I would wonder once outdoors, to a house that seemed to be made up of ancient secrets and dim light?

I carried *Lectures* up and down the hills of the town, some jagged, harsh and cliffed, others gentle, round, supple. In that bright Spanish light I walked by the water which offered itself to me in small lapping waves, and on the edge of which in the heat of the day topless Germans skipped and jumped. Through the entirety of that small Spanish town I walked, in and out of its shops, its restaurants and bars, on its dirt and cement, its black-top and stone. I walked in the morning, midday and night, by myself—always alone. I carried that book. And I didn't talk to people, the Spanish or the Germans. I did stare at the young Spanish, the beautiful young women especially, their breasts. I liked how they laughed together in groups with an ease I could see was the familiarity of family or of long and constant friendship.

I looked at the faces of the old men too, and the old women, the cracked skin of people who had always lived and worked by the sea. When they looked back at me I would dart my eyes away, afraid that one of them might actually come over and speak to me, ask me what it was I was doing in their town.

One night, forlorn, I walked over to Pablo's apartment, though it was quite late. I had been sitting in a bar re-reading something about Flaubert and his use of the semi-colon; and when I looked up from the page to take a sip of my wine I saw all the people there happily sitting in big drunken groups and it made me feel intensely alone and so I gathered myself up and walked over to Pablo's building; and when I arrived in front of it I peered up at his window and saw the light was on and though in that moment I thought of leaving—perhaps it was too late?— I forced myself to press down on his doorbell instead.

Time stopped for a second; but then he opened the door. It was hot and he was not wearing a shirt, What are you doing here? he asked. And when I just stared back without saying a word he asked me in.

And then we were inside and he offered me a glass of wine, and we started talking and it was somehow all incredibly sad. What are you doing here, in this town? I asked him.

I'm a poet, he answered. What are you doing here? and the light from the candle which sat on the low table directly in front of us flickered a bit.

I don't know, I answered.

You told me you wanted to be a writer, he said.

I don't know, I answered.

We were sitting together on pillows, on the floor, in front of the fireplace and the windows were open because it was hot and in the firebox where in the winter logs would be burning there were four or five further lit candles; and he wasn't wearing a shirt and I reached over and touched his bare shoulder in all that flickering light.

What are you doing? he asked again, only this time his voice was different.

I don't know, I answered, and my voice was different too.

And then I was kissing him, his long dark hair—its wave and curl, and I pulled myself on top of his legs, straddled him as I kept kissing his mouth. His hands moved to me and soon they were down on my pants and then his fingers were wandering their way inside them, and then finding their way inside me so that I spread my legs wider for him. I kissed him more deeply then, and moved myself closer still; but he suddenly stopped.

I made love to her, he said.

What? I asked.

Your sister, Julia.

What are you talking about? I asked.

She was only seventeen and I was twenty-one and I had heard she was in town and it was a clear and beautiful day, the sun bright; the air was crisp and cool and we walked to the park together and we lay in the grass and talked about the books and music she liked; I was annoyed by the way the bands she liked tossed the word anarchy around like a bauble and so I tried to explain some things to her, but she ignored me. She said she didn't care, that she didn't have to like what I liked or vice versa, it was pop music, sure, but it was important to her. And instead of making me angry I was glad that she'd stood up for herself. I pointed some clouds out to her then and she said something about Icarus, how he'd fallen through those very clouds and into this same grass we now lay on. She patted the grass with her small hands, her beautiful fingers, 'Right here,' she said, 'he fell right here.'

I stared into her eyes and then we walked back to your mother's apartment and I undressed her and we made love. And she scared me, your sister. There was something deep about her which seemed aged, though she looked like a child, something which made her seem much older than she was, a seriousness I didn't know what to do with. But I liked her a great deal.

You can stop now, I said. And I removed his hand from me and then I climbed off him.

And he turned his face from me now, as if in shame, so that he was facing the wall as he continued talking: The strangest thing is that after we made love—and it was making love, I've not had anything quite like that since; and maybe it was mournful too, this thing inside her that I am calling old, a depth, her eyes staring at me, looking straight into my eyes in that bed, searching me out, even though she was so young; I kissed and kissed her mouth then—but then after we made love, after that profound connection, she asked me if I'd ever had sex with your mother.

Okay, I said. You can stop now. With tears in my eyes I quickly pulled my clothes on and rose to leave.

He turned his face toward me then, I'm sorry, he said. I'm sorry.

I moved to Los Angeles where I knew my sister had lived as a child, and I found a small room, which a friend of Pablo's, another writer, had agreed to sublet to me. Pablo had appeared at the pension and guiltily offered me many things after our night together, friends' numbers and books, most of which I had not bothered to carry with me to Los Angeles, and he had promised to call a few other people he knew in LA to check in on me. I could barely face him as he spoke, rushing through his words, offering and offering and trying to make up for something he would never make up for. I could see the old widow staring out of her bedroom door, spying on us as I walked him out. I refused to have a coffee with him.

That LA room was small, with a futon bed in one corner and on the other side two long French windows that gave out to a hedge-bordered driveway. Despite their length, little light came in through those windows. The bright California sunlight was kept out of the ground floor studio apartment by an exact replica of this three story 1940s apartment building across the way. That other building, the mirror image, blocked the sun. This doubling made me feel quite sad the first time that I noticed it and so I decided to look away and stop thinking about it because otherwise I would have to start thinking about my sister again, about how things can be each other and not at the same time, and how this slippery truth had set me wandering. I knew she was in the states too, now, on the other coast, 3,000 miles away. Though I also knew she had grown up here.

There were piles of books under the windows, stacked haphazardly. There was one armchair, old velvet with worn arms. Across from it stood a big armoire with a beautiful beveled mirror. There was a little antique table on which sat an old computer with a swivel chair before it. The room was tidy, but stifling. The whiteness of the walls and the thickness of the plaster in this pseudo-Spanish building were not enough to keep the late July heat out of this small space.

And on this early Los Angeles morning I was just waking from a long restless sleep. I was slight so that even when I was all spread out I did not take up much of the space of the futon. I got up and stepped past the walk-in closet and into the bathroom where I splashed cold water onto my face and neck. I then crawled into bed again and struggled to get myself back into sleep—shut my eyes firmly tight and tried to remember last night's dream. I felt I did recall it now, or a bit of it perhaps, though it kept moving and shifting and slipping away, something about a lake, a lagoon, or was it an empty ocean beach, the beach in Spain? I lay there for a long time, that fan spinning circles above me, and watched my image spin around over and over again, a smaller version of myself on each of the fan's five blades, over and over again, as if I were chasing myself and there would never be an ending; and then, as if to block myself out, I closed my eyes though I knew I was still up there spinning.

It was later that day, driving on the Pasadena Freeway toward Echo Park, where I was set to meet another one of Pablo's friends for coffee, that I saw the girl who looked exactly like me.

As if I were following myself in my wanderings—or perhaps it was she who was trailing me—that day as I was driving the Los Angeles freeways I saw my double stare back at me from inside her own car. She looked at me from her driver's seat, through her window and into mine. She was me but stronger, and her eyes were firm and bold and bright. Overwhelmed, I turned away.

When, a moment later, I got the nerve to look back, she was already gone; in that wavering instant she had gotten ahead by two car lengths, and though I was fully shaken I tried to catch up. I sped, my heart racing, but I was unable to reach her. Soon she had zoomed fully out of sight.

Direct, she had looked straight at me, through those cars and into me, perhaps; and she was me but different, in control, somehow. I had seen this in her eyes—they were strong and clear and open; and I had felt the need to speak to her.

I was still unnerved when I walked into the coffee shop an hour later. Yet I was able to pick him out of that crowd of strangers. Adam. Pablo had told him about me and he'd called days after I arrived and I was completely alone in Los Angeles and so I agreed to meet him.

We had been sitting there for a few minutes, had both ordered our coffees, had both sat back in our chairs and I was just getting over my unease, was finally looking at his face as he focused out the door and onto the sidewalk in front—the strong jaw and thick straight hair, the glasses which made him look more serious than perhaps he was—when he turned to look at me. He was tall and moved his body forward so that he was leaning far over the table, his hands playing on its surface, when he began to speak.

I am not Pablo, he said, his eyes serious.

No, I know, I answered.

You called me Pablo. When you walked in. As you sat down. You said, Hi Pablo.

Did I? I answered. And I was truly confused, scraping my mind for the memory and wondering why, if indeed I had.

I'm very different from him, he said.

No, I can imagine, I answered.

For one thing, I will never try to convince you to do something you don't want to do.

I'm not sure I know what you mean, I said.

Well, I don't know that you noticed this, but Pablo is always trying to convince people to do things. He gets ideas. And then he tries to push them on people. Like moving to Spain. He decided he needed to leave to be a poet. It was an idea, and so he moved. He tried to talk me into going with him. Told me I would never be a serious poet if I didn't take chances. But I like to think things through. I *am* a poet. I just like to take my time. My decisions mean something to me. Adam reached over then and put his hand on my arm, *They mean something*. He looked deep into my eyes then.

I think I have to go, I said as I rose. I think I have to go now.

The second time I saw myself was at a department store. It wasn't anything fancy. I was there to buy underwear, bras, socks, panties, things I ignore for as long as I possibly can; and then I buy a lot at once. The lingerie departments are always on the top floor, or in the basement. This one was down below and after making my purchases—the agony of looking through all of that intimate wear, trying some of it on—I rode the escalator up and then went into the central space of the mall. It was then, from above me, that I heard my name. It was being called out, three times. Sandra. Sandra. And then with a bit of a question mark at the end, Sandra? Like a whisper, but loud too somehow, loud enough for me to hear it from far below. Sandra. I looked up and there I was. In a cluster. She looked exactly like me and she was in a big boisterous group and her friends, men and women both, were all laughing along with her. I stared at myself up there and then I hurried down the arcade to the escalator that would take me up to where she was. I was rushing. I ran into an old woman and did not even turn to apologize. I kept going. Up I went and when I got to where they all were, she was gone. I asked after her.

The woman, where did she go? I asked.

They stared at me, confused, and then when I repeated myself one of them asked, What woman?

The woman, I said, the woman who looks like me.

They glanced at each other. Wary. They were wary now; I could see this. Then the same short haired woman who had spoken before shrugged her shoulders and said, We don't know what you're talking about.

But I knew that she had been there. Yet, their staring pained me and so I turned and walked away.

I heard my name another time, rushed, though in a loud whisper again. Sandra. And again I was shopping for clothes. You will begin to think I am always shopping for clothes. I'm not. In fact, I rarely shop, can't stand the white light or all of those mirrors, seeing yourself reflected everywhere you turn. But I heard my name and I knew it had something to do with my sister and so I looked around. But this time I began to weep as I walked to my car. There had been nobody there.

And then I drove and drove. Those endless freeways. All that driving. There was something about it that made me feel more lost. Pablo's friend had left his old Toyota as part of the sublet and I would drive and drive. And though this felt like floating, like a not belonging, it also made me feel a part of the city somehow. Not because I got to know the city any better in this way. I didn't. I rarely got off the freeways, so this is not what I mean. I mean I felt a part of the city—like I was the blood flowing in its veins. On the freeway, I was a part of the pulsing, as I had been many years before when I constantly walked the streets of Mexico City. I was a part of the vital fluid, of what flowed and pumped and kept the city alive. That surge.

That night I drove to a bar in Highland Park. I got off the freeway on Avenue 64 and then I turned up to Figueroa where I drove some more. I saw it as I was stopped at a street light, and for some reason it called out to me and for some further reason I decided to park and go inside. I sat on a barstool and drank two drinks quickly and when a guy with long dark hair came up to ask for a beer and then began to talk to me, I flirted back. He had Pablo's sad black eyes. His lips and his chin. I took him back to my tiny apartment. And I stared into his eyes as he fucked me. And I was drunk and I began to cry. I was drunk and when he asked me what was wrong I asked him if he knew my sister. He was sweet; I could see this as he tried to figure out who she might be so that he could answer me honestly, and then I asked, insistent, Have you fucked my sister? And he looked at me with real concern in his eyes. I began weeping then, his gaze on me. And when he wrapped himself around my shoulders, shushed and shushed me to calm, and then began to rock me in his arms, I asked him to leave.

I like you a lot, he said, as he turned to go. I want to see you again.

And when I turned to face the wall, he walked out of the door.

———

I saw myself there a few more times. With my hair done up, in a silver Lexus one time. On a city bus another. That time I was in cheap clothing, looking mournfully down from that high window, the big bus window, down into my car. I tried to catch up with myself on both of these occasions, but would always lose sight of the other one. The third time I started chasing I was on the 10 freeway near Bundy, where it splits off to the 405. The other me merged over, going north, and I almost killed myself trying to reach her two lanes over. I just missed getting hit by a huge truck. I had to pull off to the side of the freeway then, I was so shaken. As the cars zoomed past me I wept with the knowledge that I had to stop myself. I wept with the thought that if I did not leave Los Angeles I was going to die. The other me, whom I kept seeing everywhere, that other one would end up killing me, whether or not she knew who I was. Whether or not she knew I existed at all.

I decided to go to my great-grandmother's house, my grandfather's mother, the ancient house in central Mexico in which he grew up. It is a place where no one asks any questions, a place for disappearing. My mother, I knew, had gone there for extended stays several times.

A couple of days later I was on a plane. I flew into Guadalajara and paid a sullen driver to bring me to Sombrarete, near the old silver mines, in the state of Zacatecas. These mines brought much wealth to the Spanish crown once, and they fought the Zacateco Indians in hard and bloody battles to keep a hold here. And then they fought the invading French too, and now, many years later I picked the most sullen driver I could find to bring me here because I knew he would not try to speak to me while he drove, and that silence was something I needed; he let me stare out of the window at the Sierra Madres in the distance, undisturbed, for the whole five hour drive.

I am in the walled-in home where my grandfather's mother lay dying in a room for many years before finally expiring—her life consisting of nothing but tiny swallows of soup and shallow breathing for more than a decade. My grandfather's sister now lies in a room dying in much the same way as her mother. Here they are used to tending to people who are barely alive. It is a place of pasts and shadows. A place to come from, but nowhere the fully living are ever supposed to end up. The now defunct silver mines are no more than a few dozen miles away. There is a small river just outside of town. The town itself is peopled by very pretty girls and boys, the mixed descendants of all those who came to mine that silver, the beautiful mestizo offspring of heedless greedy digging.

I don't know for how long I will stay in Sombrarete, in this walled in house and its dark absences. But, as I said, no one here asks me any questions, and that is a relief. My widowed aunt dresses in black and daily tends to her ancient dying mother. Her silent brother, my uncle, goes next door to the pharmacy where he is head pharmacist. We all gather each day at three, to eat our midday meal together, attended on by the old cook and her gloomy daughter. The rest of the time I wander the halls or sit in my room, and sometimes I read from the books Pablo gave me. Once or twice I have attempted to write a poem, as if to right the lie I spoke to Pablo about being a writer. But mostly I do very little. Everyone here knows it is a place to be and not be at once. A place for staring at walls, at those high old ceilings. They believe in ghosts here. The way things are and aren't present at once, my sister deeply in me, though my mother in me too. It is a place of vanishing, here, a place where you can fade. My job here is to disappear like my sister. Because, although I tried in Spain, I could not leave her, and in LA I got close to where she'd been, but then I started breaking. Maybe here, though, I can simply become one with Julia's absence. I can become a sister who disappears too. For, don't forget, I am nothing but a mirror, a replication, a reluctant resurrection. And though my sister is not here, I see her. I see Julia everywhere.

I always have.

Rocio

IT COULD BE THAT I always understood Claudia was unkind. Or it might be that I only began to see it in the dreadful way she treated my sister, in the awful way she treated my little sister. Because where Julia was concerned Claudia's cruelty was undeniable; there was no way around it, no way that you could pretend it was anything else, distraction, or hyper-sensitivity, or insecurity, or nervousness. It wasn't just anxiety or immaturity, or any of the other things we otherwise used to explain away Claudia's erratic behavior. She was also mean. And though I'm not sure when I first recognized it, I know that by the time Julia was given away it was clear to me that my mother was somebody to be careful of, to avoid even. Though she would never see it. She would come over and kiss me sometimes, jump into bed with me and force herself on me with her overbearing love, her arms tight around me, tickling me to discomfort, laughing loudly, manically attempting to make me feel that there was some special bond between us, me being her oldest. I'd lie there stiff, unable to ease into it, unable to drop my guard. I always had this thing in regard to her that I will call a wariness, and could never hide my discomfort. I'm sure it showed in my body, the way it tensed. I was afraid of her. And I made it clear I wouldn't go along with things the way Marta would. My mother terrified me. Her big hairdos and bright lipstick, her tight skirts and cleavage always showing. Her raucous laugh; there was something deranged in it and even if that had been the only thing, that was already too much for me, the way it would spring out of her, sudden, loud, savage and unexpected, making my heart leap. And the way she would publicly humiliate me, sometimes on purpose, pointing out a boy I liked, "Is this the one?" she'd yell, and then say something to him in a flirtatious voice, "Isn't she pretty?" while pointing at me, so that I'd want to kill her. Other times it was simply her manner, her way of being, the way she would talk to everyone as if they were her best friend, the grocer, or the woman selling subway tickets, joking noisily with strangers, always trying to get everyone on her side, as if life really had sides.

It was her very being that made me anxious. The way she was always drawing attention to herself, any kind of attention—good or bad—it didn't matter. It was all humiliating. It all made me want to disappear.

Yet, I often felt painfully protective of my mother, even as I was fully embarrassed by her; on a bus when she'd start, suddenly, going on about a fight she'd had with her uncle, more than two decades before, bringing it up and fully reliving the insult, "He told *everybody*, he told my *mother*, that he'd seen me with the boy at the art store. He said I was standing too closely, talking too intimately to the Indian boy, touching him, when I should have been at school," her arms flying along with her piercing voice as if she were in the midst of it again, her battle with her traitor uncle. "He was my *favorite* uncle. How *could* he?" She was almost in tears now, "My mother *believed* him!" The other passengers looking on now, some of them staring.

It was a space near death, hating and wanting to protect her at once, working hard to keep things together, all those feelings swirling inside me. "Shhhh, I know, Mamí, you've already told me all that," I would say, putting my arm around her and whispering to bring her tone down, working hard to get her to stop.

"*No*, it's not fair! It just isn't. She *believed* him!" she was weeping now, not my mother any longer, but a betrayed and angry child. All those people on that bus staring at us as I pulled her weeping face to my neck.

I never knew what would happen with Claudia. Though she would go through periods of looking strikingly normal, was even quite beautiful sometimes, she could still swallow you up in her need. In her thunderousness, her raucous emotions. Swallow you up in her compulsion to always be at the center, to draw attention to herself no matter what. Flirting with the cop on the corner, flashing her breasts as she jaywalked, shaking her ass and laughing. You never knew what to expect; I never knew what to expect. She'd start screaming at some woman she thought had cut her in line at the butcher's, savagely yelling though maybe it had been a mistake, "Who do you think you are? I've been standing here an hour!" though we'd only been there for five minutes. And those other women would look at her in shock, mostly, thinking her vulgar, back away and let her have all the room she demanded, though once or twice I saw one fight back, matching my mother in her craziness, while the others silently backed away.

It would rise up out of her suddenly, abruptly—a dizzying vertiginous mess which sent my heart leaping, my skin crawling, my fingers nervously picking, blindly scratching at my own neck.

What drove it? Drove her? It was as if she felt that if she did not blaringly exert herself, did not pound on doors to be let in, did not yell at strangers, did not sexually joke with all the cops and teenage boys, she might not be there at all. As if she doubted her own being, her selfness, and so had to make that self noisily present at all times.

And in a way maybe she was right, because when she wasn't being this loud and scary person, this abrasive needy person, bottomless, she would disappear, sitting mutely staring in the corner, blank and straight. Or for weeks, months on end not getting out of bed.

Either way, she seeped into me. So that even when she wasn't around it was as if she were, the effect from her was, how she'd undone me, the confusion she had wrought upon my life, so that I didn't know what I was getting into most of the time. I was muddled, unclear. Lost, I didn't know how to care for myself, didn't know how to keep the bad from happening, how to protect myself from badness, how to run when it approached.

Did I have a will at all? It started with them, really, my father and my mother. I didn't know how to keep them from encroaching, piling on me, taking every bit I had. But in Coahuila, when my grandmother brought Julia to us after we'd left her behind, when she told me about her carriage ride with our grandmother, I began to believe it was better to be away from my mother, from my father, far better to keep my distance from them both. It was possible to be elsewhere, I realized, to be in carriages even; there was a whole world of things outside of them. It was that night in the desert, I was nine years old, that I somehow understood I could find people to get me away from them, people to cling to. And though I don't know where I got this, this knowing how to find, somehow after that I did always manage to stumble upon people who would care for me. People who in the end could guide me away from it all, guide me away from him, away from her, tend me, get me out of there. It's no mystery I married so young. Twenty years old and I had bound myself for life, for dear life.

Perhaps I was twelve or so. That means Marta would have been about eight or nine. We were at my Grandma Marina's, my grandmother, who was constantly telling me she loved me; and though I did not so much feel it, it was so often repeated that I did at some level believe her. Grandma Marina was not affectionate, unless she'd had a bit to drink, and then it was sloppy, her love, those wet kisses, so that you did not fully trust it. She had been beautiful once, her Irish blue eyes and red hair, though now she was very heavy. I had her light eyes and I looked like my father, so I was her favorite like him. I would often drag Marta to her house after school though my grandma was not kind to her. But there was always good food, because though she was loud and overwhelming, she was a fabulous cook, so we'd go to her house after school at least twice a week.

There were some older boys on the block who began coming over. Perhaps they were the sons of one of Grandma Marina's friends, because as I said, she was big and fiery and was a great cook and had many many friends; and since she liked to drink and played the piano and sang for those people who were always dropping by to visit and eat, there were always many around, singing and drinking. So maybe we already knew those boys, had maybe met them at one of her parties. In any case, though I was very shy, Marta wasn't and so she must have been the one to let them in. And then they started coming over all the time. And since in the afternoons we were often there alone for an hour or two after we arrived, we one day started playing these games with those boys. I don't know how it began. How do things like that begin? Though we'd played simpler versions of those games before, Marta and me. It started easily enough, looking, and touching a bit maybe. Maybe we pulled down our panties a few times, or they did for us while we stood awkward and straight. I can't recall what they were like, those boys, what they looked like. I don't remember their names. Who were they? But that they were older, I am sure. I remember once on the bed, rolling around, maybe they were touching us then? I don't know, though I imagine they were because I do have a strong sense of my skin going all hot where they touched me, on my crotch, and we were giggling and their hands were on, or maybe even in our panties— the squirming away and then being caught. The wild laughter. A strange form of tag. Like little dogs. Trying to crawl away on all fours and then being pulled back by our legs, our shrieky laughter.

We were doing this, moving like this, in this, crawling and shrieking and laughing and being grabbed and pulling away and being grabbed and getting pulled back and then being grabbed again, and there was nothing strange in it, nothing wrong in it, we felt, until Grandma Marina's tenant, a middle-aged woman, maybe ten years older than our mother, ten years older than Claudia, until this woman descended the stairs outside the big window; and when she glanced in, she saw.

I will never forget the look she gave me. No one had ever looked at me like that.

Those boys were older. Her eyes made me see that. Her eyes—which seemed to stop there for a long long time, scanning the insides—gave me pause. It had been fun, electric, maybe I had even liked one of those boys, in between my legs I'd felt hot, maybe I'd dared to press myself into his hand, but her eyes made me stop.

I don't know how it ended, that game, how we got them to leave, how I got them to leave. I probably said something about our grandmother coming home soon. They probably ignored me for a while, still trying to grab onto us. I probably grew angry and stern then. Or maybe I cried. I just don't remember that part.

But her eyes I do recall, that long and weighty look, which to me seemed tinged with shame and sadness. Her eyes were big and lined in black and had caught mine for a second, though I'd quickly looked away. And then I never again, until Julian, let a boy touch me like that.

Sandra was born the year after Julia was taken away. After my sister was sent away, was given away. That means Claudia was probably pregnant with Sandra the day my grandmother Marina came for Julia. Sandra was such a serious girl. Even as a baby she was serious. She was smarter than the rest of us, too. She also seemed clear in some way, sure about what things were, what everyone meant, what each one of us was all about. And she somehow kept herself separate. Knew what was safe, in some way, and always chose that. From the beginning she mostly stayed away from Claudia. She navigated instead to my Aunt Sofia who understandably must have been missing Julia terribly then and so easily and without pause took Sandra in as her own. Maybe to heal the guilt about letting them send Julia away. Or to fill the hole Julia had left, the gap. People don't just leave. You feel them. The pain never really goes away though some people will tell you it does with time. In your heart you always feel them. I don't know how true this is, but my aunt once told me that she partially blamed herself for what happened to Julia. Told me that she felt Claudia had sent Julia away at least partially to deny her Julia's love. Sofia believed Claudia wanted to take that affection away from her because she was the detested sister. So it is understandable that Sofia decided to be clearer with Sandra; she had seen what things could become if there was no clear conviction, and so the second time around she was more decisive, was willing to fight, allowed herself to be there more completely for Sandra than she had been able to be for Julia. Because she understood fully what the loss of that love could be.

Sandra. With her you couldn't be unclear. With her you knew what things were. She insisted on it, somehow. Even as a baby. I remember going to the beach with her once. My aunt Sofia took us; my grandmother Ceci came too. My aunt rented a jeep and I recall all of us laughing as it madly bounced over the bumps in the road. Sandra would shriek wildly with each big bump and her laughter, her unbridled joy, more than anything else in that car, made us all laugh too, my aunt and my grandmother and me. It was hot. Acapulco in August. I remember lying on the sand, at the beach with little Sandra wading at my side. I was thirteen, was newly aware of my own body, lying there on the hot sand near the water, that ocean lapping at my long adolescent feet, my grand-mother and my aunt having stayed back. I am ten years older than Sandra and I was thirteen, so she was just a tiny little thing. And she looked over at me, looked into my eyes and told me this long drawn out tale about a princess and a witch. It was very sunny and the sky was an intense shade of blue; there were two or three big puffy white clouds in the distance, and their whiteness made that blue seem even brighter.

"The princess would knock on doors," Sandra said, "all the doors, all of them, and ask the people inside if they were good or if they were really the witch in disguise. And this would mean they were bad."

"The witch was hiding was she?" I asked.

"Stop *talking* to me; I'm telling you a story," she replied, serious faced. And so I looked at her very directly to show that I planned on paying attention, that I would now play by the rules, and convinced she continued, her little hand going up into the air and making the motion as she said the words: "Knock knock," she said, "Are you good, or are you really the witch in disguise?"

And as I watched her continue with the story, as I heard her slowly ask that weighty question, I saw that she was both *in* the tale and telling it at the same time, as if the story already existed before her, and she was just stepping inside it, giving it voice, though she was going to force it too, to mold and meld it; she was going to make it adhere to the outcome she willed it to have. She looked me in the eyes then and her gaze had deepened. Her own eyes had become suddenly troubled, her mouth taking on a concerned pout as if the story might in fact get away from her, get out of hand: "Knock, knock," she said more slowly still. "And this time, Rocio, inside was the witch."

She looked deeply worried and I stared fixedly back at her and then she yelled, "Bang! Close the door!" and her little hand made the motion of slamming that door shut. "Don't ever open that door again, Rocio," she said, her body fully tensed.

The sky had been clear until now, but when my eyes went up to it again there were clouds rapidly rolling in, the way they can suddenly do so in tropical climates. Those three previous white clouds had transformed and become many, were now rolling in, spinning violently, different shades of gray shifting and moving as Sandra talked. That sky suddenly tumultuous. "Don't open that door, Rocio," she warned again in her grave tone.

"I won't," I said very seriously. "I won't ever open that door."

She let her gaze wander over my face then, before re-focusing on my eyes, "I love you, Rocio," she said, her body relaxing now.

"I love you too," I said back, and I deeply meant it, and suddenly the clouds broke as if Sandra had told them to do so for effect and I grabbed her little hand and pulled her up and then, dripping through the wet sand, I led her back into the hotel lobby.

I deeply loved her, but I knew that she was strange. At seven or eight Sandra was already like a little adult. She would figure things out too, things that baffled everyone else. She could fix things. Wiggle some wires around when the TV would stop working. Find the button under the sink that we needed to push in order to get the garbage disposal going again. I seem to remember one time, my aunt Sofia and Marta and my grandmother and I all standing in the kitchen doorway watching water pour out of a broken pipe, wondering what we were going to do with all that flooding water, standing there staring in a kind of mesmerized state of inaction, when little Sandra, she must have been seven, went over and found the water valve and turned it and turned it till the water just went off. "That's what that's for," she said. The rest of us just looked at her and then at each other in amazement; we'd never even noticed that valve.

I would watch her sometimes. Her ease. The way she knew just how to move through things. What to do. Who to avoid. Where to go. How to do things. I remember seeing her once, tiny—it is strange, all of these memories I have of her, these very strong images of Sandra are from when she was quite small. Before it got messy with her, before she got confused. These stark vivid pictures of her, the way she comes back to me now, as a little girl, are clear and strong. I remember seeing her once, tiny Sandra twirling in the sun. I was reading on the upstairs patio, near the balcony that overlooked the patio courtyard where she played downstairs, when I heard something, someone talking in whispers and the voice was both familiar and strange and so I hung my head over the side, to see who it was. And I saw her there, down below me, my little sister, four or five at the time. She was there and she was talking, intently, with direct and serious eyes. I hung my head down lower to see whom she was talking to, and then lower still when I saw there was nobody with her at all. I wanted to see what it was. What she was doing. Where her adamant whispers were being directed. That deep intent talk. I saw her take a big breath in and hold it tight and then she closed her eyes and her arms went out at her sides and she faced skyward, and then her voice went sing-song and she began chanting, serious, still stern, her face going to anger once or twice. I almost said her name, almost called out to her, to save her from something, I felt, to save her from whatever that thing was that drew her, but I stopped myself because I realized she did not need my saving, because—I suddenly knew—she was beyond me, beyond anything I could do for her, beyond any-thing I could even understand. Though I was much older I already felt I was feeble in her presence. And then she began to twirl, round and round, her thick long hair flying around her like a matador's cape, swooping around her moving torso, and now the chant had changed and she was slowly counting, one, two, three, four, five… she counted to eight like that, twirling once for each number so that her mouth and her body were aligned, enacting the number eight as she said it. And then she stopped. "That's it!" she called out very seriously, and she was louder now so that I heard her clearly this time. "That's it!" she repeated, adamant. And I got the sense that she was speaking to someone, though I could not tell you whom or what that thing was. It was as it had been on the beach, when I had seen that she was both in the tale and telling it at the same time, as if the whole thing already existed before her, and she was just stepping inside it, giving it voice. There was something that bordered on enchantment in what I saw next: Sandra pulled eight big leaves from the juniper tree—she picked them carefully, examining each before pulling it off the branch—and then she picked up eight rocks one of which she stacked atop each one of those leaves. She then lit a match from a box she had near her and this terrified me, because she was tiny, too tiny for fire, I thought, but I did not try to stop her and for some reason I do not fully understand just kept on watching her instead. She lit the corners of the leafs, carefully each one, and then she watched them burn and when they were just ash she took the stones up and angrily shouted out to what-ever force was there with her, "Ouch! they're hot! I told you they would be hot!" before walking over and piling the warm little stones next to the sink where the maid, Maria, kept our wash. And then again she began speaking in whispers I could not make out, insistently, her hands gesturing fiercely from time to time.

The next day and then the next I watched Sandra do the same thing, eight days in a row, and then not again. And though I was afraid and never visited that pile of stones myself, Sandra did often for the whole of the next year, checking in on them, handling them while she whispered to herself, moving them about periodically, counting and piling in some regular way which seemed to make perfect sense to her.

There did seem to be someone. And this was not like other children's imagined friends, because she never ever openly spoke of him. She never revealed him in little child slips. Never set a place at her tea table for him, never told funny stories with him at the center like other children do with imaginary friends. This someone she spoke to was something else, something serious. I later learned to believe he was there to help, somehow. That he was someone who looked after and taught and took care of her, even in the worst of times. And though the whole thing terrified me, I began to wish I too had someone, or something, like that.

It was strange how directed and sure she always was. How intense. It was strange too how much she looked like Julia. Like Julia had come back. A stronger, lucid Julia, her dark hair and big brown eyes. Her long skinny limbs, though she was small like Julia was, her golden brown skin. She was a Julia who knew to stay away from trouble, who knew to stay away from our mother, who never ended up with Claudia's hand landing sharply on her back.

Until Sandra the adults in our lives had hardly looked at us, had very little idea, or interest really in what we did. We ran around like feral children, the wild child times three, three boundless girls competing for what little of them there was. But Sandra somehow changed this. She understood them all at some deep level and in some way this must have helped them too. She gave them clarity and definition. Gave us all a definition. Differentiated us from each other, somehow. We all knew who we were in her eyes, who we were to her, and so then to each other, and to ourselves too. Yes, she defined us. Marta had always terrified me. She was truly volcanic. I never once heard her say, That's enough. She just erupted and seeped out and did whatever she wanted, no thought beforehand or remorse after the fact. She was like my mother in that she could get into some real trouble, just walk right into it, two paths and she would always take the wrong one, like a purpose. And there was no limit to her anger, her craziness, the extremes to which she would let herself go. Yet I was never scared for her, more I was scared of her, the places she would try to drag you to. Her violence. This scar on my hand, someday I will tell you all about it.

Once, when my uncle Felix—angry over her having gone into his room again, having taken some candles and fine drawing pencils off of his desk, which she then carelessly broke and left lying haphazardly by our bed—went up to her to yell at her or maybe even slap her, she charged right back at him, challenged him in a way that was shocking and terrified him too though she was barely twelve, so that he stopped in his tracks and then backed down. It was terrible, the way she had instantly leapt up, yelling and red faced, her whole body at once ready for the attack. He simply turned, called her a nutball and shook his head in a way that spoke a real regret as he walked off, while she stood there panting still. I was sitting playing cards with Sandra and when I looked toward her with wide eyes, Sandra very simply whispered, "She's crazy, what do you want?" And somehow I had never thought about it in such simple direct terms. Oh, yeah, I thought. That does it. She's crazy. A nutball. That explains a lot.

My aunt Sofia took Sandra on without question. I would watch them together sometimes, in the kitchen, Sofia still in her slippers frying Sandra an egg, while Sandra sat intently drawing a picture, or silently reading a book, neither of them talking, neither of them having to prove they were there for each other because there they were and it felt right and easy somehow. Do you want another one, Sofia would ask sometimes when Sandra had finished, and Sandra would nod yes, or no, naturally, knowing her gesture would be read, not even having to lift her gaze to see if she'd been seen. When Sofia moved out of the family house and into her own apartment, I think because my mother had again moved back in with my grandmother, Sandra went to help her move in and then really rarely came back at all, instead living there with my aunt most of the time.

The two of them were so relaxed and comfortable together. And though I was not one of them I loved going to spend the night there. We would go shopping together, and my aunt who had a good job always took us out to nice restaurants and then at home we would sit on the couch, us three, and watch TV, laughing all together. Antonio would sometimes be there, though he did not yet live with my aunt, as they hadn't yet gotten married. And we would all play cards, using jellybeans or pistachios as chips. I was happy then, with my Aunt Sofia, who had never favored me as she had done with Julia first and then Sandra, and yet I liked her. Loved her.

I think of it often, the three of us girls, sitting on the couch eating mango or prickly pear and laughing at the TV. Together. The happy ease of that.

And now Sandra is in Sombrarete and I wonder how this can be. How did she end up in that tiny village, in my grandfather's childhood home? She was the strong and clear one, was directed, always, and now she is there and lost and I just don't understand it. She doesn't want us to go and see her, says she needs time to be alone. We hear only through my great aunt's brief calls to my aunt Sofia. She seems to do nothing for days on end, she says, and this makes me so sad that if I could I would go see her, help her, even if she doesn't want me to. But though Sara is now nearly grown, she also needs me; and I have Julian, and the house, and I cannot just up and leave my husband.

I met Julian when I was sixteen. He was a medical student and he was quiet and kind. He was serious and he came from a good family. A family like ours could have been, had it not been for all the tragedies that befell us, had it not been for all the sadness that came to inhabit our lives. Julian had a nice face, thick black hair and light skin, gentle black eyes with which he would look at me, slow and serious, for long stretches of time. His father was a sharp-tongued Spaniard and his mother was from Guadalajara, sweet and calm. I met Julian and I saw he was kind. I could right away see this in him, and that was something. For me at that time it was everything. And in many ways I think he saved my life.

I met Julian and he followed me for a long quiet time before he even tried to hold my hand. And though Marta said he was boring and called him an idiot and though my mother tried many many times to get me to break up with him, when Sandra was ten and I was twenty, we were married; and in many many ways I think Julian saved my life.

Julia

THE HOUSE IS IN THE COUNTRY, on the North Fork of Long Island, almost to the tip of it, where the land drops off to open sea. It is an area that was, until very recently, mired in poverty. The locals here are potato farmers and fishermen, have been so for generations, Edith Wharton Ethan Fromes, silent and largely cross; it's the weather, maybe, that has done this to them, the cold, those long dark winters, and the earth which lies barren much of the year. Their anger is, for the most part, turned inward, so that, for them, language—in imitation of that earth which lies desolate and ungiving for nearly six months every year—has become barren too, and is often little more than a series of grunts.

They soften a bit as spring marches into summer, for it is a vibrant march, dazzling even, lush and green with the ash and pine and maple trees newly leafing and everything blooming in a gorgeous and extravagant order, beginning with the ornamental cherry trees and dogwoods in April, followed by rhododendron and wisteria, and then the lanes of purple hydrangea in late May; peonies and asters follow suit in early summer. There are lilies then too. The marshland and pretty little inlets become inhabited by countless cranes and heron and egrets, osprey and plover and other sea birds, while small red foxes hunt rabbits or mice in the tall swaying grasses, the boundless deer eating all our gardens before prancing off through the trees. The Connecticut Sound lies on the North coast of this part of Long Island, the bay leading to the South Fork lies on the other side, with beautiful Shelter Island sitting squarely in-between the two forks. The old potato farms are now planted with berries in Spring, and then corn, tomatoes, and peaches in summer, when the tuna and bluefish run wild.

I saw this all for the first time seven years ago, when I came to spend four months here with Joaquin, who was then newly my boyfriend; we rented a cottage here with another artist couple, on the bay, and that same winter, fully charmed, Joaquin and I got this house near the Sound; we've been coming out regularly ever since.

Prices were still absurdly low then, and there was much for sale, though it is no longer like that here, the last seven years having seen an explosion of sorts. Now this area is peopled by artists and writers and most of the potato farms have given way to wineries; and the old locals have mostly gone. There are fancy restaurants with celebrity chefs which open only in the busy summer months. Joaquin, who is now my ex, was part of the quick transformation of this place; he is a well known artist, and the fact that he and a couple of others bought places here then quickly attracted many more. The fashion people followed suit about five years ago, so that the area has been written up in many magazines. Now the North Fork has become a summer draw to a large part of the New York City population who until recently only thought of Long Island as the Hamptons. But they are here now, opening restaurants and cheese shops, boutiques and hotels. The working farms that remain have all installed little stands which the New Yorkers find quaint and which sell local produce as well as things they have shipped in from elsewhere, the Mexican and Guatemalan farm workers quietly, surreptitiously even, transferring all of that distant produce into little local baskets to keep the Long Island charm. There is gelato now, down the road.

In 1964 a low level abstract expressionist, Theodore Stamos, built the house I presently live in, his notoriety lying in that he was Rothko's great friend and then the executor of his will, as a result of which Rothko lies buried in an indescript and ancient cemetery less than a mile from our house, big rock with his last name carved into it marking his grave.

Stamos was Greek, so our house is Mediterranean in style, an oddity in this area of Cape Cods and quaint Victorians though this is, of course, what attracted Joaquin and me to it. After we bought it we painted it a bright orange, a nod to his Havana and my Mexico City, but so out of place here in New York—

our big orange stone house—that everyone feels compelled to comment on it.

I like to tell myself Rothko sat in this same dining room in which I sit alone, eating fish and new potatoes night after night, thinking about the next day's work, or lack of work, and my guilt at that lack of it.

At the end of my block there is a beautiful quartz beach, the dramatic landscape having been formed by the glaciers that shaped all of this land during the last ice age, huge boulders surrounded by delicate pink quartz stones, Connecticut on the other side of that water. One block down you will see a tiny jewel of a house which sits on tall stilts, facing the beach. It is a little Tony Smith, his sculptural triangular modules on stilts, a series of three in a row, an inhabitable yellow sculpture. It turns out Smith was a friend too, of Theodore Stamos, and that is the house Tony Smith designed for Stamos before Stamos built this much larger one for himself and his sister. I imagine them here in my living room, arguing about art, drinking long into the night, Rothko and Stamos and Tony Smith. Perhaps Pollock would have made the drive up from the South Fork and would be here too, boisterously outdrinking them all.

Across from Smith's small stilt house, on the other side of the Sound, in Connecticut not far from Yale, is a much larger house which he designed for Fred Olsen, a chemical engineer with money enough for a huge compound; that house is made up of a series of separate wings and guest quarters, a Tony Smith extravaganza, with a salt water pool which looks like the polar bear enclosure at the Central Park Zoo in the middle of it all. These two very different Smith houses, as if they were his own offspring caught in a painful but enduring familial bond, look out at each other across the Sound, the large imposing compound staring down at the small though beautiful stilted house, like a proud first-born son regarding the lesser prodigal across the sea.

This house I sit in now, Stamos' big stone one, is on two perfectly laid out acres and I've spent most weekends and seven long summers tending this place, its gardens and deep insides. I know every square inch of it, where things are hidden, have planted all of its flowers and sprouting grasses, replaced birch trees where others have become infected and had to be chopped down. There is a large pool and every day from spring to fall I swim back and forth in it, twenty, thirty laps. I have entertained here, artists and curators and gallerists, occasionally other writers, friends.

There are friends who would come every year. Oliver was one of them. Joaquin and I had already been coming here for two years the first time Oliver took the Jitney out to us from New York, and as Joaquin was working, I went to pick him up at the stop. On the ten minute ride from the station to the house he raved about the farmland he'd seen on the way out to us; he'd had no idea Long Island was so rural and went on and on about a buffalo farm he'd passed, at which he'd actually seen the huge beasts roaming in groups. Oliver was from Berlin and he loved it here, all the Indian names he'd seen on the Long Island Expressway, *Hauppaug, Paumanok, Amagansett, Setauket*, loved that I arrived to pick him up in the old dented jeep, loved how over the top American it all was.

After that first year he began coming out from Berlin every summer and he would stay for weeks on end, riding my bike from yard sale to yard sale on the weekends. Jumping on the mower and driving it around a bit, joyful.

After dinner we would sit together in the screened-in porch, the fireflies lighting up the outside dark, the moths crashing against the screen, struggling to get in to the candlelight, our heads close together, giggling over the warmth of the day, our joy infused with alcohol.

Joaquin would get serious, as the two of us joked, and I'd stare over at him, trying to underline it for him with my gaze, that intimacy, the warm wash and closeness that he and I had never had. I wanted him to note it between me and Oliver, that ease, that image of something I craved and which I was beginning to suspect he and I would never really achieve. But he refused to meet my eyes, turning to his wine instead.

At dinner a few days prior I had seen a curator from a museum in Germany feed Joaquin from her fork as I was returning to the table with a platter of local fish; and as I paused in the doorway I saw Joaquin feed her back. This kind of thing happened often, the open flirtation. But this was a dinner I had spent many hours preparing, my food they were feeding each other, and their smiles as they were in the midst of that act still come back to me in sharp humiliating flashes every time I think back on that night. The fact that someone else was there, that Oliver was there witnessing, made it somehow more painful too, more real, a thing I could no longer deny, or ignore. Oliver saw me staring at them, and made some joke to lead me back into the room, draw their attention away from each other and to my stunned presence.

And then that night I got into another fight with Joaquin, though I did not address the scene I'd come in on at dinner, him and that woman, ignored it as if it had nothing to do with what was fueling my anger.

"I want a baby," I said. "I want a child! I'm tired of living just the two of us, me and you and our meaningless claustrophobic dramas."

I yelled at him.

He yelled back at me, "What is your problem? You are always, always asking for more. Look around you, Julia," he said. "This is all me. Everything you see. I have given you all of this! You should be satisfied. Especially you." He stared me down, "Anyone else would be satisfied," he added as he turned and walked away from me.

Oliver loved it here and would borrow my bike with its over-sized basket and come back from yard sales carrying the Long Island kitsch that would then inhabit his paintings. He made a joke of pop art, and was clever in it. One summer he came back from one of these bicycle outings with a huge ceramic bear, laughing at the perfection of it, its big sad eyes and hugging arms, and he gave it to me, giggling as he did so; it still sits in my kitchen, watching over me as I cook.

Since Oliver's death in that car accident that silly bear has taken on a new weight, of course. Its appearance in three of his huge canvases suddenly heartbreaking.

Two days after he gave me that ceramic bear there was a meteor shower. The most significant in eighty years, and it was big news. We'd been hearing about it on the radio for days, had read about it in the local paper too. Oliver and I were fully excited about it, though Joaquin could not have cared less. At about eleven o'clock we went out onto the long quartz driveway, already a bit tipsy from our wine, though Joaquin didn't want to join and sat aloofly at the patio table, baffled by our enthusiasm. Oliver and I lay on the quartz and looked up at the sky, anticipating. And that was already enough, somehow, lying there breathing deep and slow, looking up at that beautiful starred expanse, nothing else in the whole world but us and it, and us inside it. And then it started, the stars shooting toward us, those stars, coming at us, those shooting stars, two, three, five, until soon we couldn't count them, in every direction, shooting all over, out and in, and bright and brighter so that at a certain point even Joaquin had to look up at that sky in wonderment, remark upon it.

Later, after Joaquin had gone off to bed, a bit drunk, Oliver and I went back out to lie on the stone drive though the meteor shower had long been over. He told me about his brother. He had not wandered like Oliver, had stayed home—a dutiful son—in his parents' village, and was already married and had a child and this had somehow freed him. Oliver felt indebted to him in his freedom to move about the world. Though his father, an engineer, was angry, not happy with Oliver's choice to be an artist. Oliver was quiet for a long time and I told him that I didn't really know my father; though so far I have had three, I added. He took my hand and then I was quiet too. We looked up at the sky and an owl soared silently past. It was a fairy tale night. We stared up at that still incredibly star filled expanse and he gently took my hand in his, "I'm sorry," he said. And I did not even have to ask him why.

The fact was that I was then already tired of being the girl-friend of a famous artist, my own book unwritten. And I wanted out. I had been in love with Joaquin at one point, and had con-tinually begged to make a family with him. But perhaps it was the very obsession that drove him toward a bigger and bigger career that kept him from wanting a child; he didn't seem to want much from or for me either, nothing I could call my own, and discour-aged my writing at every turn, brutally criticizing my essays, always striving to show me that I was wrong, that he was the authority, that I was lesser than him, that he always knew more.

"I want a baby!" I cried over and over again. After a huge show at a museum, a new catalogue, another curator openly flirting with him. I would get drunk and yell at him, never about what was really bothering me, "I want a baby!" I would yell. As if that was the answer. That would fix everything.

And he would yell back. "Stop it!" He'd yell when I would fling myself at him, "Stop it!" When I would cry that he wasn't trying, that he only cared about himself, his work, his art, his production, his ego, his needs, that he didn't want a family, that I wanted a family, that he didn't want anything, really, from me…

"Stop it!!"

But after that night in our dining room the decision to leave him was quickly made.

When Oliver left for Berlin, I cried. I went back to the city, and when Joaquin followed me there I told him I was moving back into the Stamos house for a year in order to finish my book. We could sell the house when I was done. And though he argued loudly over this, the insults flying, here I am. Though now, nine months later, Oliver is dead and my book still lies largely unwritten.

When I was seventeen I would spend a difficult and at times terrifying year with my family in Mexico City, and it was then that I slept with Pablo.

My uncle David's wife hated his entire family—how deep and dark those familial hostilities can run, how fathomless the rancor—and I, as his brother's daughter, stood no chance in her home; I was despised from the first. How had he brought me into that house? A show of will, perhaps, though I know too that he loved me, that he had insisted on taking me in. But by my sixteenth year her determination and jealousy and anger had grown stronger than his love for me and I was finally sent to live with my family in Mexico City, where I was meant to stay the entirety of my seventeenth year, after which, at eighteen, no longer a minor, I could *do as I pleased*, she raged, as my uncle David looked sadly, but passively, on.

I wept the entirety of that plane-ride south.

Soon after arriving in Mexico City I moved out of the safety of my grandmother Cecilia's home and into an apartment with my sister Marta and my mother. And though it imme-diately felt somehow dangerous, at some dark level I was elated at the prospect of being near my mother. I was hungry for Claudia's love, whatever shape it took. And the freedom of that unsupervised life after the suffocating hatred of my uncle David's wife, her stifling paranoia, the sick, repressive, and punitive form it took, was thrilling. That freedom was thrilling. Though I was there when my mother brought a succession of men home in those few months I spent with her. I was there when she fell into a paralyzing depression, staring at the wall day after day, unable to eat much, or sleep, and walking the entirety of that empty apartment like a sick ghost day and night. I was there as she would wander in and out of rooms searching for her children. "We're here," I would say, "Marta and I are here." And she'd stare over at me not knowing who I was. I was there when Marta took Claudia's head in her hands and shook and slapped and slapped her, my mother staring blankly, unflinchingly, as Marta shouted, "What is wrong with you? What's wrong with you?" over and over again, before fleeing to my grandmother's house.

I called my grandmother two weeks later, for Marta had not told her anything and so it fell upon me to reveal what was going on. My grandmother Cecilia and my uncle Felix came and picked Claudia up while I was out. And then I stayed in that apartment, alone, for a couple of additional months.

It was then that I slept with Pablo. And after we made love I asked him if he'd had something with my mother. It hadn't yet occurred to me that he may have had something with my father, that that was the bond I should be asking after. What I knew, what I felt, was that there was suddenly something not right between us, though I liked him very much, now more than ever, and that was the only way I could define that chasm, how oddly he behaved toward me immediately after the intimacy of the sex we had just had. I had never slept with anybody before, and I'd felt something true and deep as I stared into his eyes while he entered me; and he'd stared back, keeping his eyes on mine as he moved slowly around inside me.

But when he immediately afterward became distant and analytical, suddenly cold, critical, it all felt driven by something that was already there in the air before us, before what had just occurred between us, bigger than us, because what we had just shared had seemed so deep, and clear and right. And so I asked him if he had slept with my mother; for anytime anything was taken from me or felt wrong or was ruined it was she who had ruined it and so I asked that question, perhaps misguided. Though maybe too it was a misplaced cry for help or else a revenge for his sudden biting coldness. Regardless of the reason, he turned on me after I asked it. And I have never seen him since.

Before leaving Mexico City, a week after my eighteenth birthday—just as my uncle David's wife had prophesied it—I asked my mother how it had happened. I asked her how, as a tiny child, she had given me away. What was it that could drive a mother to give her small daughter away, I asked. What? What had I done?

Why do you not love me?

She stared at me with such rancor in her eyes, that I physically felt it, a blow to my heart.

I saw Pablo, she said. She paused then and I looked at her; did that pause mean something? How close were my mother and Pablo? What was there between them? *We had a long talk*, she said. *I think you had better go*, she said. *I think you better leave.*

We were at my grandmother Marina's house. Marina and Rocio and Marta were there at the table; Sandra, just a girl, had moved in with my aunt Sofia, and so was not present; but none of the ones who were, not Marina nor Rocio nor Marta, said a thing to defend me. Sandra, though she was just a girl, probably would have said something to defend me.

I didn't ask Claudia what Pablo had said. And I was suddenly terrified at what Pablo might have said.

With confused shock in my eyes I stared at the group of them. There they were, and here, at the chasm, was I, the voiceless daughter of a mad woman.

A few days later I was on a plane bound for the states.

I came to New York to get far away, to try and invent myself here, and I began to wait tables and I studied art history at CUNY, and I acted as if I had no past. And now, almost two decades later, having ended it with Joaquin, I am on Long Island, starting over once again.

And though it is lonely here most of the time, until recently, I'd almost daily see Margaret, who lived down the way.

I met her at the beach one day. She was alone though she is only eight years old. "Hi," I said as the little girl passed me. "Are you going for a swim?"

"Yes, but I think there's jellyfish," she answered very matter of factly, only barely looking my way as she pulled off her shorts.

"I can help you look," I said, and as I approached my dog ran up to her. "That's Joshua," I said. "He doesn't bite."

"Why's your dog have a person's name?" she asked in a serious voice, her words clear and slow, as she finally turned fully toward me. I regarded her long red hair, and very light skin, her lovely big brown eyes staring her question into me.

"I don't know," I answered. "It just seemed right. Seemed to fit him."

"I like it," she said, and she reached out to pat his head.

"I do too," I answered and watched the two of them get to know each other. "Well, if you want to go in, go for a swim, Joshua and I can stand here at the edge and I can try to spot the jellyfish for you, tell you which areas to avoid."

"Okay," she said. "Good idea."

"And if you like, the next time I come down I can bring some vinegar, and have it ready in case you do get stung."

"That's a good idea too," she said. "I always come before lunch. When it's kinda hot, but not too hot yet." She looked over at me with cautious smiling eyes, "Pee works too," she said. "A boy at school told me." She shrugged her shoulders, "But maybe he was making it up to see if I would do it."

"You mean if a jellyfish stings you? I think I've heard that before," I said and smiled at her. "Do you live near here?"

Her hair was long and came down in beautiful red strands all about her so that in her green bathing suit she looked like a pint-sized mermaid.

"Yeah," she said, "on Aquaview Path."

"Is that so? That path is right behind my house you know."

"What house?" she asked.

"The orange one."

Her eyes lit up, "Really? The one with the pool is yours?"

"Yes, do you know it?"

"Yeah. I look at it," she said. "I see you in the pool doing laps. At least I think it's you."

"Well it must be," I said. "Yes, it's me."

"I'm Margaret," she said. "My house is the one with the trampoline."

"Is it? I'll have to look for it."

I knew it, in fact. I took that little path to the beach nearly every day. There was always a big dog tied up outside her house and this dog barked at me and Joshua, who was much smaller than him, every time we walked by, charging us though he was on a lead, the hair on Joshua's back standing up on end in a feeble attempt to make himself look more menacing. There were often loud and angry yells emanating from deep inside the house, usually from a woman, but sometimes from a man too. Emotional and hot and thick.

"Would you like to come swimming some time?" I asked Margaret. "In the pool? No jelly fish in there."

"Really? I'd like it a lot," she said.

"I would too," I answered.

And then Margaret started coming over almost every day. She'd show up in the morning and feed Joshua, walk in and right past me and to the cupboard where she would pull his food out, and then make Joshua sit at attention like I'd taught her, while she poured his food into his bowl, so that soon he would wag his tail and run in circles whenever he saw her coming toward the house, and that's how I usually knew she was approaching. Then Margaret and I would wash berries, which we would pick at while we put a puzzle together or played cards, or while we looked at books. If it was cold or raining we would bake. We'd ride into town in my jeep, sometimes, and she would help me shop for groceries, only once or twice asking for something special for herself which she very much wanted, pop tarts once, cheetos another time. We'd have lunch together at the little health food store, and she almost always ate the same thing, peanut butter and jelly on wheat bread, which they served with corn chips.

"Some people are allergic to peanuts," she said one day, her red hair falling into her face.

"Are they?"

"Yes. I feel sorry for them 'cause they can't eat peanut butter. But it makes them break out in hives if they do and that really hurts and is itchy." Margaret pushed her hair back and took a big bite, "Did you know that's why they don't give you peanuts on airplanes anymore?" she asked, her mouth full.

I loved the way she talked. Her careful enunciation, even with a mouth full of peanut butter. I stared at her then, for it hit me, suddenly, that in her she had something of Sandra.

"Why are you looking at me like that?" she asked in between bites.

"I'm sorry; it's just that you suddenly reminded me of someone I love very much. Do you like to fly, Margaret?"

She swallowed and considered before answering, "I've never been on a plane."

"Would you like to?"

"Yes. I'm going to visit my aunt one day. She lives in Colorado. We might even go there for good." She took another bite and looked up at me, "My mom says maybe we'll move in with my aunt."

"Is that right?"

"Yes. When my mom's boyfriend moves out. We'll move then too." She looked up at me, "At least I think we will."

And the thought of Margaret moving made me very sad.

We went home and jumped into the pool that day, and after I'd finished my laps Margaret stayed in the pool a while. She watched me as I dried off, looking up at me from inside the water.

"Words aren't true," she said as I dried myself.

I turned and looked at her for I felt there was something serious in her tone, in what she wanted to express.

"What do you mean, Margaret?"

"Well, I mean, they're not true."

"They're not?"

She looked at me very seriously then, and so I stopped drying myself, fully regarding her instead. She fidgeted a bit before continuing, struggling to find her way, squinted her big brown eyes as she hung on to the side of the pool.

"No. I mean, when you look at something, I mean, a tree for instance, or when you think it in your head, that's real. That's true. Because you see it. It happens. It's really something. But the word tree isn't real. Words are not real. People say things, they can say things, and it's not real."

I looked at her very seriously then, and she met my eyes for one second, but then quickly turned and swam away, her legs furiously paddling, her arms lazily hanging at her sides, her long hair fanning out around her.

It was three days later that she told me she was leaving.

"I'm going to live with my grandma for a while. We're not going to my aunt like I told you before," she said.

I was stunned. "You are?"

"Yeah." She looked sad, and reached down to pet Joshua to keep from crying. "My mom's not doing too good and it's easier for her to go to the hospital where my grandma is."

"What do you mean? She's not well?"

"No. And she's not happy. She cries all the time and always fights with her boyfriend too."

"That's not your dad?"

"No. Remember? I told you the other time." She seemed frustrated with me for not remembering. "John's my mom's *boyfriend*. I don't have a dad. That's my mom's *boyfriend*. He's not my dad. Anyway, he left. Yesterday."

We were outside, near the pool and there was a little ant mound near her. She kept petting Joshua's head but moved her leg over and began stomping the ants as she did so. "Get away from here!" she yelled.

She noticed me looking at her and she stopped stomping, though she reached down to brusquely brush two or three of those ants off her leg and then began violently scratching at the place where they'd been.

"Did you get stung?" I asked.

She nodded her head three times quickly, and looked as if she was going to cry, but swallowed it and went on instead, "They bit me," she wiped at her eyes with her pretty little hand, "My uncle came and he says Mom has to go to the hospital again and he's going to take me to stay at my grandma's in Brooklyn."

"I'm sorry, Margaret," I said.

"Why? I like my grandma." She stopped scratching and looked up at me, composed now and looking truly puzzled.

"Is she very nice?"

"Yeah. Of course. She's my grandma. Though she talks too much sometimes. And she has lots of rules. But only some days. Some days she doesn't have any rules at all." Margaret's arms went out at her sides and she sighed and then looked up at the sky.

"That must be confusing," I said.

"Oh, no. I like it." She sighed again, "I like not knowing what kind of day it will be when I wake up." She began kicking at the ants once more, then stomping them.

"I'll miss you," I said.

Her long hair fell around her lovely face.

She smiled a tight little smile then and said, "I'll miss you too. And Joshua. I'll miss Joshua a lot."

And when Joshua heard his name he looked up at Margaret and put his paw into her hand.

"Maybe when my mom's cancer gets better, we'll come back."

And I realized, as I looked into her eyes, that the whole time I'd known Margaret, I'd assumed her mother was like my mother. I'd assumed that her mother's illness was my mother's illness. When I looked at Margaret, fed and cared for her, I also saw my sister. I reached my arm out to her, "I hope so, Margaret," I said as I hugged her good-bye. "Of course you will. And I'll be waiting for you."

This house is where I've spent the last seven summers, and now this may be my last year here. Margaret may indeed come back, but I may not be here to greet her upon her return. I look around the rooms and wonder what I want to take with me and, honestly, I can't think what. For the last seven years I have made this house, have lived it, and when I look around I imagine Rothko's ghost walking its insides. Soon I will be nothing but a ghost here too, I know. I will have to give it up from the weight of all that has fallen apart in it, but no one will see any of that in this house, wonder at my time here, know that I was the one who planted those grasses, those bushes and flowers, had walls taken down and others put up... no one will see me and wonder at what killed me off in it, how it is that my spirit here died too.

Claudia

THEY WERE MY FATHER'S childhood friends, the twins. And, as he would tell it, it was a miracle that their house was saved: by the men and the water and the sand and the dirt they sent flying, their arms rapid, working madly, bodies sweating, until that fire was finally out. In the end it was only *their* room which was lost, *their* room which rose up in cinders, the girls transformed into fire and ash. Transmuted. Flesh transcended. Souls denuded. Naked rising essence. The curtains had been white and muslin, thin as light, and the flame on that candle which had been left near the open window had danced and swayed, openly flirted, until the moment that wayward breeze stirred on the wicked conjoining. Romantic billowing, a tease, the curtains sailing out, flitting mid-air for one moment, and then a partial retreat, though the slow surrendering corners bowed down into the flame. Daringly, the very tip of the thin muslin caught the fire, and that small errant corner then ruined with it the rest of that white cloth—that wicked dip, a too far motion, an irretrievably loose moment—and the whole thing fell into slippery sin; at once those nimble flames hungrily devoured the curtains before jumping greedily to the canopy that lay atop that bed, onto that yielding canopy which like all those canopies, like all those whoring canopies on the old wooden beds, hung down low and languid so as to filter light, encouraging the easy idle loll of morning, enabling prolonged comfort in the laze. The indolently shielding canopy, the loose succumbing canopy, caught the thrusting flame and took it on as it spread itself giving and compliant, supplicant and yielding, like a sinful Christian, to the fire and the flames. That ravenous fire rushed down unhindered then, a mess, and caught the bed up and the girls asleep there in it, the twins who were my father's favorite playmates, burned in the midst of guiltless sleep, of guileless girlish slumber. And then their sister who slept elder and alone, regal authoritarian across the room, that fire spread to her bed too, so that she was consumed as well.

Bodies burning, three innocent grimacing faces ablaze.

My father says he dreamt it all that very night, says they came to him inside his dreams.

From there he smelled the scorching flesh, saw the twins from down the road, engulfed, mouths stretched in fiery yells, their sister too, who at first ran away from that fire which was her burning sisters, before gluttonous flames caught at her nightgown too and soon she was wrapped in it as well, taken down as her sisters had been, and it was then, with her screams, that the adults came running in. She passed too, later that night. And their mother, my father said, could not be consoled for the rest of her life.

But then this is where the story merges with many other stories from our childhood, this is where I am not sure of what was said, where the truth and not truth blend, because he says she wandered the streets crying, calling out for her dead babies, her daughters, until they had to take her away. Where did they take her? we asked. Away, he said. He told this story often, sometimes right before bed. Though one time when he told it to us it was different. And this is the time that has stuck with me, this is the time that has come to torment me, because she had *set* the fire, he said. It had not simply been some wayward breeze joining together a dancing flame with a billowing curtain, but the mother. How could a mother be a curtain or a breeze? I wanted to ask. How could a mother so entice a flame? I wondered. This took me up for a very long time and then I had nightmares for many many nights, and when I finally got up the nerve to speak it, to mouth those words, to ask Sofia about this detail she said that I was wrong, that he had never told it like that, that he had never said the mother had done it. Because that was not a possibility. That would be insane.

I was older than Sofia but I wanted to believe her, and so I let her be the boss in this one thing. She was right. I was making it up; our father had never told it that way. Perhaps I had imagined it; maybe I had dreamt it in one of those very bad nightmares which plagued me and had me often waking up in sweats; maybe it was a story I had heard somewhere else, on the schoolyard, a nursery rhyme: *lady bug lady bug fly away home...* or a fable I had read. Maybe my father had never told it that way. He had said other things; he had spoken abstractly about death and sorrow and the space left in people's lives after a loss, how we try to fill that emptiness, with pacing or weeping, or physical labor, with alcohol or self-mutilation, or with a spinning circling mind, a mind that can not focus, though it absolutely tries, though it works and tries very very hard it cannot seem to alight on any one thing, can not focus, can not rest for more than one second on anything, not on anything at all. And maybe I had taken what he'd said and I'd turned it all into a nightmare, a nightmare that ended with daughters dying at the hands of their mother. A nightmare which had me, very often, waking up in sweats.

Maybe my father had never told it that way; maybe it was just too dark that night, there in our room, Sofia wanting me to be quiet, wanting me to stop talking so she could finally fall into her sleep, answering me brusquely and with a cold disdain. Maybe it was simply too dark in that room, in that house, all around me, and my mind was wandering to black clouds, clouds that had rolled in earlier that day, quickly taking over the sky before thunder and lightning announced the downpour that then soaked the clothing on the line, clothing which Maria, our maid, had just put out an hour earlier and which she now ran out to quickly collect.

The sky had been bright, me loafing in that kitchen, when a moment later it had gone suddenly dark and very quickly Maria was at the door cursing and when she came back in, two minutes later, arms overfull with our laundry, she dropped a shirt which when she went to pick up led her to see the baby mice that lay dead in a pile there on the floor where she had left the poison earlier that day. Her face went to disgust and so I ran over, eager but wordless, and peered down under the stove too, where I saw her eyes had gone, and I could see them there, hairless still or nearly so, in a tiny death pile and as I stared she pushed at me, moved me aside in order to get at them. The rain soaked wash had ended up on the table where she had been working on cleaning a pile of black beans when that storm had broken, and with the same plastic bag those beans had come in Maria was instantly collecting that dead brood which she then ran out to the garbage cans in back; and though she got drenched in the rain she did not say a word when she came back in.

Maybe it was simply too dark in that room, in that house, all around me, too silent which only amplified the darkness and so I spoke again, my voice breaking that silence, traveling like a warm consolation through the space of that dark room on that dim night, Today Maria killed a bunch of baby mice, I said. They were tiny, had no fur; I saw them there under the stove, their pink skin, little teeny dark eyes like seeds caught under the thin and vein-streaked lids.

That isn't true, she said.

Yes, I told her, yes it is. I saw her pick them up with a plastic bag and then I saw her carry them outside, to the trash. It was raining and she got wet.

That isn't so either, Sofia answered. Now please be quiet. I want to sleep. I need to sleep now.

And of course her rebuff made me angry and so my mind wandered there for a long time, over all of it, for a long long time. And then it was morning. And I was still alive.

And as I lay in bed that early still alive morning I wondered, what is this thing that can slip so easily in and out of lying? That makes us see things first in one way, and then another, and in our searching for the center we take from everything, from stories too, and things which we have dreamt, and then we see that all these other ways of telling are finally and in the end the same. There is no center. The one way of telling merely a cover for the others, a layering, like sand or ash or soot, a piling up of truths— or untruths. Because they do end up merging, the lies and the tales and the facts, end up merging to create one single effect full of emotion, so that my father's story had some of the fable of *la llorona* in it and to him and then to me this was the truth, seemed right, the wailing mother, the crying out for the children she had herself sacrificed. And then of Medea. The deep sorrow in that. He had read us that story as well. And my own nightmares; they all merged into one large story which seemed to encompass the rest.

I am sure I did not imagine it, my father telling the tale of a mother who could devour her children. I am sure my father could picture it himself and so then tell it, the story of a mother who in her strange love could do the things this mother had done to her girls.

But what was this fire he told us? Who were these twins with whom he had played? Had they even existed? The girls could not be laid out he said. They could not be properly laid out in white dresses, lilies in their hair, violets in cold fingers, eyes closed, lips unmoving.

One had been very beautiful, he told us. She'd had green eyes and smooth olive skin and she was odd and she was quiet, not speaking at all until she was nearly five so that her identical sister did the talking for them. The silent one staring straight as her sister spoke. And this silent twin was the one whom he had loved.

He saw her naked once, he told us. But did my father really tell us this? He saw her by the side of the river, he said. They were all going swimming, a joyful daytrip day, and they hid behind trees to change. It was hot and the air was still and heavy and he rushed in his changing and then ran to a spot from which he eagerly peered over at her; and he had seen her there, her nine year old limbs, fully there.

Where was our mother during this confession to Sofia and me? Sofia cuddled up to him as he spoke, though I found it always strange, their open love, and would lie pulled in tight like a ball at the furthest point from them on that maroon colored velvet couch, and from my position there I would watch, unblinking eyes, as he ran his fingers through her hair. Marooned and jealous of their love. I know I was. I can admit it now. I floated there jealous of that love.

Spoiled, our father was. If things were not perfect he would get angry. He did not like our noise. And I remember my mother standing straight with serious weighty eyes to keep us quiet because she was afraid of his anger. Me with the jumprope in hand, yelling at Sofia that it was my turn, *MY* turn, she was not being fair! and mother's angry eyes turning to me, Sofia mimicking them, her own eyes full of rage now, and thrust out at me, "Shhhh" she shot, and she got to keep the rope then. Though it was my turn. All of them angry with me, all of those eyes, because of his moods.

And he was withholding. Do you know what this means? He would hold his hand over my head, never really letting it rest on my nape, or allowing his fingers to run through my hair; those caresses saved for her. His moods, the way they descended on the house, how we all had to gauge and measure and fight for his love. How he would hand it out or take it, keep it to himself, self-indulgent. Yet, of course, if he ever did speak to me my insides would open up and beg for more, make a big and yawning space there for him, make plenty of room like a hunger in case he should ever decide to give a bit more…

He would come home from managing the bank, which for a long long time I confused with a funeral home; I thought it was a place of dying where he worked, a place where he tended the dead; I thought our father worked where they were all kept, those bodies. I was older, much older when I understood that a bank was a place of money, where money was handled, or something like that. Later still he went to work in Oaxaca and there he worked at overseeing the turning of forests into lumber and supervising the Indians and surveying the land and making sure that it all went smoothly for his German partner.

The German had a handsome son. He had deep brown eyes and strong cheekbones and he spoke softly and was kind. He spent a year in Mexico with his father when he was fourteen years old, Thomas. I was sixteen at the time.

Yet, regardless of my misunderstanding of where he worked, whether it was dead people or money or trees, he held all of us silent as he walked in, until we knew what we had in store that day. Sofia was perfect in it, of course, always knew just how to gauge him, how to get what she wanted, always knew what was expected and always did just what that was. And it never hurt her to do so. Perfect. My father's love for her. She would walk up to him and compliment his shoes, *My those are nice shoes you have on today*, or his hair, or she would say something about the sun falling on a tree, the light, the way it gave itself off. The nerve. It came off so fake. I couldn't. I just could not ever think of anything to say to him as he walked in, or while he sat in his big chair. And I was awkward in it when I did make an attempt, faltering speech, swallowed up words; I just wanted to be able to look into his eyes and ask him directly, Why do you not love me? Is it true what I feel, that you love Sofia more than me? I think I did ask this once, What have I done wrong? *Why do you not love me?* and he looked at me so puzzled, so pained, that I had to walk away. Cold and puzzled and pained all at once as if he just would never comprehend me, so that I dropped my head and did not wait for an answer but went into my room instead.

I just couldn't. I couldn't hold things in. I couldn't instead of saying what I wanted to say, say the things I was supposed to say.

I never even knew what those things were. I could not measure and weigh, give and withhold, decipher and control. I was not like that; and I would never learn. You will never learn, he would say often, and I knew that he was right.

Sofia always came off as so perfect. Always so good. But it wasn't really like that. I was smarter. I was better looking. I had more friends. But, of course, she had my father. And she hated me.

If I wanted to scream, I would scream. If I saw an ice cream cart and wanted one badly I would run to it, who cared if I was wearing a dress and patent leather shoes; I would skip and run and yell, my arms flailing, at the man to wait, wait, wait for me! My skirt fanning out, my skinny as a stick legs. My long black hair a dancing mess all around me. Sofia's disapproving eyes as she stood on the sidewalk. Her hair neat. She would walk up and order her treat quietly, though if it hadn't been for my mad running that truck might not have stopped there at all. And yet those eyes, her eyes, which were meant as much for our father as they were for me. A look shared with him which said, Isn't she disgusting? Isn't she too much? And it would make me want to fist my hands up and pee right there. In my thick hot anger.

But I would get her. I would torture her. At night. From the time I was tiny I would torture her though I know I was giving her the excuse to openly hate me. Why she so easily hates me still. The tricks of a child, the foolishness of a little girl, this is what I was enacting, and shamelessly she uses this to account for her hatred of me even now.

A doll my father gave her, a beautiful porcelain faced one with dark brown curls. Her mouth painted red, she had rose colored cheeks and wore a delicate white muslin dress, bows which matched the red of her lips. I imagined this doll as the twin who had burned. I imagined this doll as the green-eyed twin my father had loved. And he gave it to her. Gave it to Sofia. He gave me one too, of course, but mine was not beautiful, not nearly as nice, her face not a twin's, her hair straight instead of curled. Her eyes were not green. And so one night, I was five or six years old you understand, I told her that if she did not let me sleep with her dolly I would come over and pee in her bed and everyone would believe it had been her who had wet it. I was only five or six. No, she yelled in her stubborn four year old voice. No! And so I started walking over to her bed and as I lifted my nightgown and was about to crawl in she began to cry and she handed me her doll. I was surprised it had worked. But it did and so this went on for almost a year. Every night the exact same thing as if she forgot the script every day. She says I was mean to her in other ways too. That I stole her food, her treats, but if you look at pictures of us in those days this is hard to believe, she was so chubby and I was rail thin. Her spiteful little eyes are clear in all of those photographs, however, of that there is no question, her anger. She was already angry then and for many many years she has held on to her miserable rage.

Marcella often came home with me. She liked to eat at my house, the thin steaks and lumpy mashed potatoes that I had Maria make me all the time. The pork in green sauce which was a particular specialty of Maria's. She was a great cook. So Marcella came home with me all the time. Sofia would already be there, since her school was much closer, and usually we just ignored her. But one day I got mad at Marcella, I don't know what she did, probably something stupid; she was always doing something stupid to anger me, taking the best glass for her lemonade, or the biggest piece of cake, reaching for it without asking, or sitting in the most comfortable chair, right by the window, and refusing to move when I demanded she do so, even if I stood right over her with my hands fisted up. So on this one day I just got fed up with it and I went upstairs to change. I wanted to change into something very beautiful to make her sorry for what she'd done. And I found it, a green dress with a hem that fell well below my knees, the silky material tight around my waist and hips but then flowing out and down. But when I came down the stairs, in the skirt I'd worn for her, she was sitting in the big armchair with Sofia. They had a book in their lap and Marcella was pointing to something on the page and the two of them were laughing. I knew the book they were looking at and there was nothing funny in it. I could feel my neck and arms grow hot. And then their heads went in toward each other and Sofia's eyes shone with delight. What are you laughing at? and I hadn't meant to yell it. They looked at me in shock and their eyes registered fear for a moment, but then almost immediately Sofia began laughing and then Marcella joined her in this. And then they were both looking at me and laughing, for what seemed like a long long time; they would never stop laughing, and I grew so furious I ran back up the stairs and cut my skirt up. Began with the scissors but then pulled it apart with bare hands, long loose strands of green silk.

And then Marcella kept coming over, but I wouldn't pay her any mind. And so she would play with Sofia, would sit next to her as we ate. And when I confronted her at school one day she said, You scare me. At least your sister's nice. I wanted to shove her then, but she was with some other girls; I wanted to push her very very hard for what she'd said.

Sofia couldn't make her own friends, so she was forever stealing mine.

It was always hidden with her; she hid everything. She was sneaky. She hid everything; her anger; her affair with her boss. This was later of course, but it says a lot. She had an affair with her boss; and he was married. This is how she got that good job; this is how she got all that money. He gave her a cat; it was supposed to be very fancy, that long haired cat, but it was vicious. Fits in, no? Makes perfect sense. A vicious pussy for a vicious girl. A great furry thing who stalked the house and every chance it got slashed at your legs or your face. But because it was a good job and she helped my mother no one would have ever said a thing to her. She could do as she liked. And me, they all made me feel like an animal—I was less than that cat in that house. I never fucked my boss which is like fucking your father, yet I was the one who was made to feel like a beast.

My brothers, though, loved me. They did. We would climb together, trees and fences and things. In the courtyard and outside in the parks too. My sister hated me; my father was disapproving and my mother smothered and drowned me, but my brothers climbed trees and other things with me and they loved to go up high and they loved me loved me loved me. For a long time they did. Even if they don't now. They don't now, I know that, since they too can hold a grudge. They all get that from my father, the ability to hold on to anger, the ability to hold on to mean-spirited feelings, to hold and tend deep rancor.

In Oaxaca there was snow. I had never seen it, but my father went one winter two years before he left for good. And he saw the snow. And he came and told us. He even saw it as it fell, he told us. He told us that it fell from the sky like lace and that then it was just there, cold, and he had to wear thick coats with fur lining the inside and collar. And a hat. And also thick gloves which the German had brought him from Frankfurt.

The trees in Oaxaca were tall, and this is why he went there, to cut them down, but those trees had owls in them. The owls flew silent. And they stole children. They stole children who were out alone after dark and this of course could only mean Indian children, because they were the only children who wandered around at night, except for a very rare few other bad children. So the owls stole Indian children and all the very bad non-Indian children and they took them back to their nests where they ate them with their owlets. Pecking at chests to get at hearts first, and then when those had stopped beating they would work on the flesh. The baby owls not knowing what it was they were eating, their eyes closing with each bite of that warm flesh. The owls could be white or they could be gray with large span of wings, and yet the blood always fell red around their beaks. They flew silently in between all of those tall trees and my father walked there strong among them in his fur lined coat from out of which he could protect us. The earth white and silent like the owls in all that snow. And if we ever went there with him, went to visit him there in Oaxaca, we would have to stay close always by his side, especially at night or in the dusky light which is day on its way to becoming long night and is a time the owls like a great deal. We would have to not wander and act wild. We would have to be careful of attracting attention because there were wolves too. And jaguars. And a wild girl could easily get carried off. And so we were to stay near him and not make too much noise and be cautious and careful and quiet at all times. Because the owls or the wolves or the jaguars could carry you off if you drew too much attention. And then if we did that, drew attention, what if they killed Father too? What if because of your wildness, because of my wildness, they knew where we were and so knew where to attack and they killed not only me, not only the one making the trouble, the very very bad one who made all the trouble and maybe might deserve it, but Father and my sister too, so that there would be no one, no one to take care of my mother or to console her upon our deaths. No one to take care of my mother or our younger brothers, no one to watch over trees and help the forest and tend things for the German and help the Indians work faster and to walk among the owlets, and keep back all that wilderness and violence and in the evenings to move silently through snow.

In Oaxaca there was snow.

And yet, despite all of this, Oaxaca and the owls, and the silent angry house with its dark and judging eyes, its disapproving mouths, despite my wanting to run and not hold back, to say what came to me right now, to beg for the love I desperately needed, to demand it right now; despite all this there was nothing until M. No real trouble. Nothing I could call a slipping. There was nothing of this back and forth which he brought to my mind, nothing of this happiness that could so easily run to misery and a back and forth and back and forth. There were no pills and no doctors no dark rooms or painful shocks, none of that slipperiness of being which came to be the only sense of me. It was all normal childhood trouble, my threatening to pee, my sister's anger and resentment, my tomboyish climbing and becoming one with brothers. My father's disapproving stares. My mother's coldness which she would mask with a smothering that came from out of nowhere, that threatened to swallow me whole. She would dress me, my mother, and insist that I wear what she wanted and though it made it hard for me to climb, those thin and delicate dresses, those patent leather shoes, that tightly wound hair, nonetheless she would dress me and then when telling back the story of my young life many years later she would always catalog this as a strong proof of her love, my sheer pastel colored dresses, my tightly braided hair, shoes that were constricting, all of it meant to hold me in, all of it meant to pull me tight and keep my outline clean and clear and sharp and clasp me there. But I did love you, she still says, I would comb your hair. I would dress you in lovely clothes, rub rosewater perfume into your arms and neck. But I knew, that comb scraping hard into my scalp, that tightly wound hair, clothes meant to keep me in line.

And yet, it wasn't until M that I would forget things. It wasn't until M that I would go deep into the darkness. It wasn't until M. And the fact that I would fail to recall whole parts of my life, this too was after M, not before. I don't think it ever happened before that I would sit in a corner not moving, my mind slipping in and out of light. I recall one night, in the middle, yes, it was the middle of the night, I got up and looked for her, my daughter. What was her name? I searched and searched the house. Where was Julia? Where is she? I cannot find her; I could see her face before me now; and I began to cry. I ran back and forth down hallways, down the long hallways of our house, the house I had grown up in and in which my mother still lived; where I now once again lived with my mother, where after the tragedy of M I once again lived with my mother, and she heard me running there frantic and she came and got me as I raced back and forth up and down those long halls. It was the middle of the night and my mother gathered me up and pulled me in tight. The way she pulled me was too tight. I knew she wanted to dress me. I knew she wanted to put on an old thin dress, patent leather shoes, too small. They will not fit, I planned on telling her. If she did not listen and insisted on putting them on me I planned on yelling. I had it all planned out: They will not fit me anymore! I will not wear those frilly socks! But instead of pulling out those old clothes which I knew she kept hidden, which I knew she had there hidden, to force on me one night, instead she let me remain naked; I was naked running up and down those halls, and she let me stay that way and made me get into her bed. NO! I yelled, I have to find her. Where is my daughter? She pulled me into bed with her and I was of course afraid that she was just hiding those shoes in there, under the covers, they were too tight, but all she did was hug and shush me. She rocked and shushed and shushed me. Did not even reach toward my feet. Did not try to touch my feet. And so I closed my eyes. I let go my body a little and I closed my eyes. She's at Marina's house, she whispered. Where? And my eyes shot wide open. Marina, your mother-in-law, her grandmother, she's at Marina's house, she repeated. Don't you remember? She went there to spend the night. And while my mother spoke these words I closed my eyes again and I nodded. I nodded because I wanted to believe her. I wanted to believe she was not lying and that Julia was there, with Marina who I hated. But it had come to me in a flash. She was not coming back. She was not with Marina. She had gone. I had told them they could take her and they had come for her in a big black car. It was a car that I had never seen, where did M's family get all of those cars?

Where did M get all those cars? And they had taken her. Away. I had been afraid I would burn her. I had been afraid that I was that mother who could set fire to her own daughters. I had been afraid it was me. That the whole time it had been me who could do that. Me who was capable of that, who had done that, would do that, was going to do that; the gas. I could smell it still. And so I had asked them to take her. It was me who had asked. And now she was gone. And so I closed my eyes. I closed my eyes and I let my mother lie to me, and though for many many days I did not sleep, my body began to float there in her bed. Marooned in that big bed.

But I didn't really do it. You know that. It wasn't me. It was never my fault. It was M, I tell you. He was the badness. Until him I had never felt myself slipping. Until him everything had been just fine. It had all been alright. Just normal family fighting, just clothes that were too tight. Just those thin and fragile dresses. Just moods. My father's moods. That naked burnt up twin, her green eyes. And my sister's eyes. My father's hand in her hair and Sofia's critical judging eyes. Their anger at me always. Dark and brooding. I was just screaming. I wanted an ice cream. I wanted to sing and dance and climb. But my father's eyes. My sister's eyes: dark resentful. My mother's desperate grasping. Suffocating. My breath being taken away. That's all that it was. Being drawn out of me. Angry faces, small mean comments, just normal family life. But M. By now you understand it was M. He took it all to such places. He made me go to such depths. It was his fault. He is at fault for all of it; I could no longer breathe, would never again breathe easy and light, and he, he is responsible for all of that.

Sofia

IT WAS ALWAYS THE SAME with her, from the time she was a child. She will pretend that it wasn't. She will pretend that it was different once, that she was basically a happy, normal girl, but that at some random point things changed inside her. She will say that it was deep inside, this change. She will say that once upon a time things were smooth and calm and good, but that something happened, and that after this deep transformative shift it was all suddenly very different. That she was suddenly very different. Or, sometimes she will say it happened gradually, that things shifted slowly, over time. Though more often she will say it was sudden—a single charged event setting it all off—but regardless of which version she gives, she will always, always, try to make you believe there was a change. That it was not in her nature. That all the things that occurred after that supposed shift had nothing to do with her, her essence, who she really was. That it was something else, someone else, some outside influence which altered her and drove the initial transformation, and then continued to make her act in the ways she always did.

Mostly she will say that it was M—whom I will refer to as M out of a respect for his privacy, not because of Claudia, some presumptuous and misguided request from her, though not for him either, my respect is not at all for him, for he is loathsome too and deserves nothing even remotely resembling respect from me; my respect is for the concept, for the abstraction even, the idea, of privacy. For privacy. So, mostly she will say it was M, something he did which altered her, which caused the shift. She will blame him. It was *M*, she will say. *She* never would have done *any* of what she in fact did do if it were not for him. It was *him*, she will tell you—some way he acted, some way he treated her, something in his very nature—which pushed her to do the things she did.

She will say these things; she will say many many things, but don't you believe her. Do not listen to her, no matter how sweetly she speaks, no matter how hard she tries to convince. And if you stop to consider alone for even a minute it will become clear and obvious that she *did* do all those things, didn't she? The facts are facts, and it was she who did it all, despicable thing after despicable thing, after wicked shameful thing. Yes, she will incriminate him, but it was Claudia who did those things, not M. Her life has been written by the contemptible things she has herself done.

Anyway, I know what it is like to have that burden thrown upon you, to have to wear the mantel of her blame. I know it well because before him there was me; before there was M, there was me to blame for everything. In those days it was always something *I* did that drove her. Some mysterious way *I* treated her which caused her to be beastly, which made her act in the horrid ways she did. Some way I *looked* at her even. This is what she would say. Imagine? As if I had that much power in my gaze. It's how you *look* at me, she would say. And how you make them *all* look at me in that same judgmental way.

My mother and father, even. Imagine? As if I could control the way my parents behaved, right down to the looks they gave. I was a *child*. I was merely a girl, younger even than her.

It was insane. As if anyone had that much power over anyone else. Me, a child, over my parents. And over her too, as if some look from me would push her to act horridly, shamefully, that it would somehow drive her actions. And then, as if I could somehow, through my powerful gaze, convince everyone else in that house to use those same looks on her, and together all of us, all of our directed mesmerizing eyes, could torture and control and make her do the things she did. It really is insane. What ever happened to free will? What ever happened to self-determination? The power of the self? Please! Nearly sixty years old now and she has still not learned to take responsibility for her own actions—for her own self.

When I was fifteen my father's German partner came to live in Mexico for a year. Things were going well for him and my father in Oaxaca and Heuber wanted to be here to help guide the growth of their logging venture. He wanted to buy more land and could only do so through my father, land ownership rules still being very strict in Mexico in regard to foreign nationals.

So they came, he and his family, and they moved into the fanciest part of Mexico City, Las Lomas, that beautiful neigh-borhood full of stately old oaks and elms and large maples, and we would often go to their home on the weekend to have dinner with them. They had a wonderful cook and those dinners would go on and on. My father was already in the process of thinking about moving to Oaxaca at that point though my parents were not yet divorced and so my father went often back and forth spending more and more time in Oaxaca each visit. But for this one year he was with us more than not in Mexico City, moving back and forth only when Heuber did so, the two of them always in tandem, Heuber leading the way, though very clearly respecting and even loving my father, who was serious in a way the German seemed to like. He would put his arm around my father. They would sit and smoke cigars and talk in whispers for long periods of time.

Anyway, as I mentioned, Heuber, the German partner had come with his wife and son. He wanted his son, Thomas, to learn Spanish. It made sense, in terms of the business; he would some day take it over, Heuber hoped, a wish all rich fathers have in regard to their sons, especially if they are bright. Thomas was fourteen. He was very shy and he was quiet, and I don't think he knew what to do with my sister and me. My little brothers he understood of course, boys are boys, are simple, all like balls and cars and guns; but me and my sister were something else entirely. We were a whole other world. We would show up, at fifteen and sixteen, already beginning to dress like ladies. We would put on perfume, really do our hair up. He could barely lift his eyes to look at us. He was sweet. He was quiet. Thomas was very very shy. Yet he did begin to stare at me when he thought I wasn't looking. Those dinners were formal, but soon Thomas and I were stealing looks at each other, and then after several months we were even openly gazing. We would smile and my skin would blush and goose and thrill. I would glance up and down from my plate one-hundred times each dinner.

And Claudia didn't like this. Didn't like any of it, all of which she noticed.

Claudia noticed everything.

My friend Leticia is pregnant, she said one night at the table, and of course this drew all of the attention to her. My father asked Claudia to stop there, but she immediately began defending Lety by saying that she was deeply in love with her boyfriend, that it was love that had made her do it, and that she herself understood it. How love could make you do things. How love could make you crazy and drive what you did. My father was now quite angry and he asked her to stop again, in a sharper tone. But Claudia went on, I have told them to elope, she said; I have told them they have to make the choice of love, for love, she said. Nothing else matters, she said. I of course knew all this to be a pack of lies, because I had met Lety and it was clear that she was the worst kind of floozy, and that she went from guy to guy continually. Meanwhile, my father had grown furious. Yet while Claudia was supposedly having this very heated argument with my father, who was of course embarrassed by this outburst as well, she kept glancing over at Thomas, measuring his gaze. When my father sent her away from the table she passed very close to Thomas, looking at him to gauge his reaction.

Another time she started talking about some painting she'd seen, something erotic, a naked woman with a horse and a demon looking down at her from some height as she slept and my father gave her a sharp look to make her stop. But Mr. Heuber corrected her. She was not naked, he said, but wearing a very thin robe. He took a spoonful of his soup and asked a question, Where had she seen this painting? She did not recall, she said. He broke off a piece of bread and went on inquiring, Did she like art? Yes, she said, our grandfather, Mama's Papa, was a fantastic painter. Well, there are many wonderful museums in Germany, he said. Maybe you can visit with your father one day, he added before taking a bite of that bread he had broken off.

Mrs. Heuber turned her head decidedly away from the table at the suggestion, and my mother blushed a bit at that clear rejection, but Claudia surely did not notice it at all, because she was busy staring at Thomas, making sure she had his attention, making sure that he saw that his father was taking her in, addressing her in serious tones, though at that point she was already dating M.

It was reminiscent of when we were girls, all this, reminiscent of when she would get upset because my father and I were spending time together, how crazy jealous she would become. Only now it wasn't my father, it was Thomas. The prize was Thomas. She couldn't stand that I had his attention. Couldn't stand that I had anything at all. Though she was already seeing M then. Plus she had other boys she liked. And because she was wild many of them liked her back. Thomas was the only boy I'd ever even looked at. Thomas meant nothing to her; she had insulted him when we first met him, telling me he was still nothing but a gangly child. But now she would spring upon us as we sat in his father's library, looking at one of his father's big picture books together, draw the attention to herself with her flirtations, pulling at and playing with her hemline as she swayed her body from side to side. Or when we were in the garden, having gone off a path so Thomas could show me a nest he'd seen in a tree; then his climbing body, his legs gripping the trunk, arms pulling branches, up, up to check for speckled eggs; or else some special rare flower which was blooming. We'd be getting very quiet, our voices going to whispers, his face very close to mine, those heavy-lidded German eyes, our bodies leaning in toward each other, his fingers brushing up against my rose colored dress as he went to point, then set to touch that rare petal, when suddenly there she would be.

Everywhere. Everywhere. Everywhere. There would be Claudia.

So much as it had been when we were children. My father and I would be sitting and talking, he would be telling some story about his childhood, the silver mines, the rich uncle he had grown up with, and in she would storm, demanding attention. Or he'd be showing me something in his ledger, my brothers were still too young for this, so he'd be showing me, teaching me to keep track of things while he was away in Oaxaca, and none of this interested her, she had never shown any interest in numbers, in the regularity of math, yet in she would stomp. And because she found our talk boring she'd sit in one of his big chairs and she'd stare at the two of us together, green hatred in her eyes. Or my mother and I would finally be knitting, and it would have taken me a long time to convince her, It's okay, I can teach you, I would say, for my mother was not good at this sort of thing, had no ease with her hands, and I would have just calmed her, would just be teaching her to curl, patiently guiding her hands with my own, showing her how to move the needles in the easiest and most efficient way, whispering the directions to calm her anxious fingers, and Claudia would come storming in. Do you want to play cards? she would blurt out, holding the deck in her hands, fiddling with it, and my poor mother who was really very frustrated with the yarn could not resist; she would glance at me guiltily, but of course my mama wanted to be playing a quick and exciting game of cards. And Claudia knew this. She'd stand there staring until my mother rose to go and sit with her. My brothers ran with her too. They climbed trees while I sat alone making lace. They went to the park. They played hide and seek and kickball and climbed trees. And I did nothing to ruin it, did not complain; I did not try to get them away from her. But she, she wanted everything. Everything.

How did it happen? How could it have happened? It makes me sick to even think about it. It still makes me sick to think it. He was so shy. The way we found them. It was my brother Adrian. My eight year old brother, Adrian came and got me and led me down the hall by the hand, his finger held over his mouth, urging me to be quiet, urging me to shush. His eyes were scared and excited both; he was sort of half giggling and silencing himself at the same time, a confounding combination of actions and emotions I'd never seen in him. And when we got to the door of Thomas's room I peeked in from the side like he showed me, from the little bit of door which Adrian had pried open. I was cautious though very curious too at what it was that was in there, what it was that was causing this funny reaction in my brother.

And it was then that I saw them, though it was dim. It took only a moment to understand that Claudia was on top of him. He was lying on the bed. The adults were all downstairs. Claudia was straddling Thomas, her body moving back and forth, her skirt draped over his legs. I audibly gasped and then I pushed my way past Adrian, who looked really very scared at my reaction; I pushed past him and when he tried to reach for my arm on which to console himself—those eight year old eyes begging me to explain what it was we were seeing—I shoved him away even harder.

It was very brave of him not to cry.

I'd only ever been in Thomas's room once, to look for a book he'd misplaced. He'd wanted to show me some pictures of the area in Germany he was from, the little Christmas statues carved out of wood, the beautiful paper lanterns.

When had they snuck up there? How had it happened? I heard myself gasp and then I rushed from that doorway. Claudia had been straddling him. Had been moving back and forth. And though it was dim I had looked into his eyes as he lay on that bed. His face had turned toward me and his eyes had met mine. And terror had run through them.

And then I rushed away. I pushed Adrian, shoved to get away. And then I was downstairs—but how did I get there? how had I descended?—downstairs where I collapsed into my mother's arms, from which arms I begged to be taken home. I began to cry: I am suddenly feeling ill. I really have to go... please, I am feeling very, very sick. Mrs. Heuber stared at me but I continued, I really have to leave, now, my head, my stomach and my head.

Please, Mama, please...

And then I never went back there. I never went back to that Heuber house again.

That was Claudia.

She had to have everything. Take everything. Steal and cheat and hide. And then she would act as if she didn't understand it. Why don't you like me? You are my sister; why don't you love me? *Why do you not like me at all? Why are you always against me? Why do you not love me as you should your sister?*

I couldn't even look at her when she asked those questions. When she was feeling lonely or needed something from me and so begged, entreating, into my eyes.

Really. Why, indeed.

Look, she fucked everyone.

I don't really want to be a part of this. I don't want to be a part of the tale making, the blaming and lying and stories which don't amount to anything. If you want to know what it is all about just look at the life. She will tell you what she wants you to hear; she will lie and she will cheat and she will speak to you in a sweet voice first, for a while, and she may even fool you for a bit. But just listen closely and you will hear it start to crack. If you pay close attention you will begin to see that things just don't add up. And once it all starts to fall apart then of course it will come fast. Sometimes this cracking will come straight away, as soon as you meet her. Other times it will take longer; she will be able to hold herself together longer, for years even; but in the end she will reveal herself. She's sick. She's always been sick and she will blame M; I know she will. Because before it was M it was me, me she would blame. But the fact is that she was ghastly. The fact is that there are facts, and the fact is that she would fuck anyone and that this ended up biting her in the ass. The fact is that she had sex with M's best friend, and that when she got pregnant and then had the baby there was no denying whose it was. The fact is that in Mexico in the 1960's having a child with your husband's best friend was not exactly smiled upon. The fact is that if the child looks like the father, there will be no denying the suspicions.

Julia looked exactly like Alejandro, M's best friend. She just did.

And though in the end this may be part of the reason Claudia was so horrid to her, there is no forgiving it. Though this may be part of the reason she gave her up, there is no forgiving that either. Because, let me tell you, those *are* the facts. She *did* have sex with Alejandro. She *was* beastly to her own daughter. She *did* give her up, though I wanted to keep her. And M is somehow supposed to be to blame for all of this? He is somehow supposed to be responsible for the things that she did? As I was to blame for her miserable childhood?

I don't know.

You be the judge.

Look at the life.

What do you think?

Sandra

A CITY IS A VAST and living being. A massive breathing thing, life heaving and tugging and flowing and every fissure full of it. It is dense with shrubbery and flowers and trees, traversed by canals and rivers and lakes; it is rumored, in fact, to be built on a lake, and in the summer there is a sky so blue above it and heavy with big white clouds that it almost daily gives way to a quick and violent drench. This city is deep in a valley surrounded by peaks, volcanoes in two directions which are the earth asserting its aliveness, pulsing vibrant, virile proud—the city prophesied by an eagle and a snake warring it out in the middle of that lake, there underneath those sleeping volcanoes, those mountains of slumbering lava life. In this city there are breezes which work their way gentle down hillsides before gusting violent up and through the streets; those streets and corners dense with creatures slithering and squawking and running, lizards and birds and snakes and wild cats. This city has shimmering lights and lurking shadows, dripping pipes and darkened tunnels; bubbles and puddles and streams, gurgling and stagnant and green. It is made up of dirt and marble and lye, rock and lava and clay, all of it coming together to give evidence to this: that the city is a vast and churning living whirling thing. There are roads that were once well traveled Indian paths, paved over by colonial stones or potholed blacktop or poured and cracked cement and these mapped long ago by Indian feet roads act like the vessels in your body, the vessels through which fluids travel in your very self, and the millions of people who inhabit this city are as cells in its own limitless body, keeping it alive, all a part of the flow which travels up and down those roads and keeps the city stirring and humming with everyday life. The buildings and statues and fountains, its pyramids, houses and shacks, those monumental arches, memorials and churches all work to give definition and order as together they proclaim municipal enactment, civic entrenchment, community pride. This city is full of stray dogs who live in unseen crannies and darkened crevices and who cross the street when they see you coming, scared sad tails between their mangy legs, and old men who remind you of these pathetic dogs because they shuffle and hobble and limp, their hands busy and imaginative in their own pockets as you walk by and when you pass they stand very very still except for those hands which keep working as they whisper things into your ear which you at your age should not be hearing spilling out of shriveled cankered lips. There are women here who stand staunch on corners and sell tamales out of big steel pots, or else grilled corn with lime and chile on top, or squash flower quesadillas which they fry right there on the street, efficient sturdy hands filling and folding and reaching and frying then rapidly being wiped on an apron before offering you your food wrapped in wax paper, hot hot, while simultaneously taking your cash; and there are happy little cafés where you can stop languorous and sit at bright formica counters while you eat a warm torta and sip at a fresh juice, your eyes staring, your teenage skinny legs dangling down from that high stool as the boy who absently wipes the stove and then the blender too sneaks a look at your slowly swinging calves. On every corner nearly there are small windowless stores full of sugary treats and cigarette packs and bubbly things that you drink out of bottles, some of these little shops clean and others dingy in which built over years grime gathers in all eight corners, and you can tell something about the people's lives who run these shops just by gauging the layers of dust and whether or not it ever gets wiped up. The subways which are rapid arteries are stuffed with people, at busy times shoving dangerously together so as to get in the just closing now doors, and on these trains men come up behind you and rub hard or ever so soft into your back and sometimes even follow with their desire when you try to walk away; and it is because of this offense that you always struggle for a seat despite how difficult to get. And one time you sat right next to a boy, your knees almost touching; and your breath caught for one moment in your chest in a manner unfamiliar as your insides moved just a bit for him and you turned your face in his direction and though you tried to speak, though you wished there was something you could say your mind only wandered over dumb silence, body overcome by that thick feeling, and you remaining soundless lost him then, struck mute as he rose to go his way. And though you loved him you would never see that boy again. The women on these big city busses or subways or collective cabs look beaten down or composed, tired or so beautiful you could not have imagined their existence; their eyes are brown or black or green, hair dark and straight or curled and blonde or red. Some have shadowy circles under their eyes and are loose and languid in their motions, sleepy lidded even here; others are taut and hard and tight and sharp aware, fast eyes moving over every surface, and you wonder which type of woman you will one day be. The bus, or subway or collective cab lurches and everyone's hand reaches at the first pitch, grabbing for steel pole or some other surface, even at the body of a man or woman standing near, but your arms rise up quickly at your sides to steady without touching and you are small so that when it calms you can move between them all again.

And to wander this city, to wander this Mexico City alone is to become a part of it, somehow, to become a cell in its system, a cell, red and bold, in that blood that keeps it all moving, that keeps it going, being pulled along yourself by this life force which thrusts itself up and down those roads which were once Indian paths and which are to you like the vessels in a vast and varied heaving body full of flow.

I was a girl, just a child, when I came upon the newspaper, lying on the table and though I didn't usually look at papers this one time I did. The room was dark and the furnishing heavy. This was a room that was rarely used, though it probably had once been, where dust floated lazily in front of windows and you could lie on one of those long, dark red velvet couches and watch that dust dance heavy in the air; and in this room the paper sat, discarded, by my uncle Felix perhaps, my uncle who was always high on something I had never heard of but who was also the only artist or intellectual in that house and who too was the only one really comfortable in this dark and heavily furnished in velvet and dark wood room. Felix had long hair down to his shoulders and wore a goatee and would close his eyes there in that room; rather they would close on him, and he would nap and read and nap again. He must have left that paper there, next to a pile of books, a discarded cup of coffee, the liquid black but for a thick white oval of putrid cream floating congealed there on the surface.

The story that caught my eye was on the first page and it was about a famous photographer who worked right there at that very paper, so that the story in the paper was about someone who worked for the paper and this seemed funny and strange to me both, as if the paper were talking about itself. This photographer who was now an old man had started as a boy, just six or seven, moving through the city alone. He was like me, in that even as a child he'd liked to do things by himself, and so I kept on reading. He'd lie in bed and listen in on his little radio to police calls, the article said, and then he would rush to the sites of accidents, excited by his own presence there, because it was not so much the accidents which excited him but his own presence at them, the fact that he was not at home like other children but there in the midst of it all, and then as if to later prove it to himself, he would take photos of the bodies, usually it was bodies—in a car crash or a hanging, a drowned child, or one time a woman walking down the street with a small white coffin under her arm. I read the caption. Her tiny daughter was inside. This woman was begging for money, trying to gather enough with which to bury her daughter. There were other photos too but I stayed on that one for a long long time because I had never thought about dead children before, had never thought that a child could die, never thought about desolate mothers begging with tears in their eyes, or past tears perhaps, dry eyed begging stoic, trying to collect the money with which to bury their children. These children who had died. These children who could die; would die. Had died. There was a dead child in that tiny white coffin she carried. And that mother was desperate to put her little girl in the ground.

The story went on: the head photographer at the paper had taken an interest in this boy who would show up at the sites of all of these Mexican tragedies and so he'd asked him many questions on several different occasions: where did he live, who were his parents, where had he gotten that camera, did he not go to school? and then, finally, after a few months of this persistent boy at the edges the photographer hired him to hold his lights. And within a couple of years of this, the boy's own photos were being printed in the paper too.

I liked that. I wanted to be like the boy the famous photographer had once been, not the picture taking, but the wandering, the becoming one with the city and its life. You become one with what you see, I know, because in seeing it you and it are witnessing each other and in this mutual regard there is a strand created there between you and so you are becoming one with it. But I did not need the tool of the camera, as he had, to do this, did not need the proof that the photograph provided with which to see this transmutation, this flow of self and information between the two, me and the thing I was observing. Of course, through the actuality of the photograph it was a much simpler to see equation, made concrete through that photo and so not so abstract: your building in your photograph, your park, your running children, your food stand, your Indian beggar, your body hanging limp from a tree in Chapultepec Park. And your dead baby in a coffin, being carried under her not yet mourning mother's arm. All these things defining you through their presence as you define and give significance and carry them afield through yours. In photographs all this is clear. Proof positive of your daily life. Yet, I did not feel the need of photographs; I had no use for them. I could just wander and see it and through that active form of vision, through my eyes, the city would become mine.

I would take it, all of it, inside my body. And I would become fully a part of it too, through the act of giving myself up to it.

This city is where I was born. Where my mother was born. Where my grandparents met and were married. I held it in me, everything I saw, and so I tried to see as much of it as I could, the colonial streets, those cobblestones, and the old Aztec ruins, the newer buildings too, 50s and 60s modernist ones. I held the stray dogs and the wayward children, little Indian children wrapped in sarapes, barefoot and selling gum or candy from an open box. I held the couples kissing in the parks, sometimes the man boldly lying on top of the woman's body, grinding into her in public like that; I held the women strolling, looking in shop windows, and all the people haggling back and forth on those street corners, the man with a missing leg who played his small guitar for coins which he watched as they dropped into an old tin can he kept down at his foot. I held the girls slowly eating ice creams and the handsome teenage boys who traveled in groups and whom I knew could turn on you or each other like a pack of wild dogs. I held the tired beggars and the old women on their way to church, a mantilla on their heads; I knew a black mantilla meant you were a widow, and I held these widows deep inside myself, the churches they entered, doors wide open, entrances which gulped up those silent dark old widows and then an hour later spat them out again unaltered. I held the angry men, drunk on mezcal in the middle of the day, loudly shoving each other, rage pouring from their eyes and hands and mouths and kicking legs; I held the big hipped women, everything swinging from side to side, and the sexless emaciated ones. And though like that boy I had read about who was now an old man I could have photographed it all, I didn't need to. Because I just held it in myself and it held me. I had learned this from my sister, Julia. She was not there any longer but I held her deep inside myself, and wherever she was I knew that she held me.

There was a homeless man who lived at the end of my street for a few months the summer Julia left for good. My mother gave him food sometimes, and I knew that if Julia had been there still, she would have understood about him. One day my mother told me that he'd been a teacher long ago, that those names and long lists of numbers he drew in manic chalk up and down the length of the street actually meant something. He had been a teacher; and now he hung his pots and pans from the branches of a tree. He was black with dirt and wrapped himself in blankets even when it was most hot and he spewed furiously as she handed him his meals. Claudia would disappear for weeks at a time, who knew where she went, but for this one summer she was quiet and relatively present, and she made it her job to feed Maria's food to this long-ago teacher, food which she brought to him on our porcelain plates.

Usually he would jerk his head at the sight of her, turn his eyes away, but one day when we got there his body didn't jerk at all and he spoke softly to us, *I'm lonely; I'm lonely*, he said again and again as he rocked back and forth hugging his filthy legs. *I know*, my mother answered. *I miss her. I miss her!* he wailed. And my mother answered again, *I know, I know*. I saw his feet move about underneath his filthy blanket. *The boy, I miss the boy, skipping, jumping, I miss him*.... My mother placed the plate of our leftovers at his feet. *I know*, she said. He looked at her angrily then and kicked at the plate and the blanket lifted and I saw that he was barefoot and his feet were black with dirt and his toes were dug deep in the ground. *Holes*, he said. *Holes!* And his voice grew angry as he dug his feet deeper and deeper into that dirt, his toes digging inside it like worms. *Holes!*

What happened? I asked my mother as we turned the corner, *What boy?* She didn't look at me as she answered, *I don't know.* I pulled at her arm, *But you said, I know, you kept saying, I know. I know.* She continued to refuse to look at me as she spoke, *Because missing is missing*, she said. *It's the same pain for everyone.*

But I didn't believe her because Julia had just left and I knew what I was feeling and I knew that it simply can not be the same for everyone else.

The whites of his eyes shone through all that caked filth as he spoke the following day when we went back to exchange the empty plate for another full one. His hand darted out and back three or four times as my mother placed his food at his feet. *Inside the Casa de Azulejos you can see a painting by Orozco, Omniscience! The biggest hearted of all the muralists, not a Stalinist like the others, he had no left hand. Conscience, knowledge, humanity, do not need a perfect body, I tell you. Look at me!* And he began laughing wildly. *Omniscience! No blood on his hands!* He yelled these last words, still cackling, and when I jumped back he grabbed my mother's arm and she did not pull it away as he added, *Tell the pretty little girl that the Opera around the corner from Omniscience still has holes in the ceiling. Holes. Pancho Villa's gunshots. Tell her; she'll like that.* He looked at me directly for the first time that day, to see my reaction, but I had to turn away he was so terrifying.

As we approached a few days later he looked straight at my mother for some thirty seconds before turning his eyes away, his hand jerking back and forth as he spoke, *Carlota went mad, you know*. He glanced briefly over at my mother again. *Not the first colonial princess to do so. That's what tyranny does; makes people mad. Maddens them. She'd watch Maximilian venture out every day from her garden bed in the park as she slowly lost her mind.*

Don't talk to me about Carlota, my mother said, and he turned his head brusquely away, angrily pouting, while she set down his plate in front of him, his right hand pulling hard at his own hair while his left one fisted up beside him.

Does he use them? I asked when we got back to the house later that day. *What?* my mother asked in return. *Does he use the pots and pans? How does he cook with them? Where does he make the fire?* My mother looked at me like she had never thought to consider the question, as if the pots he hung from the trees were merely decorative. *I don't know if he uses them*, she answered. *I don't know anything about him. I just take him his food.* I looked at her: *Maybe they were his wife's.*

I was eleven the summer after my sister Julia's last visit and I began to leave my neighborhood; I began wandering the subways, the communal taxis, the buses; and because I wanted to see things, and because I was focused in this desire, I was never afraid. Eleven years old and I soon understood all of the subway lines, which color got you where, how to then return home on the bus. We lived close to the center and this is the area I liked to explore the most. I wandered the Alameda, that park which had once been an Aztec marketplace, following the crowds of people going one way toward the Bellas Artes, that huge building which is so heavy it is slowly sinking into the drained lake that lies underneath all of Mexico City, and then back to the other end of the park, to the Quemadero, the Burning Place, where during the Inquisition girls who were accused of being witches were burned at the stake. That could have been me, I thought as I stood there before it. Would have been me. I would have been a girl to be burnt at the stake. I'd walk to the Torre Latinoamericana too, which until after I was born was the tallest building in all of Mexico, and of which I had seen a picture in that newspaper article, a picture taken by the photographer boy. In that photo a woman in a red shirt is attempting suicide. She is but a tiny red dot in the picture, hard to make out dangling outside one of the hundreds of windows in the Torre, a tiny red dot full of passion, a tiny red dot who wants to die.

Omniscience is half a block up from this building, and one day I garnered the strength to wander into that fancy boutique; and I stood in front of that mural the homeless man had spoken of as all the rich Mexicans ate their lunches at the courtyard restaurant just beyond this enormous Orozco painting. I stared at that huge long haired Indian for a long time as wealthy people pushed past me on their way to the toilets. Around the corner I snuck into the bar called La Opera and stared up at the gunshots in the bronze ceiling, and it was as if the homeless man had brought me here himself. It was difficult to believe those holes had really come from Pancho Villa's gun, but they had, I knew, because it was clear to me that the homeless man did not lie and he had said that they were real; and as I stared up wondering why the homeless man had sent me there an elegant couple worked their way past me and the head waiter noticed me standing there and pushed me out the door, yelling, *What are you doing here, girl? Unless you have a lot of money you can't come in here without your parents,* and he laughed and he laughed with that rich couple as he worked his way back in. I straightened myself a bit to counter the humiliation and then I turned and made the short crowded walk to the very heart of the city, thinking of Orozco and his dream of a bloodless revolution, people bumping into me and no matter how fast I walked there was someone who wanted me to move more quickly, a few of the men even shoving me aside.

I liked the center of town the most; at the very heart of it was the national palace where I knew my grandmother worked, and into which you could walk past the guards who nodded as you entered and were polite even though they held machine guns and once in there you could look at murals painted by Diego Rivera which showed the history of the city back into Indian times, when food and other things were moved on the canals which were built into the lake which was this city in those days. The murals, those clear pictures, reminded me that this was the center of the world. I well knew that, even then. It had once been the center of an ancient empire, and those murals reminded me that most of the buildings standing here now were built from the destruction, the very rubble, the stones of that Aztec past. And yet all was not wiped out as it had been in other places in the world, because the Indians, the descendants of those shown in the paintings daily still set up their stalls there in the Zocalo as they had in ancient times when the Zocalo was all pyramids and sacred temples and aqueducts; and the markets looked virtually the same as they had then. The massive flagpole in the Zocalo spoke to this somehow as it cast its shadow which made its way slowly shifting over the whole of that square in the course of one long day, so that the two things were intertwined, the pole and the light, and the way they wrote each other, turning the whole Zocalo into a sundial, a measurement of time. On Sundays you could get a sage cleanse given to you by an ancient Toltec right in front of the Mexico City Cathedral, a timeless Indian rite performed in front of the huge catholic church. History collapses in on itself in Mexico City, I learned. Time flattens out. And on my way home, in the residential sections I could gaze into big modern houses and I would wonder about the children who lived in them, what they did all day, and why.

And when I got home and tried to describe the things I had seen to the other people who lived in my house, to my family, I had the feeling they did not see things as I did. I had the feeling that I saw colors more brightly—I could almost smell them they were so bright. I had the feeling that if I looked at something for too long it could possess me; I was always having to draw my eyes away for fear of enchantment. Things could simply be too much. Smell and sight and taste too were often overly forceful; and colors and smells and words could sometimes become confused, colors having smell and words having color that had nothing to do with the word. And because they looked at me with worried eyes, like I was strange when I said these things, like there was something deeply wrong with me, I stopped telling my family about how the word lake was a deep dark red even though actual lakes were green or blue. Or that yellow smelled like mint, that mint itself sounded like a bird-song; I stopped describing how things made me feel. I knew it best to just keep myself close and silent most of the time.

As a child I'd had someone who helped me sift through all these things, to filter and soothe, who helped me stop the vibrations when they were too much. I could not say who he was. But I do know that I would stop and breathe real slow and close my eyes and I would feel it. He would help me calm things down. I would feel him, or something I knew was him, and he would ask me to do things, to put things in a certain order, to arrange and burn corners, to make little shrines and visit them often. To say certain things and twirl and twirl; to hold my arms out from my body. In exchange he would protect me. He would calm me. He would give me an order and a clarity I could feel. I could feel it deep inside. As long as he was there I felt clear and directed and like no matter what was going on I could be soothed. And I knew who in my life I could turn to too, my grandmother or my aunt Sofia, whom to trust. He gave me that. I would talk to him. I would talk and talk to him all the time, rhythmic, like a song or a chant sometimes. And though he never spoke in words, so that I never heard his voice, I knew what he was saying. (Be careful with your mother. Keep your distance. Though he didn't exactly say it, he made this known more than once.) I knew what he wanted me to do, how he wanted me to respond, how he would protect me. I knew all this.

For some people, the old widows with their mantillas, this kind of care and guidance is like god; for me it was something else; it was this old man.

But then it began to feel perverse and wrong and so one day I didn't want him any longer. When I was twelve or thirteen I no longer felt it was right. One night I had a dream that I was drowning. I was in a boat and I was happy; I was rowing though soon someone I couldn't see took over and I lay back as they rowed me about in that boat. I was happy still, in the easy floating, and calm, so I closed my eyes. But suddenly they were moving very fast and I startled with a jolt. I stood and asked him to slow down; I was scared, I said, but he started to go faster. I begged and begged and soon I was screaming for him to slow down. *Please!* But the boat pitched and I flew into the water; I was instantly submerged there and could not breathe, though I tried to speak, a pressure growing in my chest as I descended further and further and then I was awake and I felt him lying on top of me. I felt the pressure of a body, his body, a dead weight there on my chest. I told him to leave. I said it quietly at first, but when the pressure on my body increased, I yelled it. *Leave! I don't need you anymore.* And I began to weep. And when I recovered myself, *Go away*, I said to him again, in a low and serious whisper.

The next night I was on the street, and an old man walked in slow and measured steps down the middle of the empty road right past me. That old man was maybe sixty, sleek and dignified in a long dark coat; it was odd, his slow gait, and after I stopped puzzling at this elegant man walking down the center of the street like that, how strange, I was overcome by the sense that it was him. When a street lamp shone down upon his long white hair, his handsome figure receding down the road, it came clearly to me. *That's him*, I whispered to myself as he walked away. I was sure now and it suddenly pained me that he could walk right past me without even looking my way, without acknowledging me at all; was he angry? and, heavy hearted, I watched him as he disappeared into the distance on that long and narrow Mexico City street, away from me. And then, until very much later, he did not return.

A year later, as I was wandering the city, walking in a park, I came upon a pretty girl hiding in some bushes. *Shhh*, the girl said, *or they'll find me*. The girl, like me at the time, was twelve or thirteen and so it had been about two years since the last time I had seen Julia and I had lost the old man so I was very lonely. She pulled me into the bushes and shushed me again. Then she began to giggle. *They're so stupid*, she said, *they'll never find us in here.* And I'd felt strange at that us. How had we become an us? *Come on*, the girl said, *if we run really fast they won't even see us and we can make it home while they waste their time looking for us all over the park!* The girl had shrieked with laughter then, and she had such a beautiful laugh that I wanted to laugh too though I had not seen the others she had spoken of. And then, as we ran, I began to wonder if in fact there had been a group of other kids she'd been playing with, hiding from, but I decided to believe and kept running.

She pulled me along to her house two blocks away where her father made us lunch. *Look Winnie Pooh, this is Sandra. She is my new best friend*, she said, and then she took my hand. While my hand was swinging in Marisa's her father bowed down low to me. He was round and tall and had a big beard and it was clear to me that he loved his pretty daughter very much. He made us tiny little hamburgers which we dipped in ketchup while he watched us eat. He did not eat with us.

Are you a serious girl? he asked me while we ate. And I did not know how to answer and so I looked away. *You look like a serious girl*, he said, staring directly at me as I chewed. *That's good. It's a very good quality, gravity.*

She called him Winnie Pooh and covered his face in kisses and he hugged her and I right away liked Marisa very much. I would watch them, their funny love, Marisa's long dark bangs falling into her huge black eyes while she giggled at him, the beautiful gap in her front teeth which showed when she smiled her big and naughty smile at him. I started going to her house every day and her father would cook for us and then he would watch us eat (Why did he not work? Where was her mother? It was a while before I had the answers to these questions. She had many brothers too, none of whom I ever met...). She never asked to come over to my house and it was like I had no house of my own when I was there, no sisters nor mother, no grandmother nor uncles nor aunt. It's not that I didn't mention my family, I know I must have, but it just did not matter when I was there with them. He played music very loud, a lot of opera and he would bellow along. He had recordings of poets and he would roar loudly along to them too, both in Spanish and in English. He made things he called sculptures, in miniature, maquettes he called them, and apparently they got made in large scale in other parts of the world.

Things are alive, he said one day when Marisa walked into his studio; I stayed at the doorway though I was very curious. *That's what you know when you are a poet.* He looked over at me. *Everything matters. And when you make something, if it is good, everything in it is there for a reason; every element means something, every element holds the whole within it. It has to if you are serious, if you are an artist.* He looked over at me, held his eyes on me as if waiting for a response.

I am not an artist, I whispered.

Yes, you are, he answered. *You might not know it yet, but you are.*

And when he continued to look at me I felt the blood rise through my body, and up into my head, and I felt dizzy. But then Marisa pulled me by the arm and we were gone.

Marisa and I would lie in her bed and her cat would frisk its way between us. He would knead and knead our legs or backs or arms before lying down and we would shriek with a pain tinged with delight. We would get up and peek in on her father as he worked in his studio and in his pauses he would sing loud and fling his arms around and it was as if he were a cartoon of an artist working. Marisa would laugh as we watched him. But I never laughed. And it was then that I began to realize that people do act like cartoons of what they are supposed to be, like they are performers in the play of their own lives, and if they are good and very serious at behaving like what they are intending the acting could turn real.

I would stay at Marisa's house for a couple of hours after eating, lolling and playing, sometimes an actual game, Chinese checkers or jacks or else reading comics next to each other, lying there with heads close together, passing them back and forth when we were finished. And then at around five I would go off and wander the streets again.

A few times Marisa came with me, but when she was along it was different; instead of the open wandering there had to be something to draw her out; there had to be a plan. We would always end up at a café from which we could watch the boys walk by, or those girls whose outfits Marisa criticized or else decided to imitate. She would dress me in her beautiful New York City clothes and Marisa was very pretty and she always looked much better than any of the other girls and so we got a lot of attention. She was always slightly mean to the boys and so of course they liked her. And though she tried to teach me this, I was too sensitive and could never properly do it. Sometimes we went to movies too, and since Marisa spoke English she would tell me when the subtitles were wrong, and would become infuriated by the mistakes, flinging her arm at the screen as she corrected,

That's not what he said, she would loudly whisper, *So stupid!* Often we would hold hands while we watched and once or twice she lifted mine to her face and kissed it.

One time, during a particularly sexy scene in *The Outsiders*, as Ponyboy and Cherry are about to kiss, she took my finger into her mouth and she sucked on it, soft at first but then more forcefully. And I did not make her stop but looked over at her while she did it, and when she looked at me I knew I loved her. She dropped my finger and then that never happened again.

This is where I spent my afternoons for a whole summer, before Marisa went back to her mother's apartment in New York, which she showed me in pictures before leaving, as if preparing us both for her departure. Her parents were divorced, it turned out, and Winnie Pooh lived here and her mother lived there and in the fall she went back to her mother in New York, which is where she went to school. We got in the habit of writing each other and in those letters I told her things I had never said to her or to anybody else in person; I talked to her about the homeless man and his feet digging holes in the dirt, and how I understood this; I told her that sometimes when we were together I'd pretended that she was my sister, Julia; I told her other things too, and though I missed Marisa's face, I am a specialist at missing. I got serious about school myself after she left, because by that time Rocio had gotten married to Julian who was gentle and sweet and whom I knew completely loved her. And though he was very kind to me, and though they both made me feel well loved I could not be all the time with them. And then my aunt Sofia got married too and she had a son and I couldn't be all the time with them any more either, though her husband was okay as well. Much rougher than Julian, but he was clear and direct and good; and though he was very black and white about things, and could be judgmental, at least I knew that he was good.

And so, since the ones I loved most were now married and Julia had left me for good and Marisa was now gone too, when I wasn't in school I began to really wander those streets. One day a dog appeared. He sat as if waiting outside the gate to our house and when I stepped out and then passed by it, it began to follow me. I turned around and told it to shoo at one point, and it was skittish, backed away as if hurt with its tail between its legs, so that I felt sorry for it though I turned and began walking again. But that dog kept on following me until I got on the bus which would take me to school. When I came off of the returning bus seven hours later, that dog was waiting there for me still. And then he began to follow me every day, as if it were his job, and since he was thin and drawn I began to feed him; and his tail would wag happily as he ate. After a couple of weeks I bathed him, and his cream colored fur grew soft and I saw that his ears moved alert with every sound. I began to notice that his back would shiver when I touched him, like he loved me. He would wait outside of whichever collective taxi or subway stop or bus stand I left from, so that I began to always come back in the same way I'd go because I knew he would still be waiting. And then when we got home I would feed him a bit and then again the next morning when I stepped out of the gate to leave there he would be.

I knew that dog loved me and I began to talk to him. *Hey old guy*, I would say, and his tail would wag at the sound of my voice; I wouldn't even have to touch him to get that joy filled reaction from him. I began to love that old dog back, and I would pet and pet him outside that gate as he ate.

But then one day I forgot he was behind me. How could I have forgotten that he would be behind me, that he would be following? Was I late so that I felt I had to run to catch the bus? I never ran to catch the bus, knew another one was always quickly coming, or else that I could go on a subway or a collective taxi, a pesero, so I never ran. So why on this day did I feel the need? I must have been late. And I somehow forgot he would be following me and I heard the screech of brakes and then a thud, low and flat, and my dog did not even make a sound when he was hit. The driver of the car hollered at him, *Stupid dog! He leapt right into my car!* he yelled defensively. And I ran to him and was almost hit myself. I leaned over him and his eyes met mine and in that one moment I saw that it was him. It was my old man inside that dog. *Hey, old guy*, I said, and I patted his head and his body shivered a little at my touch. And then I was crying. I was sobbing, my whole body convulsing and it took two men to carry me to the sidewalk and another one to clear that old dog away while I wept.

Maybe I could have directly asked someone about her. Maybe I could have more forcefully asked, Why was she given away? What does it mean to give your daughter away, to give your niece away, to give your sister, your granddaughter away? Because, in one way or another, all of them had done it; they had all been a part of it somehow. Maybe I should have been the one to ask, to demand an answer, to make them say it. Maybe I should have been the one to ask the question, that terrible query, that thing which we all thought about constantly, that colored our lives, that for me was a sight, and a smell and a flavor—a confused sensibility, because it was a color too—and which affected everything but which none of us openly talked about; but a coward, instead of asking I walked—I wandered the streets of my city silent. And it was many years before I could think those words directly and many more before I got the nerve to say what I wanted to say.

On the streets no one knew anything. I could walk and wander and no one knew I was a girl who believed in spirits. That I was a girl who was ruled by a long gone sister, a girl for whom vanishing seemed real and ever present, a girl whose sister had ended up that way—suddenly gone. A girl who lived in sad echoes and passion filled shadows.

And I realized as I walked that all these people wandering these Mexico City streets have secrets too. They have sisters who have been given away. They have mothers from whom they must hide. They have fathers whom they have rarely seen and aunts who take them in and old men who shield and guard them though they themselves have long been dead. All of these people on these Mexico City streets feel the warm breeze as it descends here on my arms and wraps my body in its essence, they hide under awnings during the sudden summer downpours and then in damp clothes and dripping hair they fall in love on buses and subways and collective cars.

All of these people have blistered feet and have walked on water which is what it is to walk on the drained lake that is the center of the earth which is Mexico City; and they have sung sad songs, which they now do not remember.

All of these people live in homes with uncles and grand-mothers and aunts. All of them have those who love them and those who do not. All of them know which is which, but some of these people run only to arms full of love while others go equally to the arms that are indifferent or worse still to those which hate them, only to be beaten down by this dark lack again and again. And then in their sad and stubborn and self-imposed blindness, a forced blindness, they go back just once more, over and over again....

And this was my sister, Rocio tells me, this was Julia. She did not know to stay away from her mother. Our mother. My mother. She did not know to stay away from my mother. She was always rushing toward her. Begging Claudia for love. Desperate for that demented mother love. So that Rocio was partially relieved when Julia left, was taken away, given away. Rocio was relieved, as were, I imagine, most of them.

I am tired and though I hear their voices I want to go to sleep. For now I do not wander at all as I lie in my room in my grand-father's childhood home in Sombrarete from which I can hear the beautiful mestizo children sing and call. There is a school down the road and at certain hours of the day I can hear all the children calling, can hear them singing, voices floating to me, like my sisters' voices, their childhood voices which would call out to each other, and to me too deep inside our mother's belly, as they would play in those big groups together.

I no longer wander, though I daily dream of Mexico City, and I sometimes wish that I was there, anonymous and without thought. Not plagued by sad dark thought. Instead I lie here and stare at walls and wait for Marisa who in a week's time will arrive for a visit.

And in the meantime I will think about my sister, about shadows and sadness and weight. About a girl who doesn't know what is good for her, who rushes into the arms of danger, suicidal almost, a sad red dot who goes into those brutal arms not because she wants to punish them, to hurt them, but because she deeply longs for them, even if they hurt.

Marta

SHE CAME BACK for a few months when she was eleven, and though I remember that at first it was weird between us that summer, pretty soon we began hanging out a lot, because we were only a year apart and anyway we were just kids. We'd spend our days in the street in front of the big house we lived in with my grandma, playing with the other kids who lived on the block. The boys were always kicking a ball around and we girls bossed each other like we were each other's mothers, or teased so hard that someone cried, or played jacks and jumped rope, or just strutted. Sometimes we all played together, boys and girls, kick-ball, or hide and seek or some other game we'd come up with. The older kids were good at controlling the little ones with the insane random rules they invented, and that the little ones followed as if their lives depended on it, yelling at each other loudly if one of them dared stray from those rules. And although we weren't little at all anymore we were either terrified of the older ones too or else we wanted them to love us so badly that we did whatever they said. That's also the year Julia and me went on that beach trip with our dad and his friend Pablo. We were always hanging out, actually, even if we didn't really like each other much, even though she was such a chicken she drove me crazy most of the time. We got into some trouble together too and though she was slow to follow and often scared, looking back on that year it was kind of okay, having a sister around who was about my age. When she was feeling really cowardly I just left her behind anyway. I'd go off with Bubbles and Laura and she'd look after us with her pathetic droopy eyes as we took off, still afraid but kind of wanting to come along too and sometimes she'd look so sad at being left that I'd go back for her, push her to join us; though other times I'd just feel she was too sorry and I'd take off without her. She'd pick up her book or something else equally feeble and we'd just take off and leave her like a sorry baby standing in the garden with four year old Sandra playing at her side.

Then she came back again in the summer when I was twelve and she was thirteen, though not for long that year and somehow we didn't spend so much time together. She was looking more like a teenager and I didn't like that too much, the fact that she already had breasts. She had probably even started her period by then because I did soon after she left and she was a full year older than me. I remember that her hair was really long too. I didn't much like her, and anyway, that summer she spent most of her time with my aunt Sofia so I wasn't really around her because my aunt hated me, and still does. For all these reasons, and maybe others too, I didn't see Julia much that year, though sometimes she would come out to play in the street with me and my friends. She was never really a part of the group though, was just there at the edges, looking on while we had fun.

But this was different. I was sixteen and she was seventeen and she was going to be there for a whole year. Plus for some reason she didn't hang out with Sofia any more. Maybe my aunt was married by then? I'm almost sure she was. I think maybe she'd even had her kid, my cousin Antonio. For whatever reason just a month or two after she got here Julia moved in with me and my mom. Of course then we were forced to spend a lot of time together, though I can't say we liked each other any more than before. It's just that we were sisters, so there you had it.

My mom and I lived in this apartment that Pfizer had given my uncle. Supposedly he was a pretty good salesman, though he was an asshole, so this was what he got. I hated my uncle, but he was the one my mom still actually got along with, plus he let us live in that apartment. He'd moved into a better place with his girlfriend, and since he'd never let the company know, he still got this apartment; and he just let us have it.

We'd been living there for almost a year when I noticed Claudia starting to change. It was just before Julia got to Mexico City and it was like Claudia was freaking because Julia was coming. She began to act really weird, and though she never said anything about it, I knew it was because of Julia. She began not eating. Not sleeping. Pacing around a lot. Staring off into space. Not all the time, not super bad like it had been before or like it later got, but there it already was. Claudia was better for a while just after Julia got here and maybe I even believed she was okay, but it had begun. It had already begun and a few months after Julia moved in with us, Claudia completely lost it.

I'm not sure why Julia would make her so crazy. But I know she did. I know it was her fault. I fully blame her.

When she arrived it was clear that Julia was still the same, Miss Innocent, Miss I-Never-Do-Anything-Wrong, Miss Can-I-Help-You. Miss Full-Of-Shit, if you ask me. She had them all fooled. *Oh, can I help you with that?* she'd spring up and ask my aunt when she walked in the door carrying something. *I can go with you*, she'd say to my grandma when she was on her way out the gate, headed to the market, *I'll go get the bags*, and she'd practically run for them. *How was your lunch, Sweetie?* she'd ask ten year old Sandra as she was finishing her food. She'd go get seconds for her if she said she was still hungry. *Your hair looks really good*, she'd say if someone had cut or dyed it. They'd all smile at her and nod. Sandra adored her. And Rocio was already married by then but she'd invite Julia to dinner all the time. Rocio never once asked me to dinner. Never once invited me over for anything at all. *She's sooo sweet*, I'd hear them say. It was infuriating. She was so sickly polite, overly helpful. It was pathetic. She was even that way with strangers, smiling at little kids in line at the store, making faces to make them smile back, picking things up for old women when they dropped something, giving up her seat on the subway so that I felt like shit if I didn't do it too, holding doors open, and then so many pleases and thank yous. It was disgusting. Everywhere we went. And it's not that it was phony, that's not what I'm saying. In fact it would somehow have been better if it was, she would have seemed sly then, smart and wiley, and I've always appreciated that. I like smarts. But this was pathetic; this was weak. Like she really did want to help all the time. Like she really did want everyone's approval that badly, did want everyone, even complete strangers, to like her, to think she was super nice. Why did she need to be liked so much? Why did she care? It was so sorry! Who gave a shit?

My grandma got her a part-time job at the National Palace. She'd never even asked me if I wanted a job, and I actually lived here. And then a month after getting this job Julia moved in with me and my mom. I don't remember how it happened at all; I was a kid really so I didn't question anything. All I remember is that though she would come over and stay once in a while I didn't really see her much, but then suddenly she was there all the time. And pretty soon she had moved in.

But that's what it was like with Julia. She would appear and disappear. At eleven, then at thirteen, then not a word until she was seventeen. Appearing and disappearing. Though I guess that's how it was with lots of people in our lives, including our father. Appearing and disappearing, popping in and popping out. It saved her ass that she didn't really live here, if you ask me. She never had to take anything too seriously, did she? She knew how to run away, didn't she? *I'm so concerned, I'm so concerned*, she would make you feel, *I'll help with that. How are you? You look nice today. Is that too heavy for you? Still hungry?* But in the end it was only herself she was truly worried about, saving her own ass. And she had no idea about what any of it was really like. What it was to actually live here. Suddenly, here she came. And then just as suddenly, there she went. And it made you feel like it didn't matter, like you didn't matter, like nothing, in fact, mattered to her at all. It's not like I really give a shit, don't get me wrong. I don't really care where she's coming from. It's just that the fact that everyone thought she was so sweet and innocent rubs me the wrong way. Really wrong.

So, one night, I don't know how it happened but we were at a party and that idiot Julia spotted this guy and immediately started acting super nervous. It was a party at these fancy apartments our cousins had lived in, where we'd ended up that time we took off with those boys on those bikes, two blocks of these kind of modern apartment buildings, some of them not so nice but others very posh with stores at street level and a nice playground and several shared big halls so you could really have parties there. Who knows who invited us, but there we were at this great dance party. It was fantastic, a big space and there were lights and really great music and all of these very good looking kids, the girls in their short skirts. And everyone was dancing. I think Rocio was even there; maybe she was even the one who had gotten us invited; she had the fanciest friends. I don't even know where she met these people. Modern dance classes or figure painting or some other bullshit activity she wasted her time on. So, suddenly Julia started acting like a complete idiot, looking down at her shoes in her stupid, scared, overly shy way, and refusing to dance. What the hell is wrong with you? I said. And then I noticed she was staring at this one guy out of the corner of her eye. Oh my god, her sorry assed face! Standing stiff and her eyes popping over every few seconds to look at him. I guess I can admit now that he was pretty good looking, Elias, tall with straight black hair and he had nice blue eyes, and he was with a bunch of friends and so I marched up to that guy and pointed Julia out to him and soon he was over by us and soon after that they were dancing. I don't even know why I did things like that for her. She never once introduced me to a guy. Anyway she was still living at my grandmother's at that point and this guy, Elias, showed up there one day when I was there too and I knew she must have invited him. Unless he was stalking her. Regardless, he knew where she lived and it was nowhere near where that party had been. They had obviously planned it. He had two friends with him, different ones than had been at the dance. One of these was Mario and he was really tall and had a kind of smushed in nose like it had been broken or something and long-lashed dark eyes that looked kind of sad. I liked him right away. They hung out for a bit and then a few weeks later she was living with me and my mom and Elias started coming over all the time. So maybe that's why she moved in with us, come to think of it. My mom didn't have any rules at all so you really could have guys around as much as you wanted. Claudia even cooked dinner for him and Mario and Mario's older brother a few times. And then I was going out with Mario and Claudia was having sex with Mario's brother Francisco for a while. They would all come over and though we were teenagers the only one who was having any sex at all was Claudia.

And though we now kind of had boyfriends, Elias and Mario, we would still go out all the time, Julia and me and this is where her innocent act kills me. We would go to all the clubs in the Pink Zone, those were the fanciest and most fun back then, with many different levels, each floor playing different kinds of music from disco to new wave to what we called make-out music, and they all had bars where the music was pretty low, low enough to talk, and there were always tons of people dancing in those clubs, really beautiful boys and girls running all over, the girls all wearing short short skirts and brightly colored tights and high heels, and it was on one of these nights out that Anna basically got raped by all those guys. We went home with six or seven of them. A couple of them were really handsome, but before even walking into the house Julia ran off. She just took off. Left us there just like that.

I don't talk about this much but another night it was me. We all went out together and this place was smaller but with two levels too and we were at the bar not on the dance floor, and Julia just took off at a certain point then too. I don't remember her even saying anything. Suddenly she was just gone. I remember we'd been sitting together and I had been telling them that I was going to have sex with Mario, but that I had made him think I was a virgin because he had made it very clear he expected me to be one. He had looked into my eyes and told me how he wanted to be my first, asked me to please let him, it would mean so much to him; he was almost shaking, even got teary eyed as he asked. He absolutely believed that at sixteen I was still a virgin. Sweet, the schmuck. And so I went to Bubbles with my dilemma because she always knew what was what and she told me what to do when we did finally have sex. We were in her room, lying on her bed and she told me to hold my legs really tight and then loosen them very quickly as he entered me. She made the motion with her legs as if to show me how. Closed tight, open fast and sudden.

And then you shriek. And quietly cry, she said.

But that's not what it was really like my first time, I told her. I turned on my side so that I was facing her. Her sister Laura was on the floor near us, sitting Indian style and taking it all in.

Doesn't matter, she said. She was chewing gum and she smacked it before continuing, That time you weren't lying. When you lie, you need to make it good. Tell him it hurts as he's fucking you, cry out a coupla times, he'll like that. And then afterwards let him kiss and console you. Guys like hurting you and then making you feel better afterwards.

Freaks, I said.

Yeah, she agreed. They eat that shit up, she smacked that gum again. It's 'cuz they're schizo. Good bad, good bad, it really means something to them.

Freaks, I repeated, and she just nodded.

Then she yelled at Laura to get her ass up off the floor and go get us something to drink. Didn't she see that we were thirsty here? Laura ran down to make us white wine spritzers. Don't forget the lime like last time, Dumb-ass! Bubbles yelled after her.

Bubbles was so small, thin and really really pretty, you never could believe what came out of her mouth. The shit that came out of her mouth! Her dad had gotten super strict with her and Laura after Gigi got pregnant, so now Bubbles could never go out at night, though she managed to do everything she wanted during the day. And though I did really wish she could go to the clubs with us, I didn't say it too much because I knew it would make her feel so bad.

Anyway, I really loved Mario, just loved that boy and his smushed in boxer's nose and when I told that story that night at the bar Julia acted all surprised that I was so in love with him. She looked over at me with her big scared ass look and said, I didn't know you liked him that much. She paused before continuing, You could never tell to look at you, she said.

I don't wear everything on my sleeve, like some people, I answered and then I stared her down. It was real easy to stare Julia down. She looked nervously away and so I went on, Anyway, I added, you don't know shit.

Just because she had gotten straight As in high school or something ridiculous like that she always acted like she knew everything. It really pissed me off. Bubbles would call her Professor behind her back, as in, *What would the Professor think about this?* as we were taking money from out of her dad's pockets, and Laura would laugh because for a minute she wasn't the most despised. But Bubbles would turn on her, Shut up, Laura, she would say disdainfully. And Laura would immediately shut up.

In any case, after I finished telling them about Mario, my dilemma and Bubbles' suggestion, she left. She split. She didn't even tell us she was going; she was just suddenly gone. Though for a while we thought she'd just gone to the bathroom or something. And Anna and I stayed at that bar and then Anna went home with some guy she'd seen around once or twice and I stayed a while longer and it was pretty boring all alone so I took a taxi home. At that time of night you have to take taxis, especially if you're alone. And it was then that he raped me. He told me he had a gun. Under his seat. He told me to suck him off and though I didn't feel it I forced myself to cry. I started to cry and that taxi driver jumped in the back and pulled down his pants and then tore off my panties and raped me.

I love you, I said as he was finishing. I don't know where it came from in me but I could see it, could see in that fucking beast's eyes that that was what he wanted. He really liked me; I could see it. He had said something to me about my eyes, about how pretty they were, and I could hear it in his voice, and so I forced myself to say it, though that did make me cry, saying that to him. I was really crying then but I forced myself to repeat it. I want to see you again, I said through my tears. I was so disgusted I almost threw up but I said it. My stomach turned but I tried to sound sexy. I want to see you again. But I have to get home now or my mom will be angry, I said. And that psycho got some concerned look on his face like he didn't want me to get in trouble with my mom and then he got back in the front seat and he drove me four blocks down from where we lived. Of course I'd given him a false address. I then gave him a fake number too before I got out of the car. Call me tomorrow, I said. And then he sat there and watched me as I walked into some random building, like he was my boyfriend or something! Looking after me! That fucker watched me walk in.

I began weeping then. My chest heaving. And when, after a long long time, I was sure he was gone I ran home. I ran and ran through those four long blocks. And when I got home, Julia was there asleep. There she was. Asleep.

I stayed in bed for a long time after that, many many weeks. I didn't eat and so I got pretty skinny too, but I never told anyone what happened. I never told anyone what happened. And then it was like it hadn't happened at all.

And it was around this time that Claudia began really losing it. This is also when my ulcers started so I had no patience. My insides were feeling pretty sick then and the last thing I needed was Claudia. By the time I started going out again a couple of months later she'd really lost it. We'd come home from some club, really late, and she'd be sitting in the living room just staring at the door. Like an idiot. Even after we had walked in she'd keep staring, so that it was clear it wasn't because of us she was watching that door, wasn't us she was waiting on. What are you doing?! I would yell.

I'd go right down into her face and repeat it, What are you doing?!

And she'd just keep staring.

Leave her alone, Julia would say, and I'd turn on her too.

What the hell do you know? You don't even really live here so shut up! I would run into the room I shared with Claudia and I would slam the door. And lock it.

And then that pathetic fly Julia would knock real quiet, as if she didn't want to offend me, imagine that; and she'd keep knocking on the door like that, real quiet, so that I would finally have to get my ass up and unlock it. But I wouldn't look at them. I'd just jump back into bed really fast and turn my back. And that feeble-assed Julia would lead Claudia into bed, tuck her in.

But Claudia wouldn't sleep. I'd hear her get up, two, three, four times a night and each time Julia would lead her back in, get her into bed, tuck her in. Saint Julia. That stupid hypocritical saint. And then Julia would leave the room and I would look over at Claudia and she would just be lying there staring at the ceiling. Or worse, she'd be staring over at me.

Go to sleep! I would yell. You're driving me crazy with your pathetic shit!

And then in, out. In and out of the room Claudia would go and that dumb-ass Julia would lead her back each time, tuck her in again.

One night I couldn't take it anymore. Claudia's sick staring. Her tossing and turning. Her in and outs. She never slept! I just grabbed her by the head and smacked her. I slapped and slapped her, What the hell is wrong with you? What is wrong?! Go to fucking sleep! And I smacked her again. And she did not even flinch. Her staring eyes barely blinked.

But Julia, Saint Julia came running in. Leave her alone! Stop it! she yelled.

What the fuck do you know?! I yelled back. And then I packed a bag and the next morning I left for my grandmother's house.

And then it was a long time, nearly two weeks before Julia came to talk to my grandmother. She came into the house, I heard her though I did not leave my room to say hello, and she did not even ask after me.

And then Grandma Ceci went to get Claudia and once again there she was with me, in the same house. Me and Claudia under one roof, no matter what I did. No matter where I went.

And Julia just stayed in that apartment for a long long time. Free to do what she wanted. Julia always doing her own thing. Julia always acting so innocent. So good. So concerned. Yet never really there when you needed her. Only ever there at the edges, the very corner edges.

Fucking Julia. She always found it so easy to leave.

Julia

THE PUPPETS ARE MADE to bend over. Life-sized, most are adolescent girls. And they twist and they turn in a manner which is disturbing; their young and largely naked female bodies angling in ways which look unsettling, painful, though they are meant to be enticing too, if on the fringes of the seductive, its outer edges. Still, there is an uncanniness, a sick dread which arises from the pit of your being while viewing these photographs, a dread produced by the lifelike presence of the dolls in the photos, so close to what real girls are, their pubescent girl size, their long pretty hair, though it be clumped and messy, eyes blank and unseeing, mouths slightly agape. Haggard girl puppets. Fatigued child poupée. Their sultry tangled hair. These dolls are the image of a grotesque childhood, posing for the camera with props, sometimes, as girls can tend to do, a flower or hat, a shawl and a mirror, perhaps. Yet their exhausted eyes are far away from childhood; they stare down or out; and they are unyielding. Glass eyes. The vacant blank eyes of the disturbed, of the demented… or those of death, the look of death; their eyes carry the blankness of the morally defunct.

They twist and they turn, these girls who are puppets. They pivot and bend. They are made of wood and wax with long flaxen hair; and they can be made to do ungodly things. They are not living, have never been alive, we must remind ourselves as we look at them, are not real girls at all, so does it matter that he makes them twist about like that, that he gives them such round, soft looking bellies and large breasts in the form of buttocks and such pronounced genitalia? Does it matter that he dismembers them, sometimes, removes a limb, disfigures and maims them, which we imagine might only serve to make them more alluring to the sexually demented? They are mangled child and woman both, in their size and proportion, though they are neither, of course. But they are made to look sensual, provocative, as they pose in their lace, comely in their panties and mantillas, their artificial flowers, their wigs of real hair, mussed, though adorned in fancy ribbons. They are mechanical girls, a sick sex robotic, completely nude, sometimes, except for those big bows in their lovely hair. Though they are most arousing when partially dressed, even if there be something wrong in the clothing, even if the hose are sagging, one shoe off, the mary-janes scuffed and unbuckled, the bobby-sox, though of a chaste white, stained and unevenly folded.

It seems important to repeat, for some reason, that there is often a painful looking bend to the waist, or a missing leg, that the body is most often naked, or nearly so. More disturbingly, perhaps, there are sometimes additional limbs, two pairs of legs, a second set jutting up from the torso where the shoulders should be, so that there are two vaginas instead of one, twice as much fun, for in the end, in a surrealist dream, who needs a head?

These are bodies doing what a body cannot…. What a body should not…. What a body *must not* ever be asked to do.

Hans Bellmer and his puppets stood in protest to Fascist ideals, we are told. They were a negation of Nazi perfection, it is amended in countless publications. The puppets were, at least in part, a standing up, a saying no. But did Bellmer accomplish his task of firm protest? For Bellmer was portraying the disfigurement of the female body, a disfigurement which the Nazis were in actuality enacting. On all bodies. Disfigure them all. So was Bellmer's a protest, or an illustration? Because, too, most accounts will tell us, the work was also an enactment of the love he felt for his forbidden young cousin, fifteen when she reappeared in his life after a long absence. Much younger than he, her adolescent body was one denied him through various taboos, and so in place of the desired body, that of his young cousin, he set out "to construct an artificial girl with anatomical possibilities... capable of recreating the heights of passion, even to inventing new desires."

So was it a protest or an enactment, his art? And could it, perhaps, have been both?

In a beret and sagging hose, that doll with missing limbs stands with the translucent Bellmer beside her; he is double exposed in this shot, and so he is ghost-like. His blurry spectral image stands next to his doll both illustrating and proclaiming (protesting even) the breakdown of the normal, of the acceptable, of the humane, though we know it is his sexual desire as well which has constructed this substitute girl, this puppet who stands so firm and still, if falling fully apart—having been pulled asunder and so now partial and decomposing—next to his ghostly countenance, her creator. In his wry smile we see that he delights in her, though he has also maimed her, his doll. In her he exposes his dark desire, as he brings ours forth too, his most true double exposure: that of his and our own desire merging, blurrily conjoined.

Amongst all of his work, it is in this photo, especially, that we are reminded that there is often a disfiguring ghost-father in the lives of disturbed, dismembered girls, demented girls, sick and dirty girls.... There is often a father who bends and twists and contorts, who crushes even, with his strong will, a broken daughter on the other side of that powerful paternal determination. She a filial catastrophe in his reverberating wake.

In another photo—this one set outdoors so that perhaps we can read it as a dark bucolic, a crazed unhinged bucolic—a girl with limbs on both sides of her torso, no head at all, hangs from a tree, the noose around one set of her four legs; to the left and in the background of this photograph stands a dark male figure in a long black coat, mostly hidden from sight by another large tree. His face, certainly, is fully obscured. Is this Bellmer himself, we ask ourselves, an obstructed self-portrait, that long black coat representing the artist? And is this a murder or a suicide? And can it, sometimes, be both? Is it, often, both?

Yet, he was a good man, we are told. Bellmer was an anti-fascist, it is often adamantly argued. And after successfully fleeing Germany himself, he aided the French Resistance by making fake passports for those left behind; he had made it out and to Paris, but others had not and they needed help; and so he worked for the Resistance…. It helps to know too, deepens our admiration and sympathy with Bellmer to find out that he was no show-man, that he was a solitary artist, and would remain so all his life, even after being picked up by the surrealists, even after Breton championed his art, still so after Minotaur published his photographs.

Yet his dolls look out at us with such a blank, unseeing eye. A glass eye. The eyes of the morally vacant.

Bellmer's girlfriend, Unica Zern, was a poet and painter herself. And the first poem in her book *Anagram* is entitled WE

LOVE DEATH. Unica became Bellmer's model, though it must be remembered she was his painting partner too, and was thus his firm equal; and she suffered from deep depression. She shared a psychologist with Antonin Artaud; so that in some way she and Artaud were indirectly involved in that internal dialogue, were guided in it by the same hand, that delineated drawing out of the self. And then she killed herself. In 1970 she leapt from the window of the apartment she'd long shared with Bellmer. Five years later, missing her still, he would die too. But, we must recall as well that in his body of work there are countless images of disfigured girls, of girls hanging from doorways and trees. His body of work is largely made up of their bodies dismembered. WE LOVE DEATH, Unica's first poem proclaims, and that foreshadowing makes us consider more deeply, more sadly, the subsequent act.

My grandfather, Claudia's father, was a ghost-father too, a murky spectral fact. He was a man whose daughter was disfigured *and so her thoughts could disfigure*; whose daughter was bent and misshapen *and so her thoughts could bend and misshape*; whose daughter was deformed and impaired *and so she could deform and impair*; and blighted; *and so blight*. She was a girl who would fight him at every turn; for he had left them. A girl who would not sit still, who never dressed right, who never stood in one place, who was never polite. She was a girl who had begged her father's love and had gotten nowhere; it was impious her begging; it went too far, was too much for him. Her hair was a mess, her eyes naughty, her greedy grabby hands. Hers was a body which would come to be pulled apart, over which she had no ownership, a body which was too soon offered to anyone who'd take it, a body which was then completely torn asunder before being re-configured abstract by her own mind, by its illness. Her body was confused, legs where a head should be. My grandfather, her father, was a man whose daughter often looked out on the world with mouth agape, with stone blank eyes. Her father was a man for whom daughter figures could become contorted, whose daughter was warped and distorted. She was a girl who turned into a woman who would beg for more, who would not stop, who would push and push until things were not right, until she was not right, until there was nothing in her which was right. Her hair a tangled mess, her clothes torn, or to be torn off, her body wildly fluctuating in weight and thus shape, flinging itself and being flung. Her eyes blankly staring, her mouth, after those head shocks, dumb and drooling.

I do not really know my father. He is mostly a blank, a dark absence, and one feeds the other, I know: the absence the dark, the dark the absence.

I am afraid of ghosts, though I have always lived with this one.

I barely know my father. There is no clear figure there. And I know I'm not firm in his mind either; I am blurry for him as well, a barely there form, though his blanking out is willful—for he has always known about me—and this is something I have had to wrestle with, his blanking out, his turning away. It is partially because of this that I have had to write myself. A re-figuring of the self to save my soul.

I do know him a little though, for when I was very young he would come to play cards at my grandmother Cecilia's; I didn't then know who he was, just another family friend, so I barely remember those visits. But he came again several times during my final stay in Mexico City, and by then things had changed. By then I had been living in the states with my uncle David for ten years, and my uncle, a professor who believed in the importance of truth, had a few years prior told me about him. So, though I was not yet fully convinced, at seventeen I sat in a corner of the room, petting the big cat, Paco, who lay in my lap while I observed the man I was beginning to believe was my father. It was while I watched him greeting my grandmother, her hand in his, the way they then sat and chatted and sipped at drinks, that I recalled that when I was very young he had occasionally sent gifts for me. My sisters never once received a gift from him, and this fact now worked to further convince me. I looked at him more intently. He was taller than average, thin, and wore a dark suit, no tie. His eyes were deep and he had a straight nose. Thin lips. He came with two friends and he joked with my grandmother who seemed to like him quite well; she asked after his mother and sisters and aunts for he was a family friend. He then moved to the table where a group was already playing cards. He was funny and smiled a lot and told more jokes and laughed; at one point he picked up the guitar and sang. He may well have been nervous; all that activity, all that moving around; I was certainly nervous watching him, though I was rapt. His friends, with a false and stiff cheeriness, anxiously followed his lead, laughing a bit too much, singing loudly. One of them, the shorter of the two, wore his curly hair greased back, a throwback to their youth.

He came two other times that year. And each time I watched my father unblinkingly, though not at all blankly. For my eyes have not ever been cold, have not ever been blank. Though I do sometimes wish they better hid my feelings.

I went to my aunt Sofia the night of his third visit. She knew his younger sister, she said. He came from a strict and serious home, she said, a decent family, and for many years he had been M's best friend. She didn't tell me much else, but I have added to the little she told me that night, put in details, whole stories sometimes; something we all maybe do with our fathers, insert and amend, correct and distend. So maybe I can now add that he was thrilled when he met M. He was properly shocked, at first, but then thrilled by M's bad-boy behavior, his lack of a conscience, of a moral center, of a place from which to start, that same place which tells us when to stop. At eighteen and nineteen M was always already in the middle, had always already begun when the others had not, and was quite in the midst, running and well on his way toward the edges.... And maybe my father was the one boy in his strict family who liked the thrill of that, who liked things a little edgy and dirty and slightly not right. Maybe he liked the thought of all the sex M bragged about having, all the sex he imagined himself having alongside M, his new best friend. A boy crush. Perhaps my father was excited by the thought of fucking M's girlfriends, the thought of how powerful the two of them could be together, prowling those Mexican streets, joking with the girls as they slipped an arm around a shoulder, prodding each other to go further and further, teasing the girls, playing with their hair, nuzzling in their necks, while the other one prodded and pushed. Sometimes it all happened rather quickly; they'd slow their car to a crawl and yell out at a girl from the window, M's arm partially hanging out, white shirt rolled up high at the sleeves, revealing his arms, hair greased perfectly back, a slight pompadour, his dancing blue eyes, his mouth big and laughing, while my father looked on and bit at his lips in an itchy anticipation, riding there in that car next to M. They'd pass, then turn around and come back, a cruise, the chase, that girl with the thick short hair, the huge kohl-lined black eyes, catch up with her again as she crossed the street in her tight skirt. The boys would hurriedly park, leap out of that car, and run up next to her, M putting his arm around her waist as they walked, even though she'd picked up her pace, Hey Blanca? Blanquita... do you want to go for a ride? The girl would inevitably push his arm away, That's not my name, she might brusquely answer, fully flustered. No? What are you doing later tonight? Come here... Come... and M might pull at her a bit and kiss her cheek once or twice while my father looked ardently on. After a minute or two of this teasing they hopped back in the car and were off, the girl looking about herself like a confused little bird, What had just happened?

They never chased too much, never too much, for if they started and then stopped for a bit, M told my father, the girls would come chasing back; it should never be too much effort, M told him. You are the boss. Ignore them for a week, M said, and they will come begging back. They drove past Blanca several more times, on three consecutive days, slowing down in front of her at the coffee shop where she sat with friends, wagging a finger at her, teasing her with their big smiles, blowing mock kisses, so that she blushed and turned her head away, there in front of her friends. It was soon after this that she finally opened up a bit as she talked, her hips swinging. Within a month M had fucked that short haired girl, her black kohl eyes shutting as he entered, in the servant's quarters of his mother's house.

They were handsome each, their electric lean bodies, even more so together, the power of two, and they made those girls dream of their arms embracing, strong hot shoulders, mouths kissing and whispers, their heavy with desire breath; it was never too difficult. They could see it in the girls' eyes. Some openly stared. They came fully unhinged. Those girls were distorted. They were yearning, contorted. And maybe, from M, my father soon learned that you don't have to mean it when you say it, don't have to mean it when you do it. When you sneak into her room, her into your room. Maybe, he found out, you don't ever have to mean a thing. And then M and my father walked around beaming; they smiled all the time. They had never been the dark and brooding type to begin with, were certainly not now the melancholic, sullen type. They got such attention, those two, there was nothing they could do but take it all in and absorb it. They were happy as they rushed down the street laughing. They were overjoyed as they leaned, preening, on the hood of M's car. They loved life as they drank with their arms around each other in those big groups at the bars. They liked to sing and dance too, often touching at a breast or a thigh right there, on the dance floor, before taking them home, those warm bodies, sneaking inside.

But maybe after a while, in the midst of all those girls, all those easy to get girls, my father thought he needed something different; they were older, in their early twenties now, and he needed something new. He lay there and he lay there, a cigarette in hand. And then a thought took hold of my father as he lay there on his parents' couch; and he grew excited. He thrilled as he daydreamed it, this something different, though it was clearly more complex. The thought that took hold of my father as he lay there, lighting another cigarette, the thought that took full hold of his insides, was that of fucking his friend's wife, of fucking M's wife. He got up slowly and as he put on his jacket to step out he thought that yes, he might like to have sex with M's wife; he adjusted his collar as he thought he might like that more than anything he'd ever done, more than anything he'd even allowed himself to think. And as he walked down the sun filled street, a grin played on his lips while he thought about Claudia. She was smart, and wild, though she was serious. She was sexy too, her nice hips and those tight sweaters, her full lips and staring black eyes. The beautiful young wife of his best friend. His brow furrowed a bit with the possibilities. She came from a good family, though she was perverted. He knew her sister and her mother and he'd heard she'd been perverted. By M, she herself would later tell him.

My father knew she needed what he had to offer, because, being a friend of M's he'd seen his flaws, and he could play with them; he clearly understood that he would be the first to speak to her in kind tones, in a slow and serious pitch. He was aware that she was miserable with M; everyone knew that. She was lonely, and she was yearning, too. You could see it.

So he began to speak gently to her. In her ear he sang soft songs in a warm and aching voice and recited long poems which he had memorized in school. Hadn't he wanted to be a writer once? Lorca and Neruda; he'd read Octavio Paz. Here was a real and practical use for all of that school poetry.

He did all these things, did all the things he knew how to do, whether he meant them or not.

He took her to a museum, once. Hadn't his family often gone to such places? and he could pretend to know about art; there were two or three things he could say about art, Look at the color there, the composition. See the way the yellow at the bottom appears there in that line at the top? It draws your eye up, so you see the thing as a whole. He took her hand then, and kissed each of its fingers. A whole.

Maybe he lent a sympathetic ear when Claudia complained about M. He nodded along and stroked at her arm to encourage the complaining, an easy way to relieve the aggression he felt toward his friend, an easy way to avenge. Who did M think he was, always playing leader, always pushing so hard, challenging my father's boundaries, his limits, always bossing him around? Maybe my father had grown to resent it. Maybe my father hated his friend just a little. M's wife offered a clear if indirect way to release some of the anger he felt toward his prodding friend, his pushy, bossy, cocky friend. Avenge. And, at first, all he had to do was nod and gently listen.

Soon, though, my father began to like knocking on her door for other things too, when he thought no one was looking, sneaking in while he knew M would not be there, her fingers shushing, stifling giggles as he entered, then once inside openly laughing, chasing each other down the long hall. And then, many furtive hours later, sneaking his way out.

Maybe he was on his way to her apartment that day, maybe it was because of these visits that my father smelled what was wrong. Maybe it was because of this that he smelled the gas leaking. Maybe it was because of one of these clandestine visits that he knocked down the door, because she would not open, he'd knocked and he'd knocked. He'd banged on that door. He'd yelled. He'd sensed something was wrong right away, but then he had smelled it, the gas leaking. Perhaps I was already in her belly;

maybe I was in there already and so somehow I can recall it. My father had already been coming around for a while then, for many many months, and I must have already been inside her.

When he flew in to the kitchen she was standing near the stove, staring blankly, eyes flat and unseeing: Should she leave it on? Should she go lie down in the room where Rocio was asleep, lie down next to her sleeping little girl, or should she stand right where she was, right in front of the stove, so she'd be the first to fall?

Maybe it was when he yelled at her, asked her was she crazy, pulled her away from that stove with tears streaming down his face, furious and crying he pulled at her arm, maybe it was then, on that night, that she first turned and looked at him with the fullness of the dark depth that was inside her, her eyes wet. He saw it there, that darkness. And then maybe after they'd both calmed down a little, though not fully, maybe it was then that he first fucked her with a violence. He led her to her bed and violently he did it, for he was scared and angry both. He was confused. And he was rough with her as a result. And then maybe he was only a little bit shocked, only a little bit surprised when he discovered that she liked that; she liked it like that, an angry, violent, dismembering act, a disremembering act, a ghost-father act.

Rocio

ONCE I MADE THE DECISION that I didn't want to be around M I had to constantly make excuses to avoid him. Though in reality he showed up very rarely, the way I recall it I was always on the lookout for him, and would run and hide at my friend Amanda's house when I spotted his car coming. I'd stay there, once even hiding in her closet, until I was sure he had finally gone off. But by the time I started dating Julian, not only was I too old to need to make excuses for my detachment, but now, because of Julian, M's presence didn't make me as wary either. Julian helped me feel safe somehow, at the same time that he clarified and defined my need for distance. It was as if my own conviction, my own caution, had never been enough to justify my guard, but at that point, in the physicality of another person, of a boyfriend, of Julian, I suddenly had a clear reason for not wanting to be with M. Now there was no way anyone would even attempt to convince me to spend time with him, or to go off on one of his crazy road trips.

But why should I have felt such pressure before? Just because he was my father? I should go off on some harebrained adventure with him, just because he was my dad? I should be around him as he yelled out at women from inside his car, some lewd remark, though there we were, his daughters, sitting right beside him. Once I saw him grab a complete stranger in public. She was nearly as tall as he was and had short black hair styled like a man's. Her striking eyes were done up in green eyeliner, and she had a beautiful Roman nose. "Shameless," she hissed as she slapped him, then looked directly at me as she shook her head. I was thirteen and my face burned red with the humiliation.

Julian helped me in many ways, only some of which I can put words to, only some of which I can speak about or even understand. But he did deeply help me; that I know. And there was a great relief in it, his calmness. Since the house in the desert I had somehow figured out different ways to stay away from him, from her, but now Julian made that hiding easier, gave me a safe space in which to do it. Actually, it didn't so much feel like hiding any more, but like a choice, a choice for a different way of life. Julian offered me that, his calm black eyes, his steady hands and soothing presence.

We got married when I was just twenty. A month or two before the marriage my mother pulled me into her room. Her confidences always made me uncomfortable… she simply went too far, spiteful comments directed at my uncles and aunt, anger flying out of her, or else in the middle of some mundane conversation, what I'd had for lunch, she would say something strange, "You're lucky, you're sexy like me," and she'd grab my breast. She would laugh loudly and pull me down on the bed trying to get me to giggle with her, as if we were best friends. Or she'd start kissing and hugging me so tightly that I'd have to beg her to stop.

But on this day she pulled me into her bedroom by my arm and I right away saw her wedding dress lying on the bed. She'd taken it out of my grandmother's closet and wanted to show it to me, she said. It was as if she was offering it to me, though it was all so indirect she never actually spoke the words. Why did she always have such a hard time just saying things? "Isn't it beautiful?" she asked as she took it up in her arms. It was gorgeous, that dress, all hand-worked lace, like they still make in Veracruz. It had been my grandmother's first and was very long, which was the style when she was married, tight through the waist and hips, but with a long long train. Without saying anything further my mother handed it to me and I looked down as I took it. I played that lace between my fingers for a long time, then slowly got undressed while she watched me. I then cautiously pulled that heavy dress on. It took me five minutes to get it fully adjusted, and she simply observed the slow process, not helping me until the very end, when she clasped the long line of buttons down my back. It fit me perfectly, which surprised me as I was both taller and thinner than my mother.

"It looks very good on you," Claudia said as she stared at me, her eyes carrying something heavy inside them, that too weighty gaze of hers. And so I looked away from her and toward the mirror and then I turned once in front of that mirror, a bit shyly, though I knew that it was true. It was a gorgeous dress and it fit me perfectly. My long dark hair fell messily down the front of that dress and I reached up and played with it there on its surface.

A few days later I was at Julian's house and his mother, who made beautiful clothing completely by hand, announced that she wanted to make my dress. I don't know why; I had already decided I would wear my mother's dress, but I said yes. "I would like that very much," I caught myself saying. And some part of me that I didn't at all understand deeply meant it, even after I realized the complications I'd just caused. Julian's mother put her arms around me and held me for a long time, and the gentle warmth of that embrace nearly brought me to tears; I sank into her breast and tightly closed my eyes to keep from crying.

I decided I had to immediately tell Claudia, and went home, terrified at how she might react. Her anger could be vicious. I walked into her room where she lay reading a magazine, and nervously fingered a perfume bottle while I haltingly told her what Julian's mother had offered. Strangely, she had no reaction at all. Nonetheless, I started making excuses, "I think it's good to let her," I stopped my hands restlessly working the surface of the perfume bottle and walked over to her. I bent down and awkwardly reached for Claudia's hair in consolation, fingered it as I spoke, "It'll make things easier with her after we're married…" but she cut me off.

"Of course. It makes perfect sense. Your own dress," she said tersely, without even turning to look at me.

"Okay," I answered, surprised that there'd been no real confrontation. "Then I'll ask her to go ahead and start." I dropped her hair and walked out of the room quickly, not wanting to meet my mother's eyes should she decide to look up from her magazine.

I had Sara the year after Julian and I were married. And it was a blessing. It was incredible, like an unexpected gift. The first two months of my pregnancy were difficult, they were, but then I felt so good during the rest of it, without the torture so many women describe, a relaxed ease setting into me which was an utter surprise. And then, when Sara was born she was so tranquil, in a way that everyone had always believed I was. I couldn't understand it; she never cried, and this worried me a bit. I felt there might be something wrong with that quiet little baby, my daughter. "She's just calm, like you," I remember my grandmother and aunt saying as they held that tiny thing, passing her back and forth between them, her sweet black eyes and little puckered mouth moving as if still suckling. I took her delicate hand in mine and stared at the fingernails, so small and perfect.

My few friends commented on her calmness too, how similar to me she was, "She's going to be kind, like you," Amanda said as she fed her from the little jar.

But I had never felt calm, I wanted to tell them all. I just held myself that way, close and still, so I would not be pulled into things, would not have to be in the midst of the mess, of the turmoil, of my parents' craziness. I think I had it even as a baby, a sense that I had to hold myself that way, a sense that if I didn't stay quiet and still something terrible would happen.

Do babies know things? I believe they do. I believe it was an enforced stillness I had.

Yet, I think they were right about Sara. She actually was calm. She was a happy baby too. Even I could see that. I would take her little hand and she would follow me around, not running off like other babies do. She was a peaceful baby. We would play hide and seek for hours sometimes and she always patiently waited for me to find her, never running out from her spot, exasperated that I hadn't gotten to her yet, never excitedly screaming Here I am! because I'd taken too long, not at all worried that I might never come. She would sit playing with her toys for long periods of time too, moving her dollies around, talking to them, setting up blocks and knocking them down, seeing how things fit together, putting things into a basket and pulling them out again and again while I cooked or straightened the apartment.

But I could be jealous of her too. When Julian would take her in his arms and hold her, tickle and laugh and laugh along with her, and then hold her tightly in his arms some more while having silly conversations with her, "How was your day, little Miss? Did you help your mother? Did you carry the heaviest bags for her and chop the vegetables and make the rice so we could have a nice dinner?" He'd pretend to gobble her stomach then, "A nice dinner," he'd repeat, and she'd shriek wildly while he went to gobble some more.

She looked like him, his serious Spanish black eyes and light skin, the soft dark hair which I cut just above her shoulders with bangs over those black eyes. He could play with her for hours, with her dollies even, and I'd go and insert myself in their play, sometimes, feeling envious of their easy love. I wanted it, some of it from each of them, what they were giving each other... "Me!" I would say to him, plopping into his lap like a baby myself, and he would laugh at me as if I were indeed a child, and Sara would gently move her skinny little body over and make a space for her mother.

I was twenty-one or two then, and know I acted like a child with him sometimes. I am ashamed to say it. I often acted hurt, no, injured, and he would just hold and hold me. Even before Sara was born I acted this way, deeply injured. It would start out simply enough, some small argument about the shopping, or a door that had been left unlocked, or a favor I wanted him to do me, pick something up on the way home from work. I would get so incredibly angry and he'd always gently try to make up with me so that I would end up screaming at his kindnesses,

How could he love me? I was filthy. I was dirty. A coward. We would get into long drawn out fights then and I would go on and on: I was not one to be loved, I would yell. Did he not know who I was?

"Don't you know who I am? Where I come from?" I'd be weeping.

"Stop, Rocio. You have to stop. None of that is real." His arms would reach around me tight to calm, and then he would gently pat my back.

We went to the beach for our honeymoon. A long drive through the Western part of Mexico and to the sea in Oaxaca. He had been there before and wanted me to see those beaches, their wild beauty. There were little fishermen's huts every few kilometers, from which they sold their catch; and larger palapa restaurants at which a family working the place together served ceviche or fried fish, right there on the water, the tables set up in the sand. But mostly that coast was made up of stretches of open beach and the rough sea and gorgeous inlets, very few people around. I had never been there but had of course heard that this was the state my grandfather had moved to, had heard it mentioned during my grandmother's card games many times, Oaxaca, though he had ended up high in the mountains of that state, I knew, where the forests are, not on the beaches where we now lay. I had no desire to look for it, that place where my grandfather had ended up, because it's where he'd gone when he left my grandmother, the reason he left her, perhaps; and by the time I was a child she often wondered what it would have been like if he had not gone to work with that German, if she had not encouraged him to go into the lumber business with Heuber, if he had not started leaving her for longer and longer periods of time, until finally he just didn't come back. She wondered how it would all have ended up, her two oldest children now bitter and angry, feeling eternally cast aside, my uncle Felix jobless and unwilling or unable to pursue his art, my mother lost and wild and possibly mad. But, of course, in some way it was she who had left him, when she found out he had that other woman, that other child. She would put up with a lot, but never ever that, she'd told him. And then she told him she would not have him back. But what if she had never said that, she now wondered, what if, like other women she knew, she had just kept her mouth shut? Though her guilt about how it had all turned out was nocturnal. She only ever spoke it at the end of those card games, late into the night when she thought none of us children were listening. So, on our honeymoon, when Julian asked if I wanted to go look for it, I told him I had no desire to see it, the place to which my grandfather had gone. He was nothing to me, really, or very little. I didn't know him at all, in fact, had only met him a few times. To me he was simply the man who had left my grandmother, had abandoned my mother, my uncles, my aunt. My grandfather, to me that's who he was.

After a week on the beach Julian and I took the long winding drive up the mountains to the city of Oaxaca, to see the beauty everyone talks about for ourselves. And yet, though it was close to where my grandfather had lived, I did not let him take me the extra hundred or so kilometers to his town.

Oaxaca was a beautiful city, the gorgeous copper-filled stone, the copper in the earth there giving it a dramatic green hue. All the colonial buildings and the cathedral in the main square are built of this stone and so the entire central plaza uniformly professes itself in that dramatic green color; the black cobble-stone streets are all fully intact, as are the ancient convents, and that delicious food in its thick rich sauces, a dense black mole you don't get anywhere else. Oaxaca was a beautiful city.

And I had a dream while we were in that mountain city of Oaxaca, three nights in a row, nearly identical each time, and in that dream I was not there in that city at all but back at the beach we had just left, the soft sand and little palapas. In that dream it is a misty night, dark though there is a big moon, heavy in the distance, and a shadowy figure slowly opens the door letting the breeze whip into the palapa where I lie asleep. He comes and leans into me on that bed, touches my hair and I wake, "Come," his voice whispers softly in my ear, "we can climb that mountain, there." He is a blur in that darkness, a shadow, but I obey, compelled, somehow, following him outside. I follow him though I am confused and the mountain seems made of mud and it is difficult to climb, but I drag, my feet so heavy, through it; I struggle, my heavy feet, my way up the steep and muddy cliff behind him, the ocean wild and hungry down below, the waves pounding loudly at my back. In the moonlight and the mist I can make out his outline, can see his tall silver figure leaning forward as he leads me; and I struggle, trailing, out of breath now, stumbling in places, catching myself before a fall. We reach a flat, and I am relieved, but soon feel that the mud is thinner here and it gathers in pools and my feet are sinking down into it, the hem of my long white dress falling into it too. It is my mother's gorgeous dress I am wearing, the wedding dress I tried on in front of her, and I pull its long train up into my arms, trying to save it from that mud, but it is heavy and it falls from my arms and drags and soils around me... I slip now, trying to save it, and I start to cry:

it is my grandmother's dress, a thick antique lace which gathers at the neck, and now it is filthy, the wet mud splattering all over it… "Are you okay?" the man calls back; he has not seen my soiled dress and though now I sense I know him I've still not seen his face, obscured in that lack of light.

"Please slow down… it's hard for me to keep up," I cry, short of breath, my lungs heaving, trying to contain all I am feeling. "It is all getting ruined," I gasp, and suddenly I am very tired; my legs are tired, the mud is so thick, but he insists, keeps moving forward, through that thickness… "I can't!" I call out to him, and stumble again, my legs collapsing beneath me. Is this the end, in this mud, on this strange cliff, the sea at my back? I push once more, try to rise but I cannot move, "I can't!" I call out again, begging, weeping now. "It's too heavy!" I yell, and I drop the dress from my arms. He stops and turns then, and I can see his face in the moonlight; it is Julian, and his eyes seem confused at my struggle, as if he cannot understand it, the great effort it takes for me to keep up…

"Yes you can," he says as he approaches, "You can," and though now he is before me his voice sounds very distant. "You can," and the mud has taken over my insides now because I am hearing him through it, his voice muffled, and when I reply I have to speak through it too, dense and cold and damp…

"No," I call out in my mud smothered voice. "I can't." And he takes three further steps toward me, his arms reaching. He touches me, "Take it off," he says. He looks into my eyes, "Take it off," he repeats firmly, but instead I take the hems up in my arms again, to carry it, the mud now soiling my face. "Take it off," he insists as he leans into me… and though now I am fully weeping he removes it, pulls the dress off me as he kisses my neck and shoulders, whispers in my ear; and then slowly he is on me and as he enters me I feel myself release; and it is the first time I am fully in my body while making love, the first time I can feel myself and him there too and in that dream I know what love can be. "You have to leave it here," he breathes when we have finished, looking over at the dress where it lies in a heap; I am still nodding yes when I awake…

I was newly pregnant, and I wept in that high city of Oaxaca. "How can I be a mother?" I asked Julian the next morning, "with the mother I had? How can I figure it out? I can't do it." I looked into his eyes, "I'm terrified," I said. "What if I turn into her. What if I've been fine till now, but with a baby in my belly, the commitment already made, I turn into my mother?

"What if I can't control it?" I stared into his eyes, "I can't back out now, there is nothing I can do about it now, and what if I am already her?"

"You're not, Rocio," he replied. "You must see that. You're nothing like her," and his eyes looked so worried for me, the concern long and real and deep in those black eyes; and so I cried.

And in that city of Oaxaca he put his arms around me and he rocked and reassured me, "You're not her," he said over and over again. Over and over, "You're not her."

"How can you love me?" I wept then, my face contorted; I could feel it crumbling into a struggling liquid mass, but could not stop it, "How?" and I cried and cried and Julian shushed and rocked and shushed me. And I melted into that.

He caressed my hair and then he made me drink from a glass of cool water. He told me to breathe slowly, deeply, and he asked me to shut my eyes and then he kissed me on both of my eyelids and then on my forehead too, "Shhhh, Princess," he said. He held me and made me sip more water and then I fell asleep.

And somehow, after that trip, those ten days in that state of Oaxaca, me weeping and dreaming about my mud splattered dress, his shushing and kissing and reassuring me, over and over again, each day as if it had not happened in almost exactly the same way the day before, it was done. It was done and I didn't worry about being a mother any longer. I no longer worried about being a mother. Of course I continued to worry about other things. I don't want to give the impression that my fear, my nervousness, my crazy anxious hands were all calmed. But I knew I loved the little thing I was carrying, deeply loved it, and I knew that with Julian everything would be alright.

And then when Sara was three I told Julian I wanted to go back to Oaxaca. "Where do you want to go on vacation this year?" he asked, and I answered, Oaxaca.

"I want Sara to see it," I told him. And I did.

So we went, flying in this time so that we landed in the city first, before going to visit the beaches. It again struck me as being unbelievably ancient, and colonial heavy, of course, and very very beautiful. We would eat dinner in the central square, in the Zocalo, which is where all the terraced restaurants are, across from the green Cathedral and all the municipal buildings, and Sara was only one of many small children in the restaurants there, running around and along and between their parents' legs. And then after dinner we would lick at ice creams on benches, Julian and I sitting and watching what seemed like thousands of other children playing with big balloons, tossing them like balls and chasing each other around and pausing to nibble on treats. And Sara, skinny little Sara, her shoulder length black hair with its long bangs, her thick lashed dark eyes, was one of them. Julian walked up to the vendor who held dozens of balloons and bought her one of those long over-sized ones the other children threw into the air and caught and threw into the air again for hours on end. She tossed and tossed her big balloon in imitation of the older kids, up into the air, and then laughed as it descended; and she often missed, only sometimes catching it in her still awkward toddler arms; Julian and I laughed too, watching the comic struggle in those tiny, reaching, mostly failing to catch arms.

And it struck me that night, as we lay all three in the one big bed in our room, that Sara was carefree. That she was one of many, that she was like any other child, joyful in her running and playing. And this made me both very happy and incredibly sad. Sara was normal, just an average normal child. And barring any sad disaster, she would most likely lead a quiet normal life.

The next day we sat in the same central plaza, the little Zocalo, the restaurants, the beggar children, the Cathedral, and a chubby little girl with long black curls came up to Sara and offered her her doll. Sara shyly turned away from the pretty girl, but the girl who was a bit older insisted and very soon Sara warmed up to it. I watched how Sara held the baby, not tenuous and overly hopeful, as I would have been, or harsh and terrorizing like Marta would have done, tossing it into a tree or some such thing. Sara carried it around naturally. Carefully holding it and patting at its head and talking to it a bit before the other little girl demanded it back. "It's my doll!" the little girl yelled jealously, watching Sara love it so well. Sara simply nodded and slowly handed the doll back before running to grab at my leg. I ran my hand through her soft hair as the other little girl stormed off.

The following day we drove down to the beach in a rented car; it was a long drive but Sara sucked and sucked at her pacifier and when she got a bit impatient I sang to her and then we stopped at the side of the road and I went and sat next to her in the back seat. I pointed at things out the window, and soon enough she was satisfied. At the beach, on the sand, she paused from her digging and came over and lay by me with her arms all spread out and I remembered Sandra many years before, on the beach in Acapulco with my grandmother and aunt, telling me stories about witches, warning me against them, telling me not to let them in. I looked at Sara as I remembered my sister and then I heard myself as if I were someone else, my mouth speaking before I knew what I was saying, "I won't let them in, Sara. I won't," and she looked up at me, confused. I smiled an awkward little smile at her and she smiled back and then pushed the bangs off her forehead with her hand and got up to continue her digging.

"Want to dig?" she asked, in her tiny high voice. And I thought about how she did not have the sad dark brilliance of Sandra, and then I thought that I was glad for that. She was not excessively brilliant, or worried, or angry, or sad. She did not seem to be controlled by any of the sad passions, and in that moment this made me very glad.

Yes, I said. And I got down on all fours and I dug in the sand with my daughter. I stuck my hands deep into the hot sand. Let's build a castle, I told her. Let's build a big, big one.

Sandra

THERE WERE TWO TINY BODIES lying right outside the door of my room, by the plum tree, surrounded by the fallen fruit that sat rotting on the ground. Luckily I found them before the yellow-eyed gray cat did. Though he was old, he would have made a wicked game of lazily torturing the two before gobbling them up. I spotted the pair as I approached the doorway, on my way out to the garden for fresh air, and instantly I saw one of them was dead already, its neck twisted back in an eerie position, a long line of blood extending from its beak. It was clear it had crashed into the high window above the door to my room; that window, looking like an extension of the sky, had deceived and killed it. The other small bird lay stunned near its friend, its own phosphorescent green neck intact. I looked around, and wondered where the old gray cat was; had he seen he would be upset at giving up the dainty meal, and angry with me for depriving him.

The hummingbird stirred a bit, and my heart did with it. Carefully, I reached my fingers down toward its struggling body, very gently picked it up, and cradled that ounce of life in the palm of my hand. Within moments it had managed to edge itself to the tip of my finger. It clutched me, then, with the nectar sticky claws on its delicate feet wrapping small but firm around my pinky. I could see it garnering its strength, and feel the slight shivers which gathered into a surge that ran through its body before it managed, at last, to pull itself fully together, and flutter rapidly away. But before finally departing, it first hovered near the plum tree, in front of the window that had irrevocably deceived him and his friend, who lay dead at my feet. He seemed to float there for a weighty second, and then quite suddenly the hummingbird was gone.

They'd flown toward that glass pane together, fooled by their own reflection, in the tremble of joyful spring, their bodies eager, whipping into expanding sky, wanting to merge with that other them in the window, and now one lay dead in the courtyard. Though the other had managed the brutal blow, the calamity that had killed one would probably continue to forever decenter the other. Because the one who had survived must at some level acknowledge, if not suffer, the loss of its companion for the rest of its life. Would it forever look at its own image in windows and think of its friend? Parrots and pigeons and swans, I know mate for life, and on the death of one, never go on to find another partner.

I would have to bury the one who lay dead at the foot of my patio door. Staring at it I remembered reading that the Aztecs would carry desiccated hummingbirds in pouches, as an aid to virility, and that some Indian descendants did so still. I bent down and dipped my finger into the stickiness of the blood which had rushed from the hummingbird's beak, bright red, before softly stroking the shining green throat which went luminescent pink at certain angles and that was still twisted in that ungodly bend. In the moment of my touch, I heard the low, desirous mewl of the gray cat hungrily calling to me, as if all nature were in fact connected. Yet, even if he could sense it, I knew the cat had not yet seen what lay there at my feet. I righted its neck before I picked it, gently, up.

I buried that hummingbird in a very deep hole, as I didn't want the yellow eyed Micha to unearth it. And as I placed the body in its grave, I thought of Marisa, and the fact that she would soon be on her way to see me. She'd be arriving the next day; and I was quietly waiting.

I rose from that mound and stood outside my door and then I threw small pebbles up at the high round window, one after another, softly first but then with more conviction, harder and harder until it finally cracked, ruining the illusion of sky which it created in a certain light.

In the recurring dream, my recurring dream, my father is kissing my mother, leaning down into her hand which he kisses again and again. I stand weeping in the big field. There is a pack of wild dogs coming toward me. The dogs have already eaten my sister. They have devoured Julia, and now they are coming for me; I am paralyzed and my father, in his blindness, will not see them as they eat me, because he will be bending down again to kiss my mother's hand. But he will not mean it.

Marisa arrives tomorrow and I can see her now, walking through the heavy front door of this colonial house before proceeding down the arcade that borders the interior courtyard. She will first stop, just inside the big wooden door, to talk to the cook, who will have gone out to greet her. She will introduce herself with an open smile, revealing the gap in her teeth; she will show the cook my letters, to clarify who she is, but the cook will of course already know. She will walk Marisa to her room. The one I've put her in is two doors down from mine, deep inside the house. The cook will point my door out to her as she guides her in. I see, Marisa will say, and will put her arm around the cook as she cranes her neck to try and catch sight of me inside it. But she'll decide to put her bags down, clean up a bit and change into some fresh clothes, before coming on to see me. And though I will attempt to listen to her every sound, impossibly struggling to hear her motions through the thick walls, I will let her come to me first. I will be waiting.

Will she like the high ceilings here? The big plain rooms, the thick cool walls and long shuttered windows? It will look like a storybook house to her, I know. It will seem like a fairy tale tower, the only sign of a life still beating embodied in the calls of the children playing in the schoolyard down the road, those calls rising intermittently up through the narrow, winding cobblestone streets; inside the house itself only the half alive shufflings of my black clad aunt and my silent uncle, of the serious cook, who will startle when Marisa puts her arm around her.

The girl who I was when I knew Marisa was a wanderer. She, that Sandra, was a decentered child; she was unclear about herself, and this lack of clarity had to do with her sister, the sister who was and was not there, and whom she somehow mirrored. She was confused in herself, but her sister, Julia, confused her more. Because how could a sister be and not be there at once?

I saw pictures of Julia when I was very young, a toddler perhaps, and she looked like me. In a small and halting voice I asked, "Is that me?" though the girl in the pictures was older, at least six, I believed.

"Now, how could that be you? She is a big girl," Rocio answered.

I looked into Rocio's beautiful green eyes as she put her hand to my hair; her mouth smiled but her eyes were serious, and even at that very young age I knew to look there first, to trust people's eyes the most. She bent down and gave me a kiss on the neck, "She is your sister, Silly," she added. "That's Julia."

Confused, I pushed myself into Rocio's body then, wanting it to swallow me up and hide me from my own deep fears. And then, as I stared out at that picture from my hiding place at Rocio's leg, I thought that maybe I had heard about Julia before, more than once, perhaps, that maybe I had heard that she was my sister, a hazy fuzzy fact, though I could not recall who had spoken of her, or when, or why, for I was only three or four and memory and time and reasons were all still vague and blurry and wholly imprecise.

My sister was that vanished girl in those pictures, that missing girl, that there and not there girl?

"Julia?"

"Yes."

"My sister?"

"Yes."

I was confused. I went to the mirror and saw myself there, looking just like that girl in the photos, and I wondered which one of us in fact I was. There were several pictures of her throughout our home, one in my grandmother's room, another in my aunt's, this one we were discussing now was in the dining room and I had always thought that it was somehow me there, standing next to that big tree in the photograph, but now I was understanding that my missing sister haunted many corners of that house, including hidden parts of myself.

I was told she lived with my uncle David. Why? I asked, but nobody would answer. The air grew thick and weighty, voices lowered, tones dropped, a denseness full of lack. I asked again only once or twice. Because each time it went heavy and silent and dark, as if a black cloud were descending on the house. My questions were questions ignored. And this silence was scary and blurred, of course; as the answer, I feared, could have to do with cold blooded monsters. With disappeared children and things that devour. With Saturn, yes, it was Saturn who devoured his son in the painting my uncle Felix had in his room. My sister was a terrifying nothing and blankness and a dense weight of secrets. And that is how things get confused. People get confused. Small girls get confused and decentered. Because, how could I be sure that she was not me? How could I know Julia was true? There were no facts for explaining and grasping and holding. My sister was and was not there. My mother herself was a slippery being so I knew people were unclear. I had seen my uncle David only a few times, and I only dimly, vaguely, recalled him. Did he in fact exist? Did my sister in fact exist? Or was it another one of their stories? Their you must behave stories. Like the one about cats stealing tongues. Or spirits that descend weeping in the night to steal naughty children, La Llorona. Or about Saturn eating his son. Was this another one of their dark behave tales? Or was it in fact me in that picture, made older through some trick of witch-craft? A spell that had already long ago been cast. Maria, our ancient maid, often talked about witches, about big moths and black birds who lived in the garden and were in fact witches casting their darkness. If I didn't behave I too could be disappeared. And then I too would only be a photo. I felt this, though it was unspoken. Though nothing was ever spoken. All of it was there. My sister was that vanished girl in those pictures, that missing girl, that there and not there girl.

One day I did ask our old maid, Maria, "Where is my sister? What happened to her?"

"Eat your breakfast," she said and then sprinkled a little sugar on my buttered bread to make it nicer.

"But where is she? That is her in that picture, I know. I thought it was me but Rocio said it is Julia."

"No, of course it isn't you," she said. "It is your sister." And then she shook her head. "Don't ask so many questions," she said. "It's Julia in the picture and that's all you need to know and she's no longer here so eat your breakfast." She patted my head.

"But if she's my sister why isn't she here?"

"Now, that is one question too many. Eat your breakfast," Maria said, and she went back to her stove.

I tried to take a bite of my bread, but she had unnerved me. Because if one can disappear then why not two, I wondered. Or three? Or all of us? Could we not all be easily vanished? And then who would be here to do the missing? Who would lie in bed wondering at the lack? Who would do the regretting? Who would make up stories about the life I could have lived with my sister? Who would carry all the guilt at the absence inside them? Who would lie in bed feeling as if she could not breathe any longer, as if she herself were only half there? My hand gripping at the bedclothes. The breath not coming. Where is the air? It has gone thin. My eyes won't focus, my heart rapidly beating. Why can't I breathe?

The first time I met her I was four years old. Julia was eleven. She drew a picture for me and she carried me around on her hip and she called me Little Bird. And immediately I loved her.

I lived in the house with my grandmother and aunt and one of my uncles. I had already seen the pictures, had asked my few unanswered questions, and more clearly understood it was not me in the photos. I was four and I vaguely understood that there was in fact a sister who was depicted there, though I had never met her. I was four years old and I mostly did believe it, though deep inside I had my trepidations. My uncle Felix of the terrifying Saturn still lived with us, though Adrian had long ago moved out. I was glad as he had been very mean to me on a number of occasions. He would go on to live with a succession of girl-friends, and would never move back into the big house with my grandmother again, and I was glad for that.

Felix had many girlfriends too, but they were usually even more childlike than him and it wasn't until after I was ten that he finally moved out of my grandmother's house. My mother hated him but I liked Felix a great deal. He took me to look at art, and to the archeological museums. I'd sit very straight in his car with him, straight and serious. I acted like a small adult around him, because he spoke to me like one.

"Who is Saturn?" I asked when I was nine. I turned to look over at him while he considered the answer.

We were at a stop light and he turned to look at me too, "What do you mean?"

"In the painting in your room. Why is he eating his son?"

"It's a myth," he said. But I continued to stare at him and he saw that wasn't enough. "Saturn is afraid his son will be better than him. So he eats him up so that won't happen," he then added.

"Why do you like scary pictures?"

"I don't particularly like scary pictures."

"Oh, yes you do. Scary things. You have that skull in your room and you only use that red light in there and you have Saturn too. You do like scary things."

"Well, okay. I guess I'll have to think about it." We were still at that red light and he ran his hand through his beard as he turned to face the road again.

We were on our way to pick up one of his very pretty girl-friends and when we arrived she teased him in front of me, he was so serious, and I joined in and we laughed at him together.

"Felix is in a bad mood because he didn't sleep enough," the girl said and I giggled along. "He is a sleepy grumpy bear," she said and then tickled him and he growled at her.

She grabbed his arm and nuzzled in his neck prettily and called him a grumpy bear again, and he kept up the grave composure even in the face of all that silly love. The joke was that he slept all the time, I knew. I liked that he would lie long and silent in the red velvet room and read and take naps throughout the day, on his back on that long dark red couch, sleeping and reading and sleeping all day long. I liked all of his beautiful girl-friends, interchangeable, almost, how they walked through the house on tiptoes like elegant gazelles. I liked that he was able to paint whole scenes on the head of a match, lovers holding hands around a tree, a big moon in the distance. Though he made big paintings too. I liked that he sometimes drew with me and that his girlfriends doted on him, and thought he was brilliant. I liked that they were always bribing me with treats, trying to get at him through me. And though I would later understand that he wasn't an artist in the same way as Marisa's father, still I knew he was an artist, or could have been. If my grandfather had allowed him to study art. My grandfather had not, of course, and my uncle Felix had refused to do anything else. He would paint and lie around all day. He had long hair and could be bossy, wanted everything done just so. Why even bother doing something if you're not going to do it right? he would yell. And I would be confused because he would be talking about something not important at all, like the way Maria had ironed his pants. He was fastidious, always looked dapper, even though Adrian who worked hard for the drug companies called him a lazy hippie.

My mother was and was not there. You never knew which it would be, so that you would be surprised to find her sitting at the breakfast table when you entered the kitchen. A startle first, and then a gathering of self, before you'd go to greet her. But my aunt Sofia took care of me and was constant and loving. In her room there was a big closet and it was full of beautiful clothing. Her favorite color was green, so that there were many different shades of it, in countless silk scarves and loose flowing shirts, and even slacks and shoes sometimes. There were large windows that were doors and gave onto a balcony and so her room was full of light. She had a vanity with a big silver brush and lots of different lotions for all the parts of your body and many bottles of perfume upon it. I would spray it on myself, her perfume, two or three different kinds at once when she was not looking and I would sit in front of her mirror and brush and brush my hair.

Her voice was serious, the inflections strong, and she was tall and earnest.

"Are you hungry?" she would ask me in the morning as she rubbed one of her many lotions on her legs. Or, "Do you need a new dress?" in the afternoon. She would take me out to eat in the evenings. On the weekend, sometimes, she would take me to the little country house she had bought in a small development. I would be lying about on her bed on a Saturday morning and the sun would come in her big long windows in shafts. You could really see the sky through those windows, the big white clouds making shapes above us. You could hear the children calling from the street down below, fighting or laughing or simply yelling at each other to hurry, hurry, come along. I would kick my legs around, twist myself up to a seated position and watch her as she arranged her long curls around her face and then applied her make-up.

"Why do you do that?" I asked as she swept mascara onto her already long lashes. "Why do people do that?"

"To look more beautiful," she answered very matter of factly.

"Do you like being beautiful?" I asked.

"Everyone likes being beautiful."

"I think some people like to be ugly," I answered. "They like to be mean and ugly and tough," I said.

"Do you think so?" she asked. "You shouldn't let Marta be so mean to you," she added. "You shouldn't let her bully you."

"I don't," I answered. "But she's bigger than me…."

"Come on, let's go," and she would get up from in front of her mirror and grab her overnight bag and I would shove some of my things in it and then I'd run down with her to her car where she would get in the seat beside me and off we would drive through the city and through the woods that lie to the north of it. I would swim and swim all day in the pool all the little country houses shared, while she sunned herself and napped.

I would float in that pool and look up at the faraway blue sky and sometimes there would be boys whom I liked in that pool too. I would grow shy if they looked at me, more so if they tried to talk and I would pull myself silently out of the water and go sit drip drip by my aunt, pretending that I was simply tired when she asked me what was wrong with me now.

Next to the perfume bottles on my aunt's vanity there was a picture of my sister. It was my sister in that picture, and though I mostly didn't think about it, it was there, and I saw it and it flowed into my being. My sister was that vanished girl in those pictures, that missing girl, that there and not there girl who was a spectral sister...

My aunt Sofia was not particularly affectionate, not physical at all. But my grandmother Cecilia was. I would walk into her heavily furnished room, so different from my aunt's light filled one. "Come here, my girl," she would say. "Come here my beautiful girl." And there would be longing in her voice, her long and slow inflections, and her arms would go around me and she'd kiss. As I got older I understood that she did not sleep much, my grandmother, that she was often awake in the middle of the night, worrying about everyone, cycling through the many members of our family, her children, their sins and their passions, dwelling on them, wondering how they could be sorted and fixed, working on that impossible mission all night through while everyone else in that house slept.

And though my mother's comings and goings were painful and confusing, I was young when I understood she was not a real mother. The old man made it clear. Stay away, he admonished. But I had my grandma and my aunt Sofia. My sister Rocio too, could sometimes feel like a mother.

But Julia was different. When I first saw Julia, I fell instantly in love. I didn't see the resemblance as much as I had in the pictures; yet, I knew she looked like me. Her long brown hair and big brown eyes. Her skinny legs and arms. She loved me too;

I could see that right away. She stared at me across the table that first evening as we ate; I had been too nervous and scared to sit near her; I cautiously drew my eyes up from my plate again and again to take a peek; and after we were done eating she got up and got some paper and drew a picture of a cat wearing a hat and a bow-tie to lure me over and when I shyly walked to her side she made up a silly story for me about that cat. Beginning on that night she carried me around on her hip, like a little mother. While all the adults played cards she traipsed me up and down the house, though I was already four and more than half her length. She held me in her lap often and read to me too. I would sleep in bed with her and she would put her arm around me and in the morning she would wake me up with questions, "What did you dream about, Little Bird? What do you want for breakfast, some seeds?" And she would tickle me. "What do you want to play, or should we just fly away instead?"

She would look into my eyes as she asked me these things and sometimes I would answer, "But I'm not a little bird."

"Oh, yes you are," she would insist. She would cut up fruit for me and serve it to me with a fork. She took me into the garden and played with me for hours on end. We drew and colored together. She read to me from The Archies, her favorite comic book. "Who do you like better, Little Bird?" she would ask me, "Betty or Veronica?"

"Jughead!" I would answer triumphantly.

Marta would storm into the house furiously cursing someone who had wronged her, stomp stomping, followed by one of her many angry minions and Julia would put her arms around me and keep on reading. We'd spy on Rocio and her boyfriends together too. We would watch them sit and do nothing in each other's arms for hours on end. "How boring," she would whisper.

"Yes," I would answer, but we'd keep our rapt watch. Just in case.

Sometimes we would go out, to the park. I would put my hand in hers and look at our fingers intertwined. We had the same fingers, though hers were longer.

"Do you think we look alike," I asked her once.

"Yes," she answered. "But not too much. We look a little like each other but mostly like ourselves," she added, and this confused me.

My uncle David always left spending money for her which she kept in a jar and she would take from it to buy me sweets, tamarind candy, or japanese peanuts, or cookies. She would take me out for ice creams too, all the time, always taking my hand in hers, or else I would grab her by the arm.

I would watch her lick her ice cream as we sat on a bench and I thought she was beautiful; it was a sort of vanity, I know, since we were so similar, but I couldn't take my eyes off of her. She spoke perfect English, and taught me a bit. She would put music on, the B52's or The Talking Heads and we would dance and dance, *Why won't you dance with me!* We would scream the lyrics at each other as we danced and danced, *This is not my beautiful house!* Or else with David Bowie we would pretend to be lost in space. I would sit talking or singing gibberish to her, thinking I was speaking English and she would laugh "Let the water hold me down," she would correct me, enunciating each word, or, "Ground control, Silly." And I did learn. Within a year and a half I had learned quite a bit, and by the time she came back again two years later I was really speaking English, *Come on, come on, we've really got a good thing going, Well come on, well come on!* I wanted to be more like her than I already felt I was. And that pushed me to learn. I learned fast.

She made me fall in love with her, and then one day she was suddenly gone. It was a violence to my tiny heart.

And while she was away no one talked about her. It was like she had never been there at all, so that I almost had to doubt her existence. And of course it was a relief, not to have to hear her name, but it was painful too. More painful not to, I now believe. And so again I had to go back to those old photographs. It was my sister in those pictures. Though now, of course, the photos were not nearly enough.

When she came again, I was almost six. At that point the old man had been visiting me for a while. I had begun making shrines as he instructed, little piles of perfect round rocks I found in the garden; I chanted and twirled, though never in front of Julia. I now clearly understood that she lived in the US with my uncle David, whom I knew no better than I had before, as he never came to see us so that he remained a blurry cloud in my mind, my sister's shadow father. She was a teenager then, and I thought she was amazing. She lived in Los Angeles and so was very tan and had long brown hair and wore red lipgloss I borrowed sometimes. She had big brown eyes and was always reading and was much quieter than Marta, though not as shy as Rocio. We would lie in bed together in the mornings and she would read to me from her book, and then I would run and get her mine, *Alice in Wonderland*, which I read and re-read and re-read as I wanted nothing else, and she would read that to me too. She walked around barefoot, and listened to lots of music and mostly didn't waste her time with the crazy boys Marta hung around with, though there were a couple she liked.

Maria, the maid, had come home with a long-furred black cat one day, to help with the mice, but it immediately ran for the hidden recesses under the refrigerator. Julia coaxed that cat out from under there and patiently taught it not to be afraid of her, and I befriended that cat too then. We would take him into bed with us in the morning; a glass of milk each, along with that black cat whom we would let drink from our glasses while she read to me.

Like before, she would take me out all the time. To the park, or to hang out with friends. She was not just a picture, my sister. And my aunt Sofia loved her as much as she loved me, I could see that; it was clear. So that the three of us were often together. Like Sofia was our mother. We would go to the country house on the weekends and she and I would swim and swim. Or Sofia would take us to the movies. Like a real mom. Julia wore outrageous clothing, red or purple jeans and bright velvet tops. Or these funny dresses that looked very old fashioned and black tights and big mary-janes. My uncle Felix loved her too, and he was always trying to teach her things. He would take the two of us to visit his beautiful friends, or to museums. He would talk to Julia in serious tones about the books she was reading. And she liked that he spoke to her like an adult, I could see that.

"He's nicer to you than to anyone else in the house," I told her once.

"I know that," she replied.

I was happy when she was around, but then, as before, she left a week before our classes began. I helped her pack her bag and that was somehow exciting, like I was going with her. But then the next day it was there by the door when I was brought down very early in the morning to say good-bye and I saw it sitting there and stared at that suitcase which I now fully understood I was not a part of and then I looked over at her for a moment, and she gave me a little crooked smile and then I ran to her, still in my pajamas and I wept and called out her name, said it in a damp and choking voice. And she had to peel herself away and then instantly she was gone, I was barely awake, and I cried and cried for weeks on end. Though not in front of anybody. And I didn't talk to anyone about it either, how I felt. Every day for about a month I piled and piled those smooth round rocks and made more shrines. I dug more of the stones out from the thick dirt and washed them off first to get them clean. And two weeks later one entire end of the garden had dozens upon dozens of these little rock shrines all over it, flowers and beautiful leaves drying on top of each one.

My sister was again that vanished girl in those pictures, that missing girl, my suddenly heartbreakingly gone sister.

The last time she came I was ten. She spent a whole year here then. But I was mostly with my aunt Sofia in those days as she had moved into her own apartment. She liked to have me there to keep her company and to help with baby Antonio. I'd play with him while she took a shower, or made dinner. I knew it was easier for Sofia having me around, and I really liked being there with them. I would put music on and light candles and it was like I was part of a normal family, a real family. Big Antonio liked me because I was just a kid and stayed out of their hair mostly. Julia came and spent the night a couple of times, but there really wasn't enough room for her. Sofia deeply loved her, but big Antonio made it clear that he was feeling a little crowded. Then

Julia moved in with Marta and my mom, and I didn't see her very much the rest of that year. Though I still adored her, and when I did see her, she took me out like before. And she defended me from Marta's insane rage. We would only have just arrived at Grandma Ceci's for the day, all of us, and Marta would find some reason to grow furious and chase me, threatening to beat me sometimes, and Julia would get into a fight with her about it, yelling at her to leave me alone. They came to blows over me once or twice, though when they were in the middle of it, it no longer seemed to be about me at all; instantly it was as if they had forgotten I existed, they seemed to hate each other so much, their anger sitting evident right there on the surface of their skin, the anger the only thing driving them and it easily turned into blows and heated words and fuming gasping breath. It was terrifying.

It was just a couple of months after she left the last time that I wandered into the red velvet room and saw the newspaper my uncle Felix had left lying around, that photographer boy. I had moved back in with my grandma Ceci by then, into that house that even when it was full of people you felt completely alone in, as no one fully tended you. You could wander between them, but there was no one for whom you were the one. Nonetheless, I had started to feel like I should let my aunt Sofia and the two Antonios have their family space. Though they were kind to me, I wasn't really a part of it, I knew. My mother was living with my grandmother too then, because Julia had come and told Grandma Ceci there was something wrong with her. It was that same summer, my mother there at the house all the time, slowed down and sad but physically present, that she and I would go and feed the homeless man our leftovers. I was eleven and that was the summer I started wandering the streets too. Eleven when my sister left us for good, when again she would become just a picture. But now her image was infused with my own memories, memories which I replayed over and over deep inside my own head, full of pain, full of sadness, full of a hollow empty feeling like regret, a hole left by the final vanishing of my missing sister.

There is a hammock in between the two big poplars in the garden here. I lie here and look at the shifting light as it dances through the trees. I rock myself back and forth, dragging my foot to slow myself, push again, then drag my foot; I think about things, my uncle back at the pharmacy, my aunt disappearing into her room, while I lie here with Micha dozing on my belly. I pat his back and scratch around his chin and ears and he opens his eyes ever so slowly, purring at me in a deep love vibration. I swing us a little more, my foot softly pushing, and I see the shadows playing there amongst the trees. And it strikes me as I swing in the hammock that my sister was always a shadow too. Sometimes, through her presence, the light around her shadow was brighter, sometimes, admittedly, very bright, so that the sense of shadow almost vanished. But she was somehow always tinged with darkness for me, the darkness of absence, or of her coming absence, of the painful and repeated absence of her light. I catch myself holding my breath sometimes as I lie here in this hammock. Why do I hold my breath? I have always done it and each time I catch myself doing it I think it is because I want to vanish, because I want to hold myself tight and then to be released from it all. But the cat will stir on my belly, and I will pull out of my thoughts and touch at him gently, and then I find myself breathing as he again begins to purr.

This morning he licked at my finger for a long time, there must have been something on it, because he licked and licked and suckled a bit as if he were a kitten on his mother's teat. It reminded me of when Marisa took my finger in her mouth at that movie theater. How she sucked me in that lack of light.

She walked into my room this morning. I was surprised that she was suddenly there, Marisa, though I had been waiting for her for days. I guess I had been expecting the cook to tell me she'd arrived. But nobody came; nobody warned me to prepare, and so I was lying on my bed, reading, when she walked into the room.

"Hi," she said as she made her way toward me. Her hair was short and dark, messy, bangs playing on her forehead. Her eyes were big and bright and expectant, lined in kohl, thick and black. She was tall and had pronounced cheekbones and that large gap in between her front teeth. She was still very striking.

"Hi," I said back. "How are you? How is your father?" and though it usually takes me a moment to warm up I walked right up to her and gave her a long hug.

"Good. I'm good," she answered as she embraced me. "Winnie Pooh is good too." And we walked back and sat at the edge of my bed though there were two big chairs in that room.

"I like it here," she said.

"Oh, it's strange," I answered. "I know that. It's like walking back in time." And then we talked for a while and she told me about her life in New York and how Winnie Pooh now lived there too and had sent me warm greetings.

"He liked you from the first," she said. "He said you were special."

I blushed, but then soon we were lying on that bed, facing each other, on our sides, like we had when we were just girls, and Micha came and made his way around and between us, and then he laid down by my belly and Marisa looked into my eyes and her own eyes were very serious. We talked about my family then, about the things I had told her in my letters, about the tornado in Coahuila and my double in Los Angeles, and my mother too; and I was surprised that Marisa had thought so much about it all already, and surprised too that she wanted to talk mostly about Julia.

After a pause she looked directly at me and she took some of my long hair in her hand and she said, "Maybe you should go look for her, Sandra. I can go with you. Let's just go."

"I can't," I replied.

"You can. And then maybe you can stop living other people's lives. The sad dark lives, your weight of a family. You can come stay with me in New York. And you can look for Julia. I can go with you. You can see who she is now, what she's become."

And until then I hadn't thought that was a possibility, going and directly looking for my sister.

"Sometimes I wonder if I'm mad, Marisa," I said then. "I wonder if I'm mad. Like my mother."

"You're not mad. You do this to yourself." She dropped my hair and took my hand then and the cat stirred a bit, "You can't just disappear, Sandra. Let's go. Let's go look for your sister." She looked into my eyes, "Imagine a door to the outside," Marisa added then.

"What do you mean?" I asked her.

"Imagine there is a door and you can walk through it and you can get outside. Imagine you are not trapped; imagine there is a door, and it leads outside. I can help you go through it."

I looked into her big black eyes and cried.

Marta

A MONTH OR TWO after Julia left that last visit, I decided to get the fuck out of there myself. I wanted to see what it was like to leave, to really leave. Don't get me wrong, it's not like I had never left before. I'd had many times of staying at Bubbles' house, often for weeks, sometimes longer. Once I went to the states to live with one of my dad's brothers, not David, another one, Martin, who lived in Texas. But Texas is not California and his wife was a psycho and his kids were spoiled brats and so I got my ass out of there after a couple of months. I'd kind of gone as a babysitter for my uncle's kids on account of he was rich and offered to pay me to help his wife with them, and just to kind of hang out with her, keep her company, as it turns out. And this would've been great, getting paid for hanging out, except that she was truly nuts. You know, psycho. She'd be treating me like I was her best friend, telling me all her secrets, how she had a crush on the guy at the bank, or how she'd tricked my uncle into paying for the same car repairs twice so she could pocket the extra cash, or how when she went to visit her parents in Acapulco with the kids she spent all her time in the clubs at night and hungover on the beach during the day—though Martin was my uncle she would tell me these things—and then the next moment she'd be yelling at me that I hadn't wiped her kids' butt right and that now he had a rash. I wanted to tell her to wipe her own brat's ass, but then she would have lost it and told my uncle and I wouldn't have gotten any cash for the week.

I hated my aunt and her fat whiny kids so I only lasted a couple of months, and then I lied and told my uncle Martin I missed my mom and he put me on a plane home.

But when I got back to Mexico City Bubbles had gotten really serious with her boyfriend, Fausto, and though her father had eased up on her a bit, she now never wanted to go out anymore because of the boyfriend. During the day she'd become some sort of strange housewife, hanging out at Fausto's house and cooking and cleaning alongside his mother like she was some thirty year old lady. And that was depressing, because she'd been so cool. Not that she wasn't still funny, she was, but it was different. And the worst part was that Fausto wasn't even nice to her. She'd run up to him when he walked in, actually run, throw her arms around his neck, and he'd just kind of ignore her, let her hug on him like that without so much as a hello. Okay, okay, he'd say kind of bored as she kissed at his face, smooched all over it.

What the hell was that? He certainly wasn't good looking. And he still lived with his parents. So what was the point? I didn't get it.

In the meantime Anna was getting nuttier and nuttier. She'd started doing coke or something, though she would deny it. In those days in Mexico City no one I knew did any drugs, pot was thought of as kind of out there, at least with the people I knew, so getting hooked on coke was pretty much unheard of. I'd go to her place to get her to come out with me and she'd barely open her door so that I'd have to talk to her through a little crack in it. If she did let me in she'd just lie around on her bed, half dressed like some sort of hooker and talk about guys… someone she was in love with that treated her like shit more often than not. She was always telling me about some horrible thing they did to her, and then whining, Why would he do that? and I just wanted to shake her and say, Because you're a pathetic stupid whore! I stopped going by to see her after a while.

One day I decided it was really time to go. My aunt Sofia was over visiting my grandma and she'd always thought I was a loser and a thief anyway and if someone is convinced about that in regard to you there's really nothing you can do about it, so I stole some money from her purse. Then I borrowed a little more from my grandma. When I asked her for it she looked me in the eye in that direct way she had while she questioned me about what it was for. Some shoes I saw at Suburbia. Please! I asked. I don't have anything nice! How am I supposed to change my life when I have nothing nice to wear! My grandmother appreciated shoes; she always got properly dressed before going out, and though she said Suburbia had gotten way too expensive she gave me the money anyway. And then I got some more from my mom, and I didn't tell any of them I'd gotten any from the others and then a few days later I hopped on a bus and went to Cruces in Veracruz which is where my dad lived.

I think I left a note.

I don't remember that bus ride at all, except that just before getting to the port in Veracruz, which is where I had to switch buses to get to his little town, I was suddenly in a jungle or something like one. In Veracruz I sat in the very hot, extremely humid bus stop for an hour or two waiting for the connecting bus, surrounded by all these sweaty people, many of them watching over bulky packages, while a bunch of snot-nosed, raggedy looking, greasy kids ran around like beasts. The bus finally came and I hopped on that rickety old thing and then very slowly it travelled through those towns stopping in each to let someone or other off. And then, not a moment too soon, we were in Cruces and it was my turn to get off. The whole thing had taken more than 12 hours.

But now I was in Cruces and it was very different from the city, this nothing little village, though within a day or two I realized it was the same, somehow, because I was again all mixed up in other peoples' lives. And it didn't matter in the end, I realized, if you were in a tiny village or a big city, cause all you ever really cared about were the people that were there in front of you, what they were doing and why, who you liked or hated, what you wanted to get into, and from what you'd walk away.

I got to Cruces at nine o'clock at night; it was green all around that town, though the town itself was pretty dry on account of everything had been chopped down for the town itself, but I had passed a river which was very close by and all around that water the land was lush. It was hilly in those parts too. My dad had another woman which we all knew anyway, but which I didn't understand once I met her because she was beyond ugly, skinny and no money either. She lived in some little shitty house and he took me there that night as if it was the most normal thing to take me to his woman, and she had made me dinner, which, okay, was very decent of her, but still I couldn't get over how skinny and butt ugly she was, even as I was eating her food. Her very old mother was in a back room lying on a cot, and I got the feeling that she'd been lying like that, dying, for a very long time. In the meantime my father's woman, with her thin hair that looked like scrappy hay, with her bony slouchy body, with not an ounce of sexy on her, circled around me like a nervous mouse while I ate. Her hands kept reaching out in little jerky motions to serve me. What, are you kidding? I wanted to ask M right then and there. All that playboy shit and in the end this is what you get?

The next day this group of guys came around to ask if I was the doctor's daughter. I wanted to laugh in their faces, the doctor? Sure, there was a box or two of the samples he bought cheap off of my uncle Adrian stashed in his closet, stuff he probably doled out from time to time to keep the myth going, antibiotics and fancy vitamins, but I knew that was about all the doctoring he was doing. They kept looking at me, with their mouths kind of twisted up, so that I began to get the feeling that they pretty much had his number. Anyway, the one in the middle did, that's for sure. He was thin and a bit taller than the rest of them and he held himself very straight, his shoulders back so that you could see his chest through his thin AC/DC t-shirt. He plucked his eyebrows, you could see that a mile away. So you're the doctor's daughter, he asked, his legs agile and rubbery so that he had one wrapped around the other as he talked. Leaning against the door he looked like a snake. And the way he said *doctor*, I could tell that he knew what was what for sure. He checked me out real close, to see where it was he could strike.

Who does your eyebrows? I asked, before he could attack.

He smiled a wicked smile before answering, I'll get you her number, Honey; those caterpillars on your face could use a little help.

Those boys took me to the market and I ate the best sopes and squash flower quesadillas I've ever had and Juan and I checked out all the guys there. And the really amazing thing was that most of those guys kind of flirted back, even when they were super macho. They'd act tough, but then they'd stare at him a bit too long, so that it was clear it wasn't just one thing going on there. Or else they'd tease back and forth with him, hilarious insults flying, for much longer than they had to, you know, giving him their time; very few guys ignored him outright. Someone later told me it was because the girls wouldn't have sex until they were married, so many guys did have things going with each other, but I knew that was bullshit even then. They were fucking Juan because they liked it. They liked it like that, whether they were getting any from their girlfriends or not. Plus, I knew that all the girls pretended not to be having sex, sure, but Bubbles had long ago taught me a little bit about that. You just act like he's the first one, and everyone is happy. Each and every time. And as long as they don't know about each other, the different guys you've fucked, everything is fine.

After a while my dad got really mad at me, asking why I would choose someone like Juan as my best friend and I just rolled my eyes. It was known all over that town of Cruces that Juan and my dad were good friends, maybe even special friends, and that that woman of his was nothing real. And who gave a shit anyway if you really dug someone, had a good time hanging out. And this, pretending at being something he wasn't, is what always ruined it for me with M. You never knew who he was trying to pretend for, who he was trying to impress; who gave a shit? His self-righteousness full of lies just made me insane.

But then one day when I was complaining about it all Juan said that maybe he was not so clear on things himself; that maybe it wasn't that he was lying. Maybe he was so confused inside that he really believed all that shit.

Even so, I said, it pisses me off. And anyway, why are you defending him? Juan just shrugged and went back to his beer.

That's not how the world works, Marta, my father would scold me. How do you expect things to go well for you if you only hang out with degenerates? Class it up, Girl.

As if he was really teaching me something. As if he knew what he was talking about. As if things had gone so well for him, stuck in that shitty little town.

M arranged for me to go out with the governor's niece a few times, but she was so beyond boring she put my sleep to sleep. She came and picked me up in her big car and she wasn't even hot, with her thick, unruly, brillo pad hair which it was clear she dyed way too much, and her equally thick thighs, legs like tree trunks right down to her ankles, and her flat face. Though she acted like she was something, her chest all pushed out, and then she drove us to her family ranch and as soon as we got there she yelled into the kitchen at the cook, who I couldn't even see, to make us some rabbit stew, and though I'd never eaten rabbit before and was a little taken aback, I wasn't about to tell her that.

The house isn't fully staffed right now, I'm afraid. My family is away all month, she said, and her tone made it sound like she was apologizing for something.

I don't care, I said. And then I kept snooping around the room, picking things up, inspecting them, putting them back down.

Would you like some Amaretto? she asked, and though she was really getting on my nerves with that poofed out chest of hers and her snooty face, I said yes. I liked that sweet stuff.

She served it up in these tiny little glasses and we sat around in her parlour talking, about her mostly, how her father, the governor's brother-in-law she made clear once again, had bought her an expensive apartment in Jalapa where she studied International Relations or some such thing at the University. She was planning to move to Paris some day.

Of course, I thought, and then I think I yawned; luckily the cook, a tiny hunch-backed woman, came in then and she ordered that tiny cook to set the table and then we sat down and that food was actually pretty great.

After lunch I yawned some more so she asked if I wanted to go for a swim, and I said no, but she got into her suit anyway, a painful sight, and then she took me out and showed me the ridiculous landing pad for her father's gaudy helicopter right in the middle of that huge pool.

Then she did some laps.

Afterward she drove me down the curvy hills in the dark for what seemed like an hour, dangerously sharp turns in parts of that tiny windy road so that suddenly I wasn't so tired anymore, fully awake and hanging on to the door for dear life, as if that would make a difference when we crashed. I think I released an audible sigh of relief and was truly happy to be home when we arrived. Though M did pressure me to hang out with her two or three other times. It would've been easier for me to spend time with her if she was better looking. All that money and she was still a dog. And if you're boring like that, it's best to have something to offer your guests, like good looks. I guess the food and the booze were all right.

The other person, besides Juan, I immediately loved was this girl, about my age, maybe a year or two older, so nineteen maybe, and she was mostly Indian. She cooked for this man and would make these amazing meals at her house and then deliver the food.

She was incredible, her hands, working and patting and shaping that dough as she talked and talked. She would make all sorts of things with that masa, gorditas and sopes and tortillas. It was fantastic to watch. She had very dark skin and that thick long Indian hair and she was tall. Her eyes were clear, almost black, and I loved staring into them, though she mostly didn't look back at you when she talked, and I loved that too, how she just knew you were taking it all in though she barely looked your way. She was too busy to look at you. Cooking, or cleaning up, or moving all over that little house, doing things, making things, too busy to make eye contact, her eyes fixed somewhere in front of her as she worked. She lived alone, I think, though I don't really understand that. Where were her parents? I never understood who owned the houses people lived in in that town. Or who was connected to who. I mean, some people clearly owned their houses, and there were families that were obvious families, but other parts of it were a mystery to me, and somehow you just never felt it was right to ask. Though I wanted someone to draw me a diagram; it would be titled: How the Hell We Are All Connected, and on it would be illegitimate sons and daughters, and all the kept women and young men, and the guys that had two or three families going at once. And women who were hot and had the children of three or four men. My dad's house, which was largely unfurnished, was owned by the mayor from the next town over. And this girl, Clara, her house, I don't know whose it was. Anyway, she was great. Deep and solid and I never even thought about guys or sex or anything like that when I was with her. Unless we ran into Juan together, and he was all sex so you couldn't help it, you had to think about it the moment you saw him, the way he squirmed his body around, wrapped his legs around each other and shimmied his bottom, you had to talk about it, even if it was just in a stupid way, even if Clara was around.

Clara and I would walk from one end of the small town where she lived to the other which is where the house she cooked for was, and I don't even remember what we talked about as we walked over to deliver what she'd made for the day. I just remember that we walked slow—her gait was like that, slow and measured, and she was the one who set the pace—and that I really loved being around her. She walked super straight too, with her chin held up and the only other people I've ever seen who walk like that are dancers, Rocio's friends. Maybe she was a dancer? I don't remember. But it's possible. Maybe she was. Sometimes she'd take me shopping with her, at the market, to get all the ingredients for what she was cooking that day and I liked watching her haggle with the Indian women who ran the stalls, their stuff piled all around them. God, she was an incredible cook. And she fed me. I gained weight while I was there. And I learned to cook too, though I never helped her while she worked. What I really learned was how to put things together, how to make sauces and salsas, what flavors go with what, where you should and should not use strong seasonings like garlic or lime, or acids at all. Some people use that stuff in everything, but she taught me that it's not right and just kills the other flavors.

There was this other kid there. I mean, I met some of the strangest people I have ever known in that small town. What about that place produced that? He was like a midget or something, this really short Indian kid. His name was Rafael and he was about my age, 16 or 17, but he was small so that he looked like he was twelve or thirteen, though he was broad, maybe a bit chunky is what it was. He was pretty lewd and was always pushing me on other people, like some kind of midget Indian match-maker. Like he got some satisfaction from that, though I think he liked me.

One night there was a cock fight. There was a huge build-up for quite a few days before this thing. Everyone was excited and Pedro, a neighbor of Clara's even had a cock that was going to fight, and so you really felt it when you were around him, though he was mostly a pretty calm guy. The night finally came and I have to say it was great. People were there from all of the surrounding towns and we all rode out to the ring that sat in a huge field on someone's hacienda where they did this kind of thing, and we sat in bleachers around the cockpit and the MC— yes, there are MCs at cock fights, and referees and everything else you have in any other sport—anyway, the MC would walk around the stands and pick someone to take a colored chip from a basket and this is what decided whose cock fought whose next. Sometimes it was the mayor's wife or someone like that, but usually he chose some cute kid to pick the chip—Aww, how adorable, look at sweet little Anita in her pretty braids choosing the very next cock to be massacred, Juan leaned in and whispered in my ear. Sooo cute!

And then one time it was me, since I was a guest, and that was very exciting. Though Juan just clapped and clapped with his lips puckered up while I picked that chip, mocking me, and then he rolled his eyes in my direction saying, Wow, look at the doctor's daughter!

Let me enjoy my simple little pleasures, I hissed at him.

The cocks were chosen and then carried into the ring and as soon as they got the chance they'd go at each other, fierce, to kill, but also to try and save their own lives. Their owners would very carefully tie razors to their feet, while we all watched, the whole place silent, and then they would carry their cocks out holding their torsos very tight and immobile to keep from getting slashed by those razors themselves. They'd then put the whole cock's head in their mouths and suck and then spit out, who knows what or why, and then they'd introduce the cocks to each other, getting them worked up by pushing their beaks in each other's faces five or six times, while still holding them tight. Then both owners would pull back a little and release the cocks and right away each time they angrily ran toward each other with those furious razor blades attached to their feet and immediately they went at it, leaping at each other, flying high into the air, slicing each other up, their wings flapping, their feet violently flinging out time after time, again and again, to slash. The owners crouched inside the ring, twitchy and nervous, watching, ready to push the cock back in the fight if he dared to run. One would always win, of course, though often both had to be put down. A really good cock might go on to fight again, though never, of course, the same night. But as they were going for each other, at each other, people went crazy, yelling and screaming and cheering, chugging their beers fast to try and calm down, to try and focus their nervous energy on something, anything, alcohol. And then the owner of the winning cock would have to run in and grab it without letting it slice him up in the process. The other cock would be dead, or nearly there, its head hanging limp, a bloody droopy thing.

It was a huge party, everyone drinking and gambling, and I even won some money on a cock Juan told me to bet on, though it wasn't favored. We both won and flapped our bills at each other, in each other's faces, laughing, thrilled and surprised.

Clara's neighbor Pedro was beyond nervous that night, pacing and pacing. His cock was beautiful, black with some red plumes in its crest. Pedro's cock lost, and that midget Rafael came over and sat right next to me on the other side of Juan and asked me if I'd be eating Pedro's cock covered in mole tomorrow to console him. He'd leaned into me and laughed as he said it so I made a face at him, punched him hard in the arm, and pulled away.

I saw Pedro the next day and he did invite me and Clara to eat mole at his house. That's what you do, Clara said. You make a meal out of your loss and invite your friends. So maybe Rafael hadn't just been screwing with me after all. Just maybe.

The next week there was a wedding and this was a big deal. It was some politician's daughter getting married and so people came from all over. This very beautiful family arrived from Jalapa, an eighteen year old guy, and his sister who was my age and had these big black long-lashed eyes, and a perfect mouth and was really tall and thin. And their little thirteen year old brother who was just about the most beautiful boy I'd ever seen, with eyes like his sister's, except maybe his eyelashes were even darker. And for some reason that thirteen year old and the midget Rafael immediately became friends so that I right away thought there must be something dirty about that boy. We were sitting in the main square, Juan and Clara and the gentle older brother and the sister and a bunch of other kids, and Rafael and the little brother kept coming over to me and circling and laughing and then shying away, and then coming back again, circling, until finally the little brother ran his hands through my hair, while Rafael stood back and laughed, nearly drooling, like it had been a dare.

What are you doing? His sister asked, annoyed. But I had liked it, and stared at him to let him know it.

In the morning we all went to the river and most of the older kids just laid out next to the bank and talked but I got in the water and kind of floated along on a plastic raft. I lazily kicked my legs about in that warm river and soon Rafael and the little brother had joined me, and we all three swam that raft around, up and down that gentle easy river, paddling that thing around like little kids, though there was no one on it. It's just how I used to play when I was a kid, like what I was doing was my job, only it was fun, making a hole in the dirt with a shovel or making mud pies, a job with no results except our good time. There we were pushing this raft about, letting it float us, slowly in that warm water, when suddenly I feel this kid's hand down near my crotch, his fingers gently moving around down near the elastic of my bathing suit bottom, and so I look over, real slow so I won't startle him because I don't want him to stop, but still he gets startled and pulls his hand away. I turned and looked straight ahead then, away from him and within minutes his hand went down again, and soon his fingers were rubbing at my crotch and then fidgeting to get inside, under my suit again. I spread my legs a bit and then his hand was moving around down there and it all went very hot and soon his fingers were inside me, moving rhythmically, there in that warm water, with Rafael on the other side of him. It was all I could do to keep from groaning.

This thirteen year old kid had some nerve, but god he knew what he was doing.

The next day I went to the wedding with his older brother, but he just kept talking about his little brother, how many girlfriends he already had, and the fact that they were all worried for him, him and his sister and his mother, what he might get into. I never really knew if he'd found out his brother had felt me up.

But how can a thirteen year old keep a secret like that? Rafael gave me some dirty looks, and laughed and said something about the older brother wasting his time with me and then laughed again, and I just chewed him out but kept from slapping him.

And then two days after the wedding they all left.

What the hell were you doing there with that kid? Juan asked after they were all gone.

Wouldn't you like to know? I asked him back. Next time I'll remember to take pictures.

He purred at me, that snake.

I was surrounded by boys. Apart from Clara and that governor's niece I mostly just hung out with M's friends, all these young kids. They were always at the house, even when he wasn't around. When I was younger I'd never been the draw around his friends, but now that I was older, at least with some of them I was the main attraction. We'd sit on the bed together gossiping, me surrounded, kind of yearning, something, anyway, pulsing deep inside me.

One night M came home kind of drunk and he said he was going to bed and a bunch of those kids just decided to stay over, and he asked who wanted to sleep outside in the living room with me and three of them shot their hands right up and he said, Okay, Mateo, you guys sleep outside. So Mateo—who was one of the quieter, nicer boys—and I set up a little bed for him next to the couch where I was sleeping. And in the middle of the night—both of us still awake but pretending not to be—his fingers started moving all over my stomach, real soft. I turned toward him, still pretending to be sleeping and he lifted himself up and kissed me on the mouth; and he did it surprisingly well, with his lips closed first but then slowly opening, his tongue coming after me, though he too was a kid, maybe at most fourteen. His hands started moving all over the front of me then, he was super excited, and after a minute or two he pulled my shirt back and put my breast in his mouth, my nipple, and sucked it, and then his hands were moving down my pants, were right over my crotch when I stopped him. I don't know why, I just felt like I was supposed to; he was just a kid. Plus, M was in the very next room, after all.

And then I got this creepy sense, like maybe M was watching, had been watching all along, and so I whispered at Mateo to stop. Shhhh, I said, we're supposed to be sleeping. And I took his hand and calmed him and then he fell asleep while I held his long fingers in mine, and I guess I fell asleep then too.

But then that boy started acting like he loved me or something and I had to ignore him a bit. I was seventeen by then and Mateo was just a kid.

One day, soon after, we went to his house. M had some business or other there, and he took me, or maybe we'd just been invited over to eat? and so we went, but when we got there I felt instantly sick. We walked in and his mother was real sweet, I remember that, running her hands through my hair and telling me I had beautiful eyes and then she fed me and *the doctor* the most amazing pork in green sauce I had ever had, but then I was instantly sick. My head, and I felt very tired too. All of a sudden. So Mateo starts acting like he's my boyfriend, tells his mother he'll take care of me, though my dad's supposed to be a doctor, and I notice the way he's acting though I don't know if anyone else does. So he walks me to the little guest room in back and settles me in bed, really takes good care of me, running to get me a glass of water in case I get thirsty and some pills for my head.

And then he sits at the side of the bed and starts caressing my arm, and tries to lean down to kiss me and I have to tell him I really just need to rest. And I just knew he thought he was my boyfriend or something. And then it all felt like a bit too much for me. I lay there in that bed and I had a sort of vision, me growing old in that town with this young boy. We would be married when he turned fifteen or sixteen or whatever the legal age was in that tiny backward town and he would take really good care of me until I croaked in this nothing town of Cruces.

And I decided to get the hell out of there. I thought about it all for a bit, all those young boys, how I really liked being the one in charge, and how they flocked to me, as if they knew it was possible the moment they looked at me. It felt good to be adored by all those boys, safe too, somehow, they were so sweet and young. And then I thought of M with that skinny very ugly straw haired woman of his, and his trying to get me to befriend the governor's niece, for what who knew, but I could absolutely imagine it only really had anything to do with how he might profit from it. And he had another kid too, with that skinny woman, and I haven't mentioned it yet because that baby disturbed me. It was always grabbing at him and running after him and calling him Papa and crying when he left. As if he paid it any mind at all when he was there; what was she crying about his leaving for? It was strange. He barely noticed her, but she wept when he left. I usually like kids all right, but that baby gave me the creeps, light blonde hair so that its huge head looked bald at more than two years old and its always runny nose. The way it would lick at its snot covered upper lip.

And so the next day I went and saw Clara and I told her I was leaving because she was making me fat. I'd gained something like five pounds in the month I'd been there. And then I went to see Juan and he asked if my father was running me out of town for competing with him and I called him an asshole, and he laughed his wicked laugh.

And then I asked M for some money and he gave it to me and I got on the very same buses, going back the way I came. I went home. I went home so I wouldn't get stuck there. I went home to Mexico City. I went home to Claudia.

Claudia

I TRIED PAINTING when I was seventeen, two years before the tragedy of M, the violence he caused me. It made my brother Felix very angry when I began. He was the real artist, he said, and it's true that even when we were quite small he was the one who drew while the rest of us played; while we chased each other, ran around screaming at each other, played hide and seek and got our feelings hurt with all the intricate games we made for excluding each other. While we skipped rope to sing song rhymes, *soltera, casada, vuida, divorciada, con hijos, sin hijos, no puede vivir, con uno, con dos, con tres…* on and on until we tripped up; he drew while we played hopscotch and climbed trees for hours and hours on end, while we threw balls at targets, *If it hits the first branch I will be rich; if it hits the second branch he loves me…* Felix sitting hunched over his paper, making whole little worlds of masked wrestlers in festooned rings, or tidy haciendas with men in boots and hats and animals in pens, everything clear and orderly, or else leotarded superheroes in big city landscapes. When he was a bit older, ten or so, he became obsessed with Tarzan, the movies we would watch on those endlessly boring Sunday afternoons, and so he began drawing jungles with many animals, chimps and tigers and elephants and zebras, trees and vines wrapping around them all, the pictures growing more and more ornate, extremely boy, and complex, until in some of them the entire page almost was an intricate lacework of jungle vines, the subject of the picture half hidden behind them.

Then when he was fifteen and I was seventeen I came along and started painting. And I was very good. It had been my mother's idea, an excellent way, she believed, to keep me busy and off the streets. She suggested I take a class with an old aunt of hers, her father's youngest sister; her father had been a great painter though he had died young, and his paintings hung in our house. His sister, her aunt, painted some too and taught three or four girls at once in her parlour, and though I protested loudly at first, I soon came to almost like it.

I only lasted in those classes about nine months, so not quite a year even. But I did learn. And I enjoyed going to buy my paints too, because I liked the boy who stretched the little canvases, an Indian boy a little older than me whose mother worked as a maid for the owner of the art supplies store near my aunt's house so that the boy had grown up with that owner as a father figure of sorts. That boy had thick black hair and almond shaped black eyes and big plump lips. He never spoke but he stared at me without pause whenever I came in, so I went back every few weeks to buy more paints or brushes, pencils, even if I didn't need them, or else to have him stretch a couple of canvases for me while I watched.

One day, while he was stretching a little canvas for me I walked up real close to him. His breath quickened, and I could almost see his chest jump with each hard pump of his heart.

You okay? I asked quietly.

He looked up and met my eyes but he didn't answer, so I got closer, almost touching, and when he didn't take his eyes off of me I took his hand off that canvas while holding his gaze and placed it between my legs and then pressed it there, hard, and then I led his hand inside my skirt and into my panties. He just held it there, his hand, without moving it at all for what seemed like a long long time, and as I was reaching my head in to kiss him I heard the owner's voice, and so I pulled his hand out and then stepped back a bit and let him finish stapling that canvas into place on its frame, a bit wobbly, as I watched.

The owner stepped into the room and greeted me in his overly friendly way, and then a few minutes later the boy was done and I paid.

Felix went crazy when I started painting, and of course this made it more fun for me. He would watch me work and his eyes would burn as he watched, his mouth twitching a bit.

You can't control your brush, those lines, he finally said one day, there's no distinction between foreground and background either.

At that point he was taking classes with an old man who was a friend of my great aunt's. My aunt Sabina only took girls, of course, plus she said Felix was too talented for her anyway so she sent my brother to that old man. He had studied in New York at the Art Student's League, and he was supposed to be very good. The old man lived alone and gave classes only to boys whom he hand picked from the many who came to seek him. I was always suspicious of that supercilious old man. He wanted my brother to go to an art academy in the south of the city near the University and Coyoacan, at which he himself taught once a week. He told my mother Felix could live there during the week, a kind of boarding thing so he wouldn't have to be going back and forth, but my father, on one of his visits from Oaxaca, said no.

I will not pay for my son to study to be an artist, he said very firmly when my mother and Felix presented the idea to him in his study after lunch one day. My father's dog, Abel, was there, asleep on the couch.

My mother and Felix pleaded with him, Please, Felix said. It's important to me. I heard his voice shake a bit from where I stood watching in the doorway and I thought to myself, How pathetic, he should be strong. And then Felix, in his shaky voice, added, It's the only thing I love.

Are you crazy? my father asked. All artists are delinquents, he said. Degenerates. Find something else to love, he said and turned his gaze away.

Abel stirred a bit, on his makeshift bed.

Felix took no notice of the dog, as he stood straight, staring at my father for a long long time, but my father continued ignoring him while he drank his coffee. He didn't even raise a hand to acknowledge him. After a very long and painful time Felix finally left the room.

My father and his dog went back to Oaxaca that night.

Of course Felix was furious. And he tortured the rest of us with his bad moods from then on. With his anger and his haughty disdain and superiority. With his shallow girlfriends who we had to put up with in succession and on a daily basis, and with his sick sensibility. The drugs.

But he did keep making art. I would be in the little room I'd made for myself on the roof terrace—I had set it up next to his much bigger studio in the service room on the roof, next to where Maria did our wash in those days—I'd be working there in my tiny room and he'd come over.

What are you doing? he asked the first time he came in.

What does it look like I'm doing? I answered.

It looks like you don't know what you're doing. It looks like you're doing nothing. In fact, it looks like you're wasting your time.

I think I'm doing just fine, thank you. Now why don't you go and draw your little jungle pictures and leave me alone if you don't mind. But instead of leaving he lay down on the mattress I'd had Maria help me lug up to nap on when I got bored of painting. He stared.

Go ahead, Miss Artiste, keep painting. Go on; if you were really into what you're doing you wouldn't be deterred by my presence. You wouldn't even sense I was here.

Go to hell, I answered.

I'm already there, he replied; and in some small way I felt that he was right. And then he continued to stare at me as I worked, which of course made me nervous, though I would never show it.

Eventually Felix got bored and went off; and then I quietly snuck over to his studio and watched him from the corner of his window. I went back to my room and copied what he did. His technique. He was more advanced than me; I knew that. But I was better with color. I knew what looked good with what, what could make your eye jump, what would fire it up, what could soothe it. I would put golds and pinks together to calm, red and orange right next to each other to excite, shades other people would never think to join. I could almost smell color sometimes, could taste it, and I knew what flavors went together well, what effect they would have, what would leave you wanting more, what could turn a stomach. I would start piling them there next to each other so that my mouth would pucker with the acidity, or drag with the rich like custard tones, line after thick line of different tones, textured to the point of gloppy. Felix would come in and he would be so angry at what I had done.

You're wasting paint, he would say sharply and I'd have to scream at him to leave me alone.

Get the hell out of here! Shit! I've told you a million times! I would yell.

One day, during one of my father's rarer and rarer visits home to see us, I brought him to my little room.

I want to show you something, Papa, I said after he'd had his coffee, his long serious talk with my mother downstairs.

Can I come? the eleven year old Adrian called out.

No, this is just for Papa, I answered, and then I looked at my father.

He agreed to climb the little stairway up to the roof, the stairway becoming tighter and smaller as we ascended, like a tunnel, his dog, Abel, whining a bit as we climbed, and then we went through the terrace door all three together, What, Girl? What god awful place are you taking me to? he asked. And I realized he had never been up to the service rooms.

I opened the door to my little room and showed him.

What is this? he asked while his dog sniffed about.

My paintings, I said. You're the first one to see them.

Are you crazy too? he immediately asked. Is this what you spend your days doing? What is wrong with all of you? he asked, his stupid dog looking up at me now, as if he too expected an answer. It's like you've all gone mad, he said. No one in this house has any discipline. Any ambition, any will to properly work! and he looked truly angry now. You better learn to type, Girl.

And then he told me to get rid of the paintings, to put the room back to what it was, to try and work my way back to some sense of decency; I wanted to yell at him and tell him it had been nothing but a junk room before, that he was no one to talk about decency, that he should be the one putting things back to what they were, but of course I said nothing. I swallowed it all and he stormed down the stairs, his stupid dog following on his heels, and I stayed up there for hours, fuming. But I didn't get rid of them. I left them there, those paintings.

Though it wasn't until after the tragedy of M, after I lost myself with M, after he dragged me back to my mother, dropped me there at her door in a drooling mass that I went back to them, my paintings. But at that point they no longer brought me any joy, and really only served to make me very very very sad. And then after about eight months of being back at my mother's house I tried painting again, attempted to get at what had made me so happy before, to force myself to feel, but the lines began taking over, then. I painted lines over and over again, though after months of this I realized I was not painting lines at all, but trees … over and over again, trees. They weren't lines at all. And I did this for about a year, until it began to make me extremely anxious, those trunks taking over the seemingly blank canvas, already present there before I even approached that surface, calling out to me to make them actual, to give them shape. Telling me what color to apply; I had no will in it at all. And then I would hear Rocio screaming and though I would try to ignore it sometimes I had to run down to see what was wrong.

During that time I did learn to type as well, because, though I was often very angry at my father, I did try to listen to him. I did. He was a wise man. A good successful man. I had to. He was my father. I had to listen. The painting made me very anxious but the typing I could do blind, without thought, just a series of motions, my fingers flying on the keyboard without thinking, and I liked that. I learned to type on a machine my mother bought me after my father yelled at her, and I was very very fast. Very soon, in fact, I was much faster than my mother. And accurate. I could do anything, I knew then. I could do anything as long as there was no thought. My mother got me a job at the National Palace. After his new woman the little money my father gave my mother was no longer enough. We all needed to work now. Though Felix never got a job, the rest of us worked. I myself would work a job for a year or two, give it up. Not work for a while, and then when I felt I needed to work again, or when my mother told me I had to, I simply moved to another department. There were always plenty of jobs then, plus I was smart and quick and so I always got hired fast. Though after a while I would again get bored. I would go off with my friends, to Acapulco, or Ixtapa, and I would lose my job. And then, before long, I had three daughters. I would move around a lot. Sometimes I would take them with me. Sometimes I would leave them with their grandmothers. My mother. M's mother. This is how it was. It's just how it was. Then suddenly there were four daughters; three of them were M's.

I was often angry with my father, his going off to Oaxaca, the new woman, whom I saw many times, her kids who all had beautiful clothing and nice cars; they were not even my father's own children and they got everything that was rightfully mine. She was never a wife, nevertheless she got everything that was rightfully mine.

I was very often angry at my father. But there were reasons. He came from Oaxaca once, in the early days after he'd gone there, and he had a doll for me. He held her out toward me, that doll. She was beautiful and I wanted her very badly, even though my mother thought I was getting much too old for dolls. I eagerly reached out for her before he fully handed her down to me, my arms flying out to touch. She was so pretty, her lovely lovely hair.

You can not play with it, he said. You must not even really touch it. He held her up high where I could not reach her. She is porcelain, he said. That means she is very delicate. You will break her. She must sit in your room, he said, on your dresser, he said. And she will watch everything that you do. So don't be dirty. Or bad. Don't be a bad or dirty girl. The doll is always watching and you don't want her to be ashamed, do you?

And she was, always watching.

I went to Acapulco with M. This was before the hospitals. Or was it after? Rocio was already born, I believe, though we didn't bring her. She stayed with my mother, I believe. Was it before Julia? Did M come to pick me up from my mama's house for some time out together? Is that how it was? He would just show up and I would happily jump into one of his borrowed cars and off we would go, for a day, or a week, or sometimes longer; we never knew. I was still very much in love with him then, so that I would joyfully leap into those cars. And this time, on the beach near Acapulco, a hotel on the water, the vegetation tall and wild and tropical, viney green surrounding, nearly engulfing, the little cabanas, I stirred in the middle of the night. And I saw he was not there. I reached out to touch, but he was really gone. I was half asleep still and my heart started racing, and then I sat fully up, awake now. I searched the bed more closely. Where was he? I rose, my skin buzzing, and in my long white nightgown I walked around the little pink room and then stepped out into the star filled night. I remember I saw a shooting one, that star falling long and blue and bright in that night sky, and I felt it was good luck. I stopped and made a wish, though I was very frightened, my heart racing, because I believe you must, you must take a wish that is offered to you. And as soon as I had made my wish I registered the crashing waves, loud, hard and black and loud as they are on the Pacific. I watched their dark violence play itself out upon the soft white shore for several minutes, scared, my heart thumping, not sure of myself, of my footing, and then I began wandering the gray beach all around me, and soon I was rushing around the rocks and inlets and cliffs which were lit silver by the moon, looking for him. I called out a couple of times, my voice a tremulous red, Miguel? Miguel Angel? But there was no answer. And then after another long while of this middle of the night silver light wandering, my heart having settled a bit, my senses having gotten used to the outside, my eyes having adjusted to the murky night, I heard voices. I nearly called out again, but decided not to and held it in tight instead. I crouched, like a nervous blue detective, and moved toward those whispering sounds, those dark night metallic sounds. And as I got closer I heard it was a man and a woman, and possibly another man too; were there two distinct male voices? And then through that nearly black night dim silver light I saw them, him, her, another man, bodies purple, their legs intertwined, moving, rising, falling, whispers and laughter, a moaning, a gasp, a low sound of choking. I ran, weeping scared, back toward my room, though I must have been wandering for over an hour before I'd come upon them there, in the midst of that wild act, mud green, surrounded by jungle; and I was not quite sure where I now was or how to get back.

I did find my way to the hotel and as I began moving between the cottages, trying to find the path to ours, I saw him, walking slowly in the night, a body calm, not wildly rushing as I was.

Hello, that man whispered softly as he approached me.

I answered back.

You okay? Where are you going? his deep dark voice asked.

To my room, I answered. His hand went out vermilion then, no further words; that stranger's hand reached out and he remained silent as he grabbed my nipple through my thin white nightgown and he squeezed it tight and I looked slowly up from his brown hand there on my breast and into his black eyes and he stared back at me with a firmness in those leaden eyes which matched the grip of his fingers and then he moved in toward me and kissed; and I let him. We fell to the sand there in between those pink cabanas, the green vegetation all around us, and he made love to me for a long long time, silently, not saying a word the whole time. And I was silent too.

And then he lay on top of me, inside of me, for whole minutes before kissing me one last time and slowly rising.

I have to go back to my room, he whispered.

Yes, I answered back.

And when I got back to my own room M was still gone. And the next morning we both pretended he had been there sleeping the whole night.

I am not happy about it. Any of it. But you must believe it wasn't me. You understand? There were no choices made. I didn't decide a thing, for it was M, mostly, my reacting to him. I don't know how to make you see what it is to not be able to think, or to think so much, rather, so rapidly about so many many things that you know you cannot begin to sort it, you cannot rest on any one thing, make sense of it and sort it, and you know too that to stop, you know that in order to stop it all from coming, you will have to cease the breathing and then maybe you can make a choice to stop the rushing thinking, this living. It won't stop until you cease. Your mind spins and rushes and goes to so many dark places, terrifying spaces, and spins and spins there more, and will not let you sleep. Did you know you can forget how to sleep? That you can go days, weeks sometimes, without a single moment of sleep. That breathing becomes difficult too, must become a conscious thing, like a decision each time; it catches inside you, your breath; in you must tell yourself. Now out. Your mind tells you that you might do something, that you might hurt something, yourself or someone; it counts off all the things you've done wrong, tells you *everything* you do is wicked, that all of it is bad and sinful, that you tend toward evil, that you are a dirty shameful being, that you are nothing but a thing; it tells you over and over again so that in order to stop it, you feel, if you are going to ever stop it, you feel, you yourself must stop; otherwise it will not end, and you know that it must cease. Your skin burns. It is burning. Under your skin too. It buzzes. It is buzzing, a rapid constant buzz, a burn. It must cease. But then, in the moment of turning on the gas, or of closing yourself off in your mother's garage, you were in your mother's garage, you turned the car on, doors closed, you were letting it run, the car, but then you saw them there before you, your children, your daughters, even the ones you have given away, you saw their faces, all four of your daughters, their eyes; you see their eyes, all of that confusion, there in them; they are weeping, and you must think of them, and of your mother too, wandering down to the car in her garage, of your sister seeing you there, slumped and fully defeated, completely defeated by life, by your sick life. Or into the apartment the other time you tried it, you imagine them walking into that long ago apartment, with that gas pouring out, Rocio, a toddler, asleep in her bed. Was the other one already inside you? You become confused that he is there, and so you turn it off, the gas, or he does it for you and then he leads you into bed where, though he seems angry, he climbs upon you, and there is a relief; there is a relief in that; but that other time, the second time you try it, it is you, you who turn the car off, your own determination, you who crawl back into bed in shame, by yourself, to your bed where your mind races and does not let you sleep; if only there were someone there to climb upon you, like the last time, like that other time you tried it, then you would not have time to think. And you die like this many many times, you die like this every night, every single night for months, many many months. Remembering it, thinking it, pondering it, your death. A death that never comes to give you peace so that sometimes when you forget what it is to breathe you hold yourself in that position, that not knowing how to breathe, you hold yourself there in that blank, trying hard to stay in that place of not knowing, an easy blameless end then, it would be, no sign of fault, you believe; but, somehow, you always breathe in. Out and then in, though you do not want to, out and then in yet again.

Julia

I WAS ALMOST SEVENTEEN when I was sent away from my uncle David's for good, by his wife, whose paranoid rage had fully taken over by then. Her need to control had become overwhelming and showed in how she dressed me, like a little girl still at sixteen, in how angrily she yelled at me if I walked in the door five minutes late, in those enforced little dresses; I was sixteen and I was in her home and she was not my mother and I had breasts.

And then, in her terrible anger, she finally made me leave for good. My uncle David had tears in his eyes when he stepped into my room to tell me. He stared at me for a few sorrow filled minutes before speaking. He told me I must go. I know, I mouthed. He stood just inside the doorway to my room. I looked at him from where I sat, on my bed and found my voice, I know, I whispered. He walked over to me and I stood up and he hugged me tightly, and wanting only to make it all vanish, I shut my eyes hard and hugged him back.

Soon, and very suddenly, I was on a plane with everything I owned in one suitcase; confused and bewildered I arrived in Mexico City. I would be staying at my grandmother's house. Though things were different now, for I would be there much longer, at least a full year, until I turned eighteen. At eighteen I would be an adult, I believed. I would be able to do anything, go anywhere, I believed. All roads would finally be clear and open and easy, I foolishly believed, and I would choose between those paths and wander, strong and free.

I ended up staying at my grandmother's for only one month. Though, looking back on it now, I wish I had never left there, had never ventured to my mother's house, where, like a girl in a fairy tale who must learn her difficult lessons slowly, I would spend a terrifying year. Flailing about in the deep dark forest that was my mother.

Very quickly it was revealed that my grandmother's home had been transformed into something silent, no more aunts and uncles in vital activity, which, even in the fighting, had a sure, deep draw. My uncles had moved in with girlfriends or wives. My sister Rocio had gotten married months before I arrived. My aunt Sofia had moved out too; Sandra, more often than not, stayed with Sofia. And all of this made it easy for me to leave that quiet house.

I was nearly seventeen. And my mother and Marta had their own apartment.

The first time I visited them there I took the subway. I snaked through the city's undergrounds and then walked up and out toward their place. It was a dark, cloudy day, the wind blowing all around me. I stopped at the corner store before going up, to get something to drink and a pack of these cinnamon covered cookies I especially loved, for I wanted a further moment to myself before entering their place, and felt the need to feed myself something sweet. The ancient woman behind the counter handed my cookies to me, her bony hand shaking as she did so. I carefully placed the money in her empty palm—which she partially unfurled to receive it, like an open claw—and walked quickly out while she continued to stare at me, clenching that money tight. When I came out of the bodega there was a guy with shoulder-length hair leaning back against the wall. You look lost, he said. And I guess I did, gazing up at the buildings all around me, searching out their address from where I stood. He was thin and not too tall and had soft-looking brown hair and almost black dark eyes. Without speaking I reached my hand out toward him, showed him where I had it written down, their address, and he pointed to a building across the wide boulevard before leaning back a bit to take a more serious look at me, slow and long. He then moved his head forward so that some of his hair fell on my shoulder and in a quiet voice he asked who I was going to visit, like it was a naughty secret.

My mother, I said, pulling back from him, though his draw had held me there for a second, as if he were a magnet. And though he was handsome—beautiful olive skin, and I knew I could have kept talking to him there forever, slow and easy, leaning back against that wall myself, joking and laughing and avoiding my debt—I turned and walked away, for I felt I had revealed myself.

His hair had fallen upon my arm, his warm breath spreading near my neck, deep and meaningless at the same time.

I felt his eyes still on me as I pulled at the front door he had pointed to, and I imagined him pointing still. I felt that if I turned to look back the old woman from inside the store would be standing there next to him, the two of them hunching into each other, laughing at me, at what awaited me, before transforming into two large ravens, circling the sky above, dark guides in what would soon befall me.

An older heavy-set man wearing red suspenders and a big open smile took the door from my hand and held it open for me before walking out himself. I tried to smile back though I felt near tears and so it came out as a grimace, and then I climbed the steps of that apartment building; and as I climbed my stomach felt increasingly sick. Soon I was so overcome I thought I might throw up but though my stomach was balling and cramping I forced myself forward because I knew there was no way back. I knew I would keep climbing those stairs no matter what I felt, as if my legs were leading me without consent. I leant my head down and breathed in and out three, four, five times. I tried to breathe deeply, to hold that breath down inside myself, though that made me feel somehow worse, the forced clear intention of it. I didn't know why I was suddenly sweating, but my heart was racing now too; I had no idea how I should feel at all and a part of me wanted to cry from the confusion and a part of me was angry that I could not simply feel happy that soon I would be seeing my mother, spending an afternoon with her. She was my mother. Why was I always so baffled, so overcome by my own emotions? I grabbed the banister to steady and I tried to force myself to feel a certain kind of joy then.

The apartment buildings on that block were all plain and simple modernist ones, four or five stories high at most. It was at the southern end of a nice neighborhood, and the fact that they were workers' apartments, provided by Pfizer for their better employees, meant that the places themselves were okay, though they were not particularly attractive.

I looked out a long rectangular opening in the wall, an odd shaped window which rose with the staircase, and through it saw a black cat climb along the ledge of the building across the way, like a tightrope walker, inching from the window of one apartment onto the balcony of another, and though I was scared for it and found myself holding my breath as I watched, it simply mewled joyfully as it made a circus leap and then landed gracefully on that other balcony where its bowl of food sat. Upon landing it began to greedily gulp.

I had just seen them two nights before at my grandmother's house, when I'd arrived from Los Angeles in a kind of stupor, reeling from my final days there, my uncle David's wife sitting me down in front of her while she threw ten years of my life into trash bins as I watched, my books and clothes and letters and toys, and still I was anxious. Marta and Claudia had always been able to make me nervous, of course, especially when they were together. The last time I'd been in Mexico City was when I was thirteen, and clearly things were different now; much had changed in those four years, though that same feeling had remained, an anxiousness that the two of them caused to rise inside me. The moment I walked in the door, my sister on the other side of it, a threshold I was conscious of even as I was stepping through it, everything felt vastly different. This difference had to do with the echoing cold spareness of the space, stone floors and mostly unfurnished, two nearly empty bedrooms and several long hallways, a living room with no curtains and only a stiff couch and small turntable in it; and though it was not small, that apartment, the air felt close and tight. But mostly this difference, as well as my discomfort, had to do with them, how intently they watched me, as if drawing me through that wicked threshold with their gaze—my sister's hungry eyes staring at me with a mixture of disdain and desire that made me almost shiver, an eagerness tinged with rivalrous loathing. And how immediately dark their humor was, how mocking of everything around them they instantly were. My mother in black velvet slacks and a burgundy sweater, her deep dark eyes setting themselves heavily upon me, a dim grin spreading at her mouth.

"Did you run into Humpty?" she asked as she approached. I must have looked confused, but then realized my mother meant the man who'd kindly held the door open for me. "Dumpty. The super. Filthy red suspenders?" And when I nodded a bit to acknowledge that I had indeed seen him she went on, "He's as stupid as he looks. I'll introduce you ten times before he remembers you. You'll see."

Within minutes they had told me about the "old witch" in number three with whom they were constantly fighting over noise in the stairwell; they then went on to the "stupid hippie girl" who, addicted to the drugs her father pedaled for Pfizer, had committed suicide just a month before, "Flower power, indeed," my mother said.

I stared as they talked. They were a tight little unit, swirling around their own shadowy nucleus; and I was frightened of them.

I knew what they could get into. What they thought of as normal, how much further out their idea of that concept was than it was for me. It was all written in the air in that apartment; and yet, I felt a certain pull from my mother, my blood warming. Besides, anything went here I knew: anything I wanted to do or think was okay, and after the mean and binding tightness of my uncle David's wife this sense was not only liberating, it was thrilling.

———

We sat and talked, or, rather, they talked while I awed at their acrid sharpness, though I laughed too sometimes. We went out to eat at a sidewalk café and Marta stared at me, sizing me up suspiciously. I nervously tore my napkin into little pieces while I scanned the street, avoiding her eyes; soon a group of guys walked by and my mother said, Hello Handsome, addressing all four of them as a single unit. Marta knew them a little and when one of them made some comment about her red jeans she said, Nice, no? Keep your eyes in your head Big Boy, and my mother laughed along. They exchanged glances, for the game was between them, mother and daughter, the boys some kind of instrument. I looked awkwardly away when one of them asked Marta who I was. My sister, she replied, as if he was an idiot for even asking. I'd had to sneak my time with boys in Los Angeles; this was unbelievable, my mother leaning into the conversation as we flirted, opening up a space for me and Marta to enter into. The thrill continued growing inside me as I further grasped that here I could be anything, go anywhere, think and do what I wanted. I was turning seventeen and the world was suddenly open. My mother leaned in and put her arm around me, drawing me closer as she laughed, and I leaned into her too and from her arms I smiled over at the boy who had asked my sister about me. He smiled back, You could be sisters too, he said. And my mother lit up.

I was happy then, for those few hours, though the queasiness in my stomach returned the moment I walked out of their apartment, as if there were a dark spell there which lifted once I re-crossed the threshold to the outside. As if the excitement my mother created in me, the sick desire, vanished as soon as I was past the pull of her blood, when a sort of clarity could once again descend.

––––––

Soon I was living with them.

As I said, my aunt Sofia had moved out of my grandmother's by then, plus she had a husband and a child now, a beautiful two year old son who took up all her time; and I rarely saw Sandra, who in previous years had followed me around like a little shadow; she was now always at Sofia's too, practically lived there with them, a part of that family. And Rocio had moved away as well, was now living with Julian. They'd set up their little home and her sweet baby, Sara, was softly cooing at six months old. So it made sense, somehow, for me to move in with Claudia and Marta, my mom still young and beautiful herself, and Marta only a year younger than me. I moved in with them and pretty soon Marta and I had boyfriends, and Claudia was occasionally sleeping with the brother of one of them who was only a few years older than us.

There were other men too, in and out of Claudia's life, of our apartment, doors opening and shutting, in the middle of the night, a pretense at tiptoeing, abrupt laughter, giggly shushing, odd sounds from bedrooms, from bathrooms, male bodies moving shirtless through our space, a quick and awkward glance as they slipped in and out of doors with their shoes in hand.

I never questioned it; for none of us really questioned anything. Or if we did, I don't recall it.

In the dream I am five years old and deeply confused by the sight of my grandmother Cecilia leaning over the kitchen sink, weeping. My mother stands over her, ten feet tall, a sad and looming shadow. "What have I done wrong?" my grandmother asks, and my mother's heavy arms reach toward her as the floor opens up, a hole rapidly spreading; it swallows them both. I cry out. I am in a prim white dress and I weep, running down the long hallway in a panic. But then I throw myself down, as if I know I can't escape it, know that the ground will swallow me up too; and that gaping hole draws nearer. I am in it now, falling, falling, and though she has not yet been born, my sister tumbles on top of me, Sandra and me falling through that darkness forever.

A year later I was gone. At six years old I was a world away from all of their confusion, from all of their confounding tears. I was gone, quietly disappearing into myself in the United States with my uncle David.

What did we do all day long? Maybe Claudia worked, some of the time. I did work part of that year, five hours a day at the National Palace, as a hostess, a job my grandmother had gotten for me. The girls from my department and I would stand, evenly spaced, at political meetings, looking pretty, that's all that was needed, teenage decorations, long hair and bright red lipstick, high heels too. At twenty-two Carmen was the oldest, and seemed almost ancient to us. We spent most of our time in the office, chatting, gossiping, waiting for a call.

I loved the Diego Riveras in that royal building and alone I'd go visit them often, all of Mexican history depicted on those walls, the feathered serpent Quetzalcoatl, and that so beautifully idealized by Rivera Aztec past; Cuahtemoc attempting to appease Cortes and the devastation that followed, a Spaniard branding an Indian in the face there in the left hand corner, mere chattel, followed by Trotsky and Zapata and the revolution on the tall wall in the stairwell. The artists too are in the stairs, Frida and Rivera himself, and Siquieros. There is also depicted the hoped for successful merging of those two cultures, the Spanish and the Indian, into something that could become a just and thriving future. Through a merging of those two deadly pasts. But can a phoenix rise from such dark and violent devastation? I spent a lot of time looking at the section which showed what this very center, the heart of Mexico City, had once been, the canals the Indians built on that lake because the eagle with the snake had told them to do so, there in the middle of that water, those liquid thoroughfares going on and on into the distance, the temples and the busy open markets; and there among all those people the Aztec women with babies wrapped in shawls sleeping innocently on their backs. When the Spaniards arrived they were surprised by this city, for it was larger and more well organized than any they'd seen in Spain. This fairy-tale past was my favorite section of that long mural, a sweet and dreamy Mexican fable.

At night we hung out with our boyfriends, Marta and I, with Elias and his friend Mario.

And when they'd come over we'd go out, inevitably leaving Mario's brother, Francisco, there with our mother, the two of them locked in her room.

There were loads of kids who hung in big fluid groups, and gossiped and teased and flirted and hurt each other deeply. There were lots of parties and when there weren't we went to clubs, me and Marta, though I would come home early most of the time, long before her and her friend Anna.

There was something truly wrong with Anna. She scared me more than Marta, even, because there was something I can only call an emptiness in her, something like a gaping hole. I cannot say what it was. You'd show up at her house wearing tight corduroy jeans, high heels and a loose sweater, bright red lipstick, and the very next time you'd see her she'd be dressed the same way. She bought the same eyeliner, cut her hair just like mine. She was searching for something and because of this something, this lack, she was willing to do anything, go anywhere. Marta was wild, and she was terrifying too, but even Marta wasn't like that, vacant and wanting to be filled with anything, anything. Marta was crazy, but it was on her own terms. Marta was different; she didn't care what people thought. She did what she wanted. I would watch my sister at those clubs, dancing with a wild abandon, flinging her body about as if it were not hers, an object to be cast out, to be hurled and wiped out, the lights flashing on it, on her, her hair whipping, while our mother went crazy at home.

Anna was wild too, but it was that hollowness, that need to fill that really unnerved me, because it felt as if it had no origin.

Her face was pale, and her long hair golden; she was pretty, but you never thought so. Nobody ever thought so.

And, as if to save my soul, I was always leaving in the middle of those nights out. Anna sitting empty, and Marta dancing wild. And though I knew it made them angry, I would run off by myself.

Yes, I was scared. They frightened me. They did.

I know what limitlessness is. It was during that year that I saw it in Claudia. I know what not stopping looks like, what not having an outline is, a boundary, an inside which ends at the edges. I know what not having edges is. I have seen it, that lack of line.

On a bus once, my mother began talking about Lorca, his death at the hands of the fascists in Spain; I was thrilled as she spoke, for I had just recently read him and loved his spare poetry. I think she went on to tell me about his love for Dalí, about his depression; did she mention hers to me then? Am I remembering this right? Was my mother aware at some level of what it was she had? Had she seen a shaman once? Had they talked about it all? Had he given her advice? We started listing all the things we both liked, our favorite childhood book, *Alice in Wonderland*, though she had read it in Spanish; our favorite band, The Beatles, though I was listening to other things then, David Bowie and Iggy Pop and X and The Fall; she said she wanted me to listen to Sylvio Rodriguez and Joan Manuel Serrat, socialists both; we had not ever lived together, really, and look at all we had in common! We both loved to read, shared too a favorite story, Erendira, Garcia Marquez. We were both insomniacs… and I couldn't have been happier in that moment, on that bus, riding high above those streets of Mexico City. My mother was an insomniac too!

It moved me deeply, weeks later, when she told me she'd wanted to be a painter, but that her father had not allowed her to even try. I had thought I might want to study art myself, go back to the states and study the history of art after my year there in Mexico City. When I was eighteen. One day we went together to look at Omniscience, the Orozco mural in the Alameda; she treated me to a fancy lunch at a place where this mural lines the staircase, a huge Indian with a long black braid looking down on us from that tall wall; and it was as if we were the only ones there. I reached for her hand then, as we looked up at him.

Sometimes, at night, we would listen to music together, my mother and I, sitting on the stone floor in front of the record player in that empty apartment, silly stuff, corny stuff, Cat Stevens and the Beatles and Bread, she singing those lyrics in her thick accent. But these were simply moments. Though they were instances of joy, each, what I was always trying to get back to, they were not what was most there, what made up most of our real day to day. For, what was mostly there, of course, was something else entirely.

What was there between them? I would look in on them, in bed together in the middle of the day. I never understood it, but they looked happy. Like the lovers I would later see in Godard, lazy love, Patricia and Michel in *Breathless*, him fiddling about with the covers while she holds her teddy bear, Michel asking her to take off her top while she speaks about Romeo and Juliet. Meaningless dialogue, a series of non sequiturs, none of it amounting to much other than the game of the talk and the physicality of being together. This is what Claudia and Marta were like in bed, unfettered, their legs flopping all over each other as they gossiped about this or that, created an insular language that only they were allowed into. A limited access. Marta calling my mother an idiot, my mother wondering aloud who might lend them money, Marta replying that everyone hated them both and would never give her a dime, insisting my mother beg her job back. Good-bye, I would say, leaning in to give my mother a kiss as Marta watched with withering eyes. I would leave and go to work. And sometimes when I came back six hours later they would be there, where I had left them, laughing or angrily calling each other names.

And then Marta suddenly stopped going out with me. For many weeks she stayed indoors. As if she were truly sick she spent all her time in bed, sometimes alone, sometimes with my mother. I started to go out with the girls from work, none of whom would have ever understood what I lived with my mother. We would go to bars or to parties in their different neighborhoods and I would come home very late sometimes. And on this night I yelled at my mother.

I was scared and I was tired and I told her to stop it, and then I told her to go. I pushed her out the door and I told her to go. I had been living with them for about six months at that point. And she hadn't been right for a while. When Marta and I would come home from those clubs, we would have her to deal with, Marta often exploding upon our arrival, jutting her angry face down into Claudia's and letting her have it. But when it was just me coming home late, Marta in bed all those weeks, I would alone open the door to be greeted by her gaunt ghostly face. By her wan body like an empty husk wandering the apartment alone in the night. And I would quietly, and repeatedly, lead her back into her bed.

And on this night I had already been asleep for two or three hours when her noises woke me, so I rose to look out at what it was she was doing. I stood at the threshold to the livingroom and saw that her fingers were bleeding from where she'd bitten her nails down to a nub; and she was getting ready to walk out the front door. It was just after dawn and as I walked over to where she was she looked at me and opened and closed the door three times, hesitant, halting. This had been going on for over a month at that time, maybe two. This lack of sleeping, this staring like death, this lips moving to form words which were then never spoken, this terror in the deep drawn eyes. I would wake up sometimes with her standing over me, wake up not knowing how long she'd been staring down at me as I slept. I had been tending this slippage for many many weeks; and I was tired. Still, I dragged myself over to where she stood. Where are you going? I asked. They are after me again, she whispered, truly frightened. Her shaky voice grew rushed as she continued, They would find her and if she didn't leave they'd get Marta and me too. She had to leave. Who, I asked her. And then, exhausted and growing upset at her stupefied silence I repeated it: Who? Her lips moved, but she was too undone to speak and so no sound came out; her lips kept struggling to form the words for a while, but then she stopped and looked into my eyes, searching for the answer, a confused child. I was trying not to yell, was trying not to wake Marta who was always so furious at my mother. But she was worse than I'd yet seen her, her eyes the eyes of weeks of non-sleep; and I felt very lost. She raised her gaze again so that she was staring just above my head. And still she did not answer. I turned away from her and then she did go on, her words coming out in terrified whispers, one at a time, hushed, as if someone might hear her. I looked at her to understand. They. They were coming for her and she had to leave. She said it slowly. One word, then another. Till there was a full sentence. A sentence of lunacy punctuated by that slightly swinging door. Her fingertips bloody. Grabbing at that wooden surface. She held that door tight in her hand and swung it, back and forth, back and forth, bloody back and forth in between her broken words. I looked from her, out the window, and saw that black cat, walking his fine line again, between ledge and balcony, and a part of me wished it would fall. Fine, I told her in a measured, controlled voice. But you wait till Marta wakes up. You go and wake her and tell her. Or you wait till she's up and you tell her yourself that you're going, because I will not for you. I will not do that for you. But... I... have... to... go.... Stop it, I said loudly. Loudly now. She did stop, scared, and then she stared into my eyes again. She blinked once. Then twice, and tried to form a word, though again her voice would not come. Fine, go. Go! I yelled. And I grabbed her by her hand; I grabbed her bloody swinging hand and made her let go of the door and I pushed her out. I pushed her out and yelled at her again to go. I closed the door behind her.

Marta didn't wake up and after five painful minutes I opened the door and pulled her back in from where she stood, paralyzed, staring straight exactly where I'd left her. Her lips trembled a little when I reached out to pull her in, as if I might hit her. It's okay, I said. You're okay.

I led her then, back to her bed, and for what seemed like the thousandth time that month, I lowered her in and tucked her blanket around her face. Go to sleep, I whispered. And then I leaned down and kissed her on the forehead.

Her eyes were wet, though she was not exactly crying.

The next morning I went up to the service room on the flat roof of that building. The staircase rose all the way up the five stories and at the top I found a stick which I placed in the door so it would not shut behind me. And I sat there by myself, hoping the super would not come up. I could see the bodega from up there. I imagined that long haired boy leaning back against its wall. I imagined myself there beside him, imagined myself staring into his dark eyes; I imagined kissing him, my hair fanning out and covering both of our faces, our bodies pressing together hard to disappear. I looked up above that bodega and could see the city stretching far and wide around me. I looked down again and saw that black cat on its little balcony, laid out by his empty food bowl. And then up and out again beyond the bodega I could see the tall buildings near the center. And I knew that there was a whole world out there, waiting for me.

I looked back toward the old colonial center where I worked, at the National Palace in the Zocalo. And I knew that in a few hours I would be there, a couple of offices down from my grandmother, whom I would go and greet during my break; I would kiss her warmly and I would feel the deep love flow there between us. Maybe we would share a coffee, without my mentioning my mother.

Three days later I ran gasping into their bedroom, the sound of Marta's yells calling me in. She was screaming at Claudia as I ran in. She was on top of my mother, straddling her. And she was slapping my mother repeatedly in the face.

"What is wrong with you?!" she yelled. "What?! What?" Marta shouted as she shook her, trying to force a response.

"Stop it!" I grabbed at her arms and made Marta stop and she turned on me then.

"What the fuck do you know!? You know nothing! You don't know anything about her! Or me! Or anything!"

And then the next day she was gone.

I came home a few days later, with a small present for my mother. I went to hand her the little earrings as I walked in. I brought you something, I whispered, and my mother stared at me, her eyes wide with fear. Here, I said. And I carefully took them out of the package and placed the pink coral earrings in her hand. They were carved in the shape of a rose. Aren't they pretty? I asked her. My mother nodded without looking at them, pressing down on those earrings hard, They'll look nice on you, I said. She continued to stare at me blankly, rolling them in her fingertips over and over again, pressing down as I asked her how she felt. She didn't answer and I looked down at her hand which I saw was still rolling and pressing very hard. What are you doing? I asked. Her fingers were now bleeding. Can I have those? I asked her. I can put them in your room for you, and my mother nodded, staring at me like a terrified child.

It would be another two weeks, Claudia not getting any better, before I went to my grandmother's to have the conversation I needed to have with her, another two weeks before she came and gathered my mother up and took her home to her bed. Another two weeks in which, alone, I watched my mother disintegrate in that empty apartment.

After they were both gone I continued to live in that apartment for three more months alone, and it was then I slept with Pablo. We spent the afternoon at the park and then he'd walked me home and as soon as we walked through the door he kissed me on the mouth and then he undressed me. And very quickly we were in bed and he looked at me for a long time there and then he lay himself on top of me and he turned my face toward his, staring into my eyes, deep into them, as he worked his way into me, whispering words I could not hear. Afterward he kissed and kissed my mouth, and placed his face in my neck, but then went suddenly silent. And—when I felt Pablo pulling away from me in that silence, after the love we had just made in that bed, him staring into my eyes, deep into them as he entered me, whispering words I could not hear—I ruined it with him as well.

I had never slept with anyone before, and it had meant something to me. But now I felt him suddenly distant, analytical, cold. He said something about the way I'd made love, how strongly felt, which I took to mean I was practiced, and this deeply hurt me.

"I gave myself to you," I said. And when he continued to stare without answering I repeated it, "I just gave myself to you."

And then, not able to stand his silence, feeling it as a judgment, I blurted it out, "Have you slept with my mother?" And he dropped his hand from my hair; and when he looked away and didn't answer I continued, my mouth speaking the words without my knowing what it was saying, "Is that it? Because she ruins everything, you know." He stayed quiet, "Have you slept with her?" I asked again.

I have lived all of my life like there is a catastrophe waiting to happen, and if it does not come I am afraid that I will make it happen. There is something about being here on Long Island, where days are slow and silent which makes me see this clearly. I am here, writing, but I am here disappearing as well. For I have always craved the disappearance; I can feel it in my body, now and then. I catch myself breathing in low shallow breaths, barely taking oxygen, just enough to survive. I see it when I'm lying in bed, unable to move, for hours sometimes, unable to draw myself up, until Joshua, my patient and beautiful dog, begins to whine with what sounds like real concern. It is only then that I am able to go to the paper, go to the pen, my hand finally beginning to scrawl, in the end Joshua awakening my desire to leave a mark and with his whine vanquishing my darker desire to vanish.

I miss Margaret too, I do, her sweet shy smile. I miss her patient, slow enunciation, so much like Sandra's. I miss baking with her and putting puzzles together, the way she would squeal when we finished one. I miss swimming with her in the pool and in the Sound, the way her long red hair would fan out around her. I think Joshua misses her too.

One day when we were sitting by the side of the pool she turned to me and said, "I'm happy."

We'd had breakfast together and then had changed into our suits. We washed berries to bring out by the pool. We jumped in and swam together, me doing laps, she diving and somersaulting and occasionally calling to me to watch some new trick she'd figured out, "Julia! Julia, look!" I clapped and clapped when she was able to do three underwater somersaults without coming up for air. I was truly impressed. She beamed at me, proud at the accomplishment. When we pulled ourselves out of the pool we saw that the berries were covered in ants, "Uck!" she shrieked and then we both laughed as we poured water over the berries to try to save them. Minutes later, as we lay on our towels eating those soggy berries by the side of the pool she turned to me and said, "I'm happy."

I looked at her little hand as it pushed the hair back away from her face, her sweet eyes blinking up at me. "Me too," I said. "I'm happy too."

And now I am here, alone, and I am forcing myself to finish this book because I believe I cannot do it. Because I cannot sustain a thing. All around me there is failure. It's the place from which I start. Its in the choices I make. In the choices I inevitably make. Everything a failure. I am childless. But how could I have had a child? And I see that it is me who has always been terrified of having one. It's in the choices I make. It was clear in Joaquin, in plain sight. He did not want a child. He was clear from the beginning. And still I chose him. And then I insisted on a child, though I had known all along he did not want one.

I see it like a film, a series of quick cuts, our mother with Francisco, doors closing, locks turning, the sound of shutting themselves in, Marta marching forward in her short skirt, late at night, wanting to devour as she pulls me by the arm, high heels, dancing wildly in some dark club, her hair flying. The voices floating, merging, droning in those bars, in the air, all around us;

mirrors turning, lights flashing, her body throbbing, flailing. Other hungers. The ease of forgetting, of the bodily taking over, of a desperate emptying pulsing in the air all around us, of feeling ourselves absent, of slaughtering the mind, of twisting the heart so as to live in the emptiness, of wanting that nothingness to live inside us. The sweetness of disappearing, of blanking out or being blanked. Anna's reflection, slow and glassy, in the mirrors all about us, men flocking in the dim, the lights flashing, moving, the blast of all that music, the beating, a wish to vanish, in the air and the smoke and the alcohol, loud music beating, the clawing, my mother wandering the halls, her eyes drawn, wan body, like death already, taken over. I see Anna in the red light laughing vacant, so hard she can barely hold herself together, Anna leaning forward, begging our attention, her face howling, her legs spreading, begging to be filled up, young men flocking, circling, myself always at the edges, a gazing out of windows, a searching, a scouring the outside, exterior, a dumb hope, a silly dreaming for something, anything, to come to me from else- where, a salvation, the music surging, people laughing, voices joining, me there but also distant and observing, always ready to escape. And then, finally, I am gone, running scared through the streets of Mexico City, cars flashing, headlights on me, whooshing taxis, rushing, my arm reaching, grasping for something, any- thing, running through the city haunted, feeling wicked and sullied and haunted, myself racing; I can see myself charging the final blocks to our apartment, through that city, the pale modernist buildings all around me, bolting away from my sister. But I am rushing forward too, I know, flying skin, toward my mother, feet not touching the ground, afraid of finding her not there, afraid of what she has further become while I've been away.

And so I see myself flying home to my mother, where she wanders senseless and alone, wanders those hallways, slowly falling apart.

An emptiness of being which is an overflow of too much. Too much, of torment and fear. Marta's hand rising in anger, connecting with her face, a bruise there I would tend the next day, while my mother stared at me with long sad eyes, a scared doe, those vacant drawn and startled eyes.

Yet this is when I could love my mother most. This is when, in her blanking out, in her emptying out, I could love her, her manic darkness gone, to be replaced by this, a husk. Me guiding her through the long dark halls of that apartment, tucking her in gently, she like a disappearing child, her eyes searchingly looking up at me, scared and wild, and blank, scared and blank and wild, my mother disappearing, a shell or a ghost; in her descent, this is when I could love her the most.

And then, when she was better, I left her, left them, left all of them, or felt forced to do so. I had begged her to explain it, how does one give a daughter away? How could you have given me away? How can a mother give her small child, her terrified daughter, away? Did she not know how I'd suffered? At dinner, we'd begun to fight, and I'd begged my questions at her, urging a response. She looked at me with dark scorn and she told me she'd spoken to Pablo. *He seems concerned in regard to you*, she said. And then she said perhaps I had better go. She said it would be best for everyone if I just left.

And though the implications were grave, nobody said anything to her. And then she walked away from the table and out the front door. And a few days later I told my grandmother Cecilia I was going, my beloved grandmother lying in bed, crying, begging me to forgive my mother, "She is sick," she told me. "She does not know what she says. She cannot control it. She wanders the halls looking for you, sometimes. Every two or three years, this happens. Night after miserable night for months on end, she runs up and down the halls weeping, looking for you as if she has really forgotten. She is not right. She does not know what she says, does not know what she's done. Forgive her."

And still, the next day I was on a plane. My grandmother's weeping face.

I see the failure, I do. I see it all around me, the leaves starting to fall off of these Long Island trees, the summer people gone, coming now only on occasion, for seasonal events. Gloves and scarves on little children, here for pumpkin gathering or apple picking. Fun and scary haunted houses to be visited in woods, a ghost who wanders empty halls, torments all those little children till they cry out that they are done here, that they want to go home. Their mothers console them all the way to their car, for they can be saved. Those children can go home with their mothers, for their mothers are not the ghost.

I can see it all here. The trees denuded. And all those little children make me think of Sandra. I remember her clearly, as I left my grandmother's house at thirteen. She is six, standing at the staircase, looking at me, having been brought down to say good-bye, sleepy and confused, my sister, her hand at her eyes. It is very early but I see it hit her, I am leaving, and then she is instantly at my leg, weeping, choking as she speaks my name, as she cries my name, before being torn away from me. She is the only one who wept at any of my leavings; she is the anointed one, the one who felt everything for us. And I am her in that moment, I am Sandra, watching me leave; I am six years old and I am my sister weeping and me both, a part of me left there with her, confused at six as the older me, stoic, grabs my suitcase to walk out of the door.

I see my lack in the way the days draw out; and in my wish that they would just stop. I see Margaret in that emptiness too, the child I never had; and then Joshua comes begging love. And I reach for my pen. Keep on working, because my dog and my work are all I presently have.

Before beginning this morning I sat and opened a book on Francesca Woodman for which this is the epigraph:

> A person, scattered in space and time, is no longer a woman but a series of events on which we can throw no light, a series of insoluble problems. — Marcel Proust, *La Prisonnière*

Francesca Woodman's models can confuse us: are we looking at an angel or a terrifying death? Will that woman in the doorway be discovered as a hanging, or is she divine, an exhausted spirit, perhaps, only momentarily pausing mid-flight? There are clear religious overtones here, her arms held out above her so that her body forms a high cross, a holiness suspended at the threshold, not yet having crossed to the other side. But if it is not that she is soaring and has been sacrificed instead, who has done this to her? We can only intuit into the emptiness of the stiff chair which sits before her in that room, a cloak draped upon its leg. Who once occupied that weighted absence, and where has this person gone?

And while it is not the first thing that we notice, we see that the figure in the doorway is hanging on as if she does not yet want to leave us, an affective crucifixion, her hands stubbornly gripping at the doorframe, though she averts her gaze.

In an accompanying photo Woodman seems to complicate rather than answer our questions; as a young woman sits in the previously empty chair, attentively regarding the room before her, what seems an apparition—naked and with legs flailing—flies above her. Is that angel floating in the background a cipher for something lost, for something no longer there but clearly longed for? A memory, perhaps, of a long lost sister, unsettled and with legs furiously whipping? Here, as in other images, long or double exposures give Woodman and her young models a ghostly quality; they are there and not there girls at once, spectral girls, eerie phantom girls, offering up a blurry opaque presence in those photographs. They say something to us about absence, about the spirit mark you leave when you are gone. They say something to me about my absence, about the spirit mark I left etched into my sisters when I was gone.

I know what it is to be and not be, to one day be playing in the garden, and the next be a girl suddenly gone missing, a living absence; and since that initial heartbreak I have held myself in that in-between space, where it seems, almost, that you are playing at life, that in-between place where you are just a ghost mark, so terrified of finally actually disappearing that somehow you don't allow yourself to ever be fully there at all.

This is how it is with Woodman: even when she empties out the body, puts it through formal art school exercises, double or long exposures, for instance, she somehow maintains a dream poetic, a story and the making of a story at once. She allows the body to live on the ghostly surface of the paper, a gorgeous eerie image; and it is because of this formal beauty that we can get caught up in the flow of line, the curves and light and shadow softly playing their back and forth game; yet they are never vacant, are not hollow at all, her photos. The bodies in these photographs have not been fully emptied in order to be easily manipulated, as Bellmer's have. For, even when posing in graveyards, Woodman's girls do not have that sort of stasis. We see them as girls in motion, girls playing, and recognize a life there thriving at the surface, experimenting, testing, simply trying things out. This charge of curiosity fills Woodman's images with affect, with the surge of life, her bodies fully feeling, sentient ones, though that emotive sense be deep below the surface in some of the photographs, partially hidden by the elegance of outline, or of the play of light.

In one photo Woodman and two of her models, all three of them young, stand naked save for Mary Janes and knee socks on one, as if to remind us that they are still but girls. They each hold a life size picture of Woodman's face in front of their own so that we don't know which is really her. Does this imply they are interchangeable girls, dispensable girls? It does not seem so, for we suspect one of them is truly her, and though there are no clues, we seek her out, for she is the one we really want. There is a further photo of her face, again, tacked to the wall behind them, a further Woodman setting the tone for the lie that is repetition.

That lone photo seems an overarching presence there, as the three girls before it, her symbolic offspring, have her countenance, her very selfness, stamped upon them; different as they are, different as they attempt to be, they all have her inscribed upon them, as do my sisters and I, with our mother. I can imagine those girls as my three sisters, Marta, the forward one in the Mary Janes, me the missing girl with a mere photo—a figurative talisman, a magic charm full of longing—marking my absence.

The ease with which I write my sisters and myself into that image, the ease in turning those girls into us, again leaves me to wonder whether it matters at all if one of those girls is in fact Woodman. Whether, as we move ourselves into that picture, it matters, really, if any of those girls is anyone specific at all.

How is it that Woodman's body, her ghost-girl body, is there and not there at once, sympathetic flesh and blood pumping as well as phantom spirit husk? We do recognize the formal games she is enacting, but there is also that thing both weighty and playful there below it all; beneath the elegance of surface we sense the tension in the sometimes frolicsome if not mischievous inside, a face smiling through a headstone. For it can, at times, be dark and terrifying too, Francesca's depth, as it is never fully tamed; and it seems to have a hunger for what lies there waiting on the other side; still, we are led to believe that the young Persephone will always again rise up, pomegranates being tossed in her deft and graceful hands; even if those fingers were only moments before, in a child-like curiosity, dipping deep into the river styx. If we prod her, we know she will respond… if we kiss her, beg her out of graveyards even, ask to take her by the arm and lead her from that world of dusky shadow, beg her to come and sit beside us here on this stone bench, we believe that girl will come. For, unlike Bellmer's dolls, who never approach the living, who are a terrible fantastical fact of the imagination, of some perverse desire, these are actual girls who, though they may seem untethered at times, are fully living too, searching, investigating, playing out the game of their lives in something which resembles the early childhood theater of taunts in gardens.

And is this not the space which art too inhabits? The space *between* things, that of the terrifying incomprehensibility of life as set against the possibility that the game of creation—game *as* creation—makes possible. That play we see permeating Woodman's work is a necessary in between place, the unclaimed transitional space, from which we can actively create our own lives.

Woodman's is not a body being acted upon, but a body acting, with the promise of possibility inscribed upon it; it is in the moment of taking on the theater of her own life that it can become anything, we realize; anything she does is her creation, with the potential of turning her very body into art.

So how is it that—though we see all this there thriving, pulsing at the surface of her photos—in the midst of experimenting with all that her art had to offer, at twenty-two, the fantastic, magical (though not surreal), brilliant and thoughtful young photographer, Francesca Woodman, took her own life? Twenty-two. The same age at which my mother had me, the age at which, for the first time, my mother's weighty eyes met mine.

But we know it is a deep struggle that, the taking control of the outlying voices, the reining them in, and making of them something like art.

I was wrestling with this, Woodman's work, and had grown both so frightened and excited by the parallels that I rose from my desk, jittery and surging and needing a break. I walked into the kitchen for my third cup of tea when Joshua began barking wildly, leaping about the front door. "It's just the mail," I said to soothe him. I opened the door and picked up a package; and a letter. The package I put down immediately because I saw that the letter was from my sister, from Sandra. I had to sit down. I patted Joshua to calm myself while I read it, then rubbed his ear a bit as I held it down for him to see when I had finished.

"Sandra's coming, Joshua." He put his paw on my arm; confused by my discomposure he looked up into my eyes, "My little sister's coming. She's coming to New York next week," I whispered.

Acknowledgments

I owe a special thanks to Danzy Senna, Victoria Patterson, and Dana Johnson for their constant and invaluable support. I am also deeply indebted to Chris Kraus and Hedi El Kholti. I would further like to thank Liz Welch, Karen Braziller, Dana Kinstler, Molly Barton, Markus Hoffman, Nancy Hollander, Jane Parshall, and Jeremy for all of their different but equally important forms of help with this book (and other things). Finally, my love to Beatriz Muñoz, Gabriela Rueda, Maria Elena Gonzalez, Zeynep Yucel and most of all, my darling Penelope Pardo.

LIST OF ILLUSTRATIONS

Page 31: Barnett Newman and unidentified woman standing in front of "Cathedra" in his Front Street studio, New York. © Peter A. Juley & Son Collection, Smithsonian American Art Museum.

Page 33: Marwa Abdul-Rahman, *Her Pistol Gold*, 2013. Mixed media on canvas, 144 x 69 inches. © Marwa Abdul-Rahman. Courtesy of the artist.

Page 34: Ad Reinhardt, 1966. Photograph by John Loengard. © Getty Images.

Page 73: Robert Barry, *Inert Gas Series*, Site Being Occupied by Helium, 38 cubic feet, From Measured Volume to Indefinite Expansion, 5 March 1969, Mojave Desert, California. © Robert Barry. Courtesy of the artist.

Page 74: Hanne Darboven, *Untitled*, c. 1972. Ink on ten pieces of transparentized paper, (each): 11 5/8 x 16 1/2 inches. © 2013 Artists Rights Society (ARS), New York / VG Bild-Kunst, Bonn.

Page 75: Ana Mendieta, *Arbol de la Vida [Tree of Life]*, 1976. Lifetime color photograph. 20 x 13 1/4 inches. © The Estate of Ana Mendieta Collection. Courtesy Galerie Lelong, New York.

Page 76: Agnes Martin, *Untitled*, 1998. Portfolio of 4 offset lithographs on GilClear paper. 12 x 12 inches, each. Edition of 75. © 2013 Agnes Martin / Artists Rights Society (ARS), New York. Courtesy of Pace Gallery, New York.

Page 144: Mark Rothko tombstone, East Marion, NY, 2009. © Veronica Gonzalez Peña.

Page 145: Stamos House, Greenport. © Alastair Gordon. Courtesy of the artist.

Page 146: Studio, Guilford Connecticut, 2006.Originally designed by Tony Smith in 1951 for Fred Olsen. Photograph. © Solveig Fernlund. Courtesy of fernlund + logan architects, New York.

About the Author

Veronica Gonzalez Peña is the coeditor of *Juncture: 25 Very Good Stories and 12 Excellent Drawings* and the founder of rockypoint Press, a series of artist-writer collaborations. *twin time: or, how death befell me*, her first novel, won her the 2007 Premio Aztlán Literary Prize.